The Rack

Stories Inspired by Vintage Horror Paperbacks

Stephen King   Richard Chizmar   Max Booth III

Christa Carmen   Clay McLeod Chapman

Johnny Compton   Kristin Dearborn   Philip Fracassi

Laurel Hightower   Larry Hinkle   Gwendolyn Kiste

Ronald Malfi   Bridgett Nelson   Candace Nola

Errick Nunnally   Cynthia Pelayo   Rebecca Rowland

Jeff Strand   Steve Van Samson   Mercedes M Yardley

Edited by
Tom Deady

Introduction by
Will Errickson

GREYMORE PUBLISHING

Greymore Publishing
PO Box 341
Vail AZ 85641
www.greymorepublishing.com

Cover Artwork and Design © 2024 by Lynne Hansen
Interior Design © 2024 by Greymore Publishing

ISBN-13: 978-0-9906327-7-1 (Paperback edition)

Contents

Introduction
Will Errickson

When *Paperbacks from Hell* was published in the autumn of 2017, Grady Hendrix and I did not foresee the impact our book on the history of paperback horror fiction would have on fans of the genre, or indeed the new fans it would make. Our labor of love, inspired by the blog I began in 2010 called Too Much Horror Fiction, took well over a year of research and writing, scanning lurid book covers and identifying the artists who'd made them. That golden age of mass market paperbacks, which we date roughly from the very late sixties to the early nineties, saw countless titles hot off the presses juggernauted into bookshops, drugstores, grocery checkout lanes, and airport kiosks. Horror was for the people and would be found wherever people congregated.

If you are of a certain age, you most likely have fond memories of "the rack": those wire receptacles which were crammed full of mass market paperback books in those aforementioned places. After I graduated high school in 1989, I worked at a used bookstore, and every day had to wrestle outside, and then back inside at end of day, two enormous spinner racks of dusty paperbacks, said racks precariously affixed with wobbly wheels that needed to be coaxed to the sidewalk just *so*. God damn, 35 years later and I can still feel the awkward, unwieldy weight of those ancient monstrosities!

The books on those racks were pure product, disposable, ephemeral, popular fiction and nonfiction titles that were not above appealing to a potential reader's base interests in order to get them to shell out a cool dollar-fifty, dollar seventy-five, around that, for entertainment. "I am writing for people *today*. I am writing things to be put in the book-store next month," said Michael McDowell, one of the giants of paperback horror originals, the writer behind not only Eighties novels like *Cold Moon Over Babylon* and the *Black-water* series, but also the Tim Burton films *Beetlejuice* and *A Nightmare Before Christmas*.

This type of humility belies the fact that people are redis-covering and reading books that once were considered beneath the topics of polite conversation. Who would have thought that a 1980 novel about mutant, rampaging cock-roaches, *The Nest* by Gregory A. Douglas, would come roaring back into print well into the 21st century? Who could have foretold the (unfortunately) high prices that Guy N. Smith's pulpy books of crustacean mayhem would go for in online bookseller catalogs? Or that authors as disparate as Karl Edward Wagner, Lisa Tuttle, Kathe Koja, Ruby Jean Jensen, Thomas Tessier, and David J. Schow, would see their vintage titles, all long out of print, be available once again to a reading audience a generation removed?

Horror anthologies were a great way to discover new authors, better than springing for a full novel by someone you weren't familiar with. The short story has, of course, always been considered the best showcase for horror fiction, and in that *Paperbacks from Hell* era, almost every horror writer worth their salt contributed to at least one of the countless many published then. (Off the top of my head, I can only think of a few writers who *did not* publish short stories, and they were about the biggest of the era: Anne Rice, V.C. Andrews, and John Saul. The money from the bestseller lists was probably just too good to waste time on a "lesser" pursuit!). It was in anthologies that I discovered Joe Lansdale, Poppy Z. Brite, Dennis Etchison, T.E.D. Klein, Ray Garton, and more, writers with different styles and concerns, but all who wanted to get under your skin and scar you.

The Rack, the book you have now in your hands, continues in that hallowed tradition of writers who use a variety of methods to bring you the horror goodies, but of course with some of that vintage flavor. "Ursa Diruo" by Kristin Dearborn, "The Keeper of Taswomet" by Eric Nunnally, "A Devil We Used to Know" by Johnny Compton, and "Lips Like a Scythe" by Steve Van Samson are creature features of the most intense and harrowing kind. "The Last Call of the Cicada" by Gwendolyn Kiste and "I Am a House Demanding to Be Haunted" by Mercedes M. Yardley evoke Shirley Jackson and Tanith Lee, two of the best women writers of horror and dark fantasy. "Blood of My Blood" by Christa Carmen puts a blackly comic twist on a family tradition.

Horror fiction itself plays a role in Cynthia Pelayo's "Black Pages," as well as in "Irish Eyes" by Bridgett Nelson. I've always enjoyed that kind of self-referential aspect. "Better By You, Better Than Me" by Rebecca Rowland and "Mightier Than Bullets" by Laurel Hightower address sobering reality while using the genre's fantastical elements to great effect. Of course there are some lighter-hearted tales, reminiscent of EC Comics or Robert Bloch's macabre playfulness, in "They

Look Back" by Candace Nola, "Fuzzy Slippers" by Jeff Strand, "That Chemical Glow" by Larry Hinkle. "White Pages" by Clay McLeod Chapman and "A Nightmare on Elm Lane" by Richard Chizmar remind us that childhood is a minefield of danger and threat.

"Other Things Have Happened" by Ronald Malfi blends horror film and modern technology to disturbing ends, while the tech in "Loud and Clear" by Max Booth III is charming and nostalgic, yet no less deadly for that. The haunted house, that most ancient of genre mainstays, will always be a source of grief and sadness in Philip Fracassi's "The Visitor."

And you'll even find a short work from the man who has held sway over horror entertainment for half a century now, Stephen King himself. "The Raft" was first published in an adult magazine back in the year 1982. It gained widespread attention when it was reprinted in his bestselling 1986 collection *Skeleton Crew*, no doubt a grimoire for many of the other writers in *The Rack* (it was also adapted for *Creepshow 2*). With its no-nonsense approach to a good old pulp-horror trope, it is the perfect vintage accompaniment to the new stories here.

It has been an unexpected thrill for Grady Hendrix and me to see this era of horror fiction celebrated by *Paperbacks from Hell*, the seventies and eighties—decades highly regarded as producing the greatest horror *movies* ever made—come to be so beloved, so relevant, so *inspiring* for writers today. The oldies are still goldies, still retain their ability to terrify and enlighten. *The Rack* pays homage to those glory days, but it also shows us the glory days of horror are here and now. I wouldn't have it any other way!

Introduction

Will Errickson was born and raised in Southern New Jersey in 1970. He began reading horror stories at a young age, and while in college worked in a used bookstore. There he learned to appreciate paperbacks of all genres and deepened his love of horror. In 2010 he began his blog Too Much Horror Fiction, devoted to collecting and reviewing vintage horror and celebrating the era's resplendent over art. In 2017 he co-wrote the Bram Stoker Award-winning PAPERBACKS FROM HELL with bestselling author Grady Hendrix. Today he lives in Portland, Ore., with his wife Ashley and an ever-growing library of horror paperbacks.

Black Pages
Cynthia Pelayo

THERE ARE things that linger about a person once they're gone.

The pitch of their voice, or how they laughed, which could be in between a gasp and a chuckle. How they always needed to have their music on loud each Saturday morning as they deep cleaned their home. And especially, all the objects that gave them joy and, in many ways, defined their life.

Horror paperbacks were what brought my mother joy and wonder. When we went on vacation, she'd lug a few old horror novels along, not recent ones. No. My mother preferred paperbacks from the 1970s and 1980s, with yellowed pages and garish covers. I remember going with her to the grocery store when I was little, and there they'd be, by the check-out counter, in a black wire rack that I'd spin around too fast, and she'd tell me to slow down. I would gently stop the spinning display, captivated by those creeping faces and monsters. The images on the front were horrifically whimsical, in this sort of surreal and macabre way, with menacing looking creatures peering out, or a haunted looking house in the background, begging for someone to enter.

When it came time to decide what to do with my mother's things after she died, I did what many people do, I froze. I sat in shock for a long time in her small apartment debating which of her belongings I could lug to my equally small apartment. I wanted to take her floral-patterned sofas and her velvet cushions, and her handmade pottery, and of course all the plants that hung in her windows, but I didn't have the space. I also had very little time to clear out her apartment before her landlord threatened to just dump all of her belongings, and so, I did what I could.

I made note of:

What could I throw away? Used toiletries and expired spices from the spice rack.

What should I donate? Her old furniture.

And,

What should I sell? Her horror paperback novels.

I planned to avoid her bedroom for as long as I could because that's where her home health nurse found her dead one cold morning. I was told my mother died peacefully, but her illness brought her a lot of pain, and I imagine there was very little peace for her at the end. That's how some sicknesses work, they're there and then one day, they whisk you away. I figured I'd tackle all that was in her bedroom after I had managed the rest of the apartment.

I realized quickly, no matter how tightly I hugged my mother's sweaters hanging in the coat closet in the hallway, breathing deep into the neck to catch her lavender scent it wasn't enough. She was not here. Objects can never truly capture the whole essence of the person. But at least I felt somewhat comforted being surrounded by books, while I packed up other things, because she loved those so much.

I would have to decide fairly quickly what to do with my mother's entire collection of old horror paperbacks, a collection started by my father, passed on to her, and what I imagined she wanted to pass down to me, but . . . I never really did take to them. I found them too ghoulish and grim, and maybe it was those covers and that Gothic font, the emboss and foil stamping that made the artwork leap out at me from those wire racks. While I was fascinated enough to look at them in the safety of a grocery store, I never felt quite safe picking them up or reading them while I was at home. Yet, it was important to me that whoever these books went to, they guaranteed these books would be shared and read, because that's what my mother would want.

Over time, those horror paperbacks fell out of favor, publishers folding, and other business decisions were made to stop their production altogether practically that I didn't quite understand. Mother understood some of the publishing world. Before Dad died, he worked at a small publishing company, and he published many of those books that people today buy and sell online for double, triple what they were sold for in those grocery stories. As Mother grew older, she took to purchasing as many of those books as she could find, from used bookstores and collectors. At first, I thought, it's a hobby, but it really wasn't so much of a hobby as an obsession. When I asked Mother why she cared so much about those books she said:

"I'm looking for something your father rejected a long time ago when he worked in publishing."

"Really?" I said. "What?"

She lowered her voice to a whisper, almost as if the paperbacks in the apartment could hear us. "The scariest story ever written."

When I asked her for the title of the book, she said she didn't know. When I pressed her what the book was about, she said she had no clue. So, when I finally questioned how she knew this book even existed, she smiled a sneaky little smile and said "I have proof it exists," and that's all she offered me.

Mother didn't really have a great place to store those books. It got to the point where the dining room could no longer serve as a dining room, and it just became her library. When I'd come over, we'd have all of our meals in her small kitchen, which was just fine. Still, when I walked into her tiny apartment, the first place I found myself was in the dining room, surrounded by those dark, bold, and monstrous covers. Her bedroom was just off to the side of the library, and I think she liked it that way. Mother slept with the door open, and I'd imagine her looking out of her bedroom door at night, staring down those old paperbacks that were stacked in old wooden bookshelves that she managed to get for real cheap at the thrift store. Over time, the dining room table also served as a place where she'd keep her books, stacked there in towers. They were everywhere, in piles, piled on top of one another, and on the chairs. When I told her to perhaps try using the very top of the bookshelf for space, she declined, and I found that odd given there was some good space up there to use.

I remember how the packages would come, sometimes a handful a week, sometimes just one, but there was always something on her doorstep when I arrived to check in on her as her illness progressed.

I'd walk in, hand her the mail and there she'd be, with a pair of scissors, carefully opening the envelope or the box. Sometimes the books would come in plastic, protected by packing peanuts, or bubble wrap. Other times they would just be wrapped up in old carboard. Regardless, each time

Mother unwrapped the book as if it were delicate glass. She'd hold the book out, groan with disappointment and say: "This isn't it."

"How do you know by just looking at it?" I'd asked.

"I'll know it as soon as I see it," Mother said.

But still, Mother would read each one of those books that came to her in the mail. She'd sit in her reading chair in the living room, and within a few hours the book would be completed. Once she closed the book, she'd lean back in her chair, with her eyes looking off to the distance somewhere I couldn't see and sometimes she'd say:

"That was a really good one."

Or,

"That ending sure was something!"

Or,

"Good thing the monster ate all of them."

But each and every time she'd finish with, "Too bad that wasn't the book, but I know it's coming. I know I'll find it."

"If those weren't the book you're looking for," I asked of the disappointing packages. "Then why read them all?"

My mother knit her eyebrows and stared me down like I cursed at her. "It's a book! All books should be read, and you know, maybe this is the story I need to read today," she'd point to her recently completed book. "That's what books do; they offer us something we're looking for."

I scratched the back of my head and took a seat on the sofa, legs crossed beneath me. "Do you know at least who wrote the scariest horror novel ever written?"

Mother sighed, leaned her head back, looking towards the ceiling. "Well, if I knew that then this experiment wouldn't be taking me so long, now, would it?"

I raise my palms up. "You learned something about this from Dad. What'd you learn?"

She shook her head slowly from side to side. "Well…."

There she went with her drawn out "Wells...."

She rested each of her elbows on the armrests of her chair.

She cleared her throat and then said "Your father worked for a long, long time in publishing. He edited many of those books over there," she pointed a thumb towards the library.

"He said that one day a book came across his desk that ... well, he said the pages were all black."

"Black?" I asked.

She nodded. "Black. Your father said each and every one of those pages were black."

I laughed. "Alright, so it was like a joke. Someone sent him construction paper?"

Mother shook her head. "Nope, those pages were not construction paper. There were instructions from the author that there was only one way to read that book."

I shrugged. "Okay...how?"

Mother took a deep breath and exhaled through her teeth. "The only way to read that book was to set each page on fire."

I could feel the corners of my mouth lifting. "Mom ... you don't really believe that do you?"

My mother gave me a tight-lipped smile, eased herself out of her chair, and went to the kitchen where I heard her open a drawer, the clinging and clacking of items together in her junk drawer. She entered the dining room and then she reached to the very top bookshelf where she pulled out a single black sheet of paper.

Mother then sat down in front of me in her chair, held the black sheet of paper up with one hand and with the other hand she held up a Bic lighter. She pulled down on the wheel with her thumb, and the lighter sparked once, twice, and then the flame caught. Mother held the lighter up directly to the sheet of paper and I shouted.

"Mom!"

"Shhhh. Just watch," she said, and she moved the flame back and forth across the page, back and forth, gliding all the way down until the black page faded to white and two words appeared:

"The end."

"Your father kept this last page from that manuscript. He then emailed the author and said that he was unable to accept the book, but your dad said that later on, he received a note from the author thanking him for his time and telling him that the book had been accepted and published with a small press for a limited run. I've been trying to find a copy of that book ever since."

"But why?" I asked.

"Because it's supposed to be the most terrifying thing ever written. There are words strung together in a way on those pages that are so dark the author said that no human could ever fully process the meaning. The cover is said to be so gruesome and cruel that even a glance at that glossy black front can cause someone to lose their mind…"

I interrupted. "If looking at the cover makes someone lose their mind, then what happens if someone reads the book?"

She tilts her head. "It's said you die."

"Mom! And you want to read it?"

She shrugged. "I've read all of those books over there, and I can take it. When it's time, that is. I can take it." she said.

🖤 🖤 🖤

It took some time to decide what to do with what in my mother's apartment. All of these things she bought and kept had meaning, so with each and every item I'd sit there and debate with myself? 'Do I throw it away?' 'Well, if I do, will I feel guilty?' 'Should I donate it?'

Then came the selling of the things.

I stared at those paperbacks for a long, long time debating what to do. I stand and walk over to the shelves, reading the titles, *The Tribe* by Bari Wood, the cover a strange outline of a man with three of the same faces within that form, staggered, looking out at me, a grim look on their mouths. Other titles like *The Spirit* by Thomas Page, a snowed-out cover with a small cottage in the background, and the eyes, nose, and mouth of a skull in the shape of the wind brushed snowy clouds above, *Rapture* by Thomas Tessier, a hand holding a blood dripped knife on the cover, *Nightblood* by T. Chris Martindale, and more, so much more.

Bold text. Bright colors. Ghastly green creatures. Claws digging out from graves. Wolves howling at windows in the night. And so much blood, blood dripping covers.

There was even *When Darkness Loves Us*, by Elizabeth Engstrom, a baby blue cover with a doll in the center, her face cracked right in the center, the dark gash starting in between her eyes, making its way down to her mouth. Then there's *A Nest of Nightmares* by Lisa Tuttle, a dark grey cover fading to white, in which two featherless baby birds are in profile, those pink, fleshy things resting in a nest, one with its beak open, but their eyes, their eyes weren't like bird eyes, like little black beads. Their eyes were instead these large violet marbles that looked like the galaxy swirled within. The *Hell Hound* by Ken Greenhallis a cover I tried to keep my eyes away from, but its eyes always followed me, the two bright orange orbs of a snarling white dog.

Why did my mother treasure these things so much and what was it that she found of value? And what was it that she was looking for with that black paged book?

It only took a few hours for me to find someone to purchase my mother's entire collection of horror paperbacks, and I gasped at the figure they offered to pay. That money would change my life. They are a rare book buyer and they told me these books were in high demand and they were looking forward to finding the right reader for each of them.

After I packed up the books for the buyer, I checked the top of the bookshelf, searching for that black page my mother showed me so long ago, but it wasn't there. I figured Mother must have placed it somewhere, perhaps tucked between the pages of another book, and I'd never find it at this point.

Next, it was time to enter Mother's room, and I dreaded it. I felt my arms go numb and my face grow cold, because this room is where she died. This room is where she spent so many nights aching in pain there at the end. I opened the door, and the medical equipment was all gone, the oxygen machine, and medicine bottles, and latex gloves, thermometers and more.

I sat in the chair in front of her bed where her nurse would sit, and I sighed a deep, heavy sigh.

And then, I felt my foot kick something.

I leaned over, looking under the bed and I spotted something. I reached down and felt, and I sensed a book.

Pages moved through my fingers.

I raised it to my face, and I turned away quickly from the cover, remembering what it was my mother said, the warning of one's mind spiraling in a way that would never cease.

Then I flipped through the pages carefully. Page after page was the same, each was black, and there, at the very end was that single loose black page Mother had shown me long ago before she became ill.

I don't know why my mother sought so long and hard to read this book, and I don't know if this is book helped end her life sooner than her illness would have.

All I know is I don't want this thing anywhere near me, but it's a book, right? All books should be read, and you know, maybe this isn't the story I need today, but maybe it's the story that someone else needs. And so, I tuck the book in the box for the seller knowing the book will find its right home, and its right reader.

❦ ❦ ❦

Cynthia Pelayo Cynthia Pelayo is a Bram Stoker Award–winning author. Her novels include *Forgotten Sisters*, *Children of Chicago* and *The Shoemaker's Magician*. In addition to writing genre-blending novels that incorporate elements of fairy tales, mystery, detective, crime, and horror, Pelayo has written numerous short stories and the poetry collection *Crime Scene*. The recipient of the 2021 International Latino Book Award, she holds a master of fine arts in writing from the School of the Art Institute of Chicago. She lives in Chicago with her family. For more information, visit www.cinapelayo.com.

Other Things Have Happened
Ronald Malfi

I

THERE IS an old movie house on the corner of First and
Newsom that has been boarded up for the better part of a
decade. I used to go there as a kid on Saturday afternoons, a
few dollar bills folded neatly into the side pocket of my
corduroys for whatever candy my heart desired, and I'd
spend hours in one of those dark theaters. Often, I would
watch the same movie over and over again until one of the
ushers asked me to leave. It was a second-run theater, which
meant the movies were old, the candy was stale, and the
tickets were cheap. But none of that mattered to me.

I did not begin going to this theater out of any love for
the cinema—not at first, anyway; I was only a child—but out
of necessity: Saturday was Mother's time alone in the house
with one of her male friends from the mill, and she forbade
me hanging around whenever one of those questionable
fellows appeared as if by magic on the porch, bleary-eyed
and mattress-headed, stinking of gin and looking like
someone shoved unceremoniously from a moving railway

car. She'd give me the money—or, more often, have her male companion reluctantly fork over the cash—and then instruct me not to return home until the streetlamps came on.

There were four theaters in the movie house, and each would show a different film for the better part of a month. One theater—the one by the restrooms—always ran horror movies, and as a kid, that's the theater to which I gravitated. Some of those films were very old, where the monsters were generally misunderstood and shambled around in all their black-and-white glory. Others featured creatures with faces like pot roasts, aliens with rubbery flesh and bulging, insectoid eyes, or masked, knife-wielding maniacs whose kills launched a spray of arterial blood across the movie screen. I loved them all.

I hadn't thought about that old movie house for many years, even though I still live in the same town where I grew up, and I would drive by it every day on my way to work. Once work became a thing I no longer had to contend with, I would still drive by the movie house on my way to the Bellevue Diner where I'd spend eight hours nursing a single cup of bitter-tasting coffee while reading cheap paperbacks, doing crossword puzzles, or just watching the traffic crawling up and down Newsom Road. The old movie house was right there across the street, on the corner, its doors boarded up, its ancient fish-tank ticket booth shuttered, its triangular marquee with its missing letters like a homeless man's stupefied grin.

I broke into the theater through a fire exit in the back alley. It wasn't very difficult, although I tore the cuff of my sports jacket in the process (not that it mattered anymore). I went down the musty corridor and came out in the lobby, where daylight funneled through the slats of the boarded windows in a swampy, seawater hue. There were piles of drywall heaped along the threadbare carpet, and electrical cables hung from exposed joists in the ceiling. I spied a rat scurrying along a baseboard, something black and shiny in its mouth.

There were spider webs everywhere—because of course there were—and the sight of them gave me pause. I thought of Breanne, my wife, and the state of things at our home. I watched a particularly robust arachnid traverse a web that stretched from the candy counter to a support column, and I felt a shiver ripple down my spine. In my head, I heard Breanne say, *There, there. Just relax.*

I entered the theater next to the restrooms—the one that used to show all those old horror movies—and had to activate the flashlight app on my phone, since it was so dark. And even then, I could only make out the nearest row of seats, the crimson fabric split, tufts of tallow-colored foam frothing out. The place smelled like mold, but I didn't much care as I walked down the center aisle toward the screen.

And stood there.

Staring up.

The following day, I purchased some equipment from a local AV store—a digital projector, a few HDMI cables, and several extension cords, to be precise. I took these items, along with my personal laptop and collection of hard drives, back to the theater. There was no power running to the theater, of course, but there was an electrical outlet in the alley behind the movie house that served the adjacent hardware store, and so I plugged one of the extension cords into that. Back in the theater, I set up the digital projector on a small folding table I had purloined from our basement, then hooked up the projector to my laptop with one of the HDMI cables.

I may not have started out in this life as a film buff, but those Saturdays in my youth, coming here to escape whatever carnal bedlam was transpiring at my childhood home, had manufactured me into one. I own several hard drives which I can connect to my personal laptop—hard drives packed to bursting with horror movies. Not the new ones—not the "torture porn" or the CGI-heavy splatter fests—but all the classics, spanning from the old Universal movie monsters to the slasher craze of the 1980s, and everything in between. The only thing you won't find in my collection is that curious and admittedly off-putting subgenre where giant insects attack Smalltown U.S.A. If there's a giant bug in the film—or worse, an arachnid—then you won't find it in my collection.

On that first afternoon, I played *The Blob* to a theater of one—not the original starring Steve McQueen, which is also wonderful, but the 1988 remake directed by Chuck Russell. I remember the movie poster for that film hanging up in this very movie house when I was a kid—the vague suggestion of a human body suspended behind a web of sinewy pink gelatin—and how much it had excited something inside me.

So, now, an admission: I have been doing this every day for the past three months, unbeknownst to Breanne, who thinks that when I leave the house in the morning, I am still going to my cubicle at Industrial Tile and Sheathing (or ITS, as it's embroidered on all of my corporate polo shirts). Breanne knows nothing of the incident at ITS that resulted in my...well, my unplanned and rather sudden departure, let's say. Breanne doesn't work—how could she, given her condition?—so she would be concerned if she learned of my recent unemployment. Anyway, I've got some savings tucked away until I can think of another plan.

Right now, today, I take out my cell phone while *Basket Case* plays on the screen, and text a message to myself on my phone:

think of a plan

It's a good idea, and it's smart to remind myself of good ideas so that I don't forget. And of course, since I've texted it to myself, it *returns* to myself:

> think of a plan

Yes. It's good advice. Despite the joy and comfort I have found in coming here day after day, movie after movie, I cannot keep this up indefinitely. I know that. I'm not a fool.

It is then that I look up and see a slender black shape occluding a narrow sliver of the screen. It is a figure, a person. Someone standing there in the dark, down by the screen, as if they have just materialized out of the shadows.

I stand, too—or, more precisely, I jump up from the theater seat like someone zapped with a jolt of electricity. Who is this person? Where did they come from? Am I hallucinating?

She, it occurs to me, as the figure glides up the aisle in my direction. *She*. Because it is a woman, her body ethereal and shimmery and slight of frame, and my first thought is that she is a ghost until I realize she looks that way because she is moving toward me within the light of the projector.

A strange buzzing sound momentarily filters into my ears. I hear it all around me, like a thousand flies swarming, but there is nothing there. I shake my head to clear it, and wonder once more if I'm hallucinating all of this.

"Who are you?" Ashamed to say I bark this, a measure of nervousness evident in my voice. I quickly swallow what feels like a wad of cotton and, more confidently, repeat the question: "Who are you?"

The woman stops right there in the aisle, the movie projecting in fractals of light across her body, her face. There is a sheen to her face, a shininess that makes me once more question the solidity of her. Tears, though: they are tears that stream down her face. She has been hiding in here in the dark, crying.

Immediately, I feel awful. I stammer some apology, even wave a hand at what remains of my lunch that teeters beside the projector on the foldout table—a prepackaged ham and Swiss on a questionable sub roll and half a bottle of Yoo-hoo which I purchased earlier that day at the 7-Eleven—as if presenting an offering. I'm sweating and uncomfortable in my ITS polo shirt and slacks, and I feel like someone has opened a trapdoor underneath me. Where did this woman *come* from?

"I'm sorry," she says, her voice soft. She holds up one hand, so that a snippet of *Basket Case* projects across the terrain of her palm. For one crazy moment, I wonder if she is some film starlet of the silver screen that has materialized straight out of the beam of light from my movie projector. "I was just...I think..."

Something terrible happens on the screen, and we both turn to look at it. I feel foolish, so I lean over and switch off the projector. The theater goes instantly dark and there is a winding down sound as the projector dies. I feel the heat coming off the projector, but then a coolness as the darkness settles around me. Around us.

"Oh," says the woman, whom I can no longer see. "It's dark."

I reach out and switch on the projector's light—just the light—and hold my breath as I do so, half expecting this phantom to be gone once the light comes on, confirming my madness.

But she's still there.

"I didn't mean to frighten you," I tell her.

"I didn't mean to frighten *you*," she says.

She holds up one hand again, this time to block the glare of the projector's light from her eyes.

"Sit," I say, and wave a hand toward one of the empty theater seats. I mean, they're *all* empty, but I'm trying to be polite. I even add: "Please."

She examines the seats, no doubt discomfited by the state of things—the tufts of stuffing poking from burst seams, exposed springs that look like the workings of a torture device, and the dark, incriminating stains that are visible in the projector's light on nearly every surface. Yet after a moment, she sits. I dig a Kleenex from my pocket and hand it to her; it's clean, I've only used it to wipe dust from the projector lens, yet she still hesitates. But then she accepts it, blots the streaks of tears from her cheeks, and then looks down at the Kleenex that she pinches in both hands, as if trying to divine something mystical or fortuitous from it. But it's just a Kleenex, so what could she be searching for?

She's pretty. I can tell even in the dimness of the theater, and with the outline of that stark white light from the projector illuminating her profile. When Breanne is Breanne, her features are blunt and piggish, with a snub nose and lips that pinch too tight. This woman is more delicate, like someone took great care sculpting her. I can see that even in the dark.

"It's okay," I tell her as I take a seat across from her in the aisle. "Whatever is upsetting you, this is a safe place."

"Do you work here?"

I laugh. "No one works here. It's been closed down for years."

She glances at the beam of light issuing from the projector and shining against the giant screen at the front of the theater. "What do you do here?"

"I watch movies."

"By yourself?"

"I used to watch them by myself all the time when I was a boy."

"And now you're here because...?"

I don't answer. What is there to say, really? That I got fired from my job at ITS and have been pretending to go to work so Breanne doesn't find out? That would make me sound like a crazy person, and I would like to avoid that if at all possible. There are enough crazy things going on in my life without throwing one more item on the heap. I want to ask her why *she's* here, but I don't do that, either. True, she has calmed down some, but I still feel uncomfortable asking her what has brought her to this miserable state in the first place. So, for a while, we just sit there in silence and stare at the blank white theater screen while particles of dust float in the javelin of light that issues from the projector. After a time, I reach over and turn the movie back on, and the two of us just sit like that in mutual silence while we watch the rest of *Basket Case* all the way through to the end credits.

II

Her name is Libby and she is in a bad marriage. Who am I to judge, you might ask, but I know a thing when I see it. I come to this theater so that Breanne thinks I'm still going to work—

(think of a plan)

—but I also come here as an escape. I know what it means to be trapped in a web and powerless to move, where the more you struggle, the more stuck you become. I know what it means to be trapped in the stifling claustrophobia of a bad marriage. So right from the beginning, I feel a kinship with Libby.

She got in a fight with her husband, which started out as an argument before transitioning into something physical. She touches her arm as she tells me this part, so I surmise that's the place where this man has struck her, but she does

18

not elaborate, nor does she volunteer to show me any bruises. (I do not volunteer to show her the inside of my left arm, because that would undoubtedly upset her, and it might force me to explain why I got fired from ITS, which is its own embarrassing story, sorry to say, so I just keep mum on all of that sour business.)

They have a child together, Libby and this husband of hers, which makes her situation more complex. She can't just pack up and leave without the kid, and she can't take the kid with her, because that would be some sort of violation of law. When she ran from their house earlier that day, she was in a panic. Her husband got in the family car and pursued her down First Avenue, if you can imagine such a thing. What kind of man does something like that? *This* man, apparently. Libby ran down a confusion of alleyways to avoid him, and when she found the rear fire exit to the movie house propped open—that was my doing—she ditched inside and hid in this theater in the dark. And so now here we are.

I say nothing as she relays all this to me. I'm too far from her across the aisle to lend a comforting pat on her shoulder, but that's probably for the best, because maybe such an action would be misconstrued for something else. When she's done talking, we sit there in silence. *Basket Case* has ended a while ago, and there is only the blind, white, rectangular eye of the movie screen before us, looking like a portal to heaven.

"Are you married?" she ultimately asks me.

I tell her that I am, although I do not mention Breanne by name. Nor do I tell Libby about the precariousness of my own situation. Breanne and I have got no kids, but we've got something else between us: an arrangement hinged on a dark secret, and the prospect of disrupting such an arrangement frightens me. So I pretty much keep mum on that score, too.

I let Libby talk some more. Eventually, she stops talking

about her marriage and tells me a bit about her kid—a boy whose name I instantly forget the moment she speaks it—and how she grew up in the next town over, not too far from where I grew up. She used to work as a schoolteacher but lost her job due to budget cuts. When he's not speeding down the road after his terrified wife, her husband works in banking. Most days, her kid is in school, which leaves Libby all alone in their big, empty house in the next town over. She asks why I'm in this theater, and my first instinct is to come up with a lie. But I'm not quick on my feet like that, so I just tell her the truth: that I got laid off from work and have been coming here so my wife thinks I still have a job. If Libby thinks poorly of me because of this admission, she does not say so.

We talk some more, and before I know it, the alarm on my phone beeps, and I know the streetlamps have come on and that it's time to return home. And that's when a strange thing occurs: Libby and I make a pact. A pact to return here tomorrow and watch a film together. To talk. To just share the easy comfort of another person whom neither of us know well at all.

"But first," she says, "we should clean this place up a little bit."

"I'll be here!" I announce, perhaps a bit too jovially. My palms are sweating and my heart is racing around in my chest. "We can certainly clean up a bit; I've been meaning to, anyway, to be honest. Then what movie shall we watch?"

"Pick a good one," she says.

And before she leaves, she leans across the aisle, passing through that beam of projector light, and kisses me on the cheek.

Once she's gone and I'm left alone again in that old theater, I take out my phone and text myself her name, even though I know there is no way I will forget it:

Libby

And of course, myself responds:

Libby

I shut down the projector and sit there in the dark for a while. A part of me suggests the kiss didn't happen, that it was all wishful thinking in my head. An even more repugnant part of me suggests *none of this* has happened, but I know that's not true, because I'm still holding the Kleenex damp from Libby's tears and I can see her footprints in the dusty aisle. That makes me smile, and I finally go home for the night.

III

Home is an old Victorian with shutters on the windows and a NO SOLICITING sign posted on the front door. In many ways, it's not all that different from the old movie house—cold, quiet, desolate, and shut up against the world. There are some feral cats on the porch when I arrive, which is to be expected; they whine out of hunger when they see me, but I've got nothing for them, so I shoo them away then make sure none of them dart into the house when I open the door.

I take my shoes off in the foyer and plod down the hall, wending around Breanne's hoarded stacks of newspapers and piles of old clothes she had outgrown but never got around to donating. The clothes remind me of empty husks, as if someone—Breanne, ha ha?—has come along and sucked all the fleshy people-parts out of them. I call out to Breanne but she does not respond. I've got some takeout with me—I stopped at Yung's Chinese Emporium on my way back from the movie house—and the smell of it suddenly fills the whole house.

Breanne is in the den. While it is true she is sitting on the sofa in front of the TV, her plump body packaged in gray sweatpants and a faded pink sweatshirt with a rhinestone cat on the front, I can sense that just moments before my arrival, she was suspended in her web, her massive body bristling with stiff, quill-like hairs, her eight segmented legs attuned to the minutest vibration along those silken strands. I don't often walk in on her in that state, which is a blessing, but the image is still clearly burned across the gray matter of my brain from the few times I have. Once, I opened our bedroom door to find her suspended from the ceiling, her corpulent frame wracked in spasms while she excreted a tacky gray thread from the spinnerets on her abdomen.

"I brought dinner," I say, holding up the takeout.

"Yum. How was work?"

"Oh, you know," I say. "Same old."

"Let's eat. I'm starved."

I shudder, then retreat to the kitchen. I set plates on the table, take the food from the takeout containers, and spoon it into the dishes. I need a beer, so I take a Coors Light from the fridge. I pour Breanne her usual glass of blood-red wine. My hand trembles the slightest bit as I set the wine glass beside her plate.

We eat across the table from each other like it's some sort of showdown, and we remain mostly in silence. I watch Breanne poke around the food on her plate with a pair of chopsticks, select a floret of broccoli covered in a gelatinous brown sauce, then stick it in her mouth. She chews slow and methodically, like someone in an institution just roused from a coma. There is some brownish sauce glistening in one corner of her mouth now.

This is all a ruse, of course. A facade. It's an effort to keep up pretense, although I'm no longer sure what the rationale for that might be. Breanne cannot digest Chinese food any more than I could digest a quart of motor oil. We both know this. And we both also know that Breanne will *truly* feed later tonight, in our bedroom, as she slowly works her silken strands about my body while muttering, *there, there, just relax* into my ear until she parts her chelicerae and embeds her curved fangs into the tender meat at the base of my neck. Or perhaps tonight it will be the small of my back. Or maybe my thigh.

My wife is a spider and I am her sustenance.

It wasn't always this way. To be honest, I can't remember when things changed. Did I just walk in on her and see what she really was one afternoon? Had the shock of it cast a blank spot upon my memory? Or had she whispered her terrible secret into my ear one night while we were in bed together? I can't remember now, and I chalk that lack of memory up to the amnesiac quality that comes over me whenever my wife feeds. Is there memory in our blood? Does she siphon thoughts and memories and consciousness from me as she takes her fill of me? I have often wondered.

Much in the way no one (except me) can really see Breanne for what she really is, no one can see the puncture wounds her fangs leave behind on my flesh. If they could, perhaps people would be more compassionate to my plight. They would understand why my memory fades, why I've grown weaker and weaker not just of body but of mind, and why I sometimes do perceptibly strange and erratic things.

I've tried to save myself by bringing home stray cats on which Breanne could feed. My hope was to find them cocooned in her shimmery threads suspended from the rafters of our bedroom while Breanne sucked them down to a desiccated husk. But she never touched the cats, and complained about them being in the house. I had to finally shoo them all out into the street, but in a weird twist of fate, they keep returning, scratching at the front door and purring until I feed them. So now I feed stray cats on top of everything else.

Think of a plan, my cell phone often reminds me, and so I tried to change things further. I thought that maybe if *I* could bleed *myself* and allow her to feed, I would not be captive to her nightly regiment, and all the poisons she excretes into my bloodstream during her feeding time would cease to corrupt me. Maybe (I thought) my head would clear. Maybe (I thought) I would regain some semblance of normalcy.

But not all plans are good plans. It's why I was fired from ITS. I purchased some syringes, vials, and bladder bags online, and one afternoon in the break room at the office, I went about drawing my own blood into those vials, filling those bladder bags from a puncture in my left arm. But I had gotten woozy and I spilled a lot of blood—lost a lot of blood —and then some coworkers had walked in on me, my shirtsleeve cuffed to the elbow, a syringe drooping from the crook of my arm. There was blood all over the break room table, and I had passed out in it; at the sounds of my coworkers' gasps, I ratcheted up, blood smeared along one side of my face, and shrieked like a madman.

I do not blame ITS for liberating me from my position. True, it has made things more complicated financially—my savings won't last forever and Breanne doesn't work because she is a giant spider—but it has also freed me up to spend some quality time with the one person with whom I am most comfortable: myself. And those movies, of course.

And Libby, I think now, the notion coming into my mind unbidden. Its suddenness surprises me and even thrills me a little.

I look over at Breanne, who is still pretending to eat her Chinese food across the table from me. I know that behind her eyes are a different set of eyes: eight glassy obsidian spheres arranged in a jigsaw of horror across the bristling gray nub of her head. Beautiful if seen in the right light, I'll admit, despite also being downright terrifying.

She looks at me now and says, "Why aren't you eating?"

So I eat.

I need to keep up my strength for the real meal later in the night.

IV

I arrived at the theater the following day with some cleaning supplies. I sweep the dust from the aisle, use a feather duster on the seatbacks, and scrub the vinyl arms of the seats with a heavy duty scrub brush. Midway through this process, I pause and realize Libby still hasn't arrived. That niggling voice in my head chides me for being a fool, and for fabricating a person out of nothing. I even look back at the aisle to confirm that she'd been here the day before, but I have already swept away her footprints.

"Hi."

I turn and see her standing in a darkened corner of the theater, down by the edge of the screen and beneath where the old EXIT sign would be lit if this place was getting any power.

"You came back," I say.

"I said I would."

"I've cleaned up the place."

"You did," she says, looking around. "I can tell. Thank you."

I swallow what feels like a lump of charcoal, then say, "Do you want to watch a movie?"

And that is how a pattern takes shape: Libby returns every afternoon to the theater, where we watch another one of my horror movies together. When the movie is over, we talk while the movie screen glows in the white, radiant light of the projector. She has come to share a seat beside me instead of across the aisle, and sometimes as we watch the movie, I will feel the smooth, cool flesh of her hand slide into mine.

And for the first time in my life, I think I'm feeling something strange and different inside me. Breanne has instilled within me a distrust of women. I have come to believe they are not what they purport to be. Breanne, after all, is a spider. But now I sense that *other things have happened,* and that this Libby may be altogether different from other women. From Breanne. From my mother, even.

I wonder: could there be a life for me outside of the one in which I'm currently trapped? A life—possibly—with Libby?

But what about Breanne? We have this complex, symbiotic relationship that I know she will never let me break. It would kill her to do so—literally. She must feed. So how would I even approach such a subject with her? Explain that *other things have happened?* That I have been going to the theater every day instead of the office, and that I have met a woman who is actually a woman, another person with whom I've formed a connection? A woman who does not drain me like a vampire, but instead instills in me a happiness and a complacency that has been heretofore absent from my life?

Breanne would not like that.

Breanne would not abide that.

One night, after Breanne has fed and gone to sleep, I shuck off the silken strands, wriggle out of bed, and creep downstairs where I knock back a shot of bourbon. On my phone, I text myself a question:

What will happen if I try to leave Breanne?

This time, myself replies:

> She will hunt you down and devour you whole.

I stare at my phone for a very long time, wondering if I'm starting to lose my mind. Or maybe it's the poison that drips from my wife's fangs into my bloodstream as she feeds that has corrupted my mental stability.

"You are a kind man," Libby tells me one afternoon, once the movie ends. She rests her head on my shoulder and I inhale the scent of her perfume. "It's too bad we're both married."

Does she really say that?

I believe she does.

Yes—she *does*.

I want to ask her if she'll run away with me, but in doing so, I would also have to advise that we'd have to be quick about it, no dillydallying, because there would be a giant spider on our heels. So I don't say anything, and instead just enjoy Libby's head on my shoulder. After a time, I can hear her snoring gently, and I know she has fallen asleep.

My cell phone vibrates in my pocket.

I take it out and find a message from myself:

> think of a plan

As I'm staring at it, a second message comes through, also from myself:

> something has got to be done

And then a third:

> she isn't what she seems to be and she's got
> you fooled

It's this third message that confounds me. I stare at it for a long time, trying to puzzle it out. If it is referring to Breanne, then it is a futile message, because I already know Breanne isn't what she seems to be. Of course I do.

It's when the fourth message comes through that things become clearer:

> look at her neck

And it is then, in the light of the startling white movie screen coupled with the glow from my cell phone, that I can see what appears to be a thick black hair, perhaps two inches long, poking up from the side of Libby's neck. My whole body goes stiff at the sight of it and I nearly drop my phone to the sticky theater floor. Slowly, I reach around and prod the tip of that hair with my index finger, careful not to wake her. It's tough and sharp as a pine needle, that hair. Instantly, I'm reminded of another creature-feature remake, this one from 1986 and directed by David Cronenberg: *The Fly*. Not a giant-bug-run-amok movie per se, although there are elements of that film that make it difficult for me to watch nowadays, given my current domestic situation. The hair I see protruding from Libby's neck is no different than the hair that Geena Davis finds poking up from Jeff Goldblum's shoulder in the film. It's the first indication of his physical transformation into a human fly.

I hear that buzzing noise again—the same noise I heard the first time I saw Libby approach me across the floor of this theater. The swarming of flies. Or, more precisely: a *single* fly. And isn't that apropos, to find a fly inside this rotted corpse of a movie house? It's what flies like best: a dead body.

"What are you really?" I mutter into the soft crown of Libby's head.

She sighs, cuddles closer against me, but doesn't wake.

My phone vibrates again in my hand. I look down at the text message from myself:

> it's clear now

And another:

> this is a way to freedom

And another:

> this is the plan

And then my phone goes dark.

Later, when Libby awakes, she is embarrassed at having fallen asleep. She laughs softly, but she isn't fooling me now: I can still hear that low, drumming buzz in the background of things. When I look at her eyes, I can see another set of eyes behind those: the iridescent, compound orbs of a simple housefly.

Might she be the one to liberate me?

"I don't know," I say aloud, startling myself.

Libby cocks her head and smiles. Runs a hand along the side of my face. Says, "What's that? What's that, love?"

Or does she say that?

I place my hand atop hers, holding her palm against my cheek. "I was just thinking that maybe—"

She kisses me.

Libby *kisses* me.

In my head, the buzzing rises to a cacophonic frenzy. It gets to where I have to pull away from Libby and clamp my hands to my ears, even though the sound (for the moment) is strictly inside my head.

"Hey," she says, and touches my arm. "Are you okay?"

"Just a migraine," I say, lowering my hands. "Do you think you would like to come see my house?"

"Oh," she says, and sits back a bit in her seat, as if she suddenly smells something foul. Or, more precisely, *afoul.*

"My wife is not home," I tell her.

Libby considers this. I search the side of her neck for that two-inch hair, but can no longer find it. Her eyes look normal again, too.

"Maybe that will be all right," she says finally.

And touches the side of my face again.

V

It's a Wednesday afternoon, and that's when Breanne goes to her water aerobics class. She takes the city bus to the Y and returns mid-afternoon with her hair slicked back and her body reeking of chlorine. Over her shoulder is a duffel bag with another rhinestone cat on the side. Breanne started with the water aerobics several months ago in an effort to shed a few pounds, but I'm not so sure spiders lose weight in the same fashion people do. Fat spiders are generally regarded as well-fed, happy spiders, I would think.

She is surprised to find me on the sofa in front of the TV when she returns from her class. She stands there in the doorway, her reddened face twisted into a mask of confusion, her hair practically shellacked in a waterfall down her back. I can smell the chlorine on her and it makes my eyes burn.

"What are you doing home from work so early?" she asks.

Other Things Have Happened

"There have been a few changes," I say.

Breanne's confusion turns into a scowl. "What changes? What are you talking about?"

"Other things have happened," I say.

"What does *that* mean?"

"I've brought you a meal," I tell her. My hands on my knees begin to tremble, so I tuck them beneath me, sit on them. I've got a stain on my shirt, which could be mistaken for some spilled cat food, since I fed the strays just a little while ago. "It's in the bedroom."

"You put a meal in the *bedroom*?" She's staring at me as if I've lost my mind.

"Go on," I tell her. "Go see."

Her gaze lingers on me for a moment longer. But then she turns around and lumbers back down the hall. I listen as she climbs the stairs to the second floor. Midway up the stairwell, I can hear her transformation take place, because suddenly there are eight agile legs, each one thick as a power line, knocking against the risers as the great spider ascends.

In my pocket, my cell phone vibrates. I take it out and read the message that I have sent to myself:

get ready

I stand up from the sofa and try not to drop the phone, my hands are shaking so badly. Also, there is a cold sweat that seems to have begun somewhere deep inside of me, only to ooze out of my pores like poison.

Above me, I hear the spider make its way across the floor and down the hall. I hear the bedroom door squeal open on its hinges as the great arachnid enters her feasting chamber.

One final message pops up on my cell phone:

go now go

As Breanne begins to scream, I slip the cell phone into my pocket and bolt down the hallway, right out the front door, and into an afternoon radiant with sunlight. I don't worry about why Breanne would scream at the meal I've brought for her, I only keep running. A horde of cats gives chase and follows me down the block, but I hardly notice, because I'm laughing wildly while tears stream down my face. And I keep running.

This fly has escaped.

❦ ❦ ❦

Ronald Malfi is the award-winning author of several horror novels and thrillers, including the bestseller *Come with Me*, published by Titan Books in 2021.

He is the recipient of two Independent Publisher Book Awards, the Beverly Hills Book Award, the Vincent Preis Horror Award, the Benjamin Franklin Award, and his novel *Floating Staircase* was a finalist for the Bram Stoker Award.

He lives in Maryland.

Fuzzy Slippers
Jeff Strand

AGNES HATED HER BIRTHDAY. Not just because of the relentless onward march of aging (although at sixty-two years old that was certainly part of it), but because opening presents made her so anxious. What if she didn't look surprised enough? What if she didn't look delighted enough? What if somebody in her family put a lot of time and effort into getting her the perfect gift, and her underwhelmed reaction hurt their feelings?

At Christmas, she had a shield. The house was filled with people, all of them tearing open their presents at the same time in a festival of glorious chaos. On her birthday, though, all eyes were on her. Her every facial tic was being closely observed. And the stress of it made her sick to her stomach, because there was always the fear that what lurked under the wrapping paper was a gift so atrocious, she couldn't successfully pretend to like it.

For example, these fuzzy slippers.

They were hideous. A bright orange color that looked like staring into the sun. The fuzzy part didn't resemble a shag rug so much as a lawn that had gotten out of control. Not to mention that she already had a pair of extremely comfortable slippers that *didn't* hurt her eyes.

The gift-giver was Candice. Not her favorite grandchild, but not her least favorite. Candice was legally an adult now; thus, she should have better taste than this.

"Oh," said Agnes, trying to sound elated. She knew she didn't really have sweat pouring down her face, but it felt as though the perspiration was flowing like Niagara Falls. "What a kind and thoughtful gift." She forced a smile and prayed that nobody could tell that it was forced.

"Your old slippers were looking kind of ratty," said Candice.

Agnes' old slippers were perfectly fine, but of course she didn't say anything. Her granddaughter meant well, of course, and that was all that mattered, in theory.

The disaster of the fuzzy slippers, which were the second gift in the rotation, left her anxiety-ridden for the rest of the present-opening experience. Her mouth kept twitching with each new gift, but fortunately, the slippers were the only one she had to pretend was not complete garbage. Finally, the hell on earth experience was over, and they all ate cake.

🍫 🍫 🍫

Agnes climbed onto the left side of the bed. Seven years after Rodney's passing, she'd never quite adjusted to having the entire bed to herself.

After a pleasant night of sleep, she swung her legs over the side of the bed. She was about to slip her feet into her comfy light blue slippers, but decided that she should at least *try* the ones that Candice got her. Maybe they were comfortable enough to outweigh their grotesque appearance.

They were next to her closet door. She slid her feet into them, then walked across the bedroom floor.

They were kind of scratchy. Unpleasant.

What had Candice been thinking? Perhaps she'd become an alcoholic.

Agnes let out a yelp as something bit her.

It was winter in Wisconsin. She shouldn't have to check her slippers for snakes or scorpions before putting them on! She kicked off the left slipper, sat back down on the bed, and examined her foot. There was a thin red line (not blood—it hadn't broken the skin) that went all the way around, just below her ankle.

It was as if the fuzzy slipper itself had bitten her.

That was ridiculous, of course, but it emphasized just how bad of a present it was. When Candice asked her how she was enjoying them, Agnes might very well have to be honest and say that she was not enjoying them much at all.

Well, no. She'd never do that. Maybe she'd pretend that they'd been stolen.

She cried out in pain as the right slipper bit her.

Agnes tried to kick off the slipper, but it remained firmly on her foot. This was a much more powerful bite than the first time...and, yes, she knew it wasn't really biting her, but it was doing *something* awful to her foot! She frantically kicked and kicked. The slipper wouldn't come off.

Though it was difficult for her to reach her feet these days, she managed to grab the slipper with both hands and give it a tug. It still wouldn't budge.

And now the slipper was trembling. As if it was...alive?

It made a low growling sound, more like a pit bull than a poodle.

It started to bite her, over and over. She hadn't previously noticed any teeth, but something sharp was digging into her foot. She screamed.

The slipper wouldn't come off, no matter how hard she

tried to pry it free. Blood was starting to stain the orange fuzz.

She punched it, but only succeeded in hurting her hand and foot.

"Get off me!" she shouted. The slipper did not listen to her request. She screamed for help. Unfortunately, she and Rodney had always enjoyed their peace and quiet when family wasn't visiting, and she had no neighbors within screaming distance.

The other slipper began to crawl toward her.

It was actually crawling! Moving along the floor like an inchworm!

She wished she had a fireplace poker, or a baseball bat, or a machete—something to fight off the slippers! All she had on her bed was a blanket and pillow, which weren't effective weapons.

Or were they? Violent or not, it was just a slipper. Trying to ignore the slipper that was chewing on her foot, she yanked the blanket off her bed and tossed it onto the other one, hiding it from sight.

Then she limped out of the bedroom as the slipper on her foot continued to growl and bite. It got even more aggressive as she staggered down the hallway—perhaps it was angry that she kept stepping on it.

Should she head for the kitchen, which contained knives, or the living room, which had her phone? She'd need a cover story to tell 911, since "My fuzzy slippers are trying to eat me" didn't sound credible, although she supposed they might send somebody if they thought she was in the throes of dementia.

The kitchen was the better idea.

The bite suddenly grew much more intense and vicious. She looked down and saw blood seeping all over the slippers. She had to move quickly.

The slipper seemed to get angrier and angrier as she made her way into the kitchen. She had to brace herself against the wall to keep from falling. Finally, she made it, and headed for the drawer with the knives.

"Time to die, you little creep," she said, although in her mind she used a word she would never say out loud. Not the F-word, of course, or the S-word, but, oh, she thought about how that slipper was a little bastard and didn't care how much God judged her.

Agnes opened the drawer and pulled out a long bread cutting knife. She had so many fond memories of slicing bread with this knife (rye and pumpernickel in particular), but now it would be used for a much darker purpose.

She jabbed at the slipper lightly, making sure not to poke through and injure her foot. It didn't seem to have any impact—the slipper continued to gnaw away. So she pressed the tip of the knife into a spot that she *hoped* would cause it to pass harmlessly between her first two toes, and pushed it through the slipper.

The slipper let out a high-pitched shriek. All the fuzz stood on end. For an instant, but only an instant, it stopped biting her.

Clearly it didn't like being stabbed. So she stabbed it again. And again.

With each stab, the slipper shrieked louder, and Agnes stopped caring if she was also stabbing her foot as well. She plunged the bread knife into the slipper over and over, jolts of pain searing through her foot each time. Since she didn't think the slipper itself could bleed, this was probably her blood. Not ideal, but mangling herself would be worth it if she could get this savage slipper off!

The slipper tightened its grip. A lot. This might be really bad...

Agnes screamed.

Blood spurted. Bones cracked.

And then the slipper bit her foot completely off.

She tumbled to the floor, landing hard on the linoleum. She stared at her spraying stump in horror and disbelief.

A fuzzy orange tongue protruded from the slipper, as it licked its…lips?

Then it made a gulping sound, like it was swallowing. How could it swallow her foot? Where would it go? The slipper didn't have a stomach!

"You'll go to Hell for this!" Agnes told it, not caring that she used the h-word. Some situations called for harsh profanity.

She needed a tourniquet. But she didn't think she had the tools for one, or know how to make one, or honestly quite understand how they worked. It was just something you needed after you lost a foot to keep from bleeding to death, according to something she'd read in *Reader's Digest*.

Agnes felt a lot of fear, yet also a lot of rage. How dare her birthday present attack her like this? She might not have a tourniquet, but she did have a garbage disposal, and this thing was going straight in there.

If she could stand up.

Which she couldn't, thanks to her missing foot.

She screamed again (she was doing a lot of that lately) as the other slipper, which had made its way out from underneath the blanket, chomped down on her hand. It didn't bite off her entire hand, but it did get all four fingers and the tip of her thumb. It swallowed them. Seriously, where did they go? Another dimension?

She was more concerned about the loss of her fingers themselves than the fact that her wedding ring went with them, but the ring was still a devastating loss.

The blood-covered slipper moved across her chest. Instead of biting off any more body parts, it crawled down her leg and joined the other slipper in slurping up the blood that was spewing from her leg stump. Since there was plenty of blood spewing from what remained of her hand, she wasn't sure why it made the effort.

Then it mounted the other slipper and began to thrust away.

The slippers were *getting it on* while being showered by blood! They weren't just violent, they were perverted! And they were twins, so this was fuzzy slipper incest!

Agnes turned away. She couldn't let the sight of depraved slippers engaging in carnality be the last thing she ever saw. She looked at the counter. She'd always liked that counter. She wished she'd wiped it down more thoroughly after last night's meal.

The slippers crawled on top of her and began to feast.

🐌 🐌 🐌

Grandma hadn't answered her phone, so Candice quickly drove over there and pounded on the door. Grandma didn't answer that, either.

It had been a terrible mistake to order fuzzy slippers and a cursed belt from the same online store. She'd ordered comfy fuzzy slippers for Grandma to replace the worn out light blue ones, and a belt that would squeeze her ex-boyfriend Matthew's waist until his guts popped out. But she'd received a call from customer service explaining that they'd put a curse on the wrong present.

She kept pounding on the door. "Grandma? Grandma? Please open up!"

The door opened, revealing Grandma. She was drenched in blood. Her nightgown was torn to shreds, she was missing a foot, and seemed to only have two fingers left. One of her ears had been bitten half off. She'd tied garbage bags around her wrists and ankles—were those supposed to be tourniquets?

Candice couldn't say anything. She just gaped.

"Got 'em down the garbage disposal," said Grandma.

"I'm so sorry!" said Candice.

"You should be. Your present fucking sucked."

❧ ❧ ❧

Jeff Strand is the Bram Stoker Award-winning novel of about sixty books, including DWELLER and AUTUMN BLEEDS INTO WINTER.

He hopes that readers recognize that his story was pure fiction, and that fuzzy slippers are safe and comfortable.

The Raft
Stephen King

IT WAS forty miles from Horlicks University in Pittsburgh to
Cascade Lake, and although dark comes early to that part of
the world in October and although they didn't get going
until six o'clock, there was still a little light in the sky when
they got there. They had come in Deke's Camaro. Deke
didn't waste any time when he was sober. After a couple of
beers, he made that Camaro walk and talk.

He had hardly brought the car to a stop at the pole fence
between the parking lot and the beach before he was out and
pulling off his shirt. His eyes were scanning the water for the
raft. Randy got out of the shotgun seat, a little reluctantly.
This had been his idea, true enough, but he had never
expected Deke to take it seriously. The girls were moving
around in the back seat, getting ready to get out.

Deke's eyes scanned the water restlessly, side to side
(sniper's eyes, Randy thought uncomfortably), and then fixed
on a point.

"It's there!" he shouted, slapping the hood of the Camaro.
"Just like you said, Randy! Hot damn! Last one in's a rotten
egg!"

"Deke—" Randy began, resetting his glasses on his nose, but that was all he bothered with, because Deke was vaulting the fence and running down the beach, not looking back at Randy or Rachel or LaVerne, only looking out at the raft, which was anchored about fifty yards out on the lake.

Randy looked around, as if to apologize to the girls for getting them into this, but they were looking at Deke— Rachel looking at him was all right, Rachel was Deke's girl, but LaVerne was looking at him, too, and Randy felt a hot momentary spark of jealousy that got him moving. He peeled off his own sweatshirt, dropped it beside Deke's, and hopped the fence.

"Randy!" LaVerne called, and he only pulled his arm forward through the gray twilit October air in a come-on gesture, hating himself a little for doing it—she was unsure now, perhaps ready to cry it off. The idea of an October swim in the deserted lake wasn't just part of a comfortable, well-lighted bull-session in the apartment he and Deke shared anymore. He liked her, but Deke was stronger. And damned if she didn't have the hots for Deke, and damned if it wasn't irritating.

Deke unbuckled his jeans, still running, and pushed them off his lean hips. He somehow got out of them all the way without stopping, a feat Randy could not have duplicated in a thousand years. Deke ran on, now only wearing bikini briefs, the muscles in his back and buttocks working gorgeously. Randy was more than aware of his own skinny shanks as he dropped his Levi's and clumsily shook them free of his feet— with Deke it was ballet, with him burlesque.

Deke hit the water and bellowed, "Cold! Mother of Jesus!"

Randy hesitated, but only in his mind, where things took longer—*that water's forty-five degrees, fifty at most,* his mind told him. *Your heart could stop.* He was pre-med, he knew that was true . . . but in the physical world he didn't hesitate at all.

He leaped it, and for a moment his heart did stop, or seemed to; his breath clogged in his throat and he had to force a gasp of air into his lungs as all his submerged skin went numb. *This is crazy*, he thought, and then: *But it was your idea, Pancho.* He began to stroke after Deke.

The two girls looked at each other for a moment. LaVerne shrugged and grinned. "If they can, we can," she said, stripping off her Lacoste shirt to reveal an almost transparent bra. "Aren't girls supposed to have an extra layer of fat?"

Then she was over the fence and running for the water, unbuttoning her cords. After a moment Rachel followed her, much as Randy had followed Deke.

The girls had come over to the apartment at midafternoon—on Tuesdays a one-o'clock was the latest class any of them had. Deke's monthly allotment had come in—one of the football-mad alums (the players called them "angels") saw that he got two hundred a month in cash—and there was a case of beer in the fridge and a new Night Ranger album on Randy's battered stereo. The four of them set about getting pleasantly oiled. After a while the talk had turned to the end of the long Indian summer they had been enjoying. The radio was predicting flurries for Wednesday. LaVerne had advanced the opinion that weathermen predicting snow flurries in October should be shot, and no one had disagreed.

Rachel said that summers had seemed to last forever when she was a girl, but now that she was an adult ("a doddering senile nineteen," Deke joked, and she kicked his ankle), they got shorter every year. "It seemed like I spent my life out at Cascade Lake," she said, crossing the decayed kitchen linoleum to the icebox. She peered in, found an Iron City Light hiding behind a stack of blue Tupperware storage boxes (the one in the middle contained some nearly prehis-

toric chili which was now thickly festooned with mold—
Randy was a good student and Deke was a good football
player, but neither of them was worth a fart in a noisemaker
when it came to housekeeping), and appropriated it. "I can
still remember the first time I managed to swim all the way
out to the raft. I stayed there for damn near two hours,
scared to swim back."

She sat down next to Deke, who put an arm around her.
She smiled, remembering, and Randy suddenly thought she
looked like someone famous or semi-famous. He couldn't
quite place the resemblance. It would come to him later,
under less pleasant circumstances.

"Finally my brother had to swim out and tow me back on
an inner tube. God, he was mad. And I had a sunburn like
you wouldn't believe."

"The raft's still out there," Randy said, mostly to say
something. He was aware that LaVerne had been looking at
Deke again; just lately it seemed like she looked at Deke a lot.

But now she looked at him. "It's almost *Halloween*, Randy.
Cascade Beach has been closed since Labor Day."

"Raft's probably still out there, though," Randy said. "We
were on the other side of the lake on a geology field trip
about three weeks ago and I saw it then. It looked like . . ." He
shrugged. ". . . a little bit of summer that somebody forgot to
clean up and put away in the closet until next year."

He thought they would laugh at that, but no one did—not
even Deke.

"Just because it was there last year doesn't mean it's still
there," LaVerne said.

"I mentioned it to a guy," Randy said, finishing his own
beer. "Billy DeLois, do you remember him, Deke?"

Deke nodded. "Played second string until he got hurt."

"Yeah, I guess so. Anyway, he comes from out that way,
and he said the guys who own the beach never take it in until

the lake's almost ready to freeze. Just lazy—at least, that's what he said. He said that some year they'd wait too long and it would get ice-locked."

He fell silent, remembering how the raft had looked, anchored out there on the lake—a square of bright white wood in all that bright blue autumn water. He remembered how the sound of the barrels under it—that buoyant clunk-clunk sound—had drifted up to them. The sound was soft, but sounds carried well on the still air around the lake. There had been that sound and the sound of crows squabbling over the remnants of some farmer's harvested garden.

"Snow tomorrow," Rachel said, getting up as Deke's hand wandered almost absently down to the upper swell of her breast. She went to the window and looked out. "What a bummer."

"I'll tell you what," Randy said, "let's go on out to Cascade Lake. We'll swim out to the raft, say good-bye to summer, and then swim back."

If he hadn't been half-loaded he never would have made the suggestion, and he certainly didn't expect anyone to take it seriously. But Deke jumped on it.

"All right! Awesome, Pancho! Fooking awesome!" LaVerne jumped and spilled her beer. But she smiled—the smile made Randy a little uneasy. "Let's do it!"

"Deke, you're crazy," Rachel said, also smiling—but her smile looked a little tentative, a little worried.

"No, I'm going to do it," Deke said, going for his coat, and with a mixture of dismay and excitement, Randy noted Deke's grin—reckless and a little crazy. The two of them had been rooming together for three years now—the Jock and the Brain, Cisco and Pancho, Batman and Robin—and Randy recognized that grin. Deke wasn't kidding; he meant to do it. In his head he was already halfway there.

Forget it, Cisco—not me. The words rose to his lips, but

before he could say them LaVerne was on her feet, the same cheerful, loony look in her own eyes (or maybe it was just too much beer). "I'm up for it!"

"Then let's go!" Deke looked at Randy. "Whatchoo say, Pancho?"

He had looked at Rachel for a moment then, and saw something almost frantic in her eyes—as far as he himself was concerned, Deke and LaVerne could go out to Cascade Lake together and plow the back forty all night; he would not be delighted with the knowledge that they were boffing each other's brains out, yet neither would he be surprised. But that look in the other girl's eyes, that haunted look—

"Ohhh, *Ceesco*!" Randy cried.

"Ohhhh, *Pancho*!" Deke cried back, delighted.

They slapped palms.

❧ ❧ ❧

Randy was halfway to the raft when he saw the black patch on the water. It was beyond the raft and to the left of it, more out toward the middle of the lake. Five minutes later the light would have failed too much for him to tell it was anything more than a shadow . . . if he had seen it at all. *Oil slick?* he thought, still pulling hard through the water, faintly aware of the girls splashing behind him. But what would an oil slick be doing on an October-deserted lake? And it was oddly circular, small, surely no more than five feet in diameter—

"*Whoooo!*" Deke shouted again, and Randy looked toward him. Deke was climbing the ladder on the side of the raft, shaking off water like a dog. "Howya doon, Pancho?"

"Okay!" he called back, pulling harder. It really wasn't as bad as he had thought it might be, not once you got in and got moving. His body tingled with warmth and now his motor was in overdrive. He could feel his heart putting out good revs, heating him from the inside out. His folks had a place on Cape Cod, and the water there was worse than this in mid-July.

"You think it's bad now, Pancho, wait'll you get out!" Deke yelled gleefully. He was hopping up and down, making the raft rock, rubbing his body.

Randy forgot about the oil slick until his hands actually grasped the rough, white-painted wood of the ladder on the shore side. Then he saw it again. It was a little closer. A round dark patch on the water, like a big mole, rising and falling on the mild waves. When he had first seen it the patch had been maybe forty yards from the raft. Now it was only half that distance.

How can that be? How—

Then he came out of the water and the cold air bit his skin, bit it even harder than the water had when he first dived in. "Ohhhhhh, *shit!*" He yelled, laughing, shivering in his Jockey shorts.

"Pancho, you ees some kine of beeg asshole," Deke said happily. He pulled Randy up. "Cold enough for you? You sober yet?"

"I'm sober! I'm sober!" He began to jump around as Deke had done, clapping his arms across his chest and stomach in an X. They turned to look at the girls.

Rachel had pulled ahead of LaVerne, who was doing something that looked like a dog paddle performed by a dog with bad instincts.

"You ladies okay?" Deke bellowed.

"Go to hell, Macho City!" LaVerne called, and Deke broke up again.

Randy glanced to the side and saw that odd dark circular patch was even closer—ten yards now, and still coming. It floated on the water, round and regular, like the top of a

47

large steel drum, but the limber way it rode the swells made it clear that it was not the surface of a solid object. Fear, directionless but powerful, suddenly seized him.

"*Swim!*" he shouted at the girls, and bent down to grasp Rachel's hand as she reached the ladder. He hauled her up. She bumped her knee hard—he heard the thud clearly.

"Ow! *Hey!* What—"

LaVerne was still ten feet away. Randy glanced to the side again and saw the round thing nuzzle the offside of the raft. The thing was as dark as oil, but he was sure it wasn't oil—too dark, too thick, too even.

"Randy, that *hurt!* What are you doing, being fun—"

"LaVerne! *Swim!*" Now it wasn't just fear; now it was terror.

LaVerne looked up, maybe not hearing the terror but at least hearing the urgency. She looked puzzled but she dog-paddled faster, closing the distance to the ladder.

"Randy, what's wrong with you?" Deke asked.

Randy looked to the side again and saw the thing fold itself around the raft's square corner. For a moment it looked like a Pac-Man image with its mouth open to eat electronic cookies. Then it slipped all the way around the corner and began to slide along the raft, one of its edges now straight.

"Help me get her up!" Randy grunted to Deke and reached for her hand. "Quick!"

Deke shrugged good-naturedly and reached for LaVerne's other hand. They pulled her up and onto the raft's board surface bare seconds before the black thing slid by the ladder, its sides dimpling as it slipped past the ladder's uprights.

"Randy, have you gone crazy?" LaVerne was out of breath, a little frightened. Her nipples were clearly visible through the bra. They stood out in cold hard points.

"That thing," Randy said, pointing. "Deke? What is it?"

Deke spotted it. It had reached the left-hand corner of the raft. It drifted off a little to one side, reassuming its round shape. It simply floated there. The four of them looked at it.

"Oil slick, I guess," Deke said.

"You really racked my knee," Rachel said, glancing at the dark thing on the water and then back at Randy. "You—"

"It's not an oil slick," Randy said. "Did you ever see a round oil slick? That thing looks like a checker."

"I never saw an oil slick at all," Deke replied. He was talking to Randy but he was looking at LaVerne. LaVerne's panties were almost as transparent as her bra, the delta of her sex sculpted neatly in silk, each buttock a taut crescent. "I don't even believe in them. I'm from Missouri."

"I'm going to bruise," Rachel said, but the anger had gone out of her voice. She had seen Deke looking at LaVerne.

"*God*, I'm cold," LaVerne said. She shivered prettily.

"It went for the girls," Randy said.

"Come on, Pancho. I thought you said you got sober."

"It went for the girls," he repeated stubbornly, and thought: *No one knows we're here. No one at all.*

"Have *you* ever seen an oil slick, Pancho?" He had put his arm around LaVerne's bare shoulders in the same almost-absent way that he had touched Rachel's breast earlier that day. He wasn't touching LaVerne's breast—not yet, anyway—but his hand was close. Randy found he didn't care much, one way or another. That black, circular patch on the water. He cared about that.

"I saw one on the Cape, four years ago," he said. "We all pulled birds out of the surf and tried to clean them off—"

"Ecological, Pancho," Deke said approvingly. "Mucho ecological, I theenk."

Randy said, "It was just this big, sticky mess all over the water. In streaks and big smears. It didn't look like that. It wasn't, you know, *compact.*"

It looked like an accident, he wanted to say. *That thing doesn't look like an accident; it looks like it's on purpose.*

"I want to go back now," Rachel said. She was still looking at Deke and LaVerne. Randy saw dull hurt in her face. He doubted if she knew it showed.

"So go," LaVerne said. There was a look on her face—*the clarity of absolute triumph*, Randy thought, and if the thought seemed pretentious, it also seemed exactly right. The expression was not aimed precisely at Rachel . . . but neither was LaVerne trying to hide it from the other girl.

She moved a step closer to Deke; a step was all there was. Now their hips touched lightly. For one brief moment Randy's attention passed from the thing floating on the water and focused on LaVerne with an almost exquisite hate. Although he had never hit a girl, in that one moment he could have hit her with real pleasure. Not because he loved her (he had been a little infatuated with her, yes, and more than a little horny for her, yes, and a lot jealous when she had begun to come on to Deke back at the apartment, oh yes, but he wouldn't have brought a girl he actually *loved* within fifteen miles of Deke in the first place), but because he knew that expression on Rachel's face—how that expression felt inside.

"I'm afraid," Rachel said.

"Of an *oil slick?*" LaVerne asked incredulously, and then laughed. The urge to hit her swept over Randy again—to just swing a big roundhouse open-handed blow through the air, to wipe that look of half-assed hauteur from her face and leave a mark on her cheek that would bruise in the shape of a hand.

"Let's see you swim back, then," Randy said.

LaVerne smiled indulgently at him. "I'm not ready to go," she said, as if explaining to a child. She looked up at the sky, then at Deke. "I want to watch the stars come out."

Rachel was a short girl, pretty, but in a gamine, slightly insecure way that made Randy think of New York girls—you saw them hurrying to work in the morning, wearing their smartly tailored skirts with slits in the front or up one side, wearing that same look of slightly neurotic prettiness. Rachel's eyes always sparkled, but it was hard to tell if it was good cheer that lent them that lively look or just free-floating anxiety.

Deke's tastes usually ran more to tall girls with dark hair and sleepy sloe eyes, and Randy saw it was now over between Deke and Rachel—whatever there had been, something simple and maybe a little boring on his part, something deep and complicated and probably painful on hers. It was over, so cleanly and suddenly that Randy almost heard the snap: a sound like dry kindling broken over a knee.

He was a shy boy, but he moved to Rachel now and put an arm around her. She glanced up at him briefly, her face unhappy but grateful for his gesture, and he was glad he had improved the situation for her a little. That similarity bobbed into his mind again. Something in her face, her looks—

He first associated it with TV game shows, then with commercials for crackers or wafers or some damn thing. It came to him then—she looked like Sandy Duncan, the actress who had played in the revival of *Peter Pan* on Broadway.

"What is that thing?" she asked. "Randy? What is it?"

"I don't know."

He glanced at Deke and saw Deke looking at him with that familiar smile that was more loving familiarity than contempt . . . but the contempt was there, too. Maybe Deke didn't even know it, but it was. The expression said *Here goes ole worry-wart Randy, pissing in his didies again.* It was supposed to make Randy mumble an addition—*It's probably nothing, Don't worry about it, It'll go away.* Something like that.

He didn't. Let Deke smile. The black patch on the water scared him. That was the truth.

Rachel stepped away from Randy and knelt prettily on the corner of the raft closest to the thing, and for a moment she triggered an even clearer memory-association: the girl on the White Rock labels. *Sandy Duncan on the White Rock labels*, his mind amended. Her hair, a close-cropped, slightly coarse blond, lay wetly against her finely shaped skull. He could see goosebumps on her shoulder blades above the white band of her bra.

"Don't fall in, Rache," LaVerne said with bright malice.

"Quit it, LaVerne," Deke said, still smiling.

Randy looked from them, standing in the middle of the raft with their arms loosely around each other's waists, hips touching lightly, and back at Rachel. Alarm raced down his spine and out through his nerves like fire. The black patch had halved the distance between it and the corner of the raft where Rachel was kneeling and looking at it. It had been six or eight feet away before. Now the distance was three feet or less. And he saw a strange look in her eyes, a round blankness that seemed queerly like the round blankness of the thing in the water.

Now it's Sandy Duncan sitting on a White Rock label and pretending to be hypnotized by the rich delicious flavor of Nabisco Honey Grahams, he thought idiotically, feeling his heart speed up as it had in the water, and he called out, "Get away from there, Rachel!"

Then everything happened very fast—things happened with the rapidity of fireworks going off. And yet he saw and heard each thing with perfect, hellish clarity. Each thing seemed caught in its own little capsule.

LaVerne laughed—on the quad in a bright afternoon hour it might have sounded like any college girl's laugh, but out here in the growing dark it sounded like the arid cackle of a witch making magic in a pot.

"Rachel, maybe you better get b—" Deke said, but she interrupted him, almost surely for the first time in her life, and indubitably for the last.

"It has colors!" she cried in a voice of utter, trembling wonder. Her eyes stared at the black patch on the water with blank rapture, and for just a moment Randy thought he saw what she was talking about—colors, yeah, colors, swirling in rich, inward-turning spirals. Then they were gone, and there was only dull, lusterless black again. "Such beautiful colors!"

"*Rachel!*"

She reached for it—out and down—her white arm, marbled with gooseflesh, her hand, held out to it, meaning to touch; he saw she had bitten her nails ragged.

"*Ra—*"

He sensed the raft tilt in the water as Deke moved toward them. He reached for Rachel at the same time, meaning to pull her back, dimly aware that he didn't want Deke to be the one to do it.

Then Rachel's hand touched the water—her forefinger only, sending out one delicate ripple in a ring—and the black patch surged over it. Randy heard her gasp in air, and suddenly the blankness left her eyes. What replaced it was agony.

The black, viscous substance ran up her arm like mud . . . and under it, Randy saw her skin dissolving. She opened her mouth and screamed. At the same moment she began to tilt outward. She waved her other hand blindly at Randy and he grabbed for it. Their fingers brushed. Her eyes met his, and she still looked hellishly like Sandy Duncan. Then she fell outward and splashed into the water.

The black thing flowed over the spot where she had landed.

"*What happened?*" LaVerne was screaming behind them. "*What happened? Did she fall in? What happened to her?*"

Randy made as if to dive in after her and Deke pushed him backwards with casual force. "No," he said in a frightened voice that was utterly unlike Deke.

All three of them saw her flail to the surface. Her arms came up, waving—no, not arms. One arm. The other was covered with a black membrane that hung in flaps and folds from something red and knitted with tendons, something that looked a little like a rolled roast of beef.

"*Help!*" Rachel screamed. Her eyes glared at them, away from them, at them, away—her eyes were like lanterns being waved aimlessly in the dark. She beat the water into a froth. "*Help it hurts please help it hurts IT HURTS IT HURRRRR—*"

Randy had fallen when Deke pushed him. Now he got up from the boards of the raft and stumbled forward again, unable to ignore that voice. He tried to jump in and Deke grabbed him, wrapping his big arms around Randy's thin chest.

"No, she's dead," he whispered harshly. "Christ, can't you see that? She's *dead*, Pancho."

Thick blackness suddenly poured across Rachel's face like a drape, and her screams were first muffled and then cut off entirely. Now the black stuff seemed to bind her in crisscrossing ropes. Randy could see it sinking into her like acid, and when her jugular vein gave way in a dark, pumping jet, he saw the thing send out a pseudopod after the escaping blood. He could not believe what he was seeing, could not understand it . . . but there was no doubt, no sensation of losing his mind, no belief that he was dreaming or hallucinating.

LaVerne was screaming. Randy turned to look at her just in time to see her slap a hand melodramatically over her eyes like a silent movie heroine. He thought he would laugh and tell her this, but found he could not make a sound.

He looked back at Rachel. Rachel was almost not there anymore.

Her struggles had weakened to the point where they were really no more than spasms. The blackness oozed over her—*bigger now*, Randy thought, *it's bigger, no question about it*—with mute, muscular power. He saw her hand beat at it; saw the hand become stuck, as if in molasses or on flypaper; saw it consumed. Now there was a sense of her form only, not in the water but in the black thing, not turning but being turned, the form becoming less recognizable, a white flash—*bone*, he thought sickly, and turned away, vomiting helplessly over the side of the raft.

LaVerne was still screaming. Then there was a dull *whap!* and she stopped screaming and began to snivel.

He hit her, Randy thought. *I was going to do that, remember?*

He stepped back, wiping his mouth, feeling weak and ill. And scared. So scared he could think with only one tiny wedge of his mind. Soon he would begin to scream himself. Then Deke would have to slap him, Deke wouldn't panic, oh no, Deke was hero material for sure. *You gotta be a football hero . . . to get along with the beautiful girls*, his mind sang cheerfully. Then he could hear Deke talking to him, and he looked up at the sky, trying to clear his head, trying desperately to put away the vision of Rachel's form becoming blobbish and inhuman as that black thing ate her, not wanting Deke to slap him the way he had slapped LaVerne.

He looked up at the sky and saw the first stars shining up there—the shape of the Dipper already clear as the last white light faded out of the west. It was nearly seven-thirty.

"Oh Ceeesco," he managed. "We are in beeg trouble thees time, I theeenk."

"What is it?" His hand fell on Randy's shoulder, gripping

and twisting painfully. "It ate her, did you see that? It *ate* her, it fucking *ate her up!* What *is* it?"

"I don't know. Didn't you hear me before?"

"You're *supposed* to know, you're a fucking brain-ball, you take all the fucking science courses!" Now Deke was almost screaming himself, and that helped Randy get a little more control.

"There's nothing like that in any science book I ever read," Randy told him. "The last time I saw anything like that was the Halloween Shock-Show down at the Rialto when I was twelve."

The thing had regained its round shape now. It floated on the water ten feet from the raft.

"It's bigger," LaVerne moaned.

When Randy had first seen it, he had guessed its diameter at about five feet. Now it had to be at least eight feet across.

"*It's bigger because it ate Rachel!*" LaVerne cried, and began to scream again.

"Stop that or I'm going to break your jaw," Deke said, and she stopped—not all at once, but winding down the way a record does when somebody turns off the juice without taking the needle off the disc. Her eyes were huge things.

Deke looked back at Randy. "You all right, Pancho?"

"I don't know. I guess so."

"My man." Deke tried to smile, and Randy saw with some alarm that he was succeeding—was some part of Deke enjoying this? "You don't have any idea at all what it might be?"

Randy shook his head. Maybe it was an oil slick, after all . . . or had been, until something had happened to it. Maybe cosmic rays had hit it in a certain way. Or maybe Arthur Godfrey had pissed atomic Bisquick all over it, who knew? Who *could* know?

"Can we swim past it, do you think?" Deke persisted, shaking Randy's shoulder.

"*No!*" LaVerne shrieked.

"Stop it or I'm gonna smoke you, LaVerne," Deke said, raising his voice again. "I'm not kidding."

"You saw how fast it took Rachel," Randy said.

"Maybe it was hungry then," Deke answered. "But maybe now it's full."

Randy thought of Rachel kneeling there on the corner of the raft, so still and pretty in her bra and panties, and felt his gorge rise again.

"You try it," he said to Deke.

Deke grinned humorlessly. "Oh Pancho."

"Oh Ceesco."

"I want to go home," LaVerne said in a furtive whisper. "Okay?"

Neither of them replied.

"So we wait for it to go away," Deke said. "It came, it'll go away."

"Maybe," Randy said.

Deke looked at him, his face full of a fierce concentration in the gloom. "Maybe? What's this maybe shit?"

"We came, and it came. I saw it come—like it smelled us. If it's full, like you say, it'll go. I guess. If it still wants chow—" He shrugged.

Deke stood thoughtfully, head bent. His short hair was still dripping a little.

"We wait," he said. "Let it eat fish."

Fifteen minutes passed. They didn't talk. It got colder. It was maybe fifty degrees and all three of them were in their underwear. After the first ten minutes, Randy could hear the brisk, intermittent clickety-click of his teeth. LaVerne had tried to move next to Deke, but he pushed her away—gently but firmly enough.

"Let me be for now," he said.

So she sat down, arms crossed over her breasts, hands cupping her elbows, shivering. She looked at Randy, her eyes telling him he could come back, put his arm around her, it was okay now.

He looked away instead, back at the dark circle on the water. It just floated there, not coming any closer, but not going away, either. He looked toward the shore and there was the beach, a ghostly white crescent that seemed to float. The trees behind it made a dark, bulking horizon line. He thought he could see Deke's Camaro, but he wasn't sure.

"We just picked up and went," Deke said.

"That's right," Randy said.

"Didn't tell anyone."

"No."

"So no one knows we're here."

"No."

"Stop it!" LaVerne shouted. "Stop it, you're scaring me!"

"Shut your pie-hole," Deke said absently, and Randy laughed in spite of himself—no matter how many times Deke said that, it always slew him. "If we have to spend the night out here, we do. Somebody'll hear us yelling tomorrow. We're hardly in the middle of the Australian Outback, are we, Randy?"

Randy said nothing.

"*Are* we?"

"You know where we are," Randy said. "You know as well as I do. We turned off Route 41, we came up eight miles of back road—"

"Cottages every fifty feet—"

"*Summer* cottages. This is October. They're empty, the whole bucking funch of them. We got here and you had to drive around the damn gate, NO TRESPASSING signs every fifty feet—"

"So? A caretaker—" Deke was sounding a little pissed now, a little off-balance. A little scared? For the first time tonight, for the first time this month, this year, maybe for the first time in his whole life? Now there was an awesome thought—Deke loses his fear-cherry. Randy was not sure it was happening, but he thought maybe it was . . . and he took a perverse pleasure in it.

"Nothing to steal, nothing to vandalize," he said. "If there's a caretaker, he probably pops by here on a bimonthly basis."

"Hunters—"

"Next month, yeah," Randy said, and shut his mouth with a snap. He had also succeeded in scaring himself.

"Maybe it'll leave us alone," LaVerne said. Her lips made a pathetic, loose little smile. "Maybe it'll just . . . you know . . . leave us alone."

Deke said, "Maybe pigs will—"

"It's moving," Randy said.

LaVerne leaped to her feet. Deke came to where Randy was and for a moment the raft tilted, scaring Randy's heart into a gallop and making LaVerne scream again. Then Deke stepped back a little and the raft stabilized, with the left front corner (as they faced the shoreline) dipped down slightly more than the rest of the raft.

It came with an oily, frightening speed, and as it did, Randy saw the colors Rachel had seen—fantastic reds and yellows and blues spiraling across an ebony surface like limp plastic or dark, lithe Naugahyde. It rose and fell with the waves and that changed the colors, made them swirl and blend. Randy realized he was going to fall over, fall right into it, he could feel himself tilting out—

With the last of his strength he brought his right fist up

into his own nose—the gesture of a man stifling a cough, only a little high and a lot hard. His nose flared with pain, he felt blood run warmly down his face, and then he was able to step back, crying out: "Don't look at it! Deke! Don't look right at it, the colors make you loopy!"

"It's trying to get under the raft," Deke said grimly. "What's this shit, Pancho?"

Randy looked—he looked very carefully. He saw the thing nuzzling the side of the raft, flattening to a shape like half a pizza. For a moment it seemed to be piling up there, thickening, and he had an alarming vision of it piling up enough to run onto the surface of the raft.

Then it squeezed under. He thought he heard a noise for a moment—a rough noise, like a roll of canvas being pulled through a narrow window—but that might have only been nerves.

"Did it go under?" LaVerne said, and there was something oddly nonchalant about her tone, as if she were trying with all her might to be conversational, but she was screaming, too. "Did it go under the raft? Is it under us?"

"Yes," Deke said. He looked at Randy. "I'm going to swim for it right now," he said. "If it's under there I've got a good chance."

"No!" LaVerne screamed. "No, don't leave us here, don't—"

"I'm fast," Deke said, looking at Randy, ignoring LaVerne completely. "But I've got to go while it's under there."

Randy's mind felt as if it was whizzing along at Mach two —in a greasy, nauseating way it was exhilarating, like the last few seconds before you puke into the slipstream of a cheap carnival ride. There was time to hear the barrels under the raft clunking hollowly together, time to hear the leaves on the trees beyond the beach rattling dryly in a little puff of wind, time to wonder why it had gone under the raft.

"Yes," he said to Deke. "But I don't think you'll make it."

"I'll make it," Deke said, and started toward the edge of the raft.

He got two steps and then stopped.

His breath had been speeding up, his brain getting his heart and lungs ready to swim the fastest fifty yards of his life and now his breath stopped like the rest of him, simply stopped in the middle of an inhale. He turned his head, and Randy saw the cords in his neck stand out.

"Panch—" he said in an amazed, choked voice, and then he began to scream.

He screamed with amazing force, great baritone bellows that splintered up toward wild soprano levels. They were loud enough to echo back from the shore in ghostly half-notes. At first Randy thought he was just screaming, and then he realized it was a word—no, two words, the same two words over and over: *"My foot!"* Deke was screaming. *"My foot! My foot! My foot!"*

Randy looked down. Deke's foot had taken on an odd sunken look. The reason was obvious, but Randy's mind refused to accept it at first—it was too impossible, too insanely grotesque. As he watched, Deke's foot was being pulled down between two of the boards that made up the surface of the raft.

Then he saw the dark shine of the black thing beyond the heel and the toes, dark shine alive with swirling, malevolent colors.

The thing had his foot (*"My foot!"* Deke screamed, as if to confirm this elementary deduction. *"My foot, oh my foot, my FOOOOOOT!"*). He had stepped on one of the cracks between the boards (*step on a crack, break yer mother's back,* Randy's mind gibbered), and the thing had been down there. The thing had—

"*Pull!*" he screamed back suddenly. "*Pull, Deke, goddammit, PULL!*"

"What's happening?" LaVerne hollered, and Randy realized dimly that she wasn't just shaking his shoulder; she had sunk her spade-shaped fingernails into him like claws. She was going to be absolutely no help at all. He drove an elbow into her stomach. She made a barking, coughing noise and sat down on her fanny. He leaped to Deke and grabbed one of Deke's arms.

It was as hard as Carrara marble, every muscle standing out like the rib of a sculpted dinosaur skeleton. Pulling Deke was like trying to pull a big tree out of the ground by the roots. Deke's eyes were turned up toward the royal purple of the post-dusk sky, glazed and unbelieving, and still he screamed, screamed, screamed.

Randy looked down and saw that Deke's foot had now disappeared into the crack between the boards up to the ankle. That crack was perhaps only a quarter of an inch wide, surely no more than half an inch, but his foot had gone into it. Blood ran across the white boards in thick dark tendrils. Black stuff like heated plastic pulsed up and down in the crack, up and down, like a heart beating.

Got to get him out. Got to get him out quick or we're never gonna get him out at all . . . hold on, Cisco, please hold on . . .

LaVerne got to her feet and backed away from the gnarled, screaming Deke-tree in the center of the raft which floated at anchor under the October stars on Cascade Lake. She was shaking her head numbly, her arms crossed over her belly where Randy's elbow had gotten her.

Deke leaned hard against him, arms groping stupidly. Randy looked down and saw blood gushing from Deke's shin, which now tapered the way a sharpened pencil tapers to a point—only the point here was white, not black, the point was a bone, barely visible.

The black stuff surged up again, sucking, eating.

Deke wailed.

Never going to play football on that foot again, WHAT foot, ha-ha, and he pulled Deke with all his might and it was still like pulling at a rooted tree.

Deke lurched again and now he uttered a long, drilling shriek that made Randy fall back, shrieking himself, hands covering his ears. Blood burst from the pores of Deke's calf and shin; his kneecap had taken on a purple, bulging look as it tried to absorb the tremendous pressure being put on it as the black thing hauled Deke's leg down through the narrow crack inch by inch.

Can't help him. How strong it must be! Can't help him now, I'm sorry, Deke, so sorry—

"Hold me, Randy," LaVerne screamed, clutching at him everywhere, digging her face into his chest. Her face was so hot it seemed to sizzle. "Hold me, please, won't you hold me—"

This time, he did.

It was only later that a terrible realization came to Randy: the two of them could almost surely have swum ashore while the black thing was busy with Deke—and if LaVerne refused to try it, he could have done it himself. The keys to the Camaro were in Deke's jeans, lying on the beach. He could have done it . . . but the realization that he could have never came to him until too late.

Deke died just as his thigh began to disappear into the narrow crack between the boards. He had stopped shrieking minutes before. Since then he had uttered only thick, syrupy grunts. Then those stopped, too. When he fainted, falling forward, Randy heard whatever remained of the femur in his right leg splinter in a greenstick fracture.

A moment later Deke raised his head, looked around groggily, and opened his mouth. Randy thought he meant to scream again. Instead, he voided a great jet of blood, so thick it was almost solid. Both Randy and LaVerne were splattered with its warmth and she began to scream again, hoarsely now.

"*Oooog!*" she cried, her face twisted in half-mad revulsion. "*Oooog!* Blood! *Ooooog,* blood! *Blood!*" She rubbed at herself and only succeeded in smearing it around.

Blood was pouring from Deke's eyes, coming with such force that they had bugged out almost comically with the force of the hemorrhage. Randy thought: *Talk about vitality! Christ, LOOK at that! He's like a goddammed human fire hydrant! God! God! God!*

Blood streamed from both of Deke's ears. His face was a hideous purple turnip, swelled shapeless with the hydrostatic pressure of some unbelievable reversal; it was the face of a man being clutched in a bear hug of monstrous and unknowable force.

And then, mercifully, it was over.

Deke collapsed forward again, his hair hanging down on the raft's bloody boards, and Randy saw with sickish amazement that even Deke's scalp had bled.

Sounds from under the raft. Sucking sounds.

That was when it occurred to his tottering, overloaded mind that he could swim for it and stand a good chance of making it. But LaVerne had gotten heavy in his arms, ominously heavy; he looked at her slack face, rolled back an eyelid to disclose only white, and knew that she had not fainted but fallen into a state of shock-unconsciousness.

Randy looked at the surface of the raft. He could lay her down, of course, but the boards were only a foot across. There was a diving board platform attached to the raft in the summertime, but that, at least, had been taken down and stored somewhere. Nothing left but the surface of the raft itself, fourteen boards, each a foot wide and twenty feet long.

No way to put her down without laying her unconscious body across any number of those cracks.

Step on a crack, break your mother's back.

Shut up.

And then, tenebrously, his mind whispered: *Do it anyway. Put her down and swim for it.*

But he did not, could not. An awful guilt rose in him at the thought. He held her, feeling the soft, steady drag on his arms and back. She was a big girl.

Deke went down.

Randy held LaVerne in his aching arms and watched it happen. He did not want to, and for long seconds that might even have been minutes he turned his face away entirely; but his eyes always wandered back.

With Deke dead, it seemed to go faster.

The rest of his right leg disappeared, his left leg stretching out further and further until Deke looked like a one-legged ballet dancer doing an impossible split. There was the wishbone crack of his pelvis, and then, as Deke's stomach began to swell ominously with new pressure, Randy looked away for a long time, trying not to hear the wet sounds, trying to concentrate on the pain in his arms. He could maybe bring her around, he thought, but for the time being it was better to have the throbbing pain in his arms and shoulders. It gave him something to think about.

From behind him came a sound like strong teeth crunching up a mouthful of candy jawbreakers. When he looked back, Deke's ribs were collapsing into the crack. His arms were up and out, and he looked like an obscene parody of Richard Nixon giving the V-for-victory sign that had driven demonstrators wild in the sixties and seventies.

His eyes were open. His tongue had popped out at Randy.

Randy looked away again, out across the lake. *Look for lights*, he told himself. He knew there were no lights over there, but he told himself that anyway. *Look for lights over there, somebody's got to be staying the week in his place, fall foliage, shouldn't miss it, bring your Nikon, folks back home are going to love the slides.*

When he looked back, Deke's arms were straight up. He wasn't Nixon anymore; now he was a football ref signaling that the extra point had been good.

Deke's head appeared to be sitting on the boards.

His eyes were still open.

His tongue was still sticking out.

"Oh Ceesco," Randy muttered, and looked away again. His arms and shoulders were shrieking now, but still he held her in his arms. He looked at the far side of the lake. The far side of the lake was dark. Stars unrolled across the black sky, a spill of cold milk somehow suspended high in the air.

Minutes passed. *He'll be gone now. You can look now. Okay, yeah, all right. But don't look. Just to be safe, don't look. Agreed? Agreed. Most definitely. So say we all and so say all of us.*

So he looked anyway and was just in time to see Deke's fingers being pulled down. They were moving—probably the motion of the water under the raft was being transmitted to the unknowable thing which had caught Deke, and that motion was then being transmitted to Deke's fingers. Probably, probably. But it looked to Randy as if Deke was waving to him. The Cisco Kid was waving adiós. For the first time he felt his mind give a sickening wrench—it seemed to cant the way the raft itself had canted when all four of them had stood on the same side. It righted itself, but Randy suddenly understood that madness—real lunacy—was perhaps not far away at all.

Deke's football ring—All-Conference, 1981—slid slowly up the third finger of his right hand. The starlight rimmed

66

the gold and played in the minute gutters between the engraved numbers, 19 on one side of the reddish stone, 81 on the other. The ring slid off his finger. The ring was a little too big to fit down through the crack, and of course it wouldn't squeeze.

It lay there. It was all that was left of Deke now. Deke was gone. No more dark-haired girls with sloe eyes, no more flicking Randy's bare rump with a wet towel when Randy came out of the shower, no more breakaway runs from midfield with fans rising to their feet in the bleachers and cheerleaders turning hysterical cartwheels along the side-lines. No more fast rides after dark in the Camaro with Thin Lizzy blaring "The Boys Are Back in Town" out of the tape deck. No more Cisco Kid.

There was that faint rasping noise again—a roll of canvas being pulled slowly through a slit of a window.

Randy was standing with his bare feet on the boards. He looked down and saw the cracks on either side of both feet suddenly filled with slick darkness. His eyes bulged. He thought of the way the blood had come spraying from Deke's mouth in an almost solid rope, the way Deke's eyes had bugged out as if on springs as hemorrhages caused by hydro-static pressure pulped his brain.

It smells me. It knows I'm here. Can it come up? Can it get up through the cracks? Can it? Can it?

He stared down, unaware of LaVerne's limp weight now, fascinated by the enormity of the question, wondering what the stuff would feel like when it flowed over his feet, when it hooked into him.

The black shininess humped up almost to the edge of the cracks (Randy rose on tiptoes without being at all aware he was doing it), and then it went down. That canvasy slithering resumed. And suddenly Randy saw it on the water again, a great dark mole, now perhaps fifteen feet across. It rose and fell with the mild wavelets, rose and fell, rose and fell, and when Randy began to see the colors pulsing evenly across it, he tore his eyes away.

He put LaVerne down, and as soon as his muscles unlocked, his arms began to shake wildly. He let them shake. He knelt beside her, her hair spread across the white boards in an irregular dark fan. He knelt and watched that dark mole on the water, ready to yank her up again if it showed any signs of moving.

He began to slap her lightly, first one cheek and then the other, back and forth, like a second trying to bring a fighter around. LaVerne didn't want to come around. LaVerne did not want to pass Go and collect two hundred dollars or take a ride on the Reading. LaVerne had seen enough. But Randy couldn't guard her all night, lifting her like a canvas sack every time that thing moved (and you couldn't look at the thing too long; that was another thing). He had learned a trick, though. He hadn't learned it in college. He had learned it from a friend of his older brother's. This friend had been a paramedic in Nam, and he knew all sorts of tricks—how to catch head lice off a human scalp and make them race in a matchbox, how to cut cocaine with baby laxative, how to sew up deep cuts with ordinary needle and thread. One day they had been talking about ways to bring abysmally drunken folks around so these abysmally drunken people wouldn't puke down their own throats and die, as Bon Scott, the lead singer of AC/DC, had done.

"You want to bring someone around in a hurry?" the friend with the catalogue of interesting tricks had said. "Try this." And he told Randy the trick which Randy now used.

He leaned over and bit LaVerne's earlobe as hard as he could.

Hot, bitter blood squirted into his mouth. LaVerne's eyelids flew up like windowshades. She screamed in a hoarse, growling voice and struck out at him. Randy looked up and saw the far side of the thing only; the rest of it was already under the raft. It had moved with eerie, horrible, silent speed.

He jerked LaVerne up again, his muscles screaming protest, trying to knot into charley horses. She was beating at his face. One of her hands struck his sensitive nose and he saw red stars.

"Quit it!" he shouted, shuffling his feet onto the boards. "Quit it, you bitch, it's under us again, quit it or I'll fucking drop you, I swear to God I will!"

Her arms immediately stopped flailing at him and closed quietly around his neck in a drowner's grip. Her eyes looked white in the swimming starlight.

"Stop it!" She didn't. "Stop it, LaVerne, you're choking me!"

Tighter. Panic flared in his mind. The hollow clunk of the barrels had taken on a duller, muffled note—it was the thing underneath, he supposed.

"I can't breathe!"

The hold loosened a little.

"Now listen. I'm going to put you down. It's all right if you—"

But *put you down* was all she had heard. Her arms tightened in that deadly grip again. His right hand was on her back. He hooked it into a claw and raked at her. She kicked her legs, mewling harshly, and for a moment he almost lost his balance. She felt it. Fright rather than pain made her stop struggling.

"Stand on the boards."

"No!" Her air puffed a hot desert wind against his cheek.

"It can't get you if you stand on the boards."

"No, don't put me down, it'll get me, I know it will, I know—"

He raked at her back again. She screamed in anger and pain and fear. "You get down or I'll drop you, LaVerne."

He lowered her slowly and carefully, both of them breathing in sharp little whines—oboe and flute. Her feet touched the boards. She jerked her legs up as if the boards were hot.

"Put them *down!*" He hissed at her. "I'm not Deke, I can't hold you all night!"

"Deke—"

"Dead."

Her feet touched the boards. Little by little he let go of her. They faced each other like dancers. He could see her waiting for its first touch. Her mouth gaped like the mouth of a goldfish.

"Randy," she whispered. "Where is it?"

"Under. Look down."

She did. He did. They saw the blackness stuffing the cracks, stuffing them almost all the way across the raft now. Randy sensed its eagerness, and thought she did, too.

"Randy, please—"

"Shhhh."

They stood there.

Randy had forgotten to strip off his watch when he ran into the water, and now he marked off fifteen minutes. At a quarter past eight, the black thing slid out from under the raft again. It drew about fifteen feet off and then stopped as it had before.

"I'm going to sit down," he said.

"No!"

"I'm tired," he said. "I'm going to sit down and you're going to watch it. Just remember to keep looking away. Then I'll get up and you sit down. We go like that. Here." He gave her his watch. "Fifteen-minute shifts."

"It ate Deke," she whispered.

"Yes."

"What is it?"

"I don't know."

"I'm cold."

"Me too."

"Hold me, then."

"I've held you enough."

She subsided.

Sitting down was heaven; not having to watch the thing was bliss. He watched LaVerne instead, making sure that her eyes kept shifting away from the thing on the water.

"What are we going to do, Randy?"

He thought.

"Wait," he said.

At the end of fifteen minutes he stood up and let her first sit and then lie down for half an hour. Then he got her on her feet again and she stood for fifteen minutes. They went back and forth. At a quarter of ten, a cold rind of moon rose and beat a path across the water. At ten-thirty, a shrill, lonely cry rose, echoing across the water, and LaVerne shrieked.

"Shut up," he said. "It's just a loon."

"I'm freezing, Randy—I'm numb all over."

"I can't do anything about it."

"Hold me," she said. "You've got to. We'll hold each other. We can both sit down and watch it together."

He debated, but the cold sinking into his own flesh was now bone-deep, and that decided him. "Okay."

They sat together, arms wrapped around each other, and something happened—natural or perverse, it happened. He felt himself stiffening. One of his hands found her breast, cupped in damp nylon, and squeezed. She made a sighing noise, and her hand stole to the crotch of his underpants.

He slid his other hand down and found a place where there was some heat. He pushed her down on her back.

"No," she said, but the hand in his crotch began to move faster.

"I can see it," he said. His heartbeat had sped up again, pushing blood faster, pushing warmth toward the surface of his chilled bare skin. "I can watch it."

She murmured something, and he felt elastic slide down his hips to his upper thighs. He watched it. He slid upward, forward, into her. Warmth. God, she was warm there, at least. She made a guttural noise and her fingers grabbed at his cold, clenched buttocks.

He watched it. It wasn't moving. He watched it. He watched it closely. The tactile sensations were incredible, fantastic. He was not experienced, but neither was he a virgin; he had made love with three girls and it had never been like this. She moaned and began to lift her hips. The raft rocked gently, like the world's hardest waterbed. The barrels underneath murmured hollowly.

He watched it. The colors began to swirl—slowly now, sensuously, not threatening; he watched it and he watched the colors. His eyes were wide. The colors were in his eyes. He wasn't cold now; he was hot now, hot the way you got your first day back on the beach in early June, when you could feel the sun tightening your winter-white skin, reddening it, giving it some

(colors)

color, some tint. First day at the beach, first day of summer, drag out the Beach Boys oldies, drag out the Ramones. The Ramones were telling you that Sheena is a punk rocker, the Ramones were telling you that you can hitch a ride to Rockaway Beach, the sand, the beach, the colors

(moving it's starting to move)

and the feel of summer, the texture; Gary U.S. Bonds, school is out and I can root for the Yankees from the bleachers, girls in bikinis on the beach, the beach, the beach, oh do you love do you love

(love)

the beach do you love

(love I love)

firm breasts fragrant with Coppertone oil, and if the bottom of the bikini was small enough you might see some

(hair her hair HER HAIR IS IN THE OH GOD IN THE WATER HER HAIR)

He pulled back suddenly, trying to pull her up, but the thing moved with oily speed and tangled itself in her hair like a webbing of thick black glue and when he pulled her up she was already screaming and she was heavy with it; it came out of the water in a twisting, gruesome membrane that rolled with flaring nuclear colors—scarlet-vermilion, flaring emerald, sullen ocher.

It flowed down over LaVerne's face in a tide, obliterating it.

Her feet kicked and drummed. The thing twisted and moved where her face had been. Blood ran down her neck in streams. Screaming, not hearing himself scream, Randy ran at her, put his foot against her hip, and shoved. She went flopping and tumbling over the side, her legs like alabaster in the moonlight. For a few endless moments the water frothed and splashed against the side of the raft, as if someone had hooked the world's largest bass in there and it was fighting like hell.

Randy screamed. He screamed. And then, for variety, he screamed some more.

Some half an hour later, long after the frantic splashing and struggling had ended, the loons began to scream back.

That night was forever.

. . .

The sky began to lighten in the east around a quarter to five, and he felt a sluggish rise in his spirit. It was momentary; as false as the dawn. He stood on the boards, his eyes half closed, his chin on his chest. He had been sitting on the boards until an hour ago, and had been suddenly awakened—without even knowing until then that he had fallen asleep, that was the scary part—by that unspeakable hissing-canvas sound. He leaped to his feet bare seconds before the blackness began to suck eagerly for him between the boards. His breath whined in and out; he bit at his lip, making it bleed.

Asleep, you were asleep, you asshole!

The thing had oozed out from under again half an hour later, but he hadn't sat down again. He was afraid to sit down, afraid he would go to sleep and that this time his mind wouldn't trip him awake in time.

His feet were still planted squarely on the boards as a stronger light, real dawn this time, filled the east and the first morning birds began to sing. The sun came up, and by six o'clock the day was bright enough for him to be able to see the beach. Deke's Camaro, bright yellow, was right where Deke had parked it, nose in to the pole fence. A bright litter of shirts and sweaters and four pairs of jeans were twisted into little shapes along the beach. The sight of them filled him with fresh horror when he thought his capacity for horror must surely be exhausted. He could see *his* jeans, one leg pulled inside out, the pocket showing. His jeans looked so *safe* lying there on the sand; just waiting for him to come along and pull the inside-out leg back through so it was right, grasping the pocket as he did so the change wouldn't fall out. He could almost feel them whispering up his legs, could feel himself buttoning the brass button above the fly—

(do you love yes I love)

He looked left and there it was, black, round as a checker, floating lightly. Colors began to swirl across its hide and he looked away quickly.

"Go home," he croaked. "Go home or go to California and find a Roger Corman movie to audition for."

A plane droned somewhere far away, and he fell into a dozing fantasy: *We are reported missing, the four of us. The search spreads outward from Horlicks. A farmer remembers being passed by a yellow Camaro "going like a bat out of hell." The search centers in the Cascade Lake area. Private pilots volunteer to do a quick aerial search, and one guy, buzzing the lake in his Beechcraft Twin Bonanza, sees a kid standing naked on the raft, one kid, one survivor, one—*

He caught himself on the edge of toppling over and brought his fist into his nose again, screaming at the pain.

The black thing arrowed at the raft immediately and squeezed underneath—it could hear, perhaps, or sense . . . or *something.*

Randy waited.

This time it was forty-five minutes before it came out.

His mind slowly orbited in the growing light.

(do you love yes I love rooting for the Yankees and Catfish do you love the Catfish yes I love the

(Route 66 remember the Corvette George Maharis in the Corvette Martin Milner in the Corvette do you love the Corvette

(yes I love the Corvette

(I love you love

(so hot the sun is like a burning glass it was in her hair and it's the light I remember best the light the summer light

(the summer light of)

. . .

afternoon.

Randy was crying.

He was crying because something new had been added now—every time he tried to sit down, the thing slid under the raft. It wasn't entirely stupid, then; it had either sensed or figured out that it could get at him while he was sitting down.

"Go away," Randy wept at the great black mole floating on the water. Fifty yards away, mockingly close, a squirrel was scampering back and forth on the hood of Deke's Camaro. "Go away, please, go anywhere, but leave me alone. I don't love you."

The thing didn't move. Colors began to swirl across its visible surface.

(*you* do *you* do *love me*)

Randy tore his eyes away and looked at the beach, looked for rescue, but there was no one there, no one at all. His jeans still lay there, one leg inside out, the white lining of one pocket showing. They no longer looked to him as if someone was going to pick them up. They looked like relics.

He thought: *If I had a gun, I would kill myself now.*

He stood on the raft.

The sun went down.

Three hours later, the moon came up.

Not long after that, the loons began to scream.

Not long after that, Randy turned and looked at the black thing on the water. He could not kill himself, but perhaps the thing could fix it so there was no pain; perhaps that was what the colors were for.

(*do you do you do you love*)

He looked for it and it was there, floating, riding the waves.

"Sing with me," Randy croaked. "I can root for the Yankees from the bleachers . . . I don't have to worry 'bout teachers . . . I'm so glad that school is out . . . I am gonna . . . sing and shout."

The colors began to form and twist. This time Randy did not look away.

He whispered, "Do you love?"

Somewhere, far across the empty lake, a loon screamed.

🕮 🕮 🕮

Stephen King is the author of more than fifty books, all of them worldwide bestsellers. His first crime thriller featuring Bill Hodges, MR MERCEDES, won the Edgar Award for best novel and was shortlisted for the CWA Gold Dagger Award. Both MR MERCEDES and END OF WATCH received the Goodreads Choice Award for the Best Mystery and Thriller of 2014 and 2016 respectively.

King co-wrote the bestselling novel Sleeping Beauties with his son Owen King, and many of King's books have been turned into celebrated films and television series including The Shawshank Redemption, Gerald's Game and It.

King was the recipient of America's prestigious 2014 National Medal of Arts and the 2003 National Book Foundation Medal for distinguished contribution to American Letters. In 2007 he also won the Grand Master Award from the Mystery Writers of America. He lives with his wife Tabitha King in Maine.

That Chemical Glow

Larry Hinkle

We both knew it was dangerous to cut through the old neighborhood. If there were any doubts, the rings of concertina wire atop the eight-foot fence marked with skull and crossbones "Toxic Hazard" signs put the kibosh on them quick. But after Eddie'd gone rogue and robbed Manson, our dealer, we didn't have much of a choice. It was either slink along the main roads—and get caught for sure—or try to lose those thugs in Grove Spillage. (That's the nickname Grove Village earned after the second chemical spill.) I wish I could've seen their faces when we crawled through that hole in the fence. None of them have been brave enough to follow us in. Not yet. But given a choice between admitting to Manson they let us get away or taking their chances in this toxic wasteland, I figure it's only a matter of time before they come in after us.

Fifty yards past the barrier, we hunker down behind a rusted panel van. I take in our surroundings as I catch my breath. The moonlit streets, pockmarked with potholes and rainbow-colored oil slicks, are littered with debris that puts me right back on the front lines—burned out abandoned vehicles, piles of rubble and rebar, scrap tires, and over-turned barrels. Ugly, discolored weeds grow through every crack, and trash is strewn everywhere. If you know where to look, you can still see evidence of the spills. And where they stacked the bodies.

It's a far cry from our last night here, when lights glowed in every house up and down the block as families gathered for dinner. Me and Eddie were sitting on the hood of his truck, talking shit as usual. The crickets *almost* drowned out the industrial hum from the nearby chemical plant.

And then the sirens started.

Eddie yanks my arm, pulling me out of my memories. Eddie's my twin brother. Fraternal, not identical. He's older by eight minutes and thirty-seven seconds, which he never lets me forget, but I've always been the big brother in the relationship. I'm also bigger physically; about six inches taller and 30 pounds heavier than Eddie's short, wiry frame. Most people don't believe we're even brothers, let alone twins.

Eddie's always had an edge to him. Thought joining the military might smooth it out, but that just made it worse. He came back from Afghanistan twitchier than ever, with PTSD and a serious addiction. I didn't see as much combat as Eddie, but I'm dealing with my own shit. I don't need the drugs, not like Eddie does, but they help. I guess it's in our genes. So's that "twin thing" people talk about. Which is why I blame myself for our current situation. How did I not know he'd brought a gun? I think I was even more surprised than Manson was when Eddie pulled it out.

It's tucked into the back of his pants now, the handle poking out the crack of his ass. "Give me the gun, Eddie," I say as I reach for it, but he turns and shoves my hand away.

"No way, bro." His eyes are wide, manic. "You should be glad I brought it. Those guys would've killed us if I didn't have this." He pulls the gun out and waves it around in the air.

"Seriously? The only reason they want to kill us is because you fucking robbed them!"

"Yeah, so?" He tucks the gun back into his pants. "Why do you think I brought the gun?"

It's pointless to argue with Eddie when he's like this. Besides, we have more pressing matters to deal with right now. Like finding a way out of here before those thugs find the courage to chase us down.

I sneak another peek around the corner of the van. Manson's caught up with his goons. We call him Manson because he runs his gang like a little cult, always flipping his butterfly knife and threatening to cut a swastika on someone's forehead. The way he's gesturing now looks like he's trying to decide whether it's worth hunting us down or if they should just wait until the next time Eddie needs a fix.

And Eddie always needs a fix.

I grab Eddie's arm and we shuffle up to the side of a burnt-out house, then flatten our backs against the brick. A dead tree has fallen through the garage. I can't remember who used to live here. The Millers, maybe? Doesn't matter.

There's a puddle of water on the driveway. The moon's reflection in it is rainbow-colored, probably from oil or chemicals. There's no breeze, but as I watch, the water starts to swirl, then flows *up* the driveway toward our hiding spot.

Before I can say anything, Eddie slides over to the next house. I rub my eyes, then follow him. Sticking to the shadows, we make our way further down the street, past houses with broken windows, missing doors, roofs with gaping holes. Grove Village used to be a nice middle class neighborhood, a good place to raise a family. Now it looks like a war zone.

Most everyone here worked at the chemical plant. After the

first spill, some people tried to leave, but it was already too late. Home prices crashed, and people couldn't afford to sell. After the second spill, this time with mass casualties, they didn't have a choice. The government seized the land and relocated the survivors. The neighborhood was condemned, surrounded by prison fencing and concrete barricades, and forgotten.

"Let's hole up in there for a bit," I say, pointing to a split-level hidden behind a row of overgrown hedges.

"Why that one?" Eddie looks over his shoulder to see if we're being followed. When he doesn't take off running, I assume we're not.

"It still has a front door, for one," I say. "And if I remember right, there should be a secret room under the stairs we can hide in, if it comes to that." We slip past the hedges and scurry through the front door, which I pull shut behind us.

The stench of rotting garbage washes over us as we walk through the living room, reminding me of the slums we patrolled in Kabul. I put my hand over my mouth to keep from gagging. "Maybe this isn't such a good idea," I say between coughs. I already regret picking this house.

Eddie doesn't even notice. "Wait, is this Stacy Abbot's house?" A smile spreads across his face as he looks around. "I remember spending some quality time with her in that secret room."

"I know. It's all you talked about that summer. You and your stupid stinky pinky."

Eddie laughs. "You were just jealous cuz you never got past second base that year."

I'm getting used to the smell now, taking slow, shallow breaths through my mouth like we learned in boot. If it bothers Eddie, he hasn't let on. We settle back into the shadows of the dining room. From here, I can watch the front windows, and Eddie can look out back. There's a hole in the living room ceiling, which lets in enough moonlight that we can see the hallway and both sets of stairs: one goes up to the bedrooms, the other down to the basement.

Bang!

We both jump at the sound of something falling in the kitchen.

I take a chance and turn on my phone's flashlight app, cupping the light with my hand. A rat looks at me from its seat on the countertop, unafraid. I pick up an old pop can from the floor and chuck it at the rat, and it *smiles* at me, its mouth choked with far too many teeth, some bursting through the skin of its face. *"What the actual fuck?"* I whisper as it waddles over to the sink and disappears down the drain, leaving a glistening trail of rainbow slime behind it. That smile, those *teeth*...it had to be a trick of the light, didn't it? Just my amped-up adrenaline fucking with me.

I close my eyes for a moment and shake it off. "At least we know what that smell is," I say. "There's garbage and roaches and rat shit everywhere, and black mold all over the walls. We shouldn't stay here any longer than we have to." I don't mention the vampire rat. Don't need Eddie freaking out any more than he already is.

"Fine by me." A man's voice, deep and gravelly, rumbles out from the hallway.

Eddie raises his gun. His hands are shaking so badly, I doubt he could hit anything.

"Who's there?" I ask, trying to hide the fear in my voice. I wasn't counting on anyone being in here with us. "You can come out. We don't want any trouble." I pause. "Some guys are chasing us, and we just need to hide here for a bit. That okay?"

An old man steps out of the shadows. He holds a baseball

bat in front of him. The business end has nails driven through it. I make a mental note to keep my distance.

The man's clothes are filthy. He's too skinny, and his hair and beard are patchy and thin. It's how my uncle looked during chemo. Something about him seems familiar, though. When I realize what I'd taken for dirt on his face is actually a port-wine stain, it hits me.

"Holy shit, is that you, Mr. Abbott?"

"Who's asking?" He raises the bat. Unlike Eddie's gun, it's not shaking.

"It's me, Billy Smith. We used to live around the corner. My twin brother Eddie's with me." I point over toward Eddie. "Put the gun down, Eddie. It's Stacy's dad."

Eddie lowers the gun, then nods at Mr. Abbott. His left eye's starting to twitch. Not a good sign. I wish I'd thought to take the drugs from him.

"What the hell are you doing here, Mr. Abbott?" I ask. "It's not safe. Especially at night."

"Oh, I'm not worried about that." He winks and flashes me a smile.

"I gotta take a leak," Eddie says. "That bathroom at the end of the hall still work?"

Mr. Abbott grimaces. "You don't wanna go in that one. There's a hole in the ceiling, a tree in the tub, and black mold everywhere else. You can use the one upstairs. I think some chemicals from the spill must have backed up in the toilet, though. Water's a weird color now. It shimmers in the moon-light. Moves on its own, too. Sometimes it whispers to me, late at night…" He trails off, then points to the steps. "Come on, I'll show you." Mr. Abbott starts up the stairs, Eddie right behind him.

I know Eddie's probably going up there to get high. Maybe that's not such a bad idea, all things considered. Robbing our dealer, getting chased into this toxic waste dump... And then finding Mr. Abbott here on top of all that? Maybe getting fucked up is *exactly* what we need right now. It's tempting, but I need to stay straight if we're gonna make it out of here. Especially if Eddie does more than a little bump.

I hear a door open and close upstairs, followed by muffled thumps. Stupid Eddie must have hit his head on something. Dude's always been a klutz. It's even worse when he's using.

While I wait for them to come back down, I try to decide what to do about Mr. Abbott. What's he doing here? Whole area's supposed to be off-limits. We were just lucky to find a hole in the fence. Is that how he got in? Or does he know another way, preferably on the opposite side of the neighborhood from where we squeezed through?

And what did he mean about the water *whispering* to him?

The back of my neck starts to tingle just as something, or somebody, scrapes across the floor upstairs. Something's wrong with Eddie. I can feel it. I'm already at the foot of the steps when he walks out of the shadows, followed by Mr. Abbott.

They're both smiling as they come down the stairs. Mr. Abbott takes a seat in the dining room while Eddie walks over to the couch and plops down. He pats the cushion next to him, making a small cloud of dust and rat shit. "Take a load off, Billy," he says. "Things are gonna be okay now. We don't have to worry about those guys anymore."

I don't like this. Something is definitely off with him. I can't put my finger on it, though. Not yet. "No thanks," I say. "I'll stand."

"Suit yourself."

"What do you mean, we don't have to worry about those guys anymore?"

"I mean we're good. I just need you to bring 'em here, to

the house, so I can apologize. It was all a big misunderstanding."

"Oh, pulling a gun on them and stealing their drugs was all just a big misunderstanding, huh? And your saying sorry is going to make everything kumbaya?"

Something is moving around in the kitchen. I steal a glance over my shoulder. The vampire rat is back, its fur dripping with rainbow slime. It smiles at me again. As I watch, a new fang explodes through its cheek. Jesus, these chemicals must be fucking with my head. I turn my back on it and march into the living room.

Eddie looks up at me from his seat on the couch. "It said you might need a little convincing."

"A little convincing? Are you fucking high?" I grab Eddie's chin and turn his face toward mine. It's hard to tell in this light, but he looks straight. "And who said that? This guy?" I point to Mr. Abbott. "What the fuck does he know?"

Mr. Abbot doesn't say anything, just smiles at us. His mouth has too many teeth.

I take a deep breath and collect my thoughts. Maybe this isn't so bad. I'd already been trying to think of a way to convince Eddie to give me the drugs so I can give them back to Manson. Just hadn't figured out how to do it yet. Now that it's technically his idea, though, I think I can make it work. "You want me to bring them here? Fine. Give me the drugs first." I reach for his pocket, but he knocks my hand away.

"No. If I give you the drugs, you'll give 'em to Manson, and they won't come in. And they have to come in so I can apologize, right?" He looks over at Mr. Abbott, who nods in agreement. "Besides, I don't have them."

"I'm not joking around, Eddie. I need you to give me the drugs. If we're lucky, maybe they'll let us go with just a couple broken bones."

He tilts his head and smiles. "No."

"No? Jesus, I'm agreeing with you, numb nuts! It's a solid plan. How about you give me half, then? I'll tell them they can have the rest when they come in to hear your apology." I reach for his pocket again. This time, he grabs my hand and squeezes hard enough to make my eyes water.

"I told you, I don't have them."

I jerk my hand free and shake off the pain. "Fuck! Did you take them all? You can't OD in here, man! The ambulance can't come and get you. You'll die! "

"Relax, Billy. I flushed them." His smile is wider than normal.

"You flushed them? Fuck me!" I grab the side of my head and squeeze as I pace around the room. This is bad. Like, really, *really* bad. "We're dead. You know that, right? You just signed our death warrants! What the fuck was I thinking? Fuckin' Manson was right. You *never* trust a junkie."

Eddie laughs at this. "Trust me, William, I don't need them. *We* don't need them. Not anymore." He stands up and holds his hand out. "Come on, you'll see."

Eddie knows I hate it when he uses my formal name. Whatever game he's playing, I've had enough of it. I shove his hand away. "Fuck this, I'm outta here." I push my way past him toward the front door.

Behind me, Eddie cocks the gun. I freeze.

"You're going upstairs," he says. "Now."

Mr. Abbott steps between me and the door, the bat resting on his shoulder. His skin shimmers in the moonlight.

I turn toward Eddie. He motions me toward the stairs with the gun. His skin has the same shimmer as Mr. Abbott's. His hands aren't shaking anymore, either.

"Eddie, what the fuck's going on?" I search his eyes for some sort of explanation. He stares back, unblinking. His eyes have gone black. That's when it hits me: whoever, *whatever*, this is standing before me, it's not my brother.

And when it smiles at me, with a mouth far too wide for Eddie's face, I realize it doesn't care that I know. In fact, I think it's happy that I do.

"After you." He pushes me onto the landing.

I go up two steps, then stop.

This time, the push comes from Mr. Abbott's bat. "Don't think I won't use this on you, *William*," he says. "Now get going."

At the top of the steps, Eddie grabs my shoulder and marches me toward the bathroom. "Go on. There's something in there you need to see."

"I can't see anything in the dark, Eddie. I'm gonna get my phone out, okay?" I wait a beat. When Eddie doesn't object, I reach for my phone. I turn on my flashlight app and shine it into the bathroom. There's water on the floor. Another liquid is floating on top of it, like a sheen of oil. The rainbow colors swirl, then move in a wave toward my feet. I try to retreat, but Eddie has the gun pressed into my back.

"Beautiful, isn't it?" he whispers in my ear.

"What *is* it?" My eyelids grow heavy watching the colors undulate. A purple tendril extends up from the water onto the toe of my boot. I'm helpless to stop it.

"I think it's the spill. Or it was. Something happened to it. Maybe a lightning strike, I'm not sure. It tried to show me, but it's all jumbled up. It'd been living off rodents and insects until Mr. Abbott came here a couple weeks ago, looking for pictures of his wife. He was the first human it merged with. It's been waiting for more of us to come. It wants to help us." Eddie's sigh is almost orgasmic. "It's going to make us better."

The water is weaving its way up my leg. It slides over my chest and spills up onto my neck.

I can't move.

"But first, it has to eat."

❧ ❧ ❧

He stands in the dark living room, waiting. When flashlight beams sweep through the front window, he walks onto the porch and waves. Iridescent water swirls around his feet.

"Hey, you numb nuts looking for me?" asks the thing that looks like Billy Smith.

The gang members start up the driveway. Two of them have guns. One is swinging a chain. The fourth has a baseball bat. Manson's flipping his butterfly knife. A pool of rainbow slime follows them as they approach the house.

The Billy thing laughs. His smile shows far too many teeth.

❧ ❧ ❧

Larry Hinkle is the least famous writer you've never heard of. A copywriter living with his wife and two doggos in Rockville, Maryland, when he's not writing stories that scare people into peeing their pants, he writes ads that scare people into buying adult diapers, so they're not caught peeing their pants.

His debut collection, *The Space Between*, was published in February 2024 by Trepidatio Publishing. Additionally, his work has appeared in Dark Recesses Press, *October Screams: A Halloween Anthology*, The NoSleep Podcast, and this very book, among others.

He's an active member of the HWA (his short stories made the preliminary Stoker ballot in 2020 and 2022); a graduate of Fright Club and Crystal Lake's Author's Journey short story and novella programs; an HWA mentee; and a survivor of the Borderlands Writers Bootcamp.

Stop by and visit him at www.thatscarylarry.com, or stalk him on the socials at @thatscarylarry.

I Am a House Demanding to Be Haunted

Mercedes M. Yardley

SOFIA FELL in love with a boy made of seawater.

It didn't start out as love, at first. It was more curiosity or thoughtfulness or horror. She sat in her room, curled up in her bed that was never quite warm enough, and shivered as she stared out the window.

It rained all the time, and so it was difficult to know when she was merely seeing rainwater or when she was seeing *him*. She would peer carefully, watching the streetlight's reflection in the glass, and wondered if sea-colored eyes looked back at her.

Sometimes, if she was feeling particularly brave and it was warm enough to bear, she would slip from her covers and pad across the chilly floor. She'd put her hand on the window and try to see the boy in between the colorless droplets. Was that him, there? The corner of a downturned mouth, the flutter of an eyelash? Or was it simply nothing at all?

"Nothing at all" seemed to be the answer most of the time, and she could accept that, but sometimes she caught the tell-tale sound of a soft sigh amid the pattering. She felt cool fingers reach for hers against the glass.

"Boy," she said, "why are you so sad? Are you all alone, too?"

He didn't haunt her by leaving wet footprints on the living room floor. He haunted her in small, everyday ways, like dirty water backing up in the bathroom sink and the shower stopping abruptly halfway through. He followed her in water droplets that ran down the kitchen windows and the constant drip-drip-dripping from the irrigation system that fed the tomatoes and lilac and lavender and strawberries and pansies and current bushes and all the wonderful, random wildness outside. When she wasn't looking, he opened his mouth and seawater poured out.

❧ ❧ ❧

Being a young, beautiful girl in a haunted house made Sofia a most precious thing. Boys clambered to hold her hand and girls braided her hair skillfully. They brought her special desserts in their lunchboxes and told her glorious stories. Oh, the tales they told! Of derring-do and how they spoke back to the school principal, and how lovely the robin looked sitting on its eggs today, and they would have brought her one except the nest was located much too high.

"How high?" Sofia asked. Really, she focused on the most unusual things. "How high is high enough to keep you from what you want?"

"Well, high enough to hurt when I fall," a child answered.

"Because you are afraid of pain?" Sofia questioned.

The child's brows furrowed most comically. All the children's brows followed.

"Yes, of course. I'm quite afraid of pain," the child said.

"Are you really?" Sofia asked. She turned to the other children in the group. "Are all of you afraid of pain?"

Well, obviously. Because pain *hurts,* and nobody wants to *hurt.* Isn't that frighteningly obvious, our very dear, very wonderful, oh-so-exquisite Sofia?

"Yes, obviously," she said, and turned her face toward the window. She always looked past them toward the never-ceasing rain. If only they could somehow get between her and this otherworldliness she always sought, but no. These children were made of flesh and bone. They were heartbreakingly human.

What a disappointment.

❦ ❦ ❦

Sofia readied herself for bed and lamented that she was still alive.

"Please don't feel that way," said the ghoul who lived in the wall. He had far too many eyes and his hair wrapped around his throat in a stranglehold. "There are so many wonderful things about being alive."

"Like what?" Sofia asked.

"Like food," a little dead girl answered promptly. She was missing her face. "I loved eating muffins and delicious foods at teatime. I'd come back to life for that alone."

"It's very nice not being tormented by the minions of Hell," a dark demon said. "The taunting and pricking of pitchforks and burning hellfire seems cliché, and it's rather fun at first, but like everything else, it gets old."

"That's it?" Sofia said, and her disappointment shamed them. "Treats and a little peace? Is life really worth so little?"

Melancholy little girls were all the rage in Victorian times, but it wasn't Victorian times anymore. Now it was a Great, Modern Age and Great Modern Ages needed answers.

Sad little girls become sorrowful women, and a lamenting woman breaks every man's heart.

"We will *fix* you," doctors told her. "We will make you well."

It started with tongue depressors and blood pressure cuffs. It quickly moved on to therapy and dream analysis. Then some light SSRIs, which became heavier doses of drugs. She took medications to sleep, medications to wake up, medications to boost her low moods, and then more medication to calm her anxiety. Her heart ran fast, slow, and then fast again. She gained weight before she lost her appetite and refused to eat much at all. She didn't want to do anything, but the doctors and nurses persuaded her parents that she ought to take up drawing. Reading. Fencing. Cooking. Painting. The French Horn. Yoga. Book clubs. Cooking clubs. Yarn clubs. She needed spirituality. More alone time. More time with friends. More exercise, but not so much that she became lethargic. Vitamins, but not anything that interacted with her medication.

They all interacted with her medication.

"I'm so lonely," she sobbed, and the haunted house gathered around her, watching. If only the beasts within could help. If only they could comfort her. If only the house could shift under her feet to surprise her and bang its shutters in her ear, so she never listened to droning silence. The ghosts wished to crowd into bed with her, so she never felt alone, and the demons wished to dress themselves in her body so she *extra* never felt alone.

"Let us love you," they said, and they were a clamor, a chorus, a choir. They were legion.

But Mother and Father said no. The psychiatrists and psychologists and neurologists also said no. The house isn't allowed to make any sounds, and if you say it is, well, there simply must be something horrifically wrong with you.

I Am a House Demanding to Be Haunted

Sofia spent her 17th birthday in a psychiatric hospital. The house only wanted to wish her a Very Happy Birthday, but perhaps it went overboard. Its walls ran with blood and the merry "Boom! Boom! Boom!" of the doors swinging to and fro made giant holes in the walls. The trio of brightly decorated skeletons flung the kitchen drawers open and tossed silverware to the ground with joyful cries. Oh, the sound of it hitting the tile! Oh, the way the cat joined in with hisses and shrieks! It was rapturous. It was truly a birthday celebration to remember.

"Sofia, what have you done?" Mother dabbed at her eyes and Father's mouth went in that straight line it made before something Very Serious happened. "Punching holes in the walls? Throwing knives at the cat? What has become of you?"

Sofia wailed as the police and ambulance came. Her voice blended in so nicely with the sirens that the house was pleased, until they saw tears in Sofia's eyes, and they weren't the tears of gratitude it expected.

"Where are you going?" the house whispered.

Sofia shouted and bucked and tried to wrench herself away from the men who restrained her.

"Miss, calm down or we'll be forced to give you a tranquilizer," a large and strong stranger told her firmly.

"What is a tranquilizer?" asked the house, but the man didn't answer.

"It wasn't me. Let me go. The house is haunted, I tell you! Haunted," Sofia screamed, and the house joyfully screamed back, but the medical personnel (as it said on their coats) weren't having any of it.

"This is your last warning," the big man said. "What will it be?"

Suddenly it all became clear.

"No," the strangled ghoul said.

"They're going to take her, and on her birthday," the skeletons sang.

"What if she never comes back?" asked the faceless little girl, and the house breathed in, then. A giant intake of breath, an involuntary action, and the men turned at the giant *whoosh* they heard. Sofia stilled and closed her eyes. She recognized this change in air pressure.

"Please, help me," she whispered.

The house listened.

And then chaos. Utter pandemonium. The house erupted with cold air, blowing the men back and off their feet. They hit the ground, broken puppets, and they boggled at the sheer force.

The big man, the strongest stranger, the one who threatened Sofia the most, well, he went down the hardest. Of course, he did. The house concentrated its energy on him, and there was a *snap* as his arm bent at a strange angle, and a *crack* as his head hit the stone pathway leading to the front door. Something leaked out of his skull. It wasn't just blood.

The remaining men stared for a moment, their eyes adjusting to the dark stain spreading on the dark pathway in the dark night. Their eyes traveled to Sofia, who knelt on the ground, gasping.

"She killed him," a woman hissed, and rooted around in her medical bag. There were no warnings, no posturing, no "if you are a good girl, nothing bad will happen" script this time. She simply plunged a clean hypodermic needle into a sedative, pulled the plunger, and injected it quickly into Sofia's veins.

Sofia rolled her eyes toward the woman, but then they kept on rolling. They rolled past the horrified faces of the medical men and the ghosts gathered behind them, including the new ghost who bent over his warm corpse on the ground.

"Is that me?" he asked nobody in particular. "That's a terminal wound. Nobody could survive it."

Sofia's eyes rolled past the beautiful boy made of salt water and the concerned windows of the house itself. Then they rolled into the back of her head to examine her nightmares as she passed out.

❦ ❦ ❦

Hauntings are very different in a hospital.

First off, the ghosts were exceptionally polite this time. There were no uproarious parties or off-colored jokes. Most likely these things happened in other hospitals with other hauntings. Maybe there are banshees whose shrieks herald the dead, or men who died in horrific mining accidents who wander around searching for their lost comrades, or young women who went up in flames like their great, great grandmother witches. But in this particular hospital?

Soft crying. Quiet moaning. The dead glided and tiptoed as respectfully as any live person as they visited the patients. The old tales of madness and asylums didn't fit here in Greenwood Psychiatric Hospital.

"I'm crazy," Sofia murmured. She was pumped full of drugs to keep her anxiety down and her fears sedated. Perhaps this was why the ghosts moved by so slowly.

"I'm crazy," she said as the nurses checked her heart and chest and lungs.

"No, you're not," the nurses soothed.

"I'm crazy," she whispered as she sat in the sunny room for group therapy. "Absolutely bonkers."

"It's not true," the therapist told her. "We're all working on ourselves."

"I'm crazy," she breathed, lying on her bed. The moon was

lush and bright, and was reflected in her eyes, although she couldn't see it.

The boy made of salt water came closer.

She watched him approach, and his translucent body fractured the beams of the moon in the loveliest of ways. He was quiet, and felt peaceful, and she so very wanted him to be real.

If this is madness, she thought, *then right now I embrace it.*

He stood before, this phantom of her broken mind, and she thought of all the times she had looked for him through the window in the Town That Always Rained. His eyes were luminous, and her eyes were luminous, and together they were brighter than the moon could ever hope to be.

He took her hand. It felt cool and solid, hardly phantasmic at all.

"I didn't realize hallucinations could be so convincing," she told him conversationally. If she had lost her mind, she might as well really lean into it. Her madness was giving her such soothing company.

The boy tucked her hair behind her ear.

"Is this utter loneliness?" she asked him. Her eyes stung with their own salt water. "To see things move, to hear the house whisper, to see women walking through walls and sit in chairs that don't exist. Am I so lost that my only companion is a ghost boy? I've driven everyone away. Oh, they say they support me, and they'll always be here, but how can that be? I'm so far from home and visiting is only two days a week. How can they continue to love me as they once did when I'm so irreparably broken?"

The boy rested his cool hand on her hot cheek.

"And now I've imagined you, a friend. Perhaps some future lover. A boy who is quite invisible, and silent, and isn't that just the way of it? A man nobody else can see or hear. But you're so beautiful," she said, and ran her fingers through his hair. He seemed to blush. "And I know I'm horrifically desolate. Perhaps a single, solitary, silent boy is the perfect illusion for me. I so terribly wish you were real."

"I'm perfectly real," he said, and touched his achingly cool lips to her cracked ones. Her wounds immediately filled with salt.

"Ouch," she said, but her words were soon lost in the kiss. A kiss that she could feel. Pain that didn't fade like some dream. Hands in her hair that were as real as hands could ever be.

When they parted, she listened to his ragged breathing. She put her hand on his chest and felt his heart beating fast under his colorless hoodie.

"You're real," she said.

He nodded and held her hand to his cheek.

"Yes."

"And the house, the ghosts, the demons. All of it is real, too?"

His eyes were glowing lanterns. They were will-o-the-whisps leading her through the swamps.

"Yes."

She blinked, slowly, but the moon didn't wash from her eyes.

"I'm…quite sane, then?"

He smiled, and it was the most beautiful of things. Her heart cracked open and soothing sea water rushed in to cleanse it.

"Yes."

"Oh," she said, and her reply was simple, but oh. Oh, the changes his words made in her life. It wasn't madness that had touched her, but the otherworldly. She wasn't crazy, just haunted, and while they appear the same from the outside, it put her frazzled mind at ease.

"It isn't my fault," she said, and lay in a white hospital

gown in a white bed in a white room with the seawater boy curled up behind her. The moon was their lover that night, bathing all in beauty. That night she had the very sanest of dreams.

❧ ❧ ❧

Sofia was damaged. Sofia was broken. She was Ophelia pinwheeling out the window and into the river with a splash. She was Juliet without her Romeo, begging for poison or the end of a blade. Women are beautiful as is, the people of the town thought, but a wounded woman is perfectly exquisite.

Human beings are sick, sick creatures.

They are demons despite their blushing cheeks and beautiful curls. They eat misery alive. And while Sofia went to prom and graduation and college, her friends tipped their heads back and supped from her tears.

Her college dorm was haunted, but ah, not like her home. Black mists belched from her closet and something with long fingers and even longer teeth nibbled on her ears at night. But this was nothing compared to classes, and milkshakes with students, and evenings with friends.

"I can't," Sofia cried as she trudged up the stairs to her room. The walls rippled under her fingertips, and spiders ran every which way. "They razed my flesh from my bones tonight. They asked me about politics and environmental conservation and my phobias. They wanted to discuss my past trauma. Past trauma!" she nearly howled, and when she threw herself to the floor, the bed raced to fall under her. "I don't know what they want from me. Humans are locusts. They're cannibals. They just open their mouths and eat and eat and eat."

The boy who was born from the sea of sorrows sat on the

bed beside her. He seldom had much to say, and his silence was a comfortable womb. Sofia leaned her head against his shoulder and listened to the surf.

"I think I wasn't created for this world," she whispered, and perhaps the boy was about to reply, and perhaps not. But Sofia's roommate came home and announced herself with slamming doors. Pounding feet. Exuberant exultations. She caught Sofia around the neck and hugged her tightly, and the seawater boy slipped away.

Sofia became a woman, and the boy became a man, or perhaps he had always been one. Her mother passed away and the house of haunts became hers. Sofia went on dates, but nobody compared to her nearly silent love. She did eventually live with somebody, an intriguing artist named Erik, but although he lasted longer than the others, he was still a mortal man. What could a skeleton of collagen and crystalline hydroxyapatite do against musculature comprised of sodium and chloride? When Erik twined his fingers in her hair, she felt his skin and bone caressing her keratin. They were both bags of meat, sacks of blood and flesh, and there was nothing healthy about them. They were rotting, two piles of organic material decaying second by second.

She couldn't stand it.

"I'm sorry," she said, and couldn't say any more. How could she explain it? That his sheer mortality was more than she could bear? That they created a disgusting, repulsive inevitable slide toward refuse together?

So "I'm sorry," is all she said, and "I'm sorry" wasn't nearly enough to calm Erik's fiery heart.

"But why?" he asked. "We get along well. We create beautiful things together. I don't understand why you're suddenly walking away. Is it because I don't move you?"

"It isn't that," she said. She couldn't look at him because

his eyes were full of corneas and the hands gripping hers were run through with veins. She could hear the blood saturating his body. He was a wet bag of organs. Their pulsing was more than she could stand.

"I thought you loved me," he said. His face went white, and then red. "I sacrificed everything for us. I sold my apartment and moved into this ancient pile of boards. I dealt with the rats skittering in the walls at night—"

"They're not rats," she tried to explain. "They're something else entirely."

"—to try and make this work with you. What more do you want from me?"

Their bed trembled and the walls shuddered. Sofia glanced around uneasily, but Erik only gazed at her.

"Is there somebody else?" he asked. "I don't understand otherwise."

Sofia looked at Erik's hair and eyes and hands. She saw his soul and the beautiful parts of him. His mitochondria clashed together. Cells multiplied and broke down. Cilia waved in his lungs. He was a cacophony of living tissue.

The saltwater man stood behind him. He was made of stillness. He met her eyes and smiled.

Perhaps," she told Erik, "you are the someone else."

She left the house while he packed. It only took a few hours. When she returned, the home was empty except for a few broken graphite pencils and blood oozing from the walls.

"Is that Erik's?" Sofia demanded of the house. It shook its head innocently. No, this was its blood. It materialized on its own. Sofia wandered to her room and the house cut its windows sharply to the ghoul outside, who promised never to speak of what happened.

Erik was the last man she dated. It didn't seem fair to

hold a man's hand when she was dreaming of wild surf and undertows. She started staying in the haunted house more and more, because the world outside was too loud, too garish. The sun burned her ocular nerves. Heavy grocery bags dug furrows into her skin. The comforting hands of people bruised her as they patted and patted and patted her skin.

Her bones broke. Her psyche shattered. Sofia had always been that fragile thing who lived in the darkest house on the corner, but now she was superb. Sheer perfection. She was so broken beyond almost all recognition! What joy! She must be buffeted with good will. Assaulted with the best of intentions. And when she was overwhelmed and her thin chest shuddered with panicked breaths, well then! They must draw her to them in a forceful hug and comfort the demons out of her. Whisper in her ears that she will be all right, that she will recover, that they will take care of her. She'll cover her ears and tears will drip down her cheeks, and isn't that a delight? Isn't a weeping woman the most wonderful kind?

The earth pounded with their footsteps. The air rent with their screams. They popped out at her, jump-scares in broad daylight, as they sprung from behind trees and closed cars.

Their voices were demonic. Their shiny eyes unsettling as they studied her every move.

The house had enough. It ushered her inside its safe corridors, decorated with ghosts and makeshift shrines.

"Stay with me," it said.

Sofia collapsed on her bed. The man with a seawater heart stroked her wild hair and urged her to close her even wilder eyes.

There was a knock on the door. Several. Fists rained on the wood as the people from outside howled and wailed and spit their greetings.

"Sofia! Come play with us! Join us in the sunlight."

She cringed, whimpering, and her lover's gentle arms wrapped around her.

"Stay out," a red-mouthed demon said, pressing his face to the window. "You aren't welcome here."

Still, the friendly neighbors pressed harder. They tried windows and back doors. They tried to shimmy down the chimney.

"Invite us in," they chorused. "Any little invite will do."

A woman with cropped hair burnt herbs and spices inside the house, hoping the acrid smoke would drive them away. Two ghost children painted terrifying sigils on the doors and walls, hoping the herd of humans would feel utter terror at the gory depictions and leave. A spider with broken legs poured a barrier of salt outside of the door so the people would realize there was a Very Firm Line and they shouldn't cross it.

"Are you afraid?" the house asked Sofia. "Shall we sing songs to bolster your spirit?"

So they sang, these inhabitants of the house. They sang and read from old family heirloom books with their ancestor's names written in the front. The words were ancient and confusing but there is such comfort to be found in the traditions of our fathers. The people outside rallied and the ghosts inside created a lovely, soothing nest for their very favorite Sofia.

The noise reached a critical level. Sofia bled from her ears. Her eyes rolled back, and her body went into convulsions. The screams, the screams, the people calling her name over and over and over outside…it was too much. Her mind snapped and her tortured body went with it. The man made from the ocean watched her, careful to give her room, to make sure she didn't fall from the bed. His heart seized, a tsunami of pain, as he bore silent witness.

Her jerking stopped. He cupped her soft cheek, and saltwater ran down his face.

The man stood and walked to the door. He swung it open, and the group moved in a mass outside. They writhed, they pulsed, they surged forward, seeking entrance to the home, to Sofia, to her soul.

The man stopped them with a gesture. He blinked slowly. He opened his mouth, and his voice was as everchanging as the waves.

"I banish you," he said quietly, and closed the door.

The crowd stared. They left in groups of twos and threes. One by one. Soon nobody was left at all.

The man made of seawater flowed to Sofia. Her body was contorted and peculiar, but it was just a shell. The man kissed its forehead gently.

If he was the sea, she was the sky. He was bits of shell and sunken ships and shark's teeth, whereas she was sunlight and stratosphere and cirrus clouds. She spun in the air above him and her hair floated around her face most joyously.

"It's done," the man told her.

"They're gone," the ghost children said.

"I'm free," Sofia murmured, and she drifted down into her lover's arms. Sea and sky melded together as they were always meant to.

The house hummed as it folded her into itself, tucking her inside its walls and keeping her happy and safe forever and forever.

❧ ❧ ❧

Mercedes M. Yardley is a whimsical dark fantasist who wears red lipstick and poisonous flowers in her hair. She is the author of numerous works including *Darling*, the Stabby Award-winning *Apocalyptic Montessa and Nuclear Lulu: A Tale*

Mercedes M. Yardley

of Atomic Love, Pretty Little Dead Girls, Love is a Crematorium, and *Nameless.*

She won the Bram Stoker Award for her stories *Little Dead Red* and "Fracture." Mercedes lives and works in Las Vegas.

You can find her at mercedesmyardley.com.

Ursa Diruo

Kristin Dearborn

My cousin Addie came to live with us the day after the first bear attack.

I didn't think much of it at the time—I was more distracted by this girl I didn't remember ever meeting, only six months younger than I was, who would be uprooted from her home in Southern California to come live with us in a remote corner of Idaho. She was going to hate it here. I assumed anyone from anywhere else would hate it here. In Southern California they had shopping malls and the ocean and palm trees…here we had two hikers mauled and eaten in their tent by a bear.

Dad, deputy game warden for the county, made it clear the hikers were out of towners who'd kept their food inside their tents.

My mother was a wreck, mourning a sister she'd lost touch with and a brother-in-law she didn't know in a car accident on a winding southern canyon road. It all sounded deliciously exotic. I imagined the palm trees having something to do with the crash, or maybe an earthquake. I was sixteen. Everywhere was more interesting than here.

Crouched in my dad's study, I listened through the grate that led to the kitchen, hearing my mother cry. I imagined it was *my* parents who'd been killed, probably in a tractor accident or something else excruciatingly boring; what if I were en route to Southern California?

I regretted it immediately. I didn't want that. I didn't mean it. It would be fun to see where all the movies and shows were filmed, but not at the cost of my parents. I took it back. I even stopped listening at the grate and went downstairs, slinking into the kitchen.

My mother straightened up, wiping tears away. "How are you, Jessie? You hanging in there?"

I shrugged. We'd been fixing up Addie's room all weekend, except when Dad had been called out to help deal with the bear situation. The hikers were back country camping, so no one found them for a few days, which meant the bear was still at large. Why wouldn't it be? I never understood why we had to kill animals for people's stupid mistakes.

"Why didn't you talk to Aunt Cindy anymore?" I didn't mean to ask, hadn't thought about asking, but the question fell out of me.

"She…made some choices Nana and I didn't agree with."

"She lived a rough life," my dad said diplomatically.

"So Addie's lived a rough life?"

"She's going to be very different than you and your friends, so be patient with her."

Yeah, I thought, about a million times cooler. I wondered if Santa Monica was in a valley, and if that made her a valley girl. She would see the CVS makeup selection and probably shit herself. Then get back on the bus to So Cal as fast as she could.

"Her bus gets in at eleven tonight. You staying up?" Dad said.

"Obviously."

By ten thirty, we were parked at Greyson's, the all-night diner where the Greyhounds dropped off. I brought a fantasy novel, a paperback the size and weight of a brick. I was immersed in dragons and knights when my dad opened the door and popped out of the car.

My mom, telling me to stay in the car, got out too, and screw that, I followed.

A bear sauntered across the street in the glow of a street-lamp. It was a big one, young, probably, since it wasn't covered in scars and its ears weren't torn. It wasn't rare to see bears, but we didn't much care for them when they came all the way into town.

"Just watch it. It's not doing anything. Probably been sniffing around the dumpsters," Mom said.

Because of Dad, I knew Greyson's didn't always lock their dumpsters, and sometimes got some unwelcome guests

"It looks agitated," Dad said. "Flicking his ears, anxious. I just want to call it in."

"You really think that was the bear that killed those hikers?"

Dad blew out air through his nose, the way he did when he was thinking. "I don't, actually. This guy looks young and healthy. Probably hasn't ever been into town before. Warden Keene should know we've got a bear downtown."

Mom acquiesced. "I thought I told you to stay in the car," she said to me. I shrugged at her and slid back in, book forgotten, watching the bear.

Dad went inside Greyson's to use their phone. By the time Warden Keene did a drive by, the Greyhound was here and the bear was long gone.

When I thought of So Cal I thought of blondes and hair spray and neon colors, of big shoulders, acres of shopping, manicured nails, probably sports cars and cocaine.

Addie slouched off the bus in a green jumper dress that

looked homemade, her hair brown and stringy. She *had* just been on a bus for hours and hours. Her bag didn't look big enough to accommodate the wardrobe I thought she'd bring. Hell, even I blew my hair dry and, if I was going out, teased it up a little. She looked like a young sixteen and didn't even recognize us on first pass. Mom went to her and scooped her up in a big hug, which caused Addie's shoulders to tense and her to clutch her bag even tighter. "You remember Uncle Mark and Jessie. We're so sorry for your loss, but so happy you're here."

Addie put a smile on her face, one that didn't hit her eyes.

I introduced myself even though we'd already met years ago, and stuck out my hand. The hug didn't seem to have gone over so well. She took it; her hand a cold, limp dead fish in mine. "Can't wait to show you around!" I said lamely. "There was just a bear across the street. It's gone now, which is good, we don't want them in town, but they're cool to see!" I could hear myself rambling but couldn't stop.

"A *bear*?"

"Oh yeah, we get them all the time. Usually they don't—"

"Jess, let's get her settled in before we scare her talking about bears."

"They're really not scary," I half lied.

I talked the whole way back to the house. There was the school, k-12 all in one building; was that different than her old high school? I pointed out the tiny movie theater, now with two screens. We still had the *Lion King* and *Speed* playing. It was about three hours to a city with a real multiplex, usually we just waited for the movies to trickle down to us. Then we were out of downtown, and from there we had a few farms, but national forest land quickly gobbled everything up. Our place was down a dirt road, and a long driveway Dad always bitched about plowing in the winter. Everyone had four-wheel drive for the snow.

Addie kept quiet, still clutching her one bag to her chest, and when she stepped out into our driveway, she looked up at the sky. Mom said we have some of the brightest stars in the country because we don't have light pollution here. I couldn't imagine not seeing stars like that.

"Show Addie up to her room, please," Mom said.

The phone rang as we ascended the stairs. My friends knew not to call so late, and I could only catch Dad's tone. Professional, serious, concerned. I tried to turn back, to see what they were talking about, but Mom put on her serious face and pointed upstairs.

I showed her my room, I pointed to my parents' room, showed her our bathroom (which had previously been my bathroom) and finally opened the door to her room. Once the guest room, we'd put a desk and a papasan chair in, swapped out the old curtains for some white gauzy ones. Hopefully, she liked it. She still hadn't said much.

"I know this must be different than what you're used to, but I hope you like it here. Tomorrow I'll take you down to the river and we can meet some of my friends. Do you like swimming?"

She looked like a deer in the headlights.

Downstairs, my dad was still on the phone.

"Need anything? Toothbrush? Night shirt? Glass of water?"

She nodded at the latter. I bolted from the room, intent on hearing some of the phone call. There was no use being quiet in our creaky old house, so I tore down the stairs. Mom leaned in so she could hear what was being said. I took my time getting the water. Something about bears.

Dad hung up.

"What happened?"

"Nothing," Dad said. "Game Warden Keene found the bear we saw. Dead."

Oh. "Hit by a car?"

Mom and Dad looked at one another.

"Did someone shoot him?"

"Looks like he was in a fight with another bear. We don't like the idea of them being territorial so close to downtown."

That wasn't nearly as exciting as I'd hoped, and I took the water back upstairs. Addie was sitting at the foot of the bed, taking it all in. I handed her the water, and she set her bag down to drink it down in one long swallow.

"Are you hungry?"

Her eyes flashed.

"We can go downstairs and grab something. Come on."

"I don't want to be a bother," she said.

"It's not a bother. You've been on a bus for…how long?"

"Seventeen hours."

"Jesus," I said.

Addie said she didn't want to come to the river with my friends and me because she didn't know how to swim. She also didn't know how to ride a bike, so Mom let me take her car, which was a rare treat. We all kind of forced Addie into coming. It would be good for her. The best things about Idaho are outdoors. Plus it was hot.

I gave her my old one piece to wear, she didn't seem like a two-piece kind of girl.

"I know I don't need to tell you," Mom said, out of earshot of Addie. "The bears are bugging me. If you see anything strange, just come home. And get your friends out of there, too."

Sure. I wasn't worried about it. And bears ambled out of my mind as I pulled Mom's Wagoneer up next to Kim's 4 Runner. Her parents got it for her as soon as she got her license, usually she drove us around, and I was very jealous. My parents didn't even buy new cars for themselves.

Kim dressed much closer to the way I thought Addie would be dressing. Because Brent and Shawn would be joining us, she'd done her hair and makeup, which meant she'd be prissy all day about getting her head wet. Her shorts were very short, and she'd hacked off her t-shirt to be a crop top. Addie and I looked like schlubs by comparison, just boring shorts and t-shirts. Ponytails to keep our hair out of our faces. It was going to be in the high eighties; I was here to swim and work on my tan. Flirting with Cody Keene would be a happy side effect of all that, if he was into me, which he might not be. Which would be fine. But more fine if he was. He used to date Karen Killarney, but her family moved to Boston at the end of the school year, and no one was quite sure if Cody was on the market or not. It being late July; I was losing my optimism, but there weren't many other interesting guys at our school. We walked down to the river and Addie paused. I saw it through her eyes. The water, down from the mountains, was crystal clear, and the sun refracted dappled patterns on the smooth stones beneath. There was a sandbar, the current wasn't too fast this time of year, and no recent storms meant there likely weren't any nasty snags in the deep parts.

"This isn't even the good part," Kim said. "We have to walk a little ways." She told Addie about Brent and Shawn. Kim didn't care which of them she wound up with, but she was tired of not having a boyfriend.

"Have you ever had a boyfriend?" She asked Addie point blank.

"Uh, no."

Kim frowned. "That's too bad." Then, hopefully, "Girlfriend?"

"No," Addie said.

"Do you want one?"

"Of which?"

"Oh, either."

"I don't know."

"I guess it's not too bad then. The pickings around here are pretty slim. I have to warn you. But get settled in first, figure out what you're looking for. You have Jessie and I to help you."

It was more than Mom and I had learned about Addie all day.

The boys had carried in a bunch of lawn chairs, metal with woven plastic seats, a boombox, and a cooler, presumably filled with beer. My mother sent me with a cooler full of sandwiches and water, which wasn't as fun as the boys' cooler, but necessary for a long day. They'd set up camp on a sandbar jutting out into one of the deeper, stiller sections of the river. There was a rope on the far side you could use to jump into the water. It scared the hell out of me to do it, but I always felt like I had to do it, to prove I could.

"I don't really like swimming either," Kim said to Addie. "I usually just park a chair in the water so I can put my feet in."

"The flirting is better if you actually get in the water with the boys," I pointed out to Kim.

There were Cody, Shawn, Brent, and a guy I didn't know. "Yo, check this out," Brent emerged from the water to greet us. To greet Kim. He pointed at a set of large bear prints in the sand.

"Cool." Kim's tone suggested she didn't especially care. Brent shrugged and went back to join Cody in the water. Shawn and the new guy looked like they were sharing a joint.

Addie pulled me aside. "Drugs?"

"Some weed and beer. Nothing serious."

"You don't understand. My mom...she was into all that stuff. I just...it kind of freaks me out."

I cursed mentally. "Hey, if you want to go back, we can go back. It's not the same here. This is just a little fun. No one even really gets drunk. Just a buzz."

"I've never...I don't want to try it."

"That's cool. And hey, whatever you want to do, we'll do. You were on a bus for almost a whole day. We have an excuse to leave if we need one."

"*You* don't want to leave, though."

She was right. "I come here all the time. Like, three times a week since I was nine. I can miss a day."

"No, we'll try it. Thanks for all this."

"No worries!"

It would have been better for us if we'd left.

◆ ◆ ◆

Addie was a good sport. She hung in. Even started talking a little. Told my friends she was from LA (not Santa Monica, which was a surprise to me), said her mom died in a car crash. Didn't mention her stepdad.

Cody lay his wet head on my bare stomach and told me he was so lucky to have me as a friend, which tore a little chunk of my heart out. Every time he turned to talk to me, I could feel his hot breath through the damp cloth of my bikini top.

While I was heartily distracted by what sure seemed like mixed signals, Kim and Brent "went for a walk" which I hoped for her sake meant they were frantically making out in the woods somewhere. There was an old cabin across the river, we weren't supposed to go in there, but it was a pretty good hookup spot if you wanted to walk.

Addie was talking with the new guy, Joe. He'd spent some time in So Cal and I guessed they were talking about all the cool stuff there is to do there.

Cody consumed all my attention. My heart pounded, and all I could think was that he must be able to feel it. Did he know it pounded because of him? Not, like, he was the reason for my heartbeat, but he made me so nervous. He had to know I liked him, right? I'd tried to make it pretty clear. I didn't think I was being subtle. I tried to stare out at the river, the beautiful river, but I fixated on his profile as much as I thought I could get away with. So I was completely absorbed with my crush when someone screamed, and Ashley Berns came running onto the sandbar.

These were the days before cell phones, you have to remember. We just either showed up or didn't, if someone didn't we assumed their parents had something else for them to do, they felt lazy, they were grounded…we didn't know, and I won't say we didn't care, but it wasn't our business. We'd thought Ashley would be here, and when she didn't show, we assumed something came up.

It didn't prepare us for the sight of her: blood and dirt streaked across her face, her white tank top torn and bloody, exposing her American flag bikini top. She dragged one leg behind her.

My stomach was cold in the absence of Cody's head. I was on my feet almost as fast as he was, sparing a glance for Addie. Her face had grown pale in the sunlight, her eyes haunted. I squeezed her shoulder as I passed, and she flinched.

We'd all binged the horror classics from the previous decade, starting with *Halloween*, *Nightmare on Elm Street*, *Friday the Thirteenth*, and *Texas Chainsaw Massacre*. It was the latter I thought of watching Ashley. I'd never seen fear like that on someone's face in real life. I didn't hear a chainsaw, but I expected Leatherface to be right behind her. Cody got to her first, and she crumpled in his arms. The sand along her path was scuffed by her passage and stained red. Her leg was bleeding, bleeding a lot. I scraped my memory from my babysitting classes, but this needed a combat medic, not a babysitter. Four shallow claw marks raked across her chest.

"Bear," she gasped. I scanned the sand bar behind her, the woods...someone needed to go get Kim and Brent. We needed to get Ashley to a hospital. My parents' conversation about territorial bears came back to me, the anxious looking male downtown we saw...there wasn't really anything for them out here, so there was no reason for them to bother us. Bears didn't like people, avoided us unless we fed them or—

"It ripped the door off my car," she gasped. Cody gave her some water. I shook the sand out of my towel and put pressure on the gash in her leg. I knew there was an artery somewhere near there. Would hitting it mean there was more blood? More than this?

"What can I do?" Addie appeared at my side, her voice small but steady.

Cody asked Ashley, "How did you get away?"

"Bear spray. I think I just made it mad, though. It's really big."

"There's a bunch of us. It won't bother us," Cody said.

"Kim and Brent need to get back here. Where did Shawn go?" I said.

"I'll go get them," said Joe, disappearing.

"Okay, once we get everyone, we head back to the cars—"

"I *told* you," Ashley panted. "The cars are all trashed." I didn't like the color of Ashley's skin. She was a farm girl, blonde, with white teeth. Her folks had her working outside year-round, and her complexion always was a glowing tan. Now a gray pallor crept over her skin. *Blood loss*, my brain whispered, noting that the towel I held was soaked and my hands were red. I pressed harder. "Can you shake off another towel and hand it to me?" I asked Addie. She did.

"What do you mean the cars are trashed?" Shawn appeared from somewhere, the water maybe?

"It fucked them all up." Ashley's voice was a whisper. "I thought they looked weird when I pulled in, the windows are smashed, tires flat. I opened my door and—it got me."

"I parked at Wilson's place," Shawn said. Explained why we hadn't seen his truck. "We should try for there."

"Up that hill?" Wilson's was technically closer parking, but the walk was steep. They'd asked us to stop using the path because the hillside was eroding. Last summer Melody Dansky was drunk and lost her footing and fell most of the way down, scraping her face to hell and spraining her ankle so badly she couldn't play field hockey in the fall. "Can we get her up there?"

"If all the other cars are fucked we don't have a choice."

We liked this spot because it *wasn't* close to parking. No one bothered us here. Sure it meant carrying our crap in, but it'd never been a problem before. Even with Mel's ankle, she'd been so drunk getting her up the hill was a comedy of errors. This, though, was a reality check. Ashley's eyelids fluttered, and I was transfixed by her long mascara'd lashes, the spatter of freckles standing out on her pale face.

"She's going to bleed to death if we can't get her out." I didn't say it to anyone in particular. I tried to remember when to use a tourniquet and wondered if anyone even had a belt.

Kim and Brent reappeared, and Kim screamed an overly dramatic horror movie scream at the sight of Ashley. Brent shook her.

I wanted to offer Kim some comfort, she was my best friend, but I couldn't leave my post, even if it felt more and more futile by the moment.

"We gotta get up to the truck at Wilson's."

"The bear is going to smell all that blood and come back," Brent said. Something I hadn't considered.

"There's seven of us. No way it's messing with us here," Cody said. He should have been right. But bears don't attack cars either. My dad and Cody's dad needed to hear about this.

"I've got a rifle in my truck," Shawn said.

"I think my mom's is in the Jeep," I said. Addie gawked at us. "Everyone has one out here. No one brought one today?" Usually it annoyed me when someone, almost always one of the guys, brought their gun down to the beach. It didn't happen often, if only because the sand was hell on them and it wasn't worth it to need to do that thorough a cleaning. When we were in eighth grade, Billy Long decided to show off his new rifle to some of the guys. He said it wasn't loaded, he was wrong, and now Billy lived in a facility in Spokane, probably for the rest of his life. For those of us whose parents hadn't put the fear of God in us, that incident went a long way in teaching us to respect firearms.

Everyone shook their heads no. No guns at the beach today. Ashley shuddered underneath me, seized I guess, her body shaking. Her eyes rolled back in her head.

"Don't touch her," someone said.

"Don't let her choke," someone else said.

It didn't matter because she was dying.

Someone pulled me off her leg, telling me she was gone. Impossible. This was Ashley Berns, so full of life and promise, 4-H champion for our county...

But they were right. Her chest wasn't moving. Her blue eyes stared up at the sky.

Cody pulled me away from Ashley. "Go rinse your hands," he said gently. Kim sobbed onto Brent, and in that moment I wanted to shake her. I went down to the water, wading in, rinsing my hands. I looked downriver, towards where the cars—the fucked-up cars—were parked. Hulking on the riverbank I saw a mass of brown fur…no no no. All the saliva in my mouth dried up, and it crossed my mind to disappear under the water and never come up. Surely drowning in the clean water of the Eaglebrook River would be preferable to— I pictured Ashley's bloodless face, and felt the blood spurting under my hands.

The behemoth raised its muzzle to the sky and sniffed. Not a good sign. Ashley's blood would certainly grab the creature's attention. I wished my dad were here with a ferocity I hadn't felt in a long time.

Feeling like my legs were stone, I waded back to shore.

"The bear is coming back. We need to get out of here. It's a ways down the river, but I saw it."

Kim screamed again, and I imagined the bear's sensitive ears rotating like radar discs.

"Up the hill to the truck," Shawn said.

"The cabin across the river," Kim said.

"No way. I have a rifle in the truck. We can leave in the truck."

"The cabin has a door, and there isn't a cliff to scale to get there."

"Cliff?" Addie said, quiet as a whisper.

"It's steep."

"Too steep?"

I didn't know. Maybe. I didn't know anything. Someone put one of the clean towels over Ashley, our friend Ashley, and I couldn't look at the bright colors draped over the person shape.

"I'm going for the gun." Shawn took off towards the trail, not bothering to put shoes on. Most of us left our keys in the visor of our cars, or if we were feeling sneaky, set on a rear tire. I hoped Shawn's were wherever he thought they were.

"Will the bear follow us across the water?" Addie asked. When no one answered, she said, "Is that a dumb question?"

"No! Not dumb. But they can swim, yeah."

She looked mortified.

"They shouldn't, though," Cody said. "Once it's eaten, it should go away and rest. We should dump out the cooler."

Not a bad idea, but I suspected a bunch of ham and cheese wasn't nearly as appealing as the fresh kill laid out on the beach.

"This has to be the bear who killed those hikers." Cody waded out into the water to look downstream. "We need to move. It's not coming fast, but it's coming. Shawn's gone for his rifle. Let's go to the cabin."

"We can't just follow him and leave?" Addie again, almost as pale as Ashley.

"I'm not scaling that cliff," Kim said. "It's hard, people fall. I don't want to fall and—" her gaze fell on Ashley's shroud and I worried she'd scream again.

"Okay," Brent said. "We'll cross and go to the cabin."

I looked at Cody. Our parents were the wildlife experts, but it felt like some of that should have rubbed off on us. "Yeah, okay," he said.

"I'm not a good swimmer," Addie said.

"We gotcha. Don't worry. There's only one part that's deep," said Brent.

"This is bullshit." I'd forgotten Joe was here. I still hadn't really talked to him. He carried himself as someone who'd lived rougher than any of the rest of us. "We have to fight. I'm not running."

"That thing is a thousand pounds and it's coming," Cody said. "We regroup indoors and then figure out how to fight."

"Shawn told me not to bring my piece and I believed him. Said it was safe out here."

Addie stared at him with wide eyes, and I worried he was

saying what she was thinking. Jesus, we didn't even have bear spray or an air horn. Our yelling should have been enough to make it think twice and find somewhere else to forage.

Kim waded into the water, heading for the other side. "Come on," I said to Addie. Brent and I flanked her, and for the deep spot under the rope swing, I told her to hold on to my hips. We clambered up the trail on the far side. Addie and Kim both looked wet and miserable. Cody and Joe argued on the far side.

"Cody, come on!" My heart pounded in my chest. I could go back. Save him? From here I could see the bear. It had stopped, watching the beach, in no hurry. Shawn would be back any minute now, and the gunshots would scare it away for sure.

Brent took Kim's arm, and they headed towards the cabin. "Follow them, I'll be there in a minute," I told Addie. Misery radiated off her. This was all my fault for bringing her here.

I couldn't hear as well from across the river, but Joe seemed to be panicking now. Cody split his attention from where I stood across the river, to the trail Shawn took, to downstream where the monster waited. Cody couldn't see it. I could. It paused to scratch at an ear with a massive front paw, then brought the paw to its massive mouth for a few licks.

How had I ever found these things cute?

Joe shouted something, the bear flicked its ears, and resumed its amble towards the beach. It reminded me of Michael Meyers. It didn't need to run, just walk in a focused, straight line and it would get its prey.

I knew my father would tell me I was being melodramatic. This bear had learned humans made good food and would have to be destroyed. It wasn't evil, didn't have a vendetta.

"Cody, come on!" I couldn't help myself. The bear looked over at me. "It's coming!"

"Go to the cabin! I'll be there in a minute." He shouted back.

The bear charged. One moment it was a big brown lump, shambling along on an afternoon stroll, the next it galloped with a speed you wouldn't think something so big could possess. Joe was closer to the thing, he wheeled around, a knife flashing in his hand.

It bowled him over, and he disappeared underneath it.

Some animals come in and kill quickly, making sure prey is dead and can't escape before they begin to eat. Bears don't need to. Once their meal is down, they feed. Joe screamed.

Kim's screams were performative. She wanted us to pay attention to her. To protect her.

Joe's screams were agony. Cody sprinted for the water, diving in and swimming under the moment it was deep enough. The bear watched him go before lowering its head back to its meal. Joe's screams changed. Guttural. Bubbling. Quieter. Cody surfaced, and paddled to the shallows. "Run. Go." There was no need for Cody to keep his voice down as the bear buried its face in Joe's chest.

I ran.

The cabin, with its yellow "No Trespassing" signs, sat in tall grass. The land had been cleared once upon a time but nature had been taking the cabin back as long as I'd been aware of it. It wasn't much—two rooms, this one with a wood stove and a fireplace, the other a bedroom with a mattress on the floor that teenagers swapped out every few years. The rest of the furniture had been cleared out, the floor was dirty and a little damp, covered in mouse poop. But there was a door, and the door was now closed between us and the bear.

Probably it wouldn't even come over here at all. It had

plenty to eat on our sandbar, there was no reason for it to do anything but amble off into the woods. We'd wait a bit, and be fine.

I wished I'd grabbed anything when I ran. It was cool and damp in the cabin, and I shivered in my wet bathing suit.

At least a bear wasn't snacking on my guts.

"It's going to come here and kill us all." Kim was crying, all her pretty makeup smeared on her face.

"That's not what they do," I said, trying to convince myself as well as Kim.

"Sure seems like it's what this one does," Kim snapped.

"We'll just wait a while, and one of us can go back out and check. We'll just…wait a while," I said again. How was *I* in charge here? Cody stood at the window, Brent wrapped his arms around Kim and she folded into him. Addie pressed her back against the wall, arms crossed over her chest. Her wet t-shirt and shorts had to be more uncomfortable than a wet bathing suit. I went to her.

"It wasn't supposed to happen like this."

"Did it kill Joe?"

"Yeah."

"Because he didn't run?"

"He panicked. He thought he could fight it."

"And you can't fight them?"

"No. Well, sometimes. But they're so big, most people can't."

"How long do we wait?"

"An hour maybe?"

"My mom did a lot of drugs," Addie said. I looked around, but everyone else seemed to be absorbed in their own things. "She had a lot of men come around. They were all awful. I know about violence."

I didn't. I didn't know anything about it. My dad was a conscientious hunter. I knew there were other kids less fortunate than I was, but my friends and I were sheltered. I was at a diner when a fight broke out once, but it was over quickly.

"I'm sorry." I didn't know what else to say.

"It's not your fault. This was a nice morning."

"It's usually nice here. Always nice here," I said lamely. "You're going to love it. After today, I mean. And I'm still sorry. About everything." She hadn't even wanted to come. She'd have been content hanging in the house by herself, getting her bearings, and I'd insisted she come with me.

Somehow, Kim led Brent into the bedroom and closed the door. I gaped at them.

"People cope with things in different ways," Addie said.

She was right.

I watched Cody at the window and wondered what my life would be like if I were the kind of person who coped like that. His shoulders stiffened, and he gripped the windowsill.

"The bear is here."

I started towards the back bedroom. "Leave them, let them have their fun. It won't matter if they're in there or freaking out with us," Cody said.

I went to the window beside him, and sure enough, the soaking wet bear sauntered up the path we'd followed.

The porch groaned as the ursine monster made its way up the steps. Little piggy eyes, attentive ears, huge nose working overtime scenting the air. It scratched at the cabin door and the door trembled under its inquisition.

"If that thing wants to get in, we're fucked," I whispered.

The bear meandered off the porch, that gargantuan muzzle pointed up and sniffing. It disappeared around the back of the house.

The three of us stood in silence.

"I can't do this," Cody said.

"Sure you can." I wasn't sure what he meant, or if he could or not. He looked wan and pale.

"What do we do?" Addie's voice was small.

A rhyme bounced into my head, from when I was a child: *If it's black, fight back. If it's brown, lie down. If it's white, good-night.* An over simplified rhyme to remember how to interact with different bear species. Play dead for grizzlies, black bears are pushovers and you can usually scare them off, you're basically fucked if a polar bear wants to mess with you. With no scientific reason, just a feeling, I was sure that the bear outside would appreciate if we lay down. It would make life easier for it. But fighting back too might give the bear sport. *Goodnight.*

Was that our only option?

Cody gave the textbook answer of playing dead.

"So you just…lie there and let it eat you?" said Addie.

"It's not supposed to eat you. We know this bear isn't starving," Cody's voice hitched, "so they're pretty much only aggressive when they're territorial, and if you play dead it doesn't see you as a threat."

"I don't think that's what's going on here," I said.

Glass broke in the bedroom, and Kim's scream tore through the afternoon. Wood splintered, Cody ran to the door and tugged on it. Of all the things the rundown, abandoned cabin had, the knob's lock still worked. He screamed for Brent.

Addie looked at me, her blue eyes infinite pools. "I can help," she said.

"No, no, no. Just hang back and…" I trailed off. And what? And die?

Kim's screams were guttural, piercing a part of me that would never be whole again.

"I can help. But you can't…tell on me."

"What?"

She wasn't making sense.

The bedroom door flew open, knocking Cody back and onto his ass. I chomped down on a scream as Kim tumbled through the door, reaching for us. Her hair and top were disheveled and I was embarrassed for her in the split second before the monster locked its claws into the backs of her thighs and yanked her back into the bedroom.

Addie sprinted forward.

If I were a better cousin, a stronger person, I might have been able to stop her. I think I reached for her, my mind smooth and white with panic. The bear would kill us all.

She stood in the doorway, in my old t-shirt and shorts, still dripping river water. Beyond her, in the sunlight streaming through the demolished wall, a mass of gore decorated the bed. The bear regarded her with those piggy eyes. She raised a hand to it, like Luke Skywalker commanding a lightsaber. She was fucked. We were all fucked.

The bear bellowed. I guess it hadn't seen *Star Wars* and didn't think Addie was funny.

Cody regained his senses before I did and moved towards her, to pull her back and out of harm's way. Until the bear finished with Kim and came after us.

Addie whirled on him, outstretched hands aimed at him. He flew back, smashing into the cabin's far wall.

My breathing quickened. A tiny voice somewhere where reason still held control warned me I would hyperventilate if I didn't get ahold of myself, but I'd just seen the impossible.

The bear didn't like it either, and leaving Kim, took a few steps towards Addie.

No! The cry was only in my mind, though. I couldn't move, felt the dirty floor under my bare feet. I still gulped air in ragged, unsustainable gasps.

Addie wheeled on the bear, bringing her hands up in front of her again. She didn't cower from it. She made a tearing motion, and the bear froze. Its ears laid back, eyes went wide. Its nostrils flared. It grunted. She did it again, taking a step towards the thing, setting her foot down inches from Kim's head. Brought her hands together, wrenched them, then made the tearing motion again.

The bear coughed a gout of bright blood. His own? Brent's? The creature scrabbled backwards, its claws unable to help on old hardwood. I'd never seen so much white, so much fear, in a bear's eyes. It cried out, sputtering, coughing. The thing wanted to flee but wouldn't turn its back on Addie, who took another step forward, now stepping over Kim. She made the motion a third time.

The sound the bear made will haunt me for the rest of my life. A lot of what I saw that day will—my friends being eaten by a grizzly—but their deaths were natural. Bears do what bears do. What Addie did to the bear shouldn't have worked. Shouldn't have been.

You can't tell on me.

She looked back once, and her eyes were pure black. I looked away from her, to Cody, who slumped on the floor.

The bear howled, guttural but broken. Dying. I've hunted before and since, I've taken many animal lives, usually quickly but unfortunately not always. Never have I heard a sound like the bear made.

Addie tore at the air again, and again, ripping with her hands. The bear shuddered and dropped to the bed, dropped on top of Brent's body. And the bear bled. From its mouth, nose, ears, eyes. From its asshole.

Addie took hold of Kim and dragged her through the doorway before she dropped to the floor beside my friend, head bowed.

I still couldn't catch my breath. The quiet in the aftermath of the carnage battled a ringing in my ears, one I knew would prevent passing out if I didn't get ahold of myself. I closed my eyes and focused on breath. Pushed away the barrage of thoughts: I was useless. My cousin was…what? It didn't matter because I wouldn't tell. Some of my friends were dead. I was useless and couldn't even check on Kim or Cody.

"Jessie?" Addie.

"Uh huh."

"Are you okay?"

"No. I mean yeah. I just need a minute."

"Please don't tell."

She looked like herself now. Just a tired teenager, who'd spent seventeen hours on a bus the day before only to be deposited into the worst horrors nature had to offer. I shook my head.

I hoped Shawn made it to his car.

✦ ✦ ✦

Kristin Dearborn is a life-long New Englander and horror writer was destined to write about anything that screams, squelches, or bleeds. Her first literary love was Michael Crichton. Her second, Stephen King. Dearborn earned her M.F.A. in Writing Popular Fiction from Seton Hill University and has been on the horror scene since 2010. She's the author of Faith of Dawn (2024) Downlines (2023) The Amazing Alligator Girl (2022) Sacrifice Island (2018), Woman in White (2017), many short stories, and more. When she's not unleashing a fresh new nightmare onto the page, Dearborn is probably searching for one. Or if she's taking a break from all things blood-curdling, she's likely playing boardgames, hiking the northeast, hanging out with her pets, or gallivanting the globe.

A Devil We Used To Know
Johnny Compton

ENOUGH SEASONS HAD PASSED for the seasons to no longer be what they once were. The world had changed since the thing had realized it must change its call, since it had last fed well. The cold no longer came when expected, and departed sooner than it had when the thing was younger, healthier, and when it ate slowly to indulge in the distinct flavors of blood, marrow, and above all the essence that separated the humans from other animals. In those times, its preferred prey was still developing language and had no stories to pass down that warned of something in the woods. An animal that blended not only with the trees, but the space between the trees. A predator whose call mimicked the laughter of children.

The trio of people the thing watched now were not children, but may as well have been. Upon hearing the thing's new call, they tittered like babies. No, that was an insult. Children would have known better than to laugh at this new call.

The thing's stomach was too empty to groan, giving it rare cause to be grateful for hunger. The usual, hollow noise of its starvation—the sound of stone shifting deep within a cave—might have alerted the people creeping toward it that they were in danger. Made it easier for them to spot the thing's eyes for what they were. Not part of the distant stars visible in the clearing, but darker lights that blinked just before you looked away, so fast you could convince yourself you hadn't seen them blink. If people noticed that, they might sense the shape of the thing without having to see it. Shiver at the coldness of its breath, shudder at the idea of its army of teeth, all without being aware of what made them tremble, just knowing they needed to turn back.

The people fidgeted, spoke to one another in hushed voices, but did not come closer. Were they waiting for another call? Should it oblige their curiosity, or remain patient? It could not afford to scare them away. Every second of delay was taxing, painful, but the agony of another famished season would be immeasurably worse.

It strained to remain hidden. Hiding demanded energy, as anything does, and malnourishment had exhausted the thing, as it would anything else. It had tried to sustain itself on everything from wounded birds to grubs. Larger animals could have been had, but by now were not even worth the idle effort of digestion. Spiders proved the closest thing to adequate. They at least had the wherewithal to set traps, employ deception. This made them cunning, clever, and cruel in ways that partly compensated for their diminutiveness. Still, anything that had no awareness of its soul—or even the concept of a soul—was insufficient. This included human corpses. Ideal sustenance came from living things that possessed sapience.

Not only had the world changed in the century since it last ate a proper meal, but so had the people. It had recognized this later than it should have, adjusted its call after going hungry long enough to weaken. When had the sound of laughing children become a warning to them? *How?* Joyful innocence shouldn't indicate danger. It had worked for hundreds of years as the exact opposite. A mark of safety. What better beacon of security could there be than the happiness of the young? The thing could never have guessed this call would someday make people run. Even now, its memories of the humans freezing, then fleeing from the sound seemed impossible, a misremembrance, though the thing had seen this dozens of times before accepting it must try something new.

Laughter initially seemed an essential element to an ideal call. Why would someone run upon hearing that? No other creature heard one of their own so enthralled they had to make show of it and thought, "There is a threat present." But no other creature was human. The thing had taken human intelligence and emotion for granted. What made them a delicious and invigorating diet also made them less predictable, at least after centuries of easy feeding. Maybe it was the stories it overheard them telling one another, but the thing felt it was something deeper. A newly formed and better understanding of when something in the world was out of place.

It first observed this change in the darker humans, who eventually learned to avoid its call, but it hadn't concentrated on this because the lighter ones arrived soon after, and ignored the warnings of the darker ones even when they appeared to ask for their guidance. That suited the thing well, allowed it to continue eating, maybe too hungrily. If it could change anything in its past sooner—other than its call —it would eat less. Resist gluttony, and instead take even more time to savor the hot blood, the snapping bones, and the syrupy intelligence housed in each individual's skull.

The lighter-colored ones eventually gained the same understanding as the others of darker tones, some of whom were also foreign but nonetheless intrinsically informed of the lure of the monster's call. Likely they had a similar hunter they were warned of in their homelands. The lighter ones, too, must have had cousins to the thing in the places they were from, but had either lost knowledge of such predators or elected to think such things couldn't exist.

Now humans of every shade knew not to be drawn by the laughter of children. The laughter of men and women, in their prime or long past it, also drew no one. The thing remained in denial of this for too long. Laughter in the woods may be out of place, unexpected, but it was still an attractive sound, was it not? It believed for a time that its mimicry was too imperfect, that this was what chased the humans away. Not the idea of the sound itself, but the inaccuracy of the call. It worked diligently to make it as true as possible, until the thing was sure the call was indistinguishable from that of an actual person's laughter. Still, they ran.

It adjusted, tried other calls, and discovered people were at least temporarily lured by a cry of pain. People would want to help the ones crying out. They would ask, "Are you okay? Where are you? Are you hurt?" The lack of a response beyond more crying made them wary. This, the creature understood. Their words meant something, and try as it might to form a proper reply, the only word it had mastered was, "Here." Effective enough to draw them in at first. When repeated, however, it sparked alarm. When said once, then supplanted by more wailing, it likewise made the humans concerned.

"I'll come back with help," they typically said, or something similar. Then they ran before the thing could pounce.

Its imitations of screams did not work. Nor did its attempt to match the groaning of those exerting themselves on a trek in the woods. The thing even tried coughing. Had it the capacity for such a feeling, the thing would have felt embarrassment at how long it took for it think of whispering.

No words were necessary for whispers. It was as if such sound was meant not to be understood, or mistaken for something else. A sound that people could tell themselves must be the wind rustling leaves, even when the wind was dead. A sound almost like the one the humans made when they hushed one another to listen more intently.

The thing pulled the sound from deep within its long winding throat now, with the four present humans remaining still and silent. It flittered its tongue to give the whisper the vibration of words. An approximation of language. Nothing as clear as its mastered, "Here," and that was for the better. To them it could be saying anything.

One of the men of the group came closer, separating himself from his friends. He had a large beard that seemed to pull his face down, draw his eyes into an ever-serious stare. When he blinked it looked purposeful, like he had never in his life let it be an automatic function.

"Trevor, come back here," one of the two women in the group said. She didn't sound like she meant it. Instead she seemed to want him to make a discovery, venture into an encounter that would make for a wonderful story.

Humans and their stories.

The thing could smell the man named Trevor's curiosity. His boldness. His aspiration. Things that that the soulless did not in the same way possess. No spider, clever as it may be, ever stepped toward an unidentifiable noise in the hopes that this would lead to a tale to tell. A legend its name would be attached to.

Trevor stepped into the clearing. The thing held its position. It had waited so long it thought this moment almost impossible. A deception of some kind. The human's thoughts were intoxicatingly sweet. The dormant, ever-present

135

consciousness of the man's soul—so close—was ferociously luscious, almost like it had teeth and hunger of its own, and would eat the thing if not eaten first.

Now, the thing thought.

Trevor's friends would not try to save him, it knew. They had no weapons, no real grasp of the threat in their midst. They had come here behaving as though they were playing a game, akin to the imaginary children the thing pretended to be several human lifetimes ago.

Now now NOW.

The thing in the woods fell on the human named Trevor, its four jaws wide, its tentacular tongue uncoiling, its enormous, needle-lined stomach spasming in anticipation. Its satiation at long last soon to come.

The human Trevor vanished within its mouth, and with its dorsal eyes the thing saw his friends jump back, then go stiller than the trees surrounding them, then scream. Then run. Two of them first. The last, the girl who had spoken to Trevor earlier, called his name once, as though this could save him, then followed her friends as fast as she could.

Trevor struggled in the grip of curved, hooking teeth that he could not see, within darkness that seemed an outgrowth of the night sky. Fear, pain, and bewilderment made up the parts of his screams, and the thing wished it could disgorge him and eat him anew. Eat him a hundred times over to make up for lost, hungry years. Its teeth twisted and bored through skin, muscle, cartilage, and bone. It made hideous art of its meal, saving the brain for last so the human Trevor could distantly comprehend the reshaping of his body, grasp the absurdity of his transformation more than the pain of his thousand wounds, understand that his soul was so much more than his physical vessel ever could be, while simultaneously realizing that it, too, was now nothing more than food.

The thing ate too quickly, as all things would if starved

long enough to catch sight of death. Even before it swallowed the last of Trevor's howling thoughts, it recognized this, but could not slow down, much less stop itself. It saved none of him for later. It licked its teeth clean, and as it now rested, as full as it had been in ages, it contemplated the idea of sadness over something lost. It was familiar with the concept through observation alone, having seen humans in times long gone return to the woods and cry not out of physical pain, but a different anguish. A longing for another person who had entered the forest and never returned. They would whisper names that the thing had felt in its stomach, in minds dissolving in acid.

It thought it felt something close to that now. As close as it could come to grieving. A great and hopeless desire to reverse time, relive something important and special. It could never have the human Trevor back. Never get another opportunity to take its time, pull him apart more methodically, as it would have in an earlier time. It could only ever remember him, what he provided in its desperation, and if it could have wept, it thought it might have done so this once, for this one human.

It was possible he would be its last meal. If the people were smarter, this would be the last warning they ever needed to avoid its habitat—even in packs—and to run away from any human-like call coming from something unseen. But the thing felt more assured than it had in centuries that more would come. Something about humanity now—something it tasted in Trevor's thoughts—led the thing to believe that people wanted to be fooled. Wanted to disbelieve in creatures they could not see, fight, or even properly name, while also wanting to be proven wrong about their incredulity. They sought to flout any warnings, as well, and challenge their own mortality. These deep, defiant instincts had always been part of them, but never so prevailing. Something had changed in them. It made sense. Nothing stayed the same forever.

The seasons had changed, some shorter and weaker, some longer and harsher. The humans had changed multiple times, first growing more cautious, and now, perhaps, more reckless and curious, to a degree that made the thing salivate.

Because it, too, had changed. Better, it had adapted. A stone battered by wind and rain over time is altered, but true adaptation within a lifetime requires awareness. Intelligence.

The thing returned to its shelter and slept peacefully, without fear of waking up hungry. It was sure that it would not starve again for many seasons to come.

❧ ❧ ❧

Johnny Compton, author (primarily of horror stories), HWA Member, Texan, tall person, and whiskey dilettante.

Johnny Compton is a Stoker Award nominated, San Antonio based author whose short stories have appeared Pseudopod, Strange Horizons, The No Sleep Podcast and several other publications. His fascination with frightening fiction started when he was introduced to the ghost story "The Golden Arm" as a child. The Spite House, his debut novel, was released in 2023. His second novel, Devils Kill Devils, will be released in 2024.

Johnny is also the creator and host of the podcast Healthy Fears, available on **Apple Podcasts / iTunes**, **Spotify** and most other podcasting platforms.

For more information, visit him on social media or at his website: https://johnnycompton.com/

Irish Eyes
Bridgett Nelson

I

"Why *the hell* does he wear his hair like that?"

Zane heard Cleo's stage-whisper, as perhaps he was meant to, and glanced up from his IBM computer screen at the two women passing his desk.

Cleo's companion, seeing him looking, put on a bright, insincere smile. "Oh, hey, Zane. How's it going?"

His cheeks flushed with color. "He...Hello, Minka," he replied, not daring to look her in the eye.

"Hope you're having a rad day!"

"Yeah, you too."

As they continued toward the exit, presumably for their lunch break, they burst into cruel laughter. Zane's head drooped to his chest.

He'd had a crush on Minka, with her beautiful face and mesmerizing voice, her long, honey-blonde hair, and her toffee-colored eyes, since he'd first started working at XenCorp eight months ago. Realistically, he knew nothing would come of it. A woman who looked like Minka would *never* be interested in a guy like him. Yet his traitorous heart steadfastly refused to let that kernel of hope die.

Zane trudged dejectedly to the restroom. Inside, he studied himself in the mirror, well aware he was looking at a man who knew zilch about style. He was in his thirties, and his mom's friend still cut his hair. The fact she was nearly seventy years old, and not remotely trendy, had never crossed his mind. Ethel had been cutting his hair his entire life, didn't charge him a penny, and was the last remaining tie he had to his long-deceased mother. Besides that, she always gave him leftovers from her fridge on his way out the door. Any night he had something other than a Banquet TV dinner was a win in his book.

But, yeah...his hairstyle was decidedly bowl-shaped. He ran fingers through the thick, shiny brown locks, thinking at least he didn't have to resort to a comb-over.

The rest of his body wasn't in bad shape. A bit of paunch around the middle, sure, but he certainly wasn't *offensive*.

Hell, he was proud of his broad shoulders. And, hidden beneath his coffee-colored dress pants were well-built, muscular legs. He didn't own a car and walked everywhere he went, which had its benefits. His doctor said that, despite a long history of heart-attack deaths in his family, his ticker was healthy and strong.

He turned his attention to his clothes—generic brands, but perfectly adequate. The only part of his wardrobe he splurged on was his shoes, given all the walking, so his feet were usually clad in top-of-the-line sneakers. In the office, he wore a snazzy pair of brown dress shoes he'd found on sale at K-Mart.

He may not have been Minka's dream guy, but a girl could do a lot worse.

After using the bathroom for its intended purpose, and washing his hands like the gentleman he was, Zane made his way back toward his desk. He cringed as he heard the loud bray of his boss's voice.

"Robinson! Just the man I wanted to see. Get in here!"

Zane's spirits sank further. Phil Degrassi was an asshole on the best of days, but now he sounded pissed, even for him.

Sticking his head through partially opened door, he said timidly, "Yes, Mr. Degrassi?"

"Don't just stand there! Come in. Take a seat." The words were clipped, the tone sour.

Already sure this wasn't going to be a pleasant meeting, but not having the faintest clue as to *why*, Zane shuffled into the room and sat down.

Mr. Degrassi said nothing for a long time, just looked at him. As the seconds ticked by, the uncomfortable silence grew. Approximately one-and-a-half lifetimes later, Mr. Degrassi finally spoke. "Zane, you know I like you, right?"

Knowing nothing of the sort, Zane gave an apprehensive nod.

"And you know I've always championed your work to my bosses."

It wasn't framed as a question, but, again, a confused Zane nodded his head.

Mr. Degrassi picked up a piece of paper and handed it over. "Tell me what you see."

Gripping the white sheet within his sweaty hand, Zane recognized it as a daily numbers report, something he turned in at the end of each work day. Not knowing what his boss expected, he answered, "It's the numbers report, sir."

"Yes. Yes, it is." Mr. Degrassi leaned back in his chair. "And is that your signature at the bottom?"

"Yes, that's my signature, Mr. Degrassi."

He crossed his arms over his chest and scowled. "Knowing how much I like you, and how frequently I brag

141

on you to my superiors, why the fuck would you screw me over like this, Robinson?"

Bewildered, Zane stuttered, "I…I don't. Sir?"

"Look at the sixth line, dammit!"

Wiping a drop of sweat off his brow, Zane focused on the problematic line…and silently cursed.

"Ah, so *now* you see the issue." A note of scornful satisfaction resonated in Degrassi's voice.

He saw it all right…and thought he might puke. He had mistakenly added an extra zero to the figure, inadvertently creating a multi-million-dollar mistake.

"How could you be so careless, Zane?"

Zane took a deep breath. Yes, this was certainly his error —he wouldn't deny that.

"I'm sorry, sir. It was simple mistake on my part. It won't happen again."

Degrassi's face puckered up. "A *simple* mistake? If the accounting team hadn't caught it, it could have bankrupted the company, Robinson! It's far more than a *simple mistake*."

His mistake, yes, but all reports were also supposed to be reviewed by Mr. Degrassi before they were sent to the senior team. Why the hell was he putting all the blame on Zane?

"Didn't you check it yourself?" Zane asked, blurting out the words in a rush of anxiety.

Phil Degrassi's face turned an angry red, quickly followed by an unhealthy purple. His fists clenched, and his chair squeaked as he leaned toward Zane. A vein protruded from his forehead. When he finally spoke, his voice was a gruff, vengeful purr. "Are you trying to lay *your* fuckup at *my* feet, Robinson? Because if you are, you can just pack up your desk right this minute, and get the hell out of this building. I shouldn't have to go through every goddamned line to make sure you're not an incompetent asshole. We pay you to get it right!"

Panicked at the idea of losing this job, Zane replied, "No! No, sir. Of course that's not what I was saying. I take full responsibility for my error and promise it won't happen again."

Appeased, Mr. Degrassi leaned back again and nodded. "Make sure it doesn't. Now beat it!"

II

Feeling despondent after work, Zane made his usual Friday night pit stop at the shabby tavern near his apartment. After drinking a couple of cheap, piss-tasting beers and wolfing down a very questionable cheeseburger, he slowly made his way home. As he came through the front door, Banshee greeted him with a happy meow. She rubbed against his leg, her body vibrating with contented purrs. He'd rescued the cat from a life on the streets. Although much calmer now, when he'd first taken her in, she had frequently awakened him from a dead sleep with her piercing, demanding wails—hence, her name.

These days, she was his only company.

He was so damn lonely.

After feeding Banshee and tidying up his kitchen, he watched some television, then took a long, hot shower. Sliding naked between the cool, black cotton sheets adorning his king-sized bed, he sighed. He hated all the extra space. It was a stark reminder of everything missing in his life.

Pulling the covers up to his chin, he closed his eyes. He never prayed. Religion wasn't his thing. Yet every night, without fail, he sent a very specific wish out into the universe.

He felt so alone. He had no family, no friends. It was just him and Banshee, against a world full of mean people.

A woman to pamper; a woman to cuddle; a woman to share his life...that was all he wanted.

Hoping this was the night his dreams would finally come true, he rolled onto his side, curled into a ball, and fell asleep.

❦ ❦ ❦

Zane yawned and stretched, a happy smile playing upon his lips.

He *had* to be dreaming.

Why else would a silver-haired beauty be standing beside his bed, gazing down at him with ardent adoration and desire in her violet eyes?

He reached for her. She backed away, out of his reach.

His smile turned to a frown. Was his subconscious trying to remind him how pathetic and unlovable he was...even in his dreams?

The woman let out a tinkling laugh. "You're not dreaming, my love." Her voice was enthralling—layered and nuanced, with an adorable Irish brogue and a musical quality he could listen to forever. "I'm as real as you."

Still convinced it was all a dream, he didn't react, except to study her—this woman who shouldn't be here but seemingly was.

Petite.

Delicate.

Ethereal.

Zane doubted her frame reached the five-foot mark...*but those curves!* A lavender, semi-transparent sheath draped her hourglass form. Despite her small stature, there was *nothing* childlike about her.

Silvery, shimmering hair hung to her waist in perfectly formed ringlets. Her face was lovely, heart-shaped, with full, rosy-pink lips. But it was those wide, violet eyes he found most alluring. They innocently peered at him from beneath long, dark lashes.

"Who are you?"

"I am Citrisa," she replied.

"How did you get into my apartment?"

She giggled, and Zane felt thousands of butterflies fluttering inside his abdomen. "The front door."

"It was locked."

"Yet I walked right in."

Had he locked the door? Unsure enough to argue, he pushed on. "Why are you here?"

She tilted her head to the side. "You wished for me, did you not?"

Zane sat up, suddenly wide awake. The blankets pooled around his waist, as his heart galloped inside his chest. "How in the hell do you know what I wished for?"

The encounter, dream or not, was no longer evocative—it was creepy as fuck. He nervously eyed his nightstand drawer, where a small pocketknife resided.

"You have no reason to fear me, Zane. I love you."

"You know my *name*?"

Citrisa seductively lifted the hem of her dress and crawled onto the bed with him. He was too shocked to move at first. Only as she straddled his hips did he try to push her away. She wouldn't budge.

"Of course I know your name." She leaned close and whispered into his ear. "I am your destiny, Zane. We're meant to be. I am everything you've ever wanted."

Her sweet-smelling breath on his earlobe, and that seductive voice offering his soul's deepest desires, caused a physical response—one Citrisa immediately recognized.

"Ah, I see you like my words." She smiled and moved in for a kiss.

Before she could do so, Zane wrapped his arms around

her and rolled their bodies until he was on top, his hips nestled between her spread legs. He could already feel the welcoming heat of her liquid desire. Her thighs squeezed around him—so tight, he worried she might crack a bone—and her tiny bare feet interlocked against his lower back.

"Before we consummate our relationship, you must tell me you love me." She licked his neck with her dainty tongue.

A misty moan echoed from his throat.

"I *must* hear you say it, Zane."

Her eyes were hypnotizing. Despite the urgency in her voice, Zane felt dazed, dreamy—not quite in control of his own mind. But he couldn't find it within himself to care.

Sliding inside her delicious warmth, he murmured, "I love you, Citrisa. You belong to me." His words, to his own ears, sounded flat. Emotionless.

She let out musical laugh. "Oh, but it is *you* who belongs to *me*, Zane."

Feeling more aroused than ever by her comment, Zane thrust inside this exquisite woman who had so willingly offered him her body...and the opportunity to have the life he'd always wanted.

An hour later, they were sound asleep in the center of his bed, their languid bodies intertwined, Catrisa's silver hair sparkling in the moonlight.

III

Zane awoke sated and refreshed, but realizing he was alone in the bed when he should have been snuggling his new lover made him abruptly set up. Panic set in.

Had it just been a dream? Or, had it been real, and she'd left him already? He heard a brief clang from the kitchen, and his galloping pulse slowed to a steady trot.

She was real, she was here, and she was making them breakfast.

Unable to contain his smile, Zane pulled on a pair of sweatpants and, with the eager anticipation of a teenager experiencing first love, went to find her.

Catrisa gave him a bewitching grin as he entered the kitchen. She was wearing one of his t-shirts, the navy-blue material hanging well below her knees. Long sterling curls glistened in the morning sunlight.

Zane couldn't believe this stunning woman was his. He wrapped his arms around her waist and kissed the back of her neck.

Two plates of mouthwatering food sat on the countertop. The delicious aromas caused Zane's stomach to grumble in anticipation.

This was the life he'd dreamed of—a good woman, home-cooked meals, and great sex. He couldn't stop grinning.

Pulling two glasses from the cabinet, he filled them with orange juice, put everything on a tray, and carried their feast to his small table.

Banshee slunk into the room, eyes wild. She hissed menacingly at Catrisa. The hair on her arched back stood upright.

Zane laughed...couldn't help himself. She looked ridiculous.

Passing by Catrisa's chair, Banshee screeched and swiped a paw across her shapely calf. Catrisa didn't react to the bleeding scratch, just calmly took a bite of her scrambled eggs.

"Are you okay?" he asked.

"Seems your kitty isn't my biggest fan."

"I've never seen her act that way before. I'm sure she'll come around."

Catrisa stood and went to the fridge, giving Banshee a

solid kick as she groomed herself in the doorway. The cat let out a startled yowl and darted down the hall.

"Head scritches might be a more appropriate way to forge a relationship." Zane said, his voice tight. He didn't tolerate animal abuse.

"Oh, don't you worry about us." Catrisa replied, pouring more orange juice in her glass. "Banshee and I will get along just fine. She's simply not used to competition for your attention." Zane heard her response, but had lost interest. All he could focus on was the perfectly crisp bacon and fluffy eggs covering his plate—his favorite breakfast.

"And how are you this morning, my love?" Catrisa asked, tactfully changing the subject.

"Great! I'm gonna write a book!" He wolfed down the extra-large portions she'd given him.

"Really?"

"Well, that's the weird part," he said, more than a little surprised by the declaration himself. "I woke up with the notion in my head, knowing I had to. I mean, I got by okay in school, but English wasn't my favorite subject."

Which was putting it mildly; was there anything more useless than diagramming a sentence? He wasn't a reader, either, and he sure as hell wasn't a writer. Nor was he a folk-lorist by any stretch of the imagination.

Yet, all of a sudden, he had this irresistible urge. A story, a novel. A horror novel.

"About what?" Catrisa asked, as if reading his mind.

"About the *leannán sídhe*." He took his time with the pronunciation, making sure he got it just right. *Lan-hawn shee*. Even as he said it, he wondered how he knew the term. Gaelic, wasn't it?

"Oh?" she prompted.

Like with the term and pronunciation, information seemed to have filled his brain out of nowhere. "Apparently, they're a cousin to banshees...but way worse! The Irish version of a succubus."

"I've...heard of them."

"Well, you *are* Irish. I guess you inspired me." He smiled at her.

She was so beautiful. Yet, as she picked up her glass and took a drink, her image morphed. Her clear, porcelain skin turned purple with rot. A slew of green veins crisscrossed her face. The stunning violet eyes turned black, with no discernible pupil or sclera. White, wriggling snakes and muddy-brown earthworms replaced her silvery curls.

Repulsed, Zane gasped and dropped his fork. After bending to retrieve the utensil from the floor, he saw Catrisa looking at him, her visage normal once again.

"Everything okay?" she asked.

Shaking his head to clear the disturbing image, Zane picked up a piece of bacon and crammed it into his mouth. "Sure, yeah. Everything's...fine. Didn't get much sleep last night is all. My brain is a little fuzzy this morning."

As he chewed, he felt something hairy sticking in his teeth. He pulled the bacon out of his mouth.

And gagged.

It wasn't bacon at all.

It was a rat's tail.

Sweet, smoky bacon and buttery scrambled eggs didn't fill his plate—more rat tails and a variety of other rodent parts and organs did.

He dropped the tail onto the table as his stomach clenched in horrified disgust. Dry-heaving, Zane lurched to his feet, knocking his chair backward onto the floor. He rushed to the bathroom and made it just in time to purge the contents of his stomach.

Partially digested rat bits floated in the toilet water. Sickened, Zane flushed them and headed toward the sink, intent on rinsing out his tainted mouth.

"What's going on, Zane? Is something wrong with the meal I prepared?" Catrisa appeared in the doorway.

"What the fuck do you *mean*, is something *wrong* with it? Why would you feed me goddamn *rats*, Catrisa?"

She wrinkled her nose at him, and then giggled. "You're such a goofball, Zane! Rats..." Still giggling, her fingers danced over the muscles in his back, lightly massaging the tension away.

Zane turned to her, incredulous. "My plate was full of rat tails and guts!"

A peculiar, disappointed look crossed Catrisa's face. She disappeared down the hallway and was back moments later, carrying his plate—a plate filled with nothing more than bacon and scrambled eggs.

Zane gaped at the plate. "Did you switch out the food?"

"Don't be silly. Why don't you come back and finish eating before you start writing? You need brain food."

She stared into his eyes.

He stared back.

Hers were a kaleidoscope of color.

He was hypnotized.

She took his hand. He shuffled behind her, like an innocent lamb heading to his slaughter, picked up his chair off the floor, and finished his totally normal breakfast.

Afterward, he wrote.

Catrisa made such a lovely muse.

IV

Monday morning, Zane was back at work, but could barely keep his eyes open. The weekend hadn't been particularly restful—not that he was complaining.

No, he *definitely* wasn't complaining. When he wasn't pounding out strings of words on his typewriter, Catrisa was riding him like a bucking bronco. He couldn't get enough of her, and the feelings seemed to be mutual.

It had been the best weekend of his entire life, yet he desperately needed sleep. He felt as though he'd aged a decade in two days. He'd even found a few gray hairs this morning.

"Hi, Zane! Rough weekend?" Minka asked, elbowing Cleo in the ribs as they attempted to hide their derisive snorts... poorly.

Unamused, and too tired to feel intimidated, he looked at them. *Really* looked at them.

They were loathsome creatures. He was bewildered by his attraction to Minka, wondering what he'd ever seen in such a judgmental, superficial woman. Anger flared through his belly, and a barrage of words spewed from his mouth.

"If, by *rough weekend*, you're asking whether or not I got to make love to a beautiful woman over and over again—the answer is, 'I sure as hell did!' It was *killer*, ladies." He mimicked a few pelvic thrusts, while suggestively licking his lips, to drive home the point.

The identical looks of shock and horror on their faces were comical.

Unsure where the brazenness was coming from, Zane continued, "Truth be told, my girlfriend has a better body than either of you, though those stupid boxy sweaters you're wearing makes it hard to evaluate. Why the shoulder pads gotta be so big? You defensive tackles?" He contemplatively ogled their chests. Without warning, he put one hand on each of their breasts. "Hm. Yeah, well, maybe..." he murmured, then paused, considering. His hands continued squeezing and groping. "Yeah, I'm just gonna say it...hers are definitely better. Perkier. Firmer. Perfect lollipop nipples. Makes ya just wanna suck 'em, ya know?" He made an obscene slurping sound, then shrugged and resumed typing.

They gaped at him, initially too stunned to speak, then flushing and spluttering in embarrassment and indignation.

Keeping his eyes glued to his computer screen, he casually added, "So whad'ya say you two bitches just move right along? I don't feel like dealing with your petty, junior high bullshit today." He gave them a brief shooing wave.

Minka fled, tears rolling down her cheeks. Cleo stayed for a moment, as if unsure whether or not she should attempt to fire back, then hurried after her.

Good call. Zane felt oddly satisfied by the exchange, and found he was no longer the least bit sleepy. Sitting up in his chair, his posture straight, he sifted through the work that had accumulated over the weekend.

"Mr. Robinson."

Zane stiffened upon hearing Phil Degrassi's stern voice.

"Good morning, Mr. Degrassi," he said politely.

"You *do* realize, Mr. Robinson, that, here at XenCorp, we have *strict* sexual harassment policies in place."

Oh, yeah.

"Yes, sir."

Mr. Degrassi leaned closer and said, in a venomous whisper, "If I didn't need you so desperately for the upcoming corporate visit, I'd fire you right now. If I *ever* see any inappropriate behavior from you again, I'll shove your dumb fucking ass out the window and swear on my wife's life you jumped. Got it?"

Zane gulped, his newfound confidence seeping away. "Got it."

Degrassi stroked his chin. In a self-important voice, he continued. "The president of the company will be here tomorrow. Try to dress in something nicer than thrift store hand-me-downs. And, for crying out loud, man, do something with that mop on your head."

Rendered speechless, Zane merely nodded.

Degrassi started to walk away, then stopped and turned back. "For Christ's sake, get some sleep. You look like hell."

V

Enrapt, Zane watched Catrisa slide herself up and down his very impressive erection.

Her focused intensity and dedication to the act turned him on like nothing ever had. She was a lioness, intent on taking what she was owed. Splaying her body across his chest, her lips met his in a passionate kiss. Drugs had never given him this kind of high. He basked in the comfortable, dream-like state he'd become so accustomed to since Catrisa had entered his life.

Seconds later, an orgasm ripped through him with incredible ferocity.

Afterward, he could barely get out of bed. He felt as though his entire body had become one big aching misery. Was he coming down with something? The flu?

Shuffling to the bathroom, he gazed at himself in the mirror. Dark circles rimmed his eyes. His hair appeared dull and brittle, shot with greying strands.

He looked like crap and didn't feel much better.

Catrisa, glowing with youthful energy and vigor, bounded naked into the bathroom and turned on the shower. "Want to join me?" she asked.

Zane gazed at her shapely ass. He wanted nothing more than to run his hands over those sudsy mounds under the steamy water.

But he didn't have the energy. Begging off, he hobbled back to bed, crawled in, and fell into a deep sleep.

❧ ❧ ❧

The stack of typewritten pages grew taller each day. Ten chapters already? Zane couldn't remember writing the original nine.

Also, since he'd started the project, he hadn't done one iota of research. He should probably read and assess the bullshit he'd surely written—but was scared to look.

He shambled to the kitchen, grabbing a soda from the fridge, and a bag of potato chips from the pantry.

Catrisa, who was preparing a lasagna dish for dinner, said, "You know, babe, if you ate less junk food, you might not feel so crappy all the time. That shit ages ya." Her Irish brogue was thicker than usual.

"I say this with love, sweetheart…but don't get between a man and his chips."

She shrugged and continued layering the pasta, which looked like strips of dried-out human flesh. Bile rose into his throat, but he swallowed it down and plopped his aching body onto the couch. Following the breakfast debacle a couple weeks ago, he knew his eyes were no longer trustworthy.

Taking a long swig of soda, he let out a loud, satisfied belch, and hesitantly picked up his manuscript. Skimming the first few pages, a tsunami of understanding briefly filled his mind, and he gasped in shock at the implication of what he'd written.

A moment later, the unsettling epiphany was gone. Instead, a small smile played upon his lips. He wasn't bad at this writing thing. The story was engrossing, and his prose was top-notch.

Thirty minutes later, the pages were neatly put away, and a purring Banshee was curled up beside him on the couch. As he scratched her silky ears, Zane struggled to remember a single word he'd written.

He couldn't. He just knew it was good stuff.

VI

Catrisa's bare toes crept up his pantleg to graze the skin of his shin, then teasingly worked her way up his leg until the sole of her foot pressed squarely on his crotch, massaging him to an enormous erection through his slacks.

The sensation was incredible, especially when her toes squeezed around his shaft. He looked at her, chin resting on her hand, eyes wide and innocent, a small smirk gracing her plump lips.

"If you don't stop, I'm going to embarrass myself," he said quietly, his breaths coming in short gasps.

"Well, we can't have that, can we, love?" She placed her napkin beside her water glass, glanced discreetly to the left and right, then disappeared beneath the table.

Before Zane could process what was happening, her warm mouth surrounded him. It was a struggle to maintain his dignity.

"Excuse me, sir," said their waiter, "but will your companion be returning soon? I'll be happy to take your order."

"Oh, uh…ahhhh, God." He cleared his throat, recognizing the waiter's knowing look. "She went to the restroom. Please give us a few more minutes." With a nod, the waiter walked away, just as Zane unloaded into Catrisa's mouth. The patrons at a nearby table heard the groan he was unable to contain. Their identical expressions—weary disgust—were enough to bring Zane back to reality.

"Pardon me." He gave a brief chuckle. "Bit of digestive upset."

Huffing, they turned back to their meals, just as Catrisa popped up from beneath the table, looking even more beautiful than when she'd begun the foot-play seduction.

"That was fun!" She took a sip of her water. "I feel like a million bucks!"

Zane...did not. The room was spinning. He felt suddenly weaker...flimsy. His body tilted to the side as the floor came closer and closer.

This can't be good...

❦ ❦ ❦

"Zane, m'love? Zane ...wake up."

He felt a gentle patting on his cheeks, and something wet on his forehead. As he struggled to open his heavy eyelids, he tried to remember what had happened.

The restaurant...but from a very different perspective.

He was flat on his back, the waiter standing nearby with a cluster of anxious staff, while other patrons observed curiously from their tables.

Catrisa hovered over him, her violet eyes iridescent with unshed tears.

"Hi, baby. Good to see you came back to me. How're you feeling?"

"I'm fine." His voice sounded dry and croaky, like that of a very old man.

"Ma'am, we can call an ambulance—" the waiter began.

"No, no, that won't be necessary." She waved him off, focused on Zane. "Do you think you can stand?"

"I...think so." He removed the damp cloth from his forehead.

As she helped him to his feet, his joints popped and ferociously ached. He could feel his heart galloping wildly in his chest, the palpitations making him short of breath.

"Come on, let's get you back to the car," she urged. "I'll drive you to the emergency department straightaway."

"I'm fine," he replied automatically, in that second-nature way men were conditioned to from boyhood. "Just got a little dizzy, is all."

She guided him toward the front door, the waiter trailing solicitously after, assuring them since they hadn't even ordered drinks, there was no bill to be paid.

Near the entrance, Zane glimpsed himself in an ornate, filigreed gold-framed mirror, and was so stunned, he stumbled and nearly fell again.

His cheeks were hollowed, their darkened contours giving his face an unhealthy, skeletal appearance. His eyes were sunken, his face haggard.

Even more startling was his hair—still mostly brown when he'd arrived for dinner, but now gone totally white.

VII

"Robinson, I need to talk to you!"

Letting out a long sigh, Zane shuffled his way slowly to Mr. Degrassi's office. He fell into the chair in front of the desk, and struggled to catch his breath.

Degrassi indiscreetly studied him. "I'm just going to come right out and say it. We need you to take a drug test."

Shocked by the unexpected words, Zane stupidly replied, "What?"

"What the hell else am I supposed to think, Robinson? I mean, look at you. You've aged four decades in the past month! Your behavior is erratic and entirely inappropriate. Your work is sloppy. Is it that crack cocaine shit?"

"No! I don't...I don't do drugs!"

He grabbed Zane's arm, leading him to the private en suite bathroom in his office. A company nurse waited there, wearing gloves and holding a sterile specimen cup. "Now go take a piss," Degrassi commanded. "And leave the cup sitting on the back of the toilet. I'm leaving the door open so we can keep an eye on you."

It took a while. These days, every drop of urine output was a struggle, even without someone watching.

But he finally got an adequate amount of dark amber urine inside the cup and sat it on the back of the toilet as instructed. The nurse picked it up, wrote his name and the date on the label, and departed, promising to have the results back soon.

A drug test, of all things. On him? Zane washed his hands, shaking his head with disbelief.

As he left the office, Degrassi muttered after him, "And don't be getting that girl of yours pregnant. The last thing I want my taxes to pay for is your fucked up little crack baby."

❧ ❧ ❧

The next day, Zane was not in the mood for anyone's bullshit. He was too tired and cranky.

He'd even been forced to decline Catrisa's sexual advances last night, which hadn't gone over well. Anger had flared in her suddenly black eyes for a brief moment, just before she'd smiled and assured him it was okay, these things happened. Then she'd suggested they just snuggle and watch movies.

They'd done a lot of kissing during their viewing of "The Kiss," which was pretty funny. It was sweet and innocent, and required no physical effort on his part, but he'd felt even worse afterward.

When he'd awoken in the middle of the night to see her hair writhing on the bed beside him, he'd simply rolled over and gone back to sleep, too exhausted to give it more than a second thought.

So, her hair moved on its own? So what?

This morning, as he'd left for work, she'd gifted him with a brand-new cane, "to help you walk." Though he hated to admit it, it did make getting around a little easier.

"Robinson! In my office, stat!"

Using the cane, he made his way to Degrassi. He did his best to ignore the looks from the others at their desks but still caught some of them out of the corner of his eye—Cleo's cold sneer, Minka's chagrined sympathy.

"What did you need, Mr. Degrassi?" His voice was monotone as he stood in the doorway. Flat. Any other time, he might have been nervous, but today he just couldn't seem to care.

His boss looked concerned. "I got the results of your urine test. It was clean. No drugs detected."

"I told you I wasn't doing drugs, sir."

"And I believe you. But…"

He'd never seen Degrassi at a loss for words. "But what?"

"But they said the urine they received was from a seventy-year-old man," Degrassi said. "Normally, I'd assume you'd tried to cheat the system, but I know that couldn't have happened, and the nurse agrees."

Zane waited without responding. His lack of reaction seemed to make Degrassi even more uncomfortable.

"So, here's what we're gonna do," Degrassi said, striving for briskness. "I'm giving you the day off, and you're going to call your doctor and demand an urgent appointment. Get checked out. Let me know what they say."

He nodded, unable to deny he needed medical care. "I will, sir. And…thank you."

Mr. Degrassi gingerly shook Zane's age-spotted hand,

something he'd never done before, a solemn look etched on his face.

As Zane exited the building, he realized his boss wasn't expecting a good doctor's report; he'd been saying goodbye.

VIII

"Your blood work is not even close to being within normal limits, Zane. It's as though you have the body of a seventy-year-old."

Zane laughed.

Dr. Wilkins, his long-time physician, frowned. "What could possibly be funny about that?"

"Oh, I've just heard it all before," he replied, still chuckling.

Unamused, Dr. Wilkins went on. "I'm not sure what's causing this, and as your doctor and friend, I have to tell you...you look like shit."

"I know! Why do you think I'm here?" Zane replied, agitated. Had he been able to get around without the cane, he would have paced the office like a caged animal. "I can't even walk to work anymore. I have to Uber, and that's not cheap. Peeing is a misery. My body hurts all the time. And I'd swear I've even lost a couple inches of height. I look like a goddamned hunchback! I just want to get my life back. What can I do?"

"We need to do more testing. I suspect an autoimmune disorder of some sort. But at this point, I can't even begin to guess which one." The doctor, twice Zane's age but, ironically enough, looking years younger, let out a loud sigh. "In the meantime, let's get you into physical therapy to strengthen your body. A thirty-year old man shouldn't need a cane."

"You're telling me." Zane let out a frustrated sigh of his own. "It's even affecting my sex life."

"I didn't realize you were seeing anyone. Certainly explains why you look so tired!" The doctor winked.

"It's a fairly recent development, but I'm thinking of asking her to marry me."

"Wow, must be serious—sounds like congratulations are in order!" Dr. Wilkins patted him on the back.

Zane grimaced in pain, but responded with a proud smile. "It is serious. She gives me life."

❧ ❧ ❧

Zane lay on his side, trying to breathe through the pain radiating to his left arm and jaw.

He wasn't stupid. He knew he was likely suffering a heart attack, but he couldn't seem to garner the energy to yell for Catrisa—the one person with the potential to save his life by calling nine-one-one.

Why was this happening now? He'd felt fine earlier today. His physical therapy session had gone well. He'd made some gains in his mobility.

When he arrived home, he and Catrisa had been intimate.

Which had been followed by profuse sweating.

She had likely assumed it was from their love-making and left the room to start prepping dinner.

A squeezing pain filled his chest.

The contents of his stomach roiled.

His throat felt like it was on fire.

He gasped for air.

Wheezy breaths.

Anxiety.

Pain.

He heard Catrisa humming "When Irish Eyes Are Smiling." It sent shivers down his spine.

He lost consciousness.

IX

"...too much damage..."

"...nothing we can do?"

"...matter of hours..."

Zane regained conscious slowly, hearing brief snippets of conversation between Catrisa and a man with a deep baritone voice—presumably an ER doctor—amid the steady beeps from various machines hooked to his body.

Their words didn't bode well for his longevity.

His body was a mishmash of unpleasant sensations. He could tolerate the cuffs around his lower legs that rhythmically inflated and deflated in painful squeezing cycles. A tube in his mouth aggravated his gag reflex, and he desperately wanted to pull it out. There was a tube in his dick too. Not pleasant, but he had far bigger problems.

He was dying, for fuck's sake. Yet, the thought of a tube stuck up his dickhole freaked him the hell out.

His eyes remained closed; he wasn't ready for anyone to know he was awake yet, and pushing the lids up required far too much effort from his ailing body.

Catrisa's conversation with the doctor ended. A door shut. The only sound in the room was the beeps and swooshes of the machines tasked with keeping him alive.

When a knock sounded at the door, Catrisa didn't respond. Perhaps she'd gone somewhere? The hospital cafeteria, maybe?

The door opened to the sound of a whispered voice. "We shouldn't just barge in, Phil."

Minka? Was that Minka, from work? And Phil...Phil Degrassi? His boss?

"It'll be fine," a man replied impatiently. It was Degrassi, all right.

Footsteps crossed the floor and paused at Zane's bedside.

"Gosh, he looks like…so bad," Minka blurted.

Mr. Degrassi grunted in response.

"Can I help you?" said Catrisa, who must not have left the room after all. Her tone was rich with contempt; she didn't play well with other women.

Minka, who evidently hadn't noticed her, let out a startled cry. After an awkward silence, she said, "We're so sorry. It's dark in here. We didn't see you."

Zane heard the clack of Catrisa's heels on the linoleum floor. "I'm Catrisa. Zane's girlfriend."

"You mean he *wasn't* lying—?"

Mr. Degrassi cut Minka off. "Why, hello there! Zane never told me how lovely you are."

Catrisa giggled flirtatiously as, by the sound of it, he kissed the back of her hand.

"Phil, I think we should go," Minka said tightly. "We're interrupting their time together."

"Go if you want, but I think Catrisa could use some support and company." He put on a formal business-type air. "As a representative of XenCorp, I want you to know how very sorry we all are about Zane, and assure you we'll help in any way we can."

Minka hmphed and stomped out. Had they been anywhere but a hospital, Zane was sure the door would have slammed shut upon her exit.

"Thank you," Catrisa replied. Her hand covered Zane's. She brought the limp appendage to her mouth and kissed each of his knuckles.

What little life-force was left in him dwindled.

Her voice became husky. "The doctor says he'll be gone in a matter of hours. I just…I don't know how I'm supposed to survive without him. He's all I have in this world." She sobbed.

Might want to slow that overacting roll…

"I will personally be there for you every step of the way," Degrassi said. "In fact, why don't you come and stay with me once he's gone? I've got plenty of room. There is no need for you to be alone."

His voice had gone monotone, unaware. Zane could tell he'd fallen under Catrisa's spell, the hypnotic kaleidoscope effect of her eyes.

"I'd like that very much. Thank you, Mr. Degrassi."

"Please, call me Phil."

"Phil, then. Would you mind giving me a moment?"

"Not at all. I'll be right outside."

Catrisa hovered over Zane and brushed the hair from his forehead. "Oh, how I loved you, my dear Zane." Her cold lips covered his. She lightly inhaled.

Zane's heart constricted inside his chest. Every machine attached to his body alarmed.

"But our time together is over," she whispered. "Thank you for giving me life."

Then she walked away.

He'd been discarded.

Medical personnel ran into the room, intent on saving him—strange, aged anomaly that he was.

Through the noise and chaos, from the hall, Zane heard Catrisa speaking.

"I can be everything you've ever wanted, Phil." Her words were followed by the breathless sounds of passionate kissing. "But you must tell me you love me."

A sudden haunting realization chilled him...he'd given his life to a monster.

Moments later, he was lost to the infinite void.

Epilogue

Hungry, alone, and confused, Banshee mewled loudly for her human.

She jumped onto the desk, knocking off several sheets of papers, and sniffed the rest. She could smell him on them, which was comforting despite how tainted and peculiar his scent had recently become. Banshee pawed at the papers, then turned in circles before curling up atop them.

As she drifted off to sleep, clicking sounds and anxious whispers came from the front door.

"Tell me again why we're breaking into that sleazeball's apartment? He's dead anyway, so who cares?" Cleo asked snidely.

"He has a cat, remember? He mentioned her in the lunchroom a few months ago. It's not her fault her owner was a prick. I figured I could take care of her, at least for a while." Minka continued working the lock pick. "And besides...I don't trust that girlfriend of his. I'm sure the bitch did something to him."

"The one who Phil was fawning over at the hospital?"

"That very one. She's staying at his house!" Something scraped inside the handle, and the door swung open. "Yes! Piece of cake!"

Crossing the threshold, Minka saw Banshee lying on the desk and picked her up, delighting in the cat's soft purrs. "Cleo, why don't you find her food and get some fresh water. She's probably starving." As Cleo ventured off, Minka talked softy to Banshee to keep her calm, while checking out the apartment.

The first page of Zane's manuscript was highlighted by the weak, late afternoon sunlight streaming through the window. It caught her attention.

"What's this, pretty girl?" Minka asked the cat. "Should we take a look?" She picked up the paper and began reading...

Bridgett Nelson

Faerie Lover
by Zane Robinson

*The silver-haired beauty heard his call to the
universe and answered. She slipped inside his
apartment with ease. Materializing in human
form beside his bed, she watched him sleep.*
*A cat hissed from the shadows. She hissed back. The
feline screeched and ran from the room.*
*The female turned her attention back to the slum-
bering man. While not traditionally handsome,
his looks were appealing enough to please the
Irish succubus. Yes, she thought.* I'll be happy
enough fornicating with this human male.
*Knowing she had to direct her powers precisely—she
certainly wasn't keen on becoming his slave if he
turned down her offer—the faerie waved her
hand gently over his face. He stirred. His eyes
opened, lust reflecting in the cerulean blue
depths.*
*He was already hers. The energizing strum of his
youthful essence revitalized her ancient bones.
The succubus would be his muse. His partner.
His lover.*
Her payment?
His life.
*She smirked. The rule about becoming his slave was
a frightening one, but neither she nor any other
of the succubi had ever fallen prey to it.*
No man ever turned them down.
Ever.

Bridgett Nelson is a registered nurse turned horror author. Her first collection, A Bouquet of Viscera, is a two-time Splatterpunk Award winner, recognized both for the collection itself and its standout story, "Jinx." She is also the author of What the Fuck Was That?, Sweet, Sour, & Spicy, and Poisoned Pink.

Her work has appeared in the iconic Deathrealm Spirits, Edward Lee's Erotic Horror for Horny Housewives, To Hell and Back, Evil Little Fucks, Y'all Ain't Right, Splatterpunk's Basement of Horror, Dark Disasters, October Screams, The Never Dead, Razor Blade in the Fun Sized Candy, Counting Bodies Like Sheep, Dead & Bloated, American Cannibal, A Woman Unbecoming, and several volumes of the If I Die Before I Wake series of anthologies.

Bridgett is working on her first original novel and has been contracted by Encyclopocalypse Publications to write a novelization of the cult classic film Deadgirl.

She is an active member of the HWA, was a 2022 Michael Knost WINGS award nominee, won second-place in the '22 Gross-Out contest at KillerCon in Austin, Texas, and third-place in the '23 Gross-Out contest.

She currently lives in Duluth, Minnesota, with her ball python, Indie.

Visit her website at www.bridgettnelson.com.

They Look Back

Candace Nola

THOSE DAMN STAIRS were going to end his life. Clancy Robertson knew it, just as sure as he knew he was black and bald. He stood at the top of the basement stairs, grimacing. His heart pounded in his chest and that one vein along his temple throbbed in time with his overworked heart. The stairs yawned before him, dark, steep, and deadly. The narrow wooden slats barely held his size thirteen shoes. The blank side walls where no railing clung. The concrete floor that waited to shatter his spine and crack his skull open like a rotten egg. He hated it. No. He loathed it. Loathed was much better. It suited his feelings better. Somehow loathe was better than hate.

Clancy shifted the laundry basket of work clothes to his hip and braced one large palm on the wall. Turning to one side, he began his descent, muttering and cussing the whole way. He needed to do laundry. He needed to finish clearing out his grandmother's things upstairs. He needed to do a whole lot of things, but right now, Clancy needed to get down these damn stairs without breaking his neck.

He breathed slowly through his mouth, concentrating on

each step. Left foot sought sure and stable purchase on one slat below before his right foot followed, joining it. Then he repeated the process. Left. Right. Both feet solidly on each step before he moved to the next. Sweat beaded on his shiny brow. His tongue snuck out to moisten dry lips as he went, his throat suddenly dryer than sandpaper. The bare lightbulb at the bottom taunted him, barely casting shadows back into the corners. The gray of the concrete floor mocked him, waiting to break him.

Left, step, right, step. Down he went. Clancy cursed himself. He cursed God; he cursed his grandma and his long-dead Marcia. He cursed them all for leaving him alone in this horrible house, with this terrible task, and with this dungeon of death that should not exist in any house. Halfway down now, the stairs creaked beneath his bulk as he went. He froze as his foot slipped off the narrow slat, only slightly, but his heart stopped, and his stomach dropped. He waited a moment, breathing deeply to steady his nerves, then settled his other foot on the stairs.

Cussing more violently under his breath, he continued, wanting to race down the stairs to get it over with, wanting to retrace his steps to the warm kitchen above. Clancy wanted nothing more than to be far from this house. But there was no one else. Grandma was gone. His momma was gone. Marcia passed from her cancer three years ago. There had been no one to care for Grandma when things got bad. No one but Clancy. Which meant when Grandma passed, the house passed to Clancy, along with the task of clearing it out and settling her estate.

Big tasks, grown-up tasks. Barely thirty-eight, Clancy still sometimes felt like a juvenile stumbling through life. He had an adult job, for sure. He had been married, had owned a house, did adult things, but this past year, caring for his grandma had made Clancy feel like a child of six again, let alone a man-child of middle-age that still lived for video games and hot wings. He wanted to scoff at the idea of his grandma having such power over him, even now, but the truth was, she did. She was Big Momma to the family and when Big Momma spoke, you damn well better listen.

She was not impressed by his nice car or his cushy job at the accounting firm. His sharp suits and gold chains did not do the trick, either. He was still little Clancy. Her only grandson in a world full of women and one cranky grandpa that spent most of his life in the basement or in the attic building his dolls. Those damn dolls with the too real eyes. Clancy shuddered, then breathed a sigh of relief, having reached solid ground once more. His feet settled onto the cold concrete of the basement. His thoughts had kept him wrapped inside old memories for the last few steps and for once, he was grateful.

Clancy shifted the basket to his other hip, shuffled through the dark archway into the dank deep of the basement beyond. It smelled like mildew, stagnant water, and stale paint. Rows of shelves lined the walls where the dolls sat, staring at him with those glittering eyes, judging him as he walked by. Fingers of ice walked up his spine as he trudged straight ahead. He would not look. He wouldn't dare.

Clancy kept both eyes on the back corner where the Maytag squatted like a bridge troll beneath the back stairs. The washer and dryer, both pea green from an era long gone, were covered in scratches and dents from decades of use. The space was neat and tidy, though. Big Momma insisted on the laundry area being kept clean. The back corner was swept weekly and wiped down. Heavy baskets carried upstairs and put away, and fresh loads brought down to be washed later that week. She had a system, and everyone knew it. Clothes on Saturdays, linens and towels on Wednesdays.

Clancy sighed and heaved the basket onto the top of the dryer, then set about adding detergent to the washer, pushed the buttons and dropped in his clothes. He stood there, listening to the water fill the drum, purposely delaying turning around. Once he did, he would have no choice but to see *them*. Those damned dolls, rag dolls and glass dolls, statues and figurines, porcelain dolls and baby dolls. Dolls that sang, that spoke, that had pretty hair and skin like him.

Dolls that had velvet dresses and button-down suits. Dolls with fair skin and green eyes. Dolls with tawny skin and hazel eyes. Painted dolls, carved dolls, handmade dolls. Everywhere you looked, normally not a scary thing, maybe a bit strange, but these dolls *looked back*. It made his skin crawl. It made his eyes tear up and his brain ache. *They looked back.* Clancy didn't know how else to explain it. He took a breath and slowly turned to face his foes.

There they were, all of them with their cold eyes, hard as diamonds in their enamel skulls. Staring at him, judging him. Every head cocked just so, just enough to see him without the motion being noticed. He knew they moved. He had sensed it deep down in his veins, like you can feel the subway trembling beneath a city block. His ma had never believed him. Neither did Marcia. But his sisters knew, oh they all knew from early on that something was wrong with those dolls. Grandma just tsk'd tsk'd their tall tales of leering, glinting eyes and moving limbs, but Grandpa only shook his head and shrugged, giving his sad smile before shuffling away. Grandpa knew something, but he took what he knew to his grave.

Clancy took a deep breath, refused to make eye contact with any of the tiny faces and began his march across the gray floor, ducking slightly to avoid the many heating ducts and water pipes that hung too low across the overhead beams. Like a soldier being forced to walk the pirate plank, he marched stone-faced, straight ahead to the doorway and the darkness beyond. The thudding of the washer behind him matched his heart as he felt the dolls shift ever so softly as he went, following his progress across the cold room.

He reached the doorway in seconds, ducked through, and began his climb up the narrow stairs. Thankfully, the way up was never as daunting as the way down. Up was easy. Up was safety, and light, and warmth. His long legs carried his line-backer frame up the narrow staircase, his broad shoulders almost brushing the walls. His heart slowed and his breathing eased as he reached the top. He stepped across the threshold and shivered once as ice settled in the base of his spine. A single sound had reached his ears, a quiet, high-pitched giggle, floating up from the darkness. Clancy slammed the basement door.

❦ ❦ ❦

Later that night, Clancy flopped into his granddad's old recliner. It was time to relax and watch a good movie. There was a new action flick he had been wanting to see, and it was finally on tonight. He had worked all day long cleaning and packing knick-knacks from the various mantles and cabinets around the house: ceramic cherubs, framed photos of long-dead relatives, keepsake invitations, and other such items. Big Momma had kept every school photo of every grand-child, every graduation announcement, every wedding invitation, and funeral card.

Clancy had spent all afternoon sorting the mess into piles: one to keep for the remaining relatives to sort through, one to toss, and one to donate to the Salvation Army. Big Momma had been big on donating to those less fortunate.

They all wore hand-me-downs and when finished with them, those had been donated too. Circle of life, Big Momma said. Someone could always make use of something that was trash to another. Value was in everything, no matter how old. She didn't even toss table scraps, choosing to put them in a big compost heap in the small backyard. In the spring, the compost pile would fertilize her miniscule garden.

He sighed, smiling a bit at the memories that flooded him, then picked up the remote and turned the tv on. Clancy found his movie, set the remote down beside him, lifted up his carton of Chinese takeout and began to eat, willing himself to let the stress of the day go. The movie started, and he settled in, content for now.

☙ ☙ ☙

Hours later and a loud banging reverberated throughout the house. Clancy woke with a start, confused for a moment, not remembering where he was. He jumped when the sound came again. He looked around, heart racing in his chest. Clancy sat upright in the old chair and looked around again, waiting to hear the noise once more. Ten, twenty, thirty seconds passed before BANG!! He shot to his feet that time, looking anxiously around the dark house. The television blared the nightly news in the background, his movie long since over.

Clancy stepped over to the front door, just beyond the living room, and peered through the window next to the door. He saw no one, heard no one. He squinted his eyes, peering up and down the street, trying to see through the shadows, watching for movement, but none came.

BANG!

He jumped and spun around.

"Who's there?" He called out, his deep voice rumbling in

his chest. "Better come on out where I can see you. I got a gun." He paused, listening, creeping slowly to the front closet where the coats were kept. Grandad had kept a bat in there for emergency use and right now, Clancy considered this an emergency.

BANG!!

He jumped again, then yanked the closet door open, fishing for the bat through a wall of musty parkas, peacoats, and furs. His fingers found the wooden handle tucked in the back corner and he snatched it out. He spun around when the noise sounded again, bat in hand, he began to creep toward the kitchen.

"Goddamn old-ass house," he muttered, "got me in here with a thousand damn dolls and now this?"

"Better stop playing with me!" He called out again. "I called the cops. You just better come out now." The tremble in his voice belied the bravado he was trying to convey in his tone.

BANG! BANG!

"Fuck this," he muttered, tightening his grip on the bat, ready to hit a home run on a motherfucker's head if it came to that. He wasn't scared or so he told himself. He was tired, overweight and just not cut out for this shit anymore. But his gut told him otherwise. His spine dripped with icy sweat. His armpits were rank with the stench of fear coming from his pores. His gut churned, threatening to hurl the food he had eaten all over Big Momma's kitchen floor.

A new noise met his ears. High-pitched. Shrill. Laughter.

He froze. Clancy shuddered as his asshole puckered and his balls crawled back inside him like fetuses returning to the womb. A deep moan left his lips, guttural and primal. A moan so deep and inhuman that he was not aware that he was the one making it. Fear.

Clancy stared at the open basement door, knowing full

well he had closed it on his last trip to collect his laundry. An inky abyss stared at him, unflinching at the empty threat of his wooden bat. The laughter came again, closer. Clancy's entire body began to tremble.

The pattering of footsteps began to fill the devious darkness of the stairwell. Tiny, tapping, clapping, prancing footsteps, dozens of them rushing up the narrow boards of the basement staircase. Laughter echoed around the pitch-black abyss. Clancy stared in horror, frozen, as hot rancid piss ran down his leg and soaked into his house shoes. Another horrible, terrible, rasping laugh met his ears, and that finally spurred him into action. Clancy slammed the basement door shut and tore through the house and up the stairs.

Grandad had guns in the attic. His entire collection of rifles was stored there in the gun safe for when he took his rare hunting trips. Big Momma had not wanted them where small hands could get to them. Clancy reached the second floor and bolted for the door at the end of the corridor, where the attic steps beckoned him to safety. He lumbered down the hall, knocking pictures off the walls with the bat over his shoulder, all the grace of a bull in a china shop, but he didn't care about the damage he was causing, not right then.

Small feet raced up the staircase he had just vacated. A thousand tiny patters flooded his ears. Clancy screamed and tore open the door. He slammed it shut behind him, bolted the small chain lock into place, and dashed up the narrow steps to the cold attic. Seconds later, fists rained down on the wooden door like bullets, swift and angry. A staccato of fury and evil demanding to be let in.

"Stay away from me!" He screamed, fumbling with the safe lock. "Stay away!"

"Jesus, fuck, where is that damn key?" Clancy cussed as he whipped around to his granddad's desk, tearing open drawers and scattering papers, tools, and doll parts everywhere.

"Fuck!" he screamed again, frustration overwhelming the large man as he yanked the drawers from their brackets and upended them on the desk. Sweat poured from his jowls as the fists of a hundred dolls rained down upon the door to the attic. His hands dug through the debris, searching. Clancy was gasping for breath, hoping for a miracle, when his fingers touched something cold and metallic.

"Fuck, yeah!" he crowed, triumphant. He spun back to the gun safe, jammed the key in the lock and ripped the door open. Grandad's rifles stood like silent sentries in a row, ready for their orders. Clancy clutched his chest, rubbing the ache there. His heart was pounding against his bones, demanding to be let out. Blood rushed in his ears, filling them with an ocean of noise until, gradually, his breathing slowed, and he finally noticed that the storm of fists on the door had ceased.

He paused, turning to the door, one hand still on the stock of the 12-gauge. He waited, wincing from the pain crushing his chest. His heart was still galloping away, a wild mustang on the loose. Clancy ordered himself to calm down as the silence stretched out, then he heard it.

"Clancccccyyy." The voice came through the door. A soft whisper that drew out his name a heartbeat too long.

"Let us in, Clancccyyyy." It called. A chorus of laughter fed the voice, all teasing and lilting and melodic. He shivered as it crawled up his spine and wormed into his skull, scratching the bones like nails on a chalkboard.

"It'll only hurt for a second, Clancccyyy," it called again. This time, scratching at the door, sounding like a thousand crabs skittering across a tile floor, hideous in its quiet cacophony.

"Stay away!" Clancy cried, picking up the rifle. "You all just stay away from me!"

"We can't do that, Clancccyyy. We know what you did. We know what you did to them allllllll." The voice, raspy now, evil and demonic, growing vicious and ending in a snarl.

Clancy's blood ran cold. His eyes grew wide. His hand slipped on the gunstock, slick with sweat.

"I ain't done nothing!" He called back. "You best leave me be. I ain't done nothing!"

"Now Clancy, we know better, don't we?" It tittered, amused at his denial. "We all saw what you did. Down there in the basement. Down there with all those little girls, in the dark. We saw all, didn't we, Clanccccyyy?"

Clancy finished loading the gun and advanced on the door, shouting.

"You just shut up now. You best shut the fuck up, you hear me!" His voice grew a bit stronger, forcing the fear from his lungs. "Just kids being kids. I ain't done nothing wrong." He muttered to himself, shaking his head as old memories flooded him.

❧ ❧ ❧

Decades ago, a young Clancy stood in the sub-basement, in the root cellar that Big Momma's house still had. A niche beneath the basement, just under the back porch. His grand-parent stored bushels of apples, potatoes, and onions down there all year long. The cold dirt kept the produce fresher for longer than keeping it in the house. A shelf of canned preserves in glass jars stood dusty against the back wall.

Clancy stood looking down at Wilma. Her dress, soiled. Her arms scratched. Her small neck, purple with bruises. Her glassy eyes stared at nothing and never would again. Clancy's chest heaved with rage. He only wanted to see. She didn't need to make it so hard. Clancy only wanted to see where the blood came from. His sisters wouldn't let him see, but he saw the bloody refuse in the trashcans, month after month.

Lady things they wouldn't tell him about. Private things they always spoke of but shooed him away when he came into the room. Monthly and period and tampon and pad, mystical, secret things when the blood came. He just wanted to see. Wilma had said he couldn't see because she didn't bleed there yet and it was none of his business, anyway.

Wilma and her sassy mouth. He just wanted to see, and by the time he finished, Wilma had bled. But Clancy still didn't understand. And the thing he was trying to put where the tampons go hadn't fit, at least not until she began to bleed.

Her eyes stared at him. He hated them. He hated them all. Their secret things and their female things. All their talk of being women that Clancy could not understand. He wanted to know and worse yet, when would he bleed? Would it hurt? Why did they laugh at him so much?

Her eyes, glass accusations in the dank cellar of earth. Blood seeped into the ground beneath her. Clancy kicked her, rage consuming him as those eyes continued to accuse. He looked around the room, spied the garden tools in the corner, and got an idea.

He grabbed the spade and began to dig. The ground was soft with recent rain and Wilma's fresh blood seeping through. He dug, and he cussed, and he kicked her again and again. Those damned eyes rolled back to meet his own every time. Clancy threw the spade down and looked around again. Big Momma's short trowel for her flower beds lay beneath the shelf. He grabbed it and crouched over Wilma. Slowly, he inserted it into her eye socket, a sick grin on his face.

He popped the edge of it up, just beneath the orb, and Wilma's eyeball bulged from her skull. He pushed down, adding more weight, and the eye burst free, landing wetly on her graying cheek. He grinned and did the same to the other one, then pocketed the eyes. Clancy stood, breathing easier now that Wilma couldn't accuse him anymore. He finished the shallow grave, rolled her in, and covered it. Fresh soil piled on top, a bushel of potato soil from an empty bushel, old and dry, topped it off.

Now, what to do with those eyes? He mused, rolling them around in his pocket, feeling the orbs beneath his denim against his thigh. Clancy clambered up the dirt stairs to the main basement, slowly looking for a hiding spot. Big Momma kept the basement clean and tidy, but he knew there had to be some place. He ducked beneath the stairs, but no, boxes of Christmas decorations were kept there. He turned back to the laundry area and scanned its shelves. No. Big Momma knew every inch of those shelves. She would know something was moved.

He turned again, then spotted the dolls. Granddad's dolls. The old ones just sat here, year after year. No one ever touched them. Ever. He smiled. Clancy started toward the dolls, the eyes in his hand destined for a new home.

❦ ❦ ❦

Clancy groaned that deep guttural growl once more. A man, terrified. Consumed by it. The voices tittered against the door.

"Remember now, Clancccyyy?" It rasped. Scratching followed, then more tapping, then a peculiar sound like muffled footsteps in a tunnel.

Clancy looked around the room, lowering the rifle, listening to the new sound. It was overhead, tapping, clapping, rushing patters of doll feet. An army made of porcelain and rags headed toward him through the heating vent overhead. Prancing, tapping, rushing, laughing. The voice came through once more.

"Wilma is here, Clancccyyyy. And Riley, and Terry, and Peggy Sue and Anna. Megan, Lucy, and Harriet, too. They're all here, Clancccyyy, and they all see you."

With that, the vents in the attic burst open. A flood of tiny limbs, painted on smiles, and accusing eyes rushed Clancy as he fell to his knees, screaming. He clutched his chest as they advanced, pain seizing his heart, his body and paralyzing his mind as they struck. So many eyes. Their eyes. Female eyes. Everywhere he turned, Clancy saw their eyes. He screamed and didn't stop for many minutes later.

❧ ❧ ❧

"What do you think, Sarge?" Anderson asked his boss as they surveyed the dusty attic. The body of one Clancy Robertson lay prone on his back, eyes wide, staring at nothing, the rifle by his side.

"Well, hard to say," Sarge replied. "Best I can figure, our Mr. Robertson here was planning a suicide or a robbery, but his heart gave out before he could."

"Looks that way, I reckon." Anderson said, squatting closer to inspect Clancy's frozen face. "But what do you suppose all these little cuts are?"

"Hell, if I know, but let's get out of here and let the fellas work. Them damn dolls are creeping me out."

As Anderson followed Sarge from the attic, he glanced around the room. Every free inch was crammed with dolls of all kinds, but something about their eyes made his skin crawl. He shuddered and hurried down the steps, refusing to acknowledge the faint giggle that drifted behind him as he closed the attic door.

I am **Candace Nola**, and I am a multi-award-winning author, editor, publisher, and reviewer. I write poetry, horror, dark fantasy, and extreme horror content. My books include Breach, Beyond the Breach, Hank Flynn, Bishop, Earth vs The Lava Spiders and The Unicorn Killer. I have short stories in The Baker's Dozen anthology, Secondhand Creeps, American Cannibal, Just A Girl, The Horror Collection: Lost Edition, and many more.

Beyond the Breach, won the "Novel of the Year" and my Debut Novel, Breach, was nominated for "Debut Novel of the Year", for the 2021 Horror Authors Guild awards. I am also the publisher and editor of the 2022 Splatterpunk Award Winning Anthology "Uncomfortably Dark Presents: The Baker's Dozen."

I am the creator of Uncomfortably Dark Horror, a small indie press and review platform, which focuses primarily on promoting indie horror authors with weekly book reviews, interviews, and special features. Uncomfortably Dark Horror stands behind its mission to "bring you the best in horror, one uncomfortably dark page at a time."

I also own and operate 360 Editing, which is an editing service geared toward new and indie authors to provide quality editing at affordable rates.

Find me on Twitter, Instagram, TikTok and Facebook and the website, UncomfortablyDark.com. Sign up for the Uncomfortably Dark Patreon for exclusive content, free stories, and more from myself and all of the Uncomfortably Dark authors.

Blood of My Blood
Christa Carmen

ADDISON ALDRICH STOOD across from her mother, father, three sisters, and four brothers, staring into the massive vat of blood. Her satin spike heels wobbled against the uneven stone, but Addie kept her muscles taut and her back straight, palms pressed into the pristine folds of her chiffon wedding gown. She was determined to enjoy this moment with her family, this *last* moment, before she became someone different, someone new. By marrying Marcus Weber, she wouldn't just be losing her last name—her prestigious, prominent, *powerful* last name—she'd be shedding her identity. Her place as the eldest daughter of Norton and Aleida Aldrich.

You're being ridiculous, she chastised herself. That wasn't what was happening here. Yes, she was mere hours away from marrying her fiancé of the last two years, but saying "I do" could never part her from her kin. Her blood. If anything, Marcus was the one who was facing the greatest turning point by virtue of their holy matrimony. Addie squirmed, thinking of all the ways he would need to adapt in order to align himself, body, mind, and spirit, with her tightknit, influential family.

And Marcus was the worthiest of all her suitors. Of course he was; that's why she was marrying him. He loved her, treated her kindly—if not always with the respect, or perhaps, the equality, she knew she deserved—and understood her standing in the family business. At least, he said he did. But with each month they drew closer to their wedding, Marcus had pushed her more and more, questioning how soon after they married would she relinquish her role at Aldrich Liquors, how soon would she become a housewife, bear his children. Addie shook herself, pushing the uncomfortable thoughts from her mind. Everything would work out. It always did.

Zelda, the family's maid, appeared from a shadowy passage, arms full of neatly folded handkerchiefs, rubber tubing, and a small wooden box. Addie's father reached beneath the vat and came out with a gleaming machete. Lining up the blade of the machete with a six-by-four-foot outline in the wall, he liberated a rectangular stone slab. The slab lowered to a right angle with the wall, stopped from a further downward trajectory by some unseen hinge. Norton repeated the process with a second slab, on which he placed the machete.

He patted the slab, and Zelda climbed up, after handing her various accoutrements to Eileen, Addie's youngest sister. As Eileen helped prepare Zelda for the offering, Aleida, the girls' mother, lifted a silver tray from a recess in the wall.

Atop the tray were ten crystal goblets. Aleida held the tray motionlessly while Eileen—with the help of another of Addie's sisters, Margaret—pierced the crook of Zelda's arm with a glinting needle from the box. Within moments, a line of thick, dark blood shot from Zelda's vein into the tubing, traveled through a purifier, and into the vat. Once several ounces had flowed freely, Aleida stepped forward with her tray. Norton lifted a jewel-encrusted ladle and filled each goblet with half an inch of metallic, freshly-oxygenized blood. Each of Addie's siblings—David, Ann, Richard, Margaret, Eileen, Jay, and Nelson—took one. Margaret fixed Addie with a nervous smile.

"We're so happy for you, Ads," she cooed. David reached out and squeezed Addie's arm. Addie couldn't help but feel excited. This wasn't something they partook in with any regularity. The blood was cultivated for customers only. The family came together for a blood toast at only the most special of occasions. It was a privilege to engage in their most secret commodity, their most lucrative product.

"To Addison," Norton said, when he'd filled his and Aleida's goblets. The family tightened in a circle around Addie, holding glasses aloft. "Here's to my lovely daughter on her wedding day, and to all her future successes. May she continue to move our family's legacy forward, bound forever in blood."

The sound of clinking glass filled Addie's ears, and the smile tugging at her lips felt electric. She brought the goblet to her mouth, sensing, rather than seeing, her family members do the same. The liquid hit her tongue with the thick, heady, intoxicating taste that signaled instant memories, blood toasts of the past: the birth of her youngest sister, her parents' thirtieth anniversary, her brother, David's, contract with a new line of suppliers. This blood meant wealth and power, success and protection, but also happiness. Togetherness. Unbroken bonds.

"We've had such good fortune," Aleida crooned when they'd drained the goblets' contents and returned them to the tray. Zelda remained on the slab, her skin pale, near-translucent, a wan smile on her face.

"It feels almost perverse to be celebrating another tremendous milestone," Aleida added. She hugged Addie close. Around them, Addie's father and siblings were talking and laughing. Norton slapped David across the back and started peppering her oldest brother with questions about the bachelor party two nights earlier. Eileen, Margaret, and Ann compared manicure colors and hairstyles.

"I'm so happy for you, daughter," her mother continued, then reached for the ladle, still in the vat, and pulled it from a groove in the stone. Aleida filled it with blood, raised it into the air, and dripped the liquid down, where it spattered back against the surface. "It's hard not to think of it reverently, this liquid each of us has inside our veins. It's done so much for our family. *The people who crave it* have done so much for our family."

It was only when her mother spooned another ladleful of blood into the air and they watched, mesmerized, as it pattered into the pool, that Addie heard the noise beneath her and siblings' chatter. A gasp and frantic whispering, followed by the shuffle of stiff shoes against stone. Addie looked past the vat of blood, to the mouth of the tunnel leading to this secret chamber. There, her soon-to-be-husband stood, open-mouthed, beside a gobsmacked Timothy, Marcus's best man.

Tim was holding an amber bottle of whiskey and two sparkling glasses. When he realized Addie and her mother had spotted them, the glasses slipped from his fingers, shattering against the stone. At the sound, the rest of Addie's family stopped, turned, and saw the interlopers. Addie's father let out a quiet groan and shook his head, but quickly rearranged his features into something more fitting with his genial, father-of-the-bride role.

"Marcus, my boy," he said. "Looks like you and ol' Tim were seeking a quiet place to throw a few back. You should've guessed the passageways beneath the Chateau would be tricky to navigate. Easy to get turned around. Let me show you to a place with a far better view for your revelry."

He took a step forward but something like a grunt issued forth from Addie's fiancé. "No," Marcus tried again, this time managing to get the word out. He glanced at Addie, then at the vat of blood, the motionless maid lying on the slab beside it. "Addison, what is this? What is your family *doing* down here?"

Addie looked quickly from her siblings to her parents. The expression on each familiar face was the same: regretful but resigned. *You were going to have to tell him eventually*, those looks said. *You weren't planning for it to be on your wedding day, but you don't have much of a choice in the matter now.*

Addie stepped forward. "Marcus, honey, come here."

Marcus shook his head at the same time Timothy gripped Marcus's arm and pulled him back. "Don't go anywhere near them," Timothy exclaimed. "That's some, like, human sacrifice shit going on right there. There's so much blood! And look at those goblets!"

Everyone turned to look at the silver tray. Aleida winced, as if she wished there were somewhere she could hide them. At the bottom of each glass were the dregs of the Aldrich family toast, wine-dark and as telling as a heartbeat beneath a floorboard.

"Look at the maid!" Tim continued. "She's practically dead!" His tone bordered on the verge of hysteria.

"Don't be absurd." Addie walked over to Zelda. She laid a hand on the woman's arm. "Zee's not dead. She donates blood to Aldrich Liquors all the time."

Timothy's eyes narrowed and Marcus's mouth dropped open. "She what?" Marcus asked incredulously.

Addie sighed. "You *know* my family's business provides wholesale alcohol to liquor stores across the country." She stepped forward, but again, Timothy pulled Marcus back.

Addie swallowed a lump of irritation. "But did it ever occur to you to consider just how successful Aldrich Liquors is? Sure, some of our signature lines are the top selling brands in the world. But come on, Marcus, look around."

She gestured around them, at Aldrich Mansion, at the seventy-acre estate situated on scenic Narragansett Bay in Warwick, Rhode Island. Along with the Chateau itself, all elegance and opulence, the estate boasted a Carriage House, Caretaker's Cottage, Boathouse, and stunning Chapel. Built to aid in the transportation of goods to Warwick Neck, a railway and supply tunnel led from the one-hundred-fifty-foot tower to the Mansion, allowing Addie's great-grandfather, grandfather, and now Norton himself, to distribute their products inexpensively and with minimal effort.

And this was just Norton and Aleida's estate. Each of the Aldrich children held similar property across Rhode Island. Their fortune placed them among the richest families in the United States, if not the world. Spirits were, to the Aldriches, like oil to the Rockefellers. Between 1870 and 1970, Addie's family had revolutionized the sale of liquor.

But this wasn't the entire story. Addie braced herself to tell the rest. "You don't have to look at our accounting books to figure that tequila and Chablis don't constitute the entirety of our wealth." Addie paused, looked behind her. Her brother, Nelson, smiled and mouthed, *You're doing great.* Addie took a deep breath and turned back to her fiancé. "Have you ever heard of vampires?"

At Marcus and Timothy's slack-jawed horror, Addie shook her head, annoyed by her too-blunt segue. "Not storybook vampires," she corrected herself. "Those don't really exist. I mean people who consider themselves vampires? 'Medical sanguinarians' is the term most often used.

"They drink blood willingly, from willing donors. Some do it as a religious ritual, or a fetish, and sure, there are some who operate under the delusional that they're a Romantic figure from Stoker's novel. But there are many, many others who believe there are a host of medical conditions—fatigue, headaches, excruciating and inexplicable stomach pain—that can only be treated by the consumption of human blood."

"There are thousands of sanguinarians in this country alone," Addie continued before either groom or best man could speak, "and while their behavior may be a mystery to others," she waved her hand at the vat, "it's brought us immense good fortune to provide a supply where there is such a demand. We—"

"We don't believe you," Timothy shouted.

Marcus jumped, looked at his best man, his best *friend*, and nodded his head feverishly. "Right," he agreed. "We saw with our own eyes what you were doing to Zelda."

"Zelda's fine," Addie insisted. "Like I said, she donates blood all the time. Do you think she'd still be here if we were taking advantage or, worse, hurting her?" This had gone far enough. She needed to convince him of the legitimateness of the business, before Marcus got spooked and spoiled everything. "Please, my love. This is a day for celebration. Can we talk about this later? I'll tell you everything. I'll—"

"Is this why you didn't want me getting too close to the business?" Marcus asked. He eyed Addie like she might be a concubine of Dracula's herself. "Why you hinted you'd stay involved even after we're married rather than let me take over your role with the company?"

Addie sighed again. "Yes, partly, but not because we're doing anything wrong. It's just, we don't share this part of the business with anyone outside of the family."

"So Marsha knows?" Marcus asked accusatorially.

Addie's oldest brother nodded at the mention of his wife.

"And Steven?"

"Yes," Ann said. "But Steve's a little…" Ann faltered, and

Addie felt a twinge of embarrassment for her sister. Ann's husband wasn't the sharpest stake in the shed. "Let's just say I couldn't tell Steve until three years after we were married. The new yacht I bought him went a long way toward making him understand the necessity of our most profitable product."

"This is insane," Timothy whispered loudly to Marcus. "Let's get out of here before they do to us what they did to that maid!"

After that, everything happened at once. David, Jay, and Nelson tried to approach Marcus, while Timothy attempted to pull him up the tunnel toward the main floor of the Chateau. At the same time, Ann took Zelda's arm to help her down from the slab.

"They're going to kill her!" Marcus yelled at the sight of Zelda's somewhat stilted movements. "They're out for the rest of her blood!"

Norton blocked Ann from the chaotic onslaught of limbs as Marcus flailed for the maid, and Timothy followed, yelling like a lunatic. Addie saw the next part unfold in slow motion, saw Marcus's body careen into Ann's, whose hip smacked the handle of the machete with propulsive force. The machete ricocheted like a propellor, spinning toward Timothy. One moment, the best man was whole. The next, the machete had sliced through his midsection like a steak knife through a tender cut of filet. A sheet of blood droplets flew through the air, spattering the bodice of Addie's dress.

For one, agonizing moment, Timothy remained there, upright and tottering, his wide, unblinking eyes fixed on Addie. Then, the upper half of his torso slid from his waist, spilling coils of intestine as it went. No one moved. No one breathed. An ear-splitting scream echoed off the walls of the chamber.

"Ahhhhhhhhhh!" Marcus screamed again, then let loose

with a barrage of swearing and desperate pleading. Before Addie, or Zelda, or any member of the Aldrich family could react, Marcus spun from the gory scene and sprinted up the tunnel. In mere seconds, he'd turned a corner and disappeared.

"Well, shit," Addie breathed. "That didn't go well."

Eileen giggled. "You can say that again." She turned to Norton. "What do we do now, Daddy?"

Norton wrapped one arm around Eileen and another around Addie. The tulle netting of her veil scratched at her skin.

"Don't worry," Norton said. "There are only—" He paused, turning to Zelda, "How many guests at final count, Zee?"

"Forty-two, sir."

"And how many are family or longtime business partners? People connected to us intimately, aware of our true work, our secrets?"

"Thirty-seven, sir."

"And the other five?"

Zelda looked apologetically at Addie. "The other five include him," she lowered her head to regard the two halves of Timothy. "The groom, and the other three groomsmen."

"Of course, of course," Norton mumbled. He turned to his eight children. "Well, you kids know what to do. Get going."

David, Ann, Richard, Margaret, Eileen, Jay, and Nelson started moving up the tunnel. Addie held up her hand. "Just so I'm clear, what is it we're supposed to be doing?"

"We have to stop Marcus before he can leave the property. Convince him that our business is a legit, lauded, and, most importantly, legal, enterprise, and not some front for, oh, I don't know, aristocratic vampires seeking immortality or whatever it is he thinks." He looked at Timothy again. "We also need to take care of this body. Zelda?"

"I'm on it, sir." She took the syringe and tubing that had siphoned blood from her own body not ten minutes prior and moved toward the corpse.

"What are you doing?" Addie exclaimed.

"I'm not about to waste all that blood before having Westin dispose of him, ma'am."

Addie thought about this. Zelda had a point. Besides, what did she care happened to Timothy's body? He was dead. She had to stop Marcus. With a snort of frustration, Addie started up the tunnel after her family, the sounds of Zelda grunting and breathing heavily as she maneuvered Timothy's body—or, at least, the upper half of it—mingling with the clicks of Addie's spike heels against the stone.

🍂 🍂 🍂

Addie found Ann and Margaret at the entrance to the Great Room. A fireplace crackled in the hearth and candles flickered from every surface, ready for guests to mull about after the ceremony. The light from the flames was reflected in the extensive pottery, glassware, vases, and teapots on display across the five sets of twelve shelves, stretching from floor to ceiling around the fireplace.

Addie's mother brought one-of-a-kind pieces back to the mansion from her travels around the world, and most were here in this room. Aleida's favorite item was a vase on the topmost shelf, dated from around 1870 and originally commissioned for an Indian Maharajah. The vase was so colossal, the family's butler, Westin, had to secure it with twin pieces of steel-galvanized wire.

"Have you seen him?" Addie hissed to Ann and Margaret as she joined them beneath the shelves.

"No, but we can hear him," Margaret said.

"What do you mean?"

"Listen," Ann whispered dramatically.

Addie cocked her head. From somewhere down the long corridor, Marcus's voice could be heard, growing louder and shriller with every sentence.

"—were killing her! Siphoning all her blood!" Other men's voices rose and fell, then Marcus's came again: "—just chopped Timothy in half! Right-in-fucking-half!"

"We can take them," a deep, throaty voice shouted. It sounded like Derek Messinger, Marcus's colleague at the financial firm where he worked. "Grab those muskets off the wall. Do you think they work?"

There were grunts, and the sliding of furniture, then a third voice said, "Marcus, why don't we just get the fuck out of this mansion?"

"They *killed him*, Sampson. They fucking killed him! And I know about their crazy blood business. Do you really think they're letting any of us out of here alive?"

The voices devolved into angry shouting and the movement of more furniture. Addie dragged her sisters deeper into the Great Room.

"Your fiancé is off his rocker," Ann said pleasantly, as if the whole afternoon had been one hilarious story that she couldn't wait for Gramma Aldrich to hear.

"So are his groomsmen," Margaret added. "We need to find some weapons."

"We are not finding weapons," Addie huffed. "The goal is to make them understand we're *not* insane bloodthirsty murders, not incite them to violence." Addie looked around. "I wish we were closer to Daddy's office. Maybe if I showed Marcus the ledgers, he'd understand regular people purchase the blood bottles, and that regular people volunteer to—"

Margaret grabbed Addie's arm so hard, she gasped. "What is it?" Addie asked.

Margaret put a finger to her lips.

The three women looked to the wall, where sixty pieces of glassware were vibrating on their shelves. Vases jumped. Teapots clattered. A pair of candlesticks looked to be engaged in their first dance. Addie transferred her gaze to the hallway. Angry footsteps pounded down the hall, accompanied by war whoops and frenzied shouting.

"Jesus Christ," Addie muttered. "You have got to be kidding."

"Maybe they'll run right past us," Ann said brightly.

Margaret snorted, picked up a Waterford Crystal vase, and raised it above her head.

"Okay," Addie relented, "maybe don't look for weapons *per se*, but grabbing something to keep from getting killed before we're given a chance to speak doesn't sound like the worst idea." She ran to an antique hutch and started pulling open drawers.

Ann ran to a second hutch and Margaret pulled various pitchers and candlesticks off the shelves, testing their weight against that of the crystal vase. The men were getting closer. Addie dug her hand further into the drawer and emerged with a small silver box. Inside were Mother's letter openers. *These will have to do.* She joined Margaret, who'd settled on a massive pewter candlestick, and Ann, who wielded a... a...

"What is that?" Addie whispered.

"I'm not sure," Ann replied. "Some sort of wire cutter? It's *crazy* sharp. I found it in that side table."

Before Addie could respond, the roar of the men reached a crescendo and they barreled up to the door of the Great Room. Marcus caught Addie's eye and turned on a dime. In the space of another breath, all four men were hulking in the doorframe, aiming muskets, rifles, and Great-great-Grandfather's ancient spearfishing harpoon at Addie, Ann, and Margaret.

"Well, Marcus," Addie said. "I see you're taking this whole 'blood business' thing really well."

"Stay back," Derek Messinger roared. "I don't care if you're Marcus's fiancé, Addie. I won't hesitate to use this, uh... this...this..."

Addie sighed. "It's a Semliki harpoon. From the Katanda region in Zaire. If I told you how old it was, you wouldn't believe me."

"Okay, then, yeah, this Sem-lee-key harpoon." He lifted the weapon higher onto his shoulder and glared at Ann. "Why did you kill Timothy?"

"Good grief," said Ann. "You bumped into *me* and sent the machete flying. See, like this," she added, and hip-checked Margaret, sending her careening forward. The men screeched and hop-stepped backward, away from Margaret and her candlestick, before remembering their own weapons and retraining them on the sisters.

"Marcus, you need to listen to me," Addie tried. "Every major city in the world has a 'vampire' community. They actually eschew people who engage in criminal behavior and make them look bad. We are catering to those communities. That's it. What happened with Timothy was an accident."

"A super ill-timed one," Ann quipped. Margaret stifled a giggle, and Addie shot them both a look.

"Those communities *used* to be isolated," Addie continued. "Until the Aldriches brought them together. I can show you the records. Medical consent forms from our donors." She could see Marcus considering this. "They're right in the office upstairs," she added quickly, a flicker of hope that this day, this *relationship*, could be salvaged. "I can take you there now." She tried to step forward but something stopped her, and she jerked to a halt.

"Your veil is caught on the lampshade, Ads," Margaret said. "Let me help you." She raised one of the candlesticks, and the men flinched backward. Margaret rolled her eyes and, in an exaggerated movement, brought the tip of the candlestick to where Addie's veil was caught—*See, boys, just one sister helping another with womanly things*—before pulling at the netting. The men grumbled begrudgingly, and Margaret pulled harder. The tulle hung fast, and Ann pushed her way in beside Margaret.

"Here, let me," Ann said. She wedged the wire cutter beneath the candlestick and pulled up, attempting to liberate the tulle from the silvery bead at the corner of the lampshade.

"Stop it, Ann," Margaret complained.

"Just move, and I can get it," Ann insisted.

"I said stop," Margaret tried again, but Ann was wielding the candlestick like she'd found herself in a swordfight and would stop at nothing to disarm her older sister.

Addie tried to turn but couldn't see. She dropped the letter opener and reached up, planning to abandon the veil altogether, feeing her sisters' remonstrations grow more heated, when there came the sound of sliding metal, like a knife against a sharpener, and the wire cutter Ann had been applying copious amounts of pressure to a moment earlier was suddenly aloft. It whizzed through the air toward the shelves, like something out of an Olympic precision event.

The tool's open jaws hit one side of the wire holding back Aleida's Indian Maharajah vase. Aleida's *eight-hundred-pound* Indian Maharajah vase. The wire snapped. The vase teetered, and the shelf beneath it groaned, and then it was falling to the floor. But, no, that wasn't right. Not all the way to the floor. Something was in its path. Derek Messinger's head. Which exploded in conjunction with the shattering vase, sending shards of skull and bits of brain matter across the room like shrapnel, peppering Addie's wedding dress like celebratory rice. Or confetti.

"Oops," Margaret and Ann said in unison, but it was drowned out by the screams of the three men as they sprinted from the room.

Addie looked at her blood-and-brain-spattered dress then back at her sisters.

"*That* was your attempt at convincing them we're not bloodthirsty murderers? Jesus fucking Christ, you two." She groaned and shook her head, then hurried from the room after Marcus, flicking gobs of brain from her lacy sleeves and muttering under her breath.

She found Marcus at the top of a double staircase at the back of the Chateau, trembling and crying. There was no sign of Sampson or the final groomsman; Addie never could remember his name. She held up her hands to show she carried no weapon, but Marcus cowered from her. Addie stopped several feet from him and sat on the top step. She rubbed a splotch of blood from her left ring finger, where, by now, there should have been a diamond.

"Marcus, *you know me*," she whispered. "You know I wouldn't be involved with something cruel or barbaric. What happened to Timothy and Derek were—"

He jerked his head up at her, and she stopped. What could she say to get through to him? Before she could decide on something, Marcus spoke first. "Vampires or not," he whined, "you were never going to step down, were you? Never going to give me your role in the business."

Addie sighed. "No," she admitted. "Not completely. You would have been brought into the fold, of course. But I was always going to stay on. All the Aldrich children do, male or female."

"That's bullshit, Addison!" Marcus exploded. "That's

worse than supplying blood to weirdo vampire freaks. You were supposed to be a stay-at-home mother. Raise our children."

Addie felt her own blood chill. "I see," she replied. She stood. "Come on, then. Let's find your last two groomsmen and my family. It's time we send them all home, call this thing off."

At Marcus's confused expression, Addie said, "We have much bigger issues than your misconceptions of my family." Her stomach sank at this revelation, but Addie was never one to turn from the truth once she'd found it.

As she went to descend the right-hand portion of the staircase, footsteps came pounding up the left. Sampson and the forever nameless groomsmen reached the top and charged toward her, screaming at the top of their lungs, wielding musket and rifle. In a flash, Addie weighed her options: turn and run or drop to her knees and cover her head. She started to turn but Sampson was already on her, grabbing one shoulder. The tip of the musket pressed into her back.

We're at the south staircase, Addie remembered. *The one David, Richard, Jay, and Nelson used to chase me up all the time.*

Addie shook off Sampson and grabbed the rail. Spinning her hands around, she dropped forward in a half-flip that, though she hadn't performed since childhood, came back to her in a torrent of muscle memory. She hung upside down, the skirt of her dress swaying, relieved to have put a wrench in those two would-be-warriors' mad dash to attack her. But... that was odd. Why did her feet feel so cold?

Addie looked down and saw bare toes. Frowning, she turned one hand on the railing, then the other, spinning herself halfway around. Through the wood posts of the railing, she spotted Marcus first, face whiter than her gown, silent tears streaming down his face. She shifted her grip one bar to the left, and there it was: the answer to what had happened to her shoes.

The satin was no longer cream but a deep cherry red. Each five-inch spike heel was embedded—to the sole—into the undersides of Sampson's and the anonymous groomsman's chins. Sampson's lips were parted slightly, so she could see the upward trajectory of the heel through his mouth, rammed like a spike through hard earth by her bid for escape. Both men were on their knees, but as she watched, they slumped to the ground, first Sampson, then the other.

Addie returned her gaze to Marcus. The horror on his face had hardened into something different. Something dangerous.

"I'm going to kill you," he said.

Addie let go of the rail.

She dropped the ten feet to the floor with her dress billowing around her like a sail. The landing sent bolts of pain up both ankles, but she was up in an instant. Marcus was sprinting down the stairs like an angry bear.

Addie ran through the Chateau, first yanking the top layer of her thick skirts free then tearing the veil from her hair. The gauzy fabric floated behind her like a ghost. *Fitting, since my marriage is dead*, Addie thought, *along with half the wedding party.*

There were voices up ahead, and she ran toward them, through the pillared, high-ceilinged hall, past the kitchen, where Chateau staff would be putting the finishing touches on the elaborate menu, and toward the east side of the mansion. To the Chapel.

To salvation.

Where her family—her blood—would be gathered.

Addie saw the pews first, then clusters of her relatives—Gramma Aldrich with Aunt Edith and Aunt Alta. Ann and Margaret had made their way here as well and were gesticulating wildly to Addie's brothers, no doubt filling them in on the magic trick they'd witnessed in the Great Room—*Behold! Derek Messinger's Exploding Head!*

Addie's parents were by the altar, conversing with Uncle Winthrop, who'd been meant to officiate the ceremony. When Addie careened into the aisle, there was a gasp. Everyone turned at the same time. But Addie didn't stop, just sprinted to the front of chapel and up the five wide steps to the altar. She needed a higher vantage point for when Marcus burst into the room.

"Darling, are you all right?" Aleida asked.

Addie turned to her mother, trying to catch her breath. "I'm fine," she said a moment later. She gestured to the back of the room. "But Marcus is coming. I... I couldn't get him to listen. To understand. He thinks we're monsters. That *I'm* a monster. The groomsmen, they're all dead."

Aleida and Norton started to make their way to her, but before they reached the stairs, a flash of black shot out from the door to the sacristy. Marcus. He'd found the side entrance rather than follow her through the back.

Addie tried to run, but in his rage, Marcus was too fast for her. He grabbed her by the shoulders and flung her backward. A chalice—actual wine, not blood—crashed to the floor, spilling its burgundy contents.

Marcus's hands were around her throat before she could yell out. He dragged her to the back of the altar. The crucifix loomed above them, so large and hulking, it blocked much of the light from the stained-glass window behind it. Addie felt Marcus's hot breath on her neck and closed her eyes.

"A good metaphor, isn't it?" he sneered, "your little side business. Because you would have bled me dry."

"No," Addie choked out. She clawed at his arms.

"Yes. Bled me of my manhood, all so you could continue being a part of your family's disgusting enterprise. You killed my friends. *You sell blood*." He lifted her by the neck and gave her a little shake. Addie felt the pillars above them trembling. "Now your blood must spill. What were our vows for today? I give ye my Body, that we Two might be One. Well, we're two becoming one alright. Only one of us is leaving this chapel."

Addie heard a commotion, saw movement in the distance through her darkening vision. Her family was coming. Her kin, her blood, would save her. But before anyone could charge the altar, Marcus lifted her away from the wall several inches and slammed her with all his force into the wooden paneling.

The pillars groaned. A cable snapped like a piano wire. Marcus's grip around her neck slackened. And then, with a shriek of collapsing metal and wood and glass, the crucifix swung down like a pendulum. At the exact moment the metal point pierced Marcus's chest, the statue of a saint fell back through the stained-glass window. Brilliant shards fell around Addie and Marcus like a miracle. Rain after a drought. Then, thanks to the largest image within the glass— a rose, symbolic of the blood shed for humanity's salvation— the rainbow of glass turned red.

And the rainstorm matched the hue of Marcus's crucifix-impaled heart.

Though no longer contained within the cage of his body, it gasped out a few final beats. There were screams. Someone fainted. Gramma Aldrich let out a cackle of disbelieving glee. Out of the corner of her eye, Addie saw Zelda hurry from the room in the direction of the supply closet. *Can't waste all that blood*, Addie thought she heard her say before she disappeared. Marcus's body crumpled to the wine-soaked ground.

Slowly, Addie crawled down from the altar. In an instant, all seven of her siblings were upon her. Aleida and Norton joined the fray, and soon, aunts and uncles and trusted business partners surrounded them, asking what they could do to help.

When Addie felt a little less shaky on her feet, she risked a look around. The Chapel was in shambles. She thought of the bodies that littered the Chateau, covering the staircase and the floor along the Great Room's hearth. The union that was almost forged between her and Marcus, wholly distinct from how it had existed—love, respect, *equality*—in her head. Then, she thought of the staff in the kitchen, waiting to serve the five-course meal. The drinks that were supposed to flow, the conversations, the revelry, the gifts, and the dancing and merry-making.

Addie lifted her gaze to meet the eyes of her friends and family. In her periphery, she could see Zelda bend over Marcus Weber and start the steps to extract what remained of his blood.

"'Weber' will look way better on a specialty bottle than it would at the end of my name," Addie said and smiled. She grasped her sisters' hands. "I don't want to waste *any* of this... come on, let's get on with the celebration."

🦇 🦇 🦇

Christa Carmen lives in Rhode Island and is the Bram Stoker Award-nominated author of the short story collection Something Borrowed, Something Blood-Soaked. She has a BA from the University of Pennsylvania, an MA from Boston College, and an MFA from the University of Southern Maine.

When she's not writing, she keeps chickens; uses a Ouija

board to ghost-hug her dear, departed beagle; and sets out on adventures with her husband, daughter, and bloodhound–golden retriever mix. Most of her work comes from gazing upon the ghosts of the past or else into the dark corners of nature, those places where whorls of bark become owl eyes, and deer step through tunnels of hanging leaves and creeping briars only to disappear.

You can find her at christacarmen.com.

The Keeper Of Taswomet

Errick Nunnally

THE SLOW WHINE of a cicada cut through the warm air and mixed with the other chirps and clicks of insects. A light breeze came in from across the marsh, tickling tall dry grass. The dense green could barely be seen through a narrow corridor in the trees surrounding the last house on the lane.

Joshua shot out of the back of his home, cutting across the lawn and into the trees before the screen door banged shut. He wore the summer-ready haircut of most twelve-year old boys: buzzed short on top and close on the sides, his brown hair lightened by the sun. The day was especially warm, so he wore his favorite, tank top: light blue with Mjölnir on the front. Partway down his skinny biceps, his skin went from its usual fish-belly pale to cinnamon-toasted, exposing what his mother referred to as a 'farmer's tan.' The youngster was an anachronism, belonging instead to the days when scores of children roamed through nature, picking it apart, living in it and on it. These days, most of his friends were more interested in music or the latest dramas of the latest pop stars.

He rushed to check on the well-hidden, briny pool he'd

found just before lunch, a gift born of the marsh that defined so much of his life. Joshua was fortunate, he enjoyed the area to a degree that other kids did not. Taswomet Marsh made summers the best time of year, and it made school bearable. The natural wonder's proximity bent the school's science program to its will. And Joshua loved it.

A trip to the hardware store and chores with his father had kept him from exploring the discovery further earlier in the day, but the precious gift of extra daylight during the summer meant he had some time after dinner.

He wound through the oak and pine wood, rooted in a sandy surface, cutting through to the well-worn path that meandered along the greater portion of the marsh. Insect cries intensified in constant whirrs and clicks. He imagined the long shadows were the devastating ice clubs of frost giants and Joshua danced around them. He slowed when he reached the next path, exposed to the setting sun.

Bright light and heat slammed his face and arms as he eased the pace, picking his way along the narrow path that cut through low brush too thick to pass otherwise. He'd promised to get back before sunset, so he didn't dally when a plover snapped out of the tall grass, capturing his attention. It beat quickly into the sky, then broke into the tree line before he could determine whether it was a western or a white-rumped.

The backpack he wore added a layer of unneeded warmth to the small of his back. It contained his notebook, sample bags, a small shovel, and other knick-knacks for research and sample collection. He shrugged the bag off and carried it by the handle. Just ahead, there was a less worn path cutting towards the marsh proper. Softer soil gave beneath his shoes as he wound his way through the flora to the pool, pushing tall grasses and thick underbrush aside. The stink of mosquito repellant stung his nose. It was necessary to wear in the marsh, but he always felt like his mom laid it on too thick. Still, he was fortunate to be part of a new generation allowed to roam, to drift away and explore only to return when hunger saw fit to remind him. As long as it happened before dark.

He crouched down at the edge of the hidden pool and peered into the dark water. Just below the surface, he could make out eight gelatinous sacks about the size of large raviolis and trending in color from brown to translucent to gray. He couldn't tell if there were more of them deeper in the water, but it didn't matter. He only wanted one for his project. Being careful not to fall in, and using a heavy-duty zip-locking bag, he scooped up one of the sacs and as much of the brackish water as he could. He only wanted a sample, something to study. Of all the species he knew that reproduced in this manner—he presumed they were egg sacs—this one escaped him. It looked like the egg case of a catshark, but more square and smaller. The marsh was a cornucopia of ecology accentuated by the sea.

Joshua held the bag up to the sunlight and peered through the odd mass. Inside the sac, a tiny creature lay curled into a tight ball. It twitched in the glare. Overhead, two ospreys observed the marsh in widening circles. Joshua was anxious to get his find settled into the glass habitat he'd constructed in his room. He'd dubbed the thing a "terraquarium" since it approximated, as best he could manage, the mixed environment of the marsh. He was going to have the best summer project on display when school started again.

Thoughts of the future danced in his mind as he hurried home, the kind of open-ended musings only a twelve-year-old could think of; a future of discovery and fortune.

Nora checked the harness around her pelvis for the last time, tightening the buckles so that the pressure felt even and snug. Then she flicked on the headlamp strapped to her forehead and pulled on thick, leather gloves up to her elbows. She hated the gloves, they limited dexterity. And the hole in the wall was even less endearing. They'd widened it as much as they could without compromising the integrity of the foundation. With some irony, she noted that her best protection—the face-cage helmet—wasn't an option at all. Her size, the reason she was going into that hole, was the same reason the damn thing wouldn't stay on her head when she was lying flat on her belly. Every cage she wore dropped down as soon as she looked up, the visor slid down and ground into the bridge of her nose. Excepting the thick, wavy hair she kept raked back into a practical bun, her head wasn't going to get any larger.

Most people thought Nora's hair was a dye job or assumed she was Puerto Rican, Dominican, or some other ethnicity they knew nothing about. Migrating to Boston from the Cape had mitigated some of her circumstances, but not all of them. Bearing the skin color equivalent of a latte still had responsibilities she wasn't interested in exploring for even half the time they were thrust upon her.

She looked at Hardy and nodded. He held the other end of the chord she was clipped to. He was the junior officer here and the most likely candidate for belly-crawling hole duty, but his size put the kibosh on any plans such as that. As soon as the hole had been widened to its limits, Nora began to wordlessly gear up.

Inside the hole, they could still hear the plaintive mewling of...some kind of canid, she was sure. A litter of them, most likely. The sounds had been heard, off and on, for over a week until the owner of the property decided it was worth a call to Animal Control. At the mouth of the opening, she listened again and reassured herself it wasn't the giggling whoop that haunted her sleep as it had haunted the streets of one of Boston's poorest neighborhoods a year prior. The owners of that particular sound had carved a wild swath through the population, eating anyone in their path.

She crawled forward.

🍂 🍂 🍂

Nora's phone rang a third time and for a third time she looked at a 508 number she didn't recognize. She hated picking up unknown calls. Chasing creatures large and small around the southern reaches of Boston derailed her life often enough without further distractions. But a third attempt…

"Hello."

"Nora! Holy shit, girl, took you long enough to answer."

"Who is this?"

"Wow, you don't recognize the voice, huh?"

"I'm hanging up now."

"Wait! It's Tom. Tom Liddelle."

Tom. Tom from high school. *Little Tom Thumb*, another congenital outcast in their hometown. For a while, anyway. The sort of person she fell in with or they fell in with her. Until they reached escape velocity. For Tom, that had been a late growth spurt.

"Oh. Uh, hi."

"Yeah, hello, Nora. Good to hear your voice."

Okay, then. Nora tried to remember why she had dated Tom for as long as she did and the memories came hard. The experience with him hadn't been one that stuck out in her mind as worth remembering. In her memories, at this moment, he was mostly a grey area; a nice enough guy, but they hadn't meshed well.

"Sooooo what's up, Tom?"

"Well, for one thing, it's Deputy Liddelle, nowadays."

She could hear the grin in his voice. She recalled that he'd wanted to be a cop, but she couldn't come up with the *why* other than the opportunity to have authority over others. "Congratulations."

"Uh, thanks. I hear you're in animal control up there in the big city. You always were into nature and stuff."

Nature and stuff. She sighed.

"Okay, okay, hear me out. I was hoping you'd do me a favor and come back to the old town and take a look at something for me. Animal related. A case, consult on a case."

Nowadays, law enforcement requests brought to mind a cascade of memories: grisly crime scenes, dog fighting, breeding gone awry, death, a bite powerful enough to masticate metal, fear. She'd seen more in the past year and a half than any animal control officer should ever have in a lifetime.

"I don't know, Tom—"

"C'mon, Nora, I know about that thing with the dogs you were involved with—"

"*Dogs?* Not dogs—"

"And that you haven't taken a break since then. Take few days off, take a look at this situation I've got, give me some credibility, and then relax on the beach."

Nora gathered herself, reigned in anger and spoke calmly. "They weren't dogs, Tom."

"Look, that's what the report said, Nora, and the newspapers. What do I know? Nothing. That's why I'm calling you."

Tearing flesh and pulverizing bone had been nothing to the creatures. They were not dogs, they were something new. "You have people there for this sort of thing—"

"Everyone's tied up in the search, they're spread out. They've cleared this area and the local game warden doesn't believe it's an angle worth looking into. They've moved on."

Probably with good reason, Nora thought. Tom was ambitious, if not overly talented, he *wanted* more than he could prove he deserved, more than he was capable of delivering. And he couldn't see it. He'd always been that way, she recalled.

"Please? There's a kid missing and I think this is a lead, and I need your help proving it, Nora."

Goddamn it, Tom. "Fine. I'll put in and head down tomorrow. Promise."

"Oh, Jesus, thank you, Nora, thank you. I know it'll make all the difference."

She hoped it would, more than Tom knew. After the fiasco last year, the director of her department had personally let her know that she could take time off whenever she wanted, but she'd been too freaked out. Days became weeks, weeks months, and so on. If she stopped moving, stopped going to work, the fear would catch up. At least this way, she could get out of the city and keep running.

❦ ❦ ❦

Out of the city. *Out.* It was a slippery concept in Boston, something the Gods of Traffic Patterns actively tried to foil. Especially going to the Cape. The only thing that would make it more epic would be solving doom-laden riddles and slaying dragons along the way. Dragons. *Monsters.* She slapped the dash, found some music and turned it up. Summer was on the wane, but humidity hung in the air and it was only going to get worse near the marshes. Still, she refused to button up and rely on the air-conditioner. The natural environment was to be experienced, not fought. Oftentimes, either choice led to humanity's detriment.

Traffic eased and started moving at a more favorable clip. Nora slid the sunroof of her Toyota compact open and stuck her hand out, savoring the feel of the wind sluicing through her fingers. Only seventy some odd miles to go before she drove back into her childhood...

❧ ❧ ❧

Nora checked the text from Tom one more time on her phone to verify the specific address. As she pulled onto the small road leading into the neighborhood near the marsh, she couldn't shake a stunned feeling. So close to where she grew up—where they grew up. Tom had said so, but she never imagined it'd feel like this, a further taint added to her memories.

They'd passed the house hundreds of times back then, it was the "last house." The last house before the marsh proper began. Taswomet sprawled along the southwestern coast of the Cape, a living breathing organ of Mother Earth, veins and arteries of salty water and nitrogenous silt sprawled out of it, penetrating the land and bringing with it life. The scientific verification of how vital this ecology was came late to humanity. The idea that the marshes were a kind of natural wasteland begging for development had lasted for too long—in some ways it still did. Entire species of both flora and fauna died out under the capitalistic onslaught.

By the time Nora was born, development had been brought to a halt or, at least, kept at bay. And when she'd started exploring the marshes, taking a serious interest, some species were starting to come back. Not all of them, unfortunately. The eelgrass was going to be gone soon, but osprey had made a modest comeback. You had to pay attention, but they were there, circling the marsh, telling evidence that their diet of local fish wasn't killing them anymore, that humanity hadn't fully broken the chain of custody yet.

She pulled up to the Nantucket-grey house and didn't

immediately see Tom but noticed the tell-tale colors of the county sheriff's vehicle down the drive. Nora steered into the driveway, crunching gravel, rolling slow, when Tom came into view. He stood on the side porch, thumbs hooked into his duty belt.

He looked sharp, but cliched to Nora, an approximation of law enforcement. She felt pity, then cut that emotion off. It was Tom's special way of worming behind her defenses, how she'd been foolish enough to date him for as long as she had in high school. Still, he was fit and bore a thick mustache under his nose now. It suited him, this dress-up, he seemed comfortable in his own skin and for that she was grateful.

When she cut the engine, silence dropped over the area like a wet blanket. Too quiet. No insects, no rustling of small creatures in the forest periphery, no birds. Nora opened the door and stood at her vehicle, lost in thought. When Tom spoke, it made her jump, the quiet was too much.

"Nora? You okay? You seem…rattled."

"Hey, Tom. Yeah. I'm fine. It's just…quiet."

"Yeah, it's eerie. Right? It doesn't get any better inside."

Nora mounted the stairs, painted grey with white accents to match the home, and instinct took over as it always did in the presence of a uniformed man. She stuck her hand out for a shake, and they shared an awkward moment where Tom tried to hug her. A little dance, a quick embrace and he backed off.

The house was a two-story affair, wood shingles, decorative white trim, neat. Just as it had been when she was twelve years old, roaming the area for quahogs and oysters, marking summertime in sight of the open waters just beyond the surrounding forest.

"Here." He held out a pair of the blue booties intended to preserve a crime scene. He slipped on his own pair.

"Thanks."

Then Tom led the way. The inside of the house was all angles like most of these colonials near the beach. Lots of wood details, muted reds and blues, a shining floor. The floor featured the usual scuffs, but something more ragged, in addition. There were odd dents and gouges leading towards what she assumed was the kitchen.

"You noticed that." Tom nodded toward the floor. "We'll come back down and I'll show you more, but you should see it from the beginning."

Nora nodded, choking back a brief strike of panic. So far, there were none of the usual triggers typically associated with a crime scene, but she could smell something. A musty, old sea scent mixed with the unmistakable smell of viscera. Faint, but present.

"Hold on, Tom."

He turned.

"How bad is this?"

"Oh! Sorry. It's not as bad as it was the day before yesterday. All the, uh, bodies are gone, of course, but the scene hasn't been sanitized or anything. It's an ongoing investigation. We've been more preoccupied with the missing kid." He narrowed his eyes at her. "I thought you'd done this sort of thing before?"

"Not often, but I have. That doesn't make it any easier."

"Ah. Sure. Sorry. This way?" He tilted his head up the stairs.

"Fine."

There was a landing at the top of the stairs that extended nearly the width of the house. At either end were bedrooms.

"The master—Roger and Wendy Fairmann's room—is that way." Tom indicated the right. "This in the center is the guest room, untouched. And that," he waved to the left, "was the son's room, Joshua. Come this way first." He moved towards the right.

Nora braced herself again, shutting down 'human' in her mind and reminding herself that humans were simply animals, like any other. She looked down. There was a beige carpet runner the length of the landing and small bloody spots led from the stairs to the master, or vice versa. On the edges of the carpet, more of the dings and scratches.

The room remained intact, but the bed was a reddish-brown encrusted mess. Any neatness in the surroundings only accentuated the slashed bed and chunks of synthetic filler scattered amongst the wide blood stain.

"Jesus, Tom." Nora exhaled and blew it out slowly, surprised that she'd been holding her breath. "Who could do this?"

"That's the thing, Nora, I don't think it's a 'who' so much as a…'what.'"

Nora edged up to the bed and peered down. The pillows were slashed, spatters of blood moved outward from the main mess at the center. Even without the bodies, it was horrific. There was no discernible pattern, it wasn't so much that it looked like the Fairmanns exploded as they seemed to have been blended on the spot.

"It's like some freaky devil cult movie from the seventies. Remember those boys in tenth grade?"

Nora's mind clicked back and forth from what Tom was saying to what she was seeing. The cresting wave of irrational thought and pure emotion trembled inside her as she forced calm and focused on the situation in front of her. There were no bodies, no need to view that violence first-hand. She was only here to help a childhood friend.

"Please, that was bullshit. Small-town Satanic panic. Drinking beer while wearing black and listening to heavy metal do not cultists make."

"Whatever. Their son is missing. What if it is some kind of cultist mess?"

A detective, he is not, she thought. "No offense, Tom, but I don't think you're the only one that has considered that."

Tom hummed the affirmative by making a sarcastic folksy sound that matched his uniform.

She looked down and around the bed, along the wall-to-wall carpeting, noting the little blood dots that were impossible to see close to the bed because of the spatter, but coalescing on the way out of the room. "Tom, I don't know what could have done something like this."

"Just keep an open mind, Nora, I need someone with your background to see what I saw. C'mon."

She flexed and relaxed her hands, shook out the muscles of her arms, and rolled her shoulders. She prayed that Joshua's room was benign, a typical boy's room whose only unusual aspect was the absence of the boy.

Nora stepped around Tom and let loose a long, quiet sigh of relief.

Inside Joshua's thankfully bloodless room, the difference in upkeep was notable. Despite the usual chaos of a boy's room, there was damage. He'd been working on some kind of habitat on a table above his dresser. It was shattered, mud and plants strewn across the floor. The wildlife that had been kept within were dead. She could see snails and small crab carcasses. On shelves around the room, other shells rested—oyster, quahog, horseshoe crab—no doubt collected while exploring. One shelf held a collection of dried eggshells. She recognized quail and robin, but the others were lost to memory. In between, on the walls, posters of birds, fish, and one of Thor, raising his hammer to a lightning storm. A wave of nostalgia passed over her.

"Yeah, this room…" Tom said.

"What?"

"Reminded me of you. All this stuff; this kid was a nature nut too."

"Yes, he was," Nora muttered. *Still is*, she silently hoped.

Other shelves held books about the local wildlife. Nora looked at the twin bed, covers tossed off, sheets ruffled, but stiff. The bedding had a slight shine, as if they'd been starched. She slipped an antennae-like probe from a pocket and poked at the sheets. Yes, stiff. Coated with...what? She peered closer and noticed the coating flaked when prodded.

"What is this, has it been analyzed?"

"Uhm, yeah. The folks at the lab said it was a protein or something."

"A protein or something." She stared at Tom, willing him to be more specific.

"C'mon, Nora, that's not my thing, I don't remember those forensic particulars. What I remember them sayin' is that it wasn't very complex. Like dried egg whites."

It does look like dried egg whites, Nora thought.

Joshua's room was carpeted like his parents, but Nora could see the scratches and dents on the boy's dresser that matched the others. Still, nothing that resembled animal droppings or markings that she could recognize. "Chrissakes, Tom, I got nothing here that looks like the passage of an animal."

"There's more. Follow me." He walked out.

Nora stood for a few beats longer, taking in the room and the faint, musty scent of the sea hovering in the air. The windows were closed, the smell was trapped. Her skin crawled, and she walked towards the doorway. Tom thumped down the stairs.

By the door, there was a bright blue backpack flopped over, its contents spilling out. Ziploc bags, a small trowel, a few plastic vials, and a notebook. She picked the book up. There were a few more things inside like a small flashlight, magnifying glass, a hat. But it was the notebook that held her attention. A field guide. Joshua had taken notes, studied the nature around him, made small crude sketches. He was a true scientist, curious and thoughtful. The last entry was about a briny pool he'd discovered along with a hastily scribbled map and sketch of what he'd found inside it. Nora's eyes wandered over the shattered glass and small animal carcasses.

"Nora?"

She jumped, unable to shake the creepy feeling the house and surrounding area were giving her. "Be right there!" She shoved the notebook into her cargo pocket and headed downstairs. Later, she planned to take a tour, following Joshua's routes. Maybe she'd find something the previous investigators had missed. Clearly they hadn't had much interest in Joshua's book. Them or the mysterious kidnapper.

Tom waited at the base of the stairs. "Okay, the dents and scratches. Right? Here and here, going down the stairs. See the bottom? More. Around the stairs, towards the kitchen. C'mon."

She entered the kitchen and skidded to a halt, trying to make sense of the scene.

"Weird. Right?"

Weird was appropriate. Directly ahead of the doorway, the stainless steel of the dishwasher had been crumpled inward. On the other side of the counter, to her left, the back door was still on its hinges, but the bottom was shattered. Splinters of wood pushed outward. *Outward.*

"See that? The goddamned door is broken out. Something went *outside* through here."

"I…yeah, I see that." Whatever it was, it had been just small enough to fit through the doorway, but tall enough to take out nearly the bottom half.

"Okay, now look out here." Tom wrestled the door open and stepped out onto the back porch.

More dents and scratches marked the wood but left none

had been on the tile floor. The marks went in a straight path down the stairs, pointing towards the tree line. Nora stood at the bottom of the stairs, her eyes fixed on the forest, and clamped down on a full body chill.

She felt a tingle in her feet, her legs. *Run*. The singular thought cut through her mind.

A loud rasp and click made her jump and she spun toward the sound. Tom had un-holstered and extended a collapsible baton.

"There's nothing here, Nora, you don't have to be so jumpy. Look, check this out." He thumped the porch with the baton and once more, then pointed.

Nora mounted the stairs and peered down to where Tom indicated. The dent his baton had left was nearly identical to the existing indentations. "Okay, what does that mean?"

Tom spread his arms. "I don't know. That's why you're here. Animal was my first thought after seeing what happened to the Fairmanns."

She swallowed and took a deep breath. "I didn't see any evidence that would *prove* an animal, Tom."

"What? No evidence?" He swept his arms toward the door, then the floor without taking his eyes off her.

"I mean: whatever this was didn't leave anything behind that clearly indicates whether it was or was not an animal. No shedding of any sort, no recognizable prints, no notable feces or urine." She licked her lips, already regretting her next question. "What about the bodies, did they show evidence of bite or scratch marks?"

"That's the thing, Nora, there wasn't much body left. All that blood upstairs? The only things that remained were shredded pajamas, hair, teeth, some bones—most of them shattered or picked at."

"Picked at?"

"Yeah, marks like a saw or something."

"You just put your finger on it. Tools. People are shit."

Tom growled in frustration. "Whatever killed them, left these prints and did not know how to use a fucking door."

"Was the door locked when you found it?"

"People *still* don't lock their doors here, Nora."

"Two grisly murders and a missing boy. So, a person could have just walked in through the back door?"

"Nora…"

"Why would an animal take a child and how could it do it without hurting the kid?"

"I don't know! Maybe it was a person with an animal, for Christ's sake, maybe they used a goddamned animal, maybe the kid ran. To me, it's distinct, it stands out, it's the odd thing in this situation and what we might want to focus more attention on, but no one believes it's worth looking into, no one believes *me*!"

"All right, all right." She raised her hands and wondered if she'd be able to relax on the beach after this. Or at all, ever. The hurt on Tom's face was clear, he cared, he wanted to help. And Nora was sure, Tom wanted to be recognized for his efforts, to succeed where he had not before. To be respected. If he was right about any of this, then he'd deserve some recognition for seeing what others had not. The process had overrun any consideration for Tom's hunch. At the moment, procedure dictated that the search for the missing boy was priority, and not the murders. That might change soon, but by then, if an animal was involved, the trail would be even colder.

The dents did remind her of tracks she'd seen thousands of times when she was growing up here. Along the sandy shores, always near the ocean or an inlet. Impossible in this situation, in this location. At this size. But she'd been reevaluating her understanding of the word 'impossible' since last year. Then another thought came to her.

Tom continued to grumble in the background, shifting around, thinking with his body.

"Tom, shush."

"Huh?"

"Just...hold still for a minute, don't say anything."

"Wh—"

"Sshh!"

He shut. The silence enveloped them again. She could hear insects in the distance, but no birds chattering, leaping from branch to branch. Nature was closing back in slowly. But where had it gone lately? Surely they'd thoroughly searched the surrounding woods, but that wouldn't have driven nature away, merely up. The authorities had found nothing while looking for a young boy. Nora looked for something else. She moved with deliberate steps to the edge of the yard, peering down the entire way. At the trees she looked up. Still nothing. A snapping sound from behind startled her.

Nora glared at Tom. He stood near the porch, his hand hovering near his holster. He'd just unsnapped the catch.

"Sorry. You're making me a little nervous, I guess." He popped it closed and held his hands away from the holster.

Resuming the search, she picked her way along the edge of the underbrush and found a dead robin. Then another bird, a finch, along with other tiny bodies scattered amongst the trees and thick shrubs. Here and there, larger insects, more easily seen: beetles, dragonflies, a few bees, a Pelecinid wasp—all dead.

Nora thought about the shattered terrarium, the dead animals. Neglect was a possibility, but Joshua gave no indication of being that kind of boy. He didn't dabble, he was all in.

Nora looked at the trees again, peered into the forest. "If this was an animal, it's toxic to the environment, to other creatures. It's so quiet because all the insects and birds and otherwise around here are dead."

"But I can still hear bugs whining and shit."

"They're coming back, but whatever was here died. There're dead birds along the edge of the property, insects—I bet I could find a few small mammals if I started digging through the brush. Frankly, I don't want to touch anything; this scares the piss out of me."

"Hey! That's evidence. Right?" Tom's eyes lit up.

"No, nothing immediately concrete. Nothing without extensive testing to see if it was a chemical agent, whether it was something the Fairmanns did or a natural phenomenon. There's no animal that I can think of whose very presence kills."

Nora clenched and unclenched her teeth. The dentist had warned her of the grinding and she struggled to break the habit. While she was pushing up on her jaw and working the muscles to relax them, she saw a face peering at them from the trees.

◆ ◆ ◆

"You! Step into the clearing right here, with your hands up! Do it n—God damn it."

It happened fast, almost in one breath. Nora was used to reacting to animals, reading them, but people weren't necessarily part of her repertoire. The man in the forest bolted, Tom unholstered his service weapon and gave chase.

"Tom, wait!"

Deputy Tom Liddelle crashed into the forest, yelling for the man to stop. And before Nora thought too hard about it, she launched herself after them.

The man they chased wore dark clothing—at least one layer too many for the weather and he moved like he knew the forest, cutting left and running deeper in rather than towards the nearest open coast. Tom and Nora knew the forest too.

Tom ran with his weapon up as they weaved through the trees. Nora hoped he wouldn't do something stupid and fire at the man. Their quarry only made fleeting appearances in and out, behind bushes and old growth tree trunks. Nora gained on Tom and he, in turn, closed on the strange figure. Their quarry was balding, Nora could see, his hair more salt than pepper. Old, but wiry.

The man in black broke wide to circle a clump of low growth. Tom crashed right into it, bounding over the initial growth and high-stepping through it.

What the hell was he doing? Nora followed the man, going wide. She was a runner, familiar with the surroundings, and starting to wonder what the hell she would do if she caught the guy. Close enough now to hear his labored breathing over her own, a sudden commotion caught her attention on the left. Tom exploded from the undergrowth and barreled into the man. Both deputy and quarry tumbled to the forest floor, the stranger hitting the ground hard.

Nora ground to a halt at the scene as the deputy sprang to his knees and secured the suspect by jamming his pistol into the back of his neck and shouting, "Don't you move, mother-fucker!" The old man's face mashed into the dirt.

"Tom!" Nora shrieked, unsure of what would happen next.

With one knee in the guy's back, his foot in the suspect's crotch, and a free hand on the back of the man's neck, Tom holstered his gun. Then he expertly forced the old man's arms back and slapped the cuffs on before hauling him to his feet.

Tom asked, "What's your name?"

Nora could see that he truly was an old man. A long nose

and close-set hangdog eyes, white eyebrows and stubble to match. The stranger's lips twitched and his icy blue eyes darted left and right, taking both Nora and Tom in.

"Hey! This'll all go a lot easier if I know your name, old timer." Tom gave the guy a little shake.

The old man mumbled in a wheezy croak like he'd forgotten how to use his voice. After a few stuttering attempts while catching his breath, he ground out, "Paul."

"Bullshit." Tom jerked the old man again, rifling through his pockets, coming up with nothing. "But it'll do for now. Let's go, *Paul*, no more running, start walking."

The deputy huffed and started taking deep breaths. Nora didn't know whether he was doing it to calm down or catch his breath. She wasn't sure what to do. She wasn't a cop, didn't have a bulletproof vest or a utility belt for fighting crime, no human-type weapons. The situation reminded her that she didn't have her gear on her, just her usual folding knife and pocket-size flashlight, collapsible probe, a pen—things she could always have in her pockets. Stuff that had nothing to do with stopping bad guys, but her full pack provided her comfort as good as any child's lovie.

Nora itched to ask questions, to find out what Tom was thinking, what 'Paul' knew, why he was lurking in the woods near the Fairmann's home. When they broke into the clearing near the house, she had to ask, "What now?"

Tom slipped on a nasty grin and said, "Now we ask our friend Paul here a few questions. Like, what were you doing in the woods?"

"Nothing."

Tom pinned him with a skeptical look. "Oh? Just happened to be stumbling through the forest, off-trail, and came on the scene. Eh? How about you save us all some trouble and tell me where Joshua is."

"Who?"

Tom fished a photo out of his chest pocket and shoved it in Paul's face. "Joshua, *Paul*, the kid you took. Where is he, why'd you take him?" Tom spun Paul around and thumped him against the Sheriff's car. "Talk. Now. Make this easier on yourself."

Paul shook his head and kept touching his chin to his chest. His eyes watered and he looked like he was going to cry. "There's no time, no time."

"What? What do you mean? No time for what?"

"No time for this, no time, I have to take care, get back." The old man barely acknowledged Tom, but Nora wasn't sure Tom even noticed. The old guy was staring into some middle space, referring to something she couldn't be quite sure was reality.

"Get back to what, huh? Look at me, Paul, talk to me, I'm right here."

"I have to get back to the children, to Basatan, I have to keep them safe."

"Where is Joshua?" Tom shouted, sticking a finger in the old man's chest, forcing Paul to focus.

"I don't know Joshua. Only Basatan."

"What is that, explain, what is it? It's no place nearby. I know every beach, cove, and inlet around here, and that ain't one of 'em. Is it an island, one of the little islands, a boat? What?"

Was that the name of a person? Nora wondered.

"They need tending," Paul mumbled.

Children. He'd said 'children.' Plural. Joshua was the only kid missing that we know of.

It was the last straw for Tom. He cocked one arm back and was about to take the old man's head off when Nora hooked his elbow and held him back.

"Damn it, Tom, you can't do that!"

"This guy knows something, Nora, and I'm gonna find

out what."

"Let me talk to him."

"What?"

"You heard me. Desperate times, right?" In her thoughts she added, *Like I'm going to stand here and watch you beat up an old man in handcuffs.*

"Fine. Make it brief." Tom looked up over the tree line. The sun was sinking fast, shadows crept from the forest like the talons of an inhuman hand come to claim the backyard.

"Give us some room."

"No."

"*Tom*, back up. He's cuffed."

He backed, jaw convulsing with barely restrained anger.

Nora looked Paul in the eyes, waited for him to focus. His mouth hung slightly open and she could smell his awful breath, the scents coming off his body. He smelled like the deep, the kind of humid and salty smell of the Atlantic. The area seemed to be saturated with it. A line of drool slipped over his bottom lip. Slowly, he came to see her. She could see flecks of diamond in his eyes. They were beautiful, the only thing about him that seemed bright and present when he paid attention.

"Paul, my name's Nora Tuttle, I'm an animal control officer, a preservationist, I keep animals safe. Do you understand?"

"Safe?"

"Yes, safe. Are you trying to keep something safe? Maybe I can help."

"Safe," Paul repeated. "Yes, safe. I care for them, I keep them safe, I preserve them. Basatan. But someone took one, took one away. There were a...a...a hundred, now there's nine-nine."

"Who took one? Joshua?"

"I don't know, I don't know, it's too late, it's too soon." Paul looked at the house, tears blooming in his eyes.

"Did he take an animal, is that what you care for?"

"Animal? No. More than us." Paul became more animated, impassioned, back straight and proselytizing. "Us—we are the animals, a mistake, temporary. *They* are the legacy, the future, it is their future—"

"Okay, that's enough." Tom stepped back in.

"Tom. Let him talk."

"No, enough of this shit. He's cuffed, now he's getting stuffed; we don't have time for babbling old men."

"He knows something about this, Tom; I think you were right."

The deputy paused, seemingly taken aback at being told he was correct, that she agreed with his assessment, even if only a little bit. But he had no patience for teasing it out of the old man. Everything about him suddenly softened and he turned to face Nora, his shoulder to Paul.

"Nora, look, it's just that I don't think this is going t—"

Paul bolted.

❦ ❦ ❦

Nora was sweating hard. Even though the air was cooling, the humidity was still strong and it dragged moisture out of everything. Paul hit the forest at a dead run with Tom in close pursuit. Again.

It had to be different for Nora this time, however, she needed it to be different. Instead of heading into the forest again, she dashed to her car and snatched her gear bag from the back seat. She could hear Tom alternately shouting at Paul to stop and using his radio to call in. Shrugging her tight pack on, she started after Tom and Paul, feeling more secure than before.

The pursuit cut to the right, this time, Paul was headed for the coast or the trail that hugged the coast. She caught sight of Tom in no time and began to close the distance.

She shouted to him. "He's headed for the trail!"

"I know!" Tom's voice huffed and held the tremor of someone on the run.

She could see a dark stain of sweat down the center of his back. A garbled voice came to her ears, squawking from Tom's radio, something about locations. She caught the word 'hours.'

"Shit!" Tom growled more comments into his mic while Nora caught up.

The light becameg muddier as they went and Nora felt the agitation of fear. This was going against her instincts, this mad pursuit into the woods. Even if she were armed, she wasn't foolish enough to believe a gun would guarantee her self-preservation. Adrenaline tempered the sense of fear, but it was creeping back. People often referred to it as the fight or flight response, but there was another option: freeze. She was determined not to freeze, but she sure as hell could turn back and embrace flight. Whatever had killed the Fairmanns might be out here somewhere, might be something Paul was involved with, and she had no interest in finding out for sure.

Ahead, arms straight behind his back, the spry old man turned left around a thicket, a similar move to earlier. Tom, once again, charged into the mass, but this time he went down hard in the brambles. Wrens pinwheeled into the air and Tom cried out in pain.

He was a big boy; Nora wasn't too worried about a few prickles teaching Tom a lesson. She rounded the brush that had crept upward, creating a natural wall in the forest, a sort of apartment house for nature's winged is what the deputy had slammed into.

Paul was nowhere to be seen and the smell she'd noted on him was thicker now, enveloping everything as if they were running down the throat of some leviathan. The humidity of the atmosphere became cloying and terrible, no air moved. In the distance, insects buzzed and birds worked out their cacophony. Tom struggled to his feet, cursing, and pulled himself out of the thick.

"God damn it!" He swiped at his face and neck, wiping off debris and insects.

There'd be no succor there, Nora knew, the damage had already been done and without a shower, he was going to be itchy for the rest of the night.

"Where'd he go? Which way?"

Nora shook her head and turned a slow circle. It was nearly dark, Paul was wearing all black, a dingy approximation of a suit, and he'd gone silent. It made no sense.

Tom unclipped his duty flashlight and Nora reached out to stop him.

"No, not yet. You turn that on and our night vision will be completely shot, better to wait. Just listen." The forest had a blue veil drawn over it, twilight that was difficult for human eyes, but it'd be impossible if they needed to adjust after the bright beam of a Mag Light. Around them, the transition from day to night was almost complete in the animal world.

Tom said under his breath, "He's got to be nearby. This is ridiculous."

They heard rustling far off, nothing distinct, not the crashing of human feet, for sure.

A scream cut through the air, a terrified and painful screech that sliced up their nerves and made them recoil.

"What the shit?" Tom recovered first, unholstered his weapon and snapped the flashlight on. "It came from over here. C'mon!"

Nora looked away, determined not to be blinded as Tom

rushed in the direction of the scream. "Screw that, let's get the hell out of here and wait for backup."

"That was the old guy, I guarantee it! He's close!"

Shit. Nora reached for her flashlight but opted against it for now. Instead, she followed Tom at a reasonable pace, picking her way more carefully than he, unwilling to simply abandon him or trudge through the forest alone.

Ahead, Tom stood stock still, swinging his flashlight left and right, alternating between the surrounding woods and the ground. She saw, in her peripheral vision, a glint from Tom's panning light. She moved toward it and peered through the blue-tinged light at Tom's handcuffs. Red spatters marked the restraints and the surrounding ground. She had a sickening feeling as her stomach dropped out and she began to honestly listen to what her instincts were telling her.

Nora slipped her small flashlight from her pocket and pointed it down before flicking the LED on.

"Tom." She managed to say through clenched teeth and a constricting throat.

He backed over to her, still panning his light, pistol at the ready.

"Look," she said.

They were standing in the blended remains of Paul, bits and pieces of him strewn about the forest floor, blood and bone in amongst the low growth. She saw a finger, shredded clothing, a shoe that was still occupied and now that they were still and quiet, she could hear it.

❧ ❧ ❧

"What the fuck is that?" Tom whispered.

"We need to leave." Nora hissed.

"Not as long as I have a badge and a gun." Tom continued to search the trees with his light.

Duty had its limits, as far as Nora was concerned. This problem was bigger than one lawman with an animal control sidekick. But she couldn't leave alone. As much as she hated to admit it, Tom had a gun and that was their best defense for now. Until she was sure it was a futile defense, here she would stay.

There was a rasping sound, of hard things rubbing together and something that sounded like a pot of spaghetti hitting a bowl. Bright pink, fleshy tendrils burst out of the undergrowth, right at their feet. Tom startled backwards into her and he lost his footing. The report of his weapon was deafening as his rump hit the forest floor. The bullet zinged off into the trees, a useless projectile. The tendrils resembled a network of veins and gathered up the rest of Paul's remains before withdrawing back into the brush. Nora's eyes followed their progress, eerily fascinated by the familiarity of it.

"What the fuck was that!?" Tom panned flashlight and weapon, searching for a target as he shuffled backwards on his butt, away from the proboscis.

A flesh-like proboscis. That was it. "Nema... *Nemertean.* A ribbon worm?" Nora remained aghast, unsure of herself, whether to run or stick with Tom.

"What?"

"It's a kind of sea worm. Blind. It inverts its guts in search of food."

"I will not believe a worm wrecked that house."

"I don't think it's a worm." Nora's eyes remained locked on the spot where the probe seemed to have originated from.

The sounds of slurping mastication had stopped and the brush rustled. Something broke from the greenery inside the cone of Tom's light. It was black, a dull chitinous texture of ridges and spikes, low slung between more than four legs. It was as tall and wide as a kitchen table. Two heavy claws were held against its lower body in front of two twitching plates. Beneath the plates, a trail of cloudy ichor dribbled from its open mouth in a nest of antennule that were furiously drawing in what flesh remained of the old man's foot. The things were hideously efficient, stripping the leather shoe away and then deftly removing meat from bone.

Both of them were transfixed by the size of the carapace, the inexorable motion of the mouth as the beast swayed rhythmically on its appendages. Nora realized that it was blind at the same moment the front plates slurped open and the proboscis exploded outward. She danced back, out of reach, but Tom, still on the ground, could only scramble. The tendrils slopped over his feet. He screamed and fired directly into the mass of the thing in front of them.

Wild shots hit it, bullets left gouges in the exoskeleton, but didn't penetrate. Where it seemed to have some effect, however, was at the base of the unspooled guts. The mass twitched and the monster reacted violently, reeling in its probes. Tom gasped in pain and Nora glanced down to see blood on his leg where the thing had touched him.

Hoplonomenta. Her mind fired on every bit of biology she could recall about such things. *The thing had a damned stylet spike in that fleshy mess*. She hoped it didn't carry a toxin and decided this might be a good time to point out the obvious: "Run!"

Nora hesitated long enough to see Tom get to his feet before tearing off towards the coastline. The trees were thick here, the thing would be slowed. If they could make it to the trail, it led to a research cabin. From there, they'd have some kind of fortification. She was through listening to Tom or following his lead. This was her plan and she wasn't going to waste precious moments explaining it to him. It was time for him to keep up with her.

She didn't look back and instead let her ears do that work. Tom huffed behind her, his heavier footsteps slamming the ground in a counter rhythm to her own. She breathed evenly, kept her eyes ahead and used her flashlight to plot their path. Further back, she could hear the thing rumbling through the forest. Every so often, she'd hear it collide with a tree, making a dull thump in the night and then the staccato sound of its multiple legs striking the ground would remind her to keep up the pace.

Tom's breath was becoming ragged, uneven. She could hear his footsteps starting to echo the unbalanced pace of his breathing. He wasn't going to make it to the trail, they needed some kind of defense.

It was so large, she thought, *but it's not built like a coconut crab.*

Nora slowed a bit and started looking for likely candidates.

"What are you doing?" Tom gasped. He spun on his heel and fired a few rounds into the dark.

"Cut it out, I think it's blind! There! That one's for you. This one's for me. Climb!"

The thing was closer than she'd thought, its multiple legs moved far more efficiently than expected at this impossible size. She dug a strap out of her cargo pocket and pulled it over her head, then clipped the mini Mag Light to it for an instant head lamp. A glance confirmed that Tom was looking to start his climb. She wasted no more time and started climbing her tree, getting one good grip, using her legs and always keeping one hand glued to a branch. Repetitive, machine-like, focused on the task at hand. One slip...

The bizarre thumping sounded just below. It had arrived.

❦   ❦   ❦

Tom had not mounted his tree. He crouched behind the trunk, aiming at the hideous thing. He started squeezing off steady shots, each one finding their mark as he growled through clenched teeth. Each strike made the thing twitch and turn towards the shots.

"Tom, stop, get up the tree! It's just figuring out where you are!"

The lawman's only response was to drop a magazine and slap a new one in. He started firing again. The crab-like thing turned in his direction and rumbled forward. This time, it didn't open its forward plates. Instead, it unfolded the deadly claws it carried low-slung to its armor. The organic rasping and clacking made her skin chill.

Tom's rage melted from hot to cold in an instant. He danced around the tree, dodging the creature. It was faster than they were but couldn't maneuver around the trees as well. The deputy's face was pale, sweat soaked his chest and back. He was starting to limp.

Oh, God, Tom. "Climb, damn it!" *Before it's too late.*

Tom made a desperate dash and turn between two trees nearby, wheeling around and jumping for the branches of the tree Nora had pointed out for him.

The thing struggled to reorient itself, managed the turn and closed on him as he scrambled to get up the tree.

It paused as Tom mounted the lowest branch and pulled, scrabbling with one foot and raising the other. He raised one leg and reached for a higher branch when the thing's claw snapped out and claimed his right foot. He screamed, struggled briefly and broke free with a sudden jerking motion that sent him out of the thing's reach.

The deputy moved as if he'd made a clean escape, but when he went to place his right foot on a branch, the appendage he needed wasn't there. There was a confused tumble, and he nearly lost his balance, grabbing at branches to arrest his fall. He froze and stared incredulously at the empty end of his leg.

It had snapped his foot off just above the ankle. A gout of blood splashed down across the beast as it stripped the remnants of Tom's boot away and consumed his flesh.

She saw this, knew it had happened, and Nora could only grind her jaw down and keen in the back of her throat. Tom gasped, struggled for a deep breath and started howling. He was experiencing something Nora hoped she'd never see again, promised herself she'd never let happen to her. His skin resembled a plain white candle, an oily sweat swam down his face in rivulets mixed with tears of anguish and sorrow. He was slipping fast into shock. Part of him was gone and it was being *eaten*.

"Tom!" She repeated his name until he looked at her, into her light and squinted. She pulled the lamp off and shone it on herself. "Look at me, look at me. See? It's Nora. Okay? You're gonna be okay. Listen, listen to me. You need a tourniquet; you have to staunch the bleeding. Do you understand?"

Tom looked down at this dripping stump and sobbed, slumping in a precarious position on his branch.

Nora screamed at him. "Tom! God damn it, remove your belt and tie your leg off, tie it off tight!"

Below them the thing slowly circled the tree, picking at the ground where Tom's blood was pooling.

Nora felt a burning in her stomach, smelled the awful truth coming from both Tom and the thing on the ground. The humid, salty sea and blood. All a reminder of humanity's inextricable connection to the ancient past.

"Tom! *Please*. I need you to *try*, I need you to live. *Please*. Do it now." She sobbed at him, unable to keep her voice even.

Tom looked up into her light, his face so white and moist as to be obscured by the brightness. All she could really see where his mustache, eyebrows, and rheumy eyes. With slow and deliberate movements, he reached to his waist and unbuckled his belt.

The thing below rasped and made a slurping sound, pressed up against Tom's tree. The two plates exploded open, and the probes shot up the tree, entangling the lower half of Tom's body. He moaned and grabbed the nearest branches, clinging with what strength he had left before the tree limbs snapped and he plummeted to the forest floor.

For a moment, he had the breath knocked from him and he struggled to sit up, legs pumping to disentangle from the tentacles. In a burst of speed, it reeled him in and surged forward, its antennule beginning their gruesome work, stripping Tom's clothing away and tearing at the tender flesh beneath. He screamed, unburdened by shame or any other constraints. She could see the veins pulse in his neck as he struggled like a wild animal, reduced to a subhuman state as the thing, in turn, pushed him further down the food chain. The powerful claws unfolded from beneath the carapace and descended on Tom's flailing torso. The sounds of bone and softer things being minced overtook his voice and Nora couldn't bear to watch anymore. She turned away and climbed higher.

❧ ❧ ❧

Nora brought her knees up to her chest and choked off a sob. Then she clicked off her flashlight. She didn't want to make any kind of sound, draw any sort of attention to herself. Her mind didn't drift, it jolted back to Franklin Park in Boston, the hunt, and forced retreat. Being chased. The animals, a dog-breeding experiment gone awry. They'd bred monsters, demons. Ghosts who claimed the park with an insatiable hunger. She wished detectives Pushoffski and Roman were here with her, even though what was left of Pushoffski had retired and Roman could still be a bit racist when cornered. Pushoffski's full-disability retirement had to be going smoother than this and as long as Roman was at the top of the social food chain, he was satisfied.

This. Right now. The matter at hand. It was time to survive, get back in that space and move the agenda forward. She uncapped her hands from her ears, unaware that she'd done it in the first place. The sounds of Tom's horrifically efficient end were still strong. The hushed breath of the ocean working with the marsh came on a light breeze. The marsh was close. *Now*. She knew what to do, where to go. Time to move, not wait.

Nora flicked on her lamp and eyed the trees around her. She didn't want to descend anywhere near that monstrosity below. Measuring the distance, she got her feet beneath her and aimed for the next copse of trees, a dense collection that would provide some protection on the ground. She paused, unwilling to forget what the thing was doing below her, but needing to know it was still busy. Then she jumped.

Smaller branches and needles slapped her in the face before she was even close to the tree. An electric shock of panic ran through her as she began to fall, feet pedaling to find support, hands grasping desperately. Her fingers closed around a branch that slipped fast through her palm, another branch thumped her shoulder and her feet slipped. She pinballed before getting a thick branch into her armpit to stop her fall short.

Branches and bark fell away as she scrambled for purchase, swinging herself around the trunk. When she was sure of not falling, she paused to listen again. Silence. No buzzing of insects or the flapping of startled wings. Everything sounded muffled, far off. She swallowed and stole a glance down the tree. There was nothing there. When the sounds of mastication resumed, terror nearly caused her to spring out into the air.

Nora shimmied down the tree and peeked around the thick trunk. Almost twenty feet away, the thing was making short work of what was left of Tom, its backside to her. As it rendered the pieces in front of it, a stream of shit escaped its backside and spattered on the forest floor. A glimpse of what may have been Tom's arm, moving steady into the mulcher of its pharynx, brought a shiver to Nora's skin, despite the humid heat.

Her mind scattered, coming up hard against the impossibilities of it all. *Where did this thing come from? Why now? Why me again? Never mind. Survive.*

She turned and picked her way through the copse, slipping around trees, watching her step. The underbrush near the marsh could be impenetrable. And noisy.

The masticating sounds behind her stopped. She didn't. It was her cue to run. She broke into a dash, knowing the thing was following, that the open marsh was ahead. She needed a lead to make good time on the trail. It would be faster than her in the open.

Nora careened through the forest, arms up, fists clenched. Branches pulled at her clothing and raked her face, snapping back or breaking as she passed. She focused on keeping her footing, high-stepping through the underbrush as needed, dodging rocks and roots, ignoring the bizarre cadence of thumps behind her. When she burst out of the woods, she almost overshot the trail. Stumbling to turn, her feet got tangled in the tall grass and she went down hard.

Never look back.

Nora slammed her palms on the ground and forced her weary weight up and forward, picking up speed quickly on the clear path. The familiarity of the trail gave her hope until she heard the thing exit the woods behind her. It tore down the path, its outward edges dragging on the growth to both sides. She hoped the obstruction was slowing it down. The trail wound along the edge of the marsh, tacking in and out with the softening coast and uneven tree line. The research cabin was less than a quarter-mile away and she moved at a dead run.

Her lungs burned with effort. Fatigue from all the running before, the panic, climbing. It all wore heavy on her body. She exercised and ran occasionally before encountering the genetically impossible chimeras in Boston. Since then, she ran regularly, taking kickboxing classes, dedicating herself to resistance training. Several extra pounds of fat melted away over the months to be replaced by lean muscle. For all her efforts, this was pushing her new limits. She didn't run on fear, but she heard its cheer and responded.

Another bend and she could see the station. *One-hundred yards*. It was a single story, small windows and deck, brown shingles, dark. Unoccupied. *Locked*. As she approached at a dead run, she had no idea what she would do here. She'd hoped the small structure, a tiny oasis of civilization, would provide the answers, but nothing obvious came to mind. *Fifty yards*. Along the side, there was a shed just large enough for the trash barrels and firewood. *Ten yards.* She vaulted onto it, scrabbled up the structure, and rolled on to the roof.

She lay on her back, gasping for air, and snapped off the headlamp. The first indications of bruises to come tingled all over her body, a cut across her palm burned, scratches tingled wherever her skin had been raked. The night sky, clear and full of stars, pitch black but for the lights of other galaxies, spread from horizon to horizon in a beautiful dark smear. The world wouldn't stop turning, no matter how hard she wished it. A cramp pinched her side.

Nora heard it coming. She didn't move.

It rumbled up to the side of the cabin and began circum-navigating it. Once around and a half more. Then it stopped. She listened, straining to hear it over the gentle whoosh of the surrounding grasses and the nearby ocean. Then the chitinous rasping, slurping sound, and the proboscis slapped over the side of the roof opposite her. She could see the stylet as it dug into the tiles of the roof. Smaller probes snaked out from the sides of the worm-like appendage, splayed again like a network of veins. She moved, shimmying to the center of the slightly pitched roof, noting that the thing couldn't reach dead center, thankful it had started probing on the other side of the building.

She cradled the capped vent in the center of the cabin's roof, trying to think. Probes slapped the surface of the roof again and dragged over the side. It moved and repeated the action, testing its way around the building, tasting for Nora. The whole structure shook once, then again more violently. Crunching and splintering sounded below before the building shook again. Then she realized what she was holding and pried the cap off, flinging it out into the night. It tumbled into the grass. The thing stalked off to where the cap had landed and probed the area. Nora, surprised that it had been distracted, pulled her attention back to the cabin. Shrugging out of her pack and snapping on her head lamp, she slipped through the hole and onto the rafters inside. From there, she surveyed the inside.

Tables, bunks, cabinets. Nothing obviously useful.

"C'mon, Nora, there's something here, there's gotta be something here..." *Electricity?* She had no idea how to harness that. Besides, this place was off the grid and—

The generator. It ran on fuel. There was fuel here. Inflammable fuel. And a wood stove for heat. Wood for heat meant tools to harvest wood.

Nora dropped into the space just as the thing slammed into the side of the cabin, shaking dust and bits of wood loose. She scrambled around inside, finding a jerry can of fuel. Two axes leaned against the wall, near the bathroom in the back.

The cabin shuddered again, and a door popped open. The thing shot probes into the room and Nora rolled backwards onto a table. It was too large to fit through the doorway, and it seemed bigger than before. She held still while its glistening reach slapped around the floor beneath her.

Nora clenched her teeth and hissed. "You're gonna burn, motherfucker." She popped the top off the can and dumped fuel onto the floor, coating the proboscis. A thin wave of fuel spread slowly toward the door. The thing's ersatz tongues twitched in the oily mess and the mass of it shivered. Nora capped the can, grabbed an axe, and prepared to break out a window once she made a few sparks from her magnesium fire starter. She patted her pockets.

"Shit. Shitshitshit..."

The striker was in her pack. On the roof. The worms retracted, returning to the monstrosity trying to wedge itself through the doorway. As fast as she could manage, Nora rolled off the table and pushed it to the center of the room, beneath the tiny vent. The disgusting sound of the thing's plates rasping open and the sloppy gurgle of probes being shot out made her squeak and jump on the table once again. The probes wrapped around the legs of the table and pulled.

As the table screeched a few inches across the floor, she pitched over, onto her back. A panic shot through her and she stopped thinking about what she wanted to do. She put the axe down and her fingers flew to her belt. She unclipped it and pulled the thick canvas through a few loops. The table screeched again, she was almost out of escape's reach and into the devil's coils.

One end of the belt went through the can's handle then back through belt loops. She stood, the table screeched again and she nearly lost her balance. The probes retracted with a hair-raising slurping sound as she scooped up the axe and jumped. The thing's tongues shot out again and slopped across the table, overturning it.

Nora hung from the rafters by the axe handle, the head of the tool hooked over the support beam. She hauled herself up with two overhand grabs and swung her feet up to the adjacent rafter for leverage. She managed to balance the axe on the beam and work herself around and on top. Then she unhooked the can and pushed it through the hole. The building shuddered again and there was a sickening crack followed by more splintering and the structure lurched. She clung to the rafters as a window shattered. A deafening crunch signaled the end of a load-bearing beam. The structure tipped precariously.

Nora slid the axe and can onto the roof and followed. She rifled through her pack for the fire starter. With the little tool shoved into a breast pocket, she unscrewed the cap on the can and crawled towards the edge of the roof. Everything was pitched in the direction she was heading, making a head-long plunge possible if she weren't careful.

The building shook again and it dropped another foot. The probes slurped out directly in front of her. She screamed and threw herself to the side as the central stalk of the tentacular nightmare slammed against the plastic jerry can. Branching probes snaked around her legs and she screamed again, struggling to hang on to the can and free her legs.

She thrashed backward, throwing herself wildly, letting animal instincts guide her, listening to fear. She spotted the axe and flailed in that direction. When she glanced down, she saw the stylet had embedded itself into the can. Fuel was leaking out of a gash in the side and the open spout, dribbling down the roof, over the edge.

Lucky.

Her fingers glanced off the fiberglass handle of the tool and she surged, stretching to wrap her palm around the base of the axe.

A sickening tug had her sliding down the roof, towards the thing. She dragged the axe, let go of the can and, using both hands, brought the tool around in a whizzing arc. The axe bit through some of the worm-like thing wrapped around her legs as well as the roof. Her slide stopped against the head of the axe. The smell of the ancient sea bit into her nose as sludge-like blood from the severed probes leaked. The stench burned through the membranes of her nose and into her brain. She kicked the axe free and slammed it down again. The probes slid away, dragging the can over the edge.

Nora dug the striker out of her pocket, her adrenaline fatigued hands shaking. A few jittery strokes and sparks lit the fuel. Flame charged across the roof and over the edge. When a burst of fire shot up, she dared to glance over the side. The thing turned in a circle, ablaze. Its claws clacked wildly as it spun, slamming into the cabin. The entire wall collapsed, and Nora struggled to find purchase, but instead found herself tumbling in the air, over the beast.

She hit the ground hard, trying to roll, knocking the wind out of her. A sharp pain bit her side and the muffled crack of something breaking inside her body filled her ears. The main problem surged back in as the thing began spinning in her direction. It was incapable of rolling or patting to smother the flames.

She lunged for the axe, inches from her reach. The handle slid into her palm. Her fear goaded her on, guiding her, screaming at her to press on. Ignorant of any pain she felt, Nora raised the axe two-handed and howled in senseless hate at this thing that had eaten its way into existence. As it turned, exposing back and sides, she slammed the sharp blade down, biting deep into the carapace.

Two things happened at once. The thing turned and pulled away. Nora wasn't going to let go of her weapon and it pulled her too. She sailed off her feet, helpless in the face of its strength, and tumbled into the grass again. She sat up and screamed in defiance at the creature, the heat of the fire around her.

It trembled in place and wailed in return. The scream warbled in pitch, matching her own, then ascended into a higher note. The edge of anguish shook her from the blinding rage she felt, her eyes locked on the thing as it collapsed, its spiny back plates, vibrating. Through the flames, she could make out a hazy shape. The back peeled open like a beetle unsheathing its wings, and a thin, darkened figure rose. An innumerable number of tiny tendrils buried in its flesh trailed behind to anchor the form in place. Membranes and probes penetrated and covered the body, its eyes, its head. One flail of its arms and the caul surrounding it parted. The figure sucked a wet breath and shrieked. The missing boy howled in pain and despair as he began to burn in earnest, inextricably tied to the thing beneath him.

Nora recoiled and crawled backward to the edge of the marsh where it met the sea. When her fingers touched the water, she turned and heaved, emptying her stomach, an attempt at purging the guilt and sorrow she felt watching this boy die a second, hard death. Pain shot through her side with every ragged breath as she clutched her ribs. The screaming behind her tapered until all she could hear was the crackling of fire and feel the powerful heat at her back. The marsh around her burned bright.

Thoughts of Joshua—that he'd been inside that thing all

this time—pushed disorienting waves of nausea through her. She could feel his notebook pressing into her thigh.

I will damn well finish this too.

❦ ❦ ❦

Errick Nunnally was born and raised in Boston, Massachusetts, and served one tour in the Marine Corps before deciding art school was a safer pursuit. He enjoys art, comics, and genre novels. A graphic designer by day, he has trained in Krav Maga and Muay Thai kickboxing.

His work has appeared in several anthologies of speculative fiction. His work can be found in APEX MAGAZINE, FIYAH MAGAZINE, GALAXY'S EDGE, LAMPLIGHT, NIGHTLIGHT PODCAST, and the novels, LIGHTNING WEARS A RED CAPE, BLOOD FOR THE SUN, and ALL THE DEAD MEN.

He has a short novel THE QUEEN OF SATURN AND THE PRINCE IN EXILE (April 2025 from Clash Books).

Visit erricknunnally.us to learn more about his work.

The Last Call of the Cicada

Gwendolyn Kiste

IT's the first week of June when the bugs are everywhere.

They're buzzing through the smoky air of our town, their wings limned in orange, their eyes burning red. The latest brood of cicadas.

I'm with my best friends Elle and Autumn when we spot the first ones in the trees. We're walking to the grocery store on a Tuesday afternoon, and the whole town is scowling at the sky.

"Disgusting things," says the store manager as we stroll in through the automatic doors and head to the produce section. There are three cicadas exploring the oranges and lemons on an endcap.

"I hope they find what they're looking for," I say, as we peruse the aisles for Jiffy cornbread mix and lunchmeat and boxes of red and green Jell-O.

"Nuisances," we hear the locals say as we pass by, and we're not quite sure if they're talking about the bugs or about us.

Me and Elle and Autumn, three best friends since we were in preschool. Three women who were never very good at doing what we were told. We're hanging over the edge of middle-age now, too old to be wives and mothers, too young to be gray-haired spinsters.

This town doesn't know what to do with us, as if it should do anything at all.

On our way out the door, brown paper bags in our arms, a cicada dive-bombs a nearby family. The young mother lets out an ear-splitting screech, and her little pink-cheeked daughter does the same, a pair of workers rushing to their aid, all of them convinced this is a crime against nature as opposed to just being nature.

"Nobody understands them," Autumn says as we cross the parking lot. "Those bugs just want to be left alone."

I can't help but grin. "Doesn't everyone?"

As we walk home, Elle starts murmuring an old song we made up back when we were just girls. Autumn and I keep pace beside her, humming along too.

🐞 🐞 🐞

Cicadas in the farmhouse, cicadas in the weeds
Cicadas in the sky, going where the moonlight leads
Cicadas in the treetops, peering in your room
All those shiny scarlet eyes, sealing up your tomb

🐞 🐞 🐞

The bugs are waiting for us outside after dinner. They dart past, that buzz in their bellies louder than thunder.

"I don't know why the locals are so surprised," Autumn says, as we laze in the backyard, a pitcher of lemonade at our side. "They should have known this was coming."

Elle and I laugh because she's right. Every seventeen years, the cicadas descend on our town. That's the rule, like it or not. All you needed to do was look at a calendar. It's the summer of 1982, and this Biblical plague is right on schedule.

I flip on the nearby transistor radio, a Todd Rundgren song crackling through the pale speakers, nearly drowned out by the bugs.

"I've always loved locusts," I say, curling up in an Adirondack chair.

"They're not technically locusts," Elle tells us, her lips pursed. "They're cicadas. There's a difference."

"I know that," I say with a grin. I just like to get Elle going. She's always the first one to correct us anytime we're wrong, a walking textbook of a girl.

Autumn, however, isn't like Elle. She doesn't care about facts and figures. She's more worried about what waits beyond this town, beyond this world. "Do you think the cicadas recognize our faces?" she asks. "Do you think they'll miss us after they're gone?"

I only laugh and shake my head. As for me, I'm just worried about paying the bills. I gaze up at the peeling shingles on the roof and the gutters that haven't been cleaned in more summers than I can count. Even so, I love it here—I've lived in this house all my life. My grandmother took care of me when I was little, and I took care of her when she was older, a lump of cancer gobbling her up from the inside out.

"You girls have fun," she told us on her way out, because she already knew what we would do. The three of us banded together and made a place of our own. A makeshift home for a makeshift family.

The sun dissolves in the sky, and it's time to bid farewell to the day. Upstairs, our narrow beds are lined up in a row like a cabin at summer camp. That's sometimes exactly how this feels. As though we never bothered to leave behind our favorite parts of growing up. And honestly, why should you abandon the best memories of you? Why is everyone so eager to end up sad and bored anyhow?

With the curtains drawn, Elle is asleep in an instant, but Autumn and I lie awake for a while, listening to the mournful melody of the cicadas outside.

"Can you hear them, Lara?" she asks, and I feel her watching me in the dark. "They're speaking to us. I think they've been speaking to us all these years."

I clutch the bedsheet tighter. "I wish I knew what they were saying," I whisper, but no matter how long I listen, I can never quite decipher the words.

The next morning, we realize we forgot the milk and butter, so together, we return to the grocery store. Things haven't gotten any better.

"Somebody stop them," a man with fright-white hair shrieks, as the cicadas fill up a row of overhead light fixtures, half the store going dark, our own personal eclipse.

A teenage worker tries and fails to shoo them away with a broom. He recoils, as a few tumble down on him. "They're tiny monsters," he calls out, his face scrunched up like a crushed cabbage.

"Yes, they are," I say to myself, and smile.

In the cereal aisle, all the boxes are bulging open, the cardboard stippled and shimmering with movement. Elle stands back, her arms crossed, her eyes wide, but Autumn isn't afraid, not of this, not of anything. She steps forward and tears open one of the box tops, dumping all the contents on the floor.

A hundred cicadas come crawling out.

The Last Call of the Cicada

"You can measure a life in cicadas," Elle says that night, as we watch them sneaking across the windows, blotting out the moon. Autumn and I know instantly what she means. Their life cycles take so long that by the time you see them again, you're basically a different version of you.

We met the bugs for the first time when we were six years old, all of us recent kindergarten graduates, our hair in pigtails, half-moons of dirt caked beneath our fingernails. The world was so new to us then, so ripe and ready for the taking. Everything seemed possible, even magic.

Especially magic.

"Do you think we'll ever learn to fly like them?" Autumn asked, and I only hoped one day we might.

🍂 🍂 🍂

Each morning at breakfast, Elle continues with her list of fun facts we never asked to learn.

"The cicadas live in the earth from the time they're larvae," she says, like she's reciting out of a textbook. "They're beneath us all the time, growing up and growing old."

This makes me smile. I've never spoken it aloud, but the truth is I admire the cicadas. The way they wait patiently in the dark, their filmy wings just waiting to unfurl.

There are other things happening in the dirt here. This is a town of coal mines, of hardhats and hard hearts, every face on every corner smeared with a long day's work.

"You girls will marry miners, no doubt," our school-teachers used to tell us, but we always just giggled, because we knew we'd do no such thing.

"I don't want to get married at all," Autumn said back when we were still in grade school, and Elle and I nodded eagerly next to her.

Ask anyone around here, and they'll tell you the coal mines will last for generations to come, but we're not so sure.

"Does anything really last forever?" Autumn asks.

After all, we can only empty out the earth for so long before it empties us.

It's Sunday night, and I lie awake in bed, listening to the high-pitched buzz outside, thinking how we're not all that different from bugs. Cicadas burrow into the earth like men. They just require no chisel or lamplight to guide the way.

The next day, we get back to work, toiling away at minimum wage. I wish we could live like cicadas, tucked quietly in the ground, but we make do, cobbling together a living, me as a part-time accountant, Elle selling Avon, Autumn picking up an occasional nightshift at the steel mill in the next town over. It's not much, but it's enough, the three of us surviving from one paycheck to the next.

Except for the times when a few of the locals decide to give us a gift we can't return. Graffiti on our garage. A broken window. A poison pen letter. It's always the same. We're the strange ones, the unwelcome ones, the girls who refused to grow up.

And in a small town, there's no greater sin than the sin of being different.

"They want to drive us out," whispers Elle, but I only grit my teeth.

"This is where we belong," I say, resolve hardening in my heart. We're not going anywhere.

But maybe they are.

❧ ❧ ❧

Cicadas never bite, cicadas never sting
Cicadas want to live their life, learning how to sing

The Last Call of the Cicada

But you sneer and snoop and swat at them, you just won't leave
them be
So now they're coming after you until they make you see

🍂 🍂 🍂

We're having lunch at the diner downtown when a dozen cicadas end up in the fryer.

"Call it the daily special," somebody hollers, but it mostly makes me sad those cicadas didn't live long enough to take to the sky and explore the clouds.

"Poor things," I say, as the waitress pours our coffee.

She scoffs at me. "You weirdos belong with those bugs."

I just shrug. "Maybe."

Autumn lets out a laugh, sharp as glass. "They certainly seem more polite than all of you."

The waitress snaps her tongue and shuffles on to the next table. The three of us lean over our steaming mugs, not saying much. It's always been this way. We're restless in spirit, our parents used to say, and restless in body. The girls no one trusts.

People don't trust the cicadas either. And this time around, I don't entirely blame them. It's a different swarm, and maybe they've got different intentions. They seem to be watching us a little more closely this time. They cover up windows and they cover up trees.

They seem eager to cover up the locals too. One of the cicadas pops out of the fryer, his eyes red and determined, and he goes right at the cook, digging into the soft flesh of his arm. There's a choir of screams and a splash of blood, and I sigh because with gore spewed all over the counter, we're never going to get our blue-plate specials now.

"They're not supposed to do that," Elle says blithely, as the cook flails through the door and scampers out into the street, the cicada still burrowing into him.

Autumn takes a sip of her coffee. "I don't think those cicadas like this town too much either."

The three of us sit back in our booth and grin, as one by one, the bugs materialize out of the fryer and the light fixtures and from behind the walls, all of them dead-set on the same thing: nesting in the locals' skin. Soon, the other patrons and all the servers are dashing out into the street, their flesh peeling away, their screams gone ragged, leaving us alone to enjoy our coffee in peace.

When we're done, we toss a two-dollar tip on the counter. It seems like the polite thing to do.

🐞 🐞 🐞

The cicadas came back for the second time when we were twenty-three. It was 1965, smackdab in the middle of a decade of chaos, a decade of change, the whole world ready to open up like the leaves of a lotus flower.

Except as it turns out, the promise of the 1960s never quite reached this part of West Virginia.

"The future always seems to forget all about us," Autumn said with a huff.

By then, we were all living in my grandmother's house, and so long as we locked our doors at night and kept our heads down, things weren't so bad. At least we were together.

"It could be worse," I said, as I gripped Autumn's hand, and she took Elle's, a daisy chain of girls.

And when the cicadas came, they taught us a thing or two. We learned how to listen a bit more carefully. We learned how to close our eyes and make-believe. Sometimes, we were even sure our feet would glide off the floor, just an inch, just enough it felt like flying, but nobody else ever noticed. The locals could peer straight through us and still not see what we are. The bewitchery of girls is taken for granted. It's a fault to be forgiven, a sin to un-teach in Sunday school.

Not that we're asking anyone for forgiveness.

❦ ❦ ❦

Now the cicadas have returned again, and we're forty years old. It's not really so bad, not really so old—there are probably decades left ahead of us—but it doesn't feel that way. Instead, if you listen to the sour-faced locals, the three of us are already superfluous, our lives as discarded as the cicada husks littering our yards.

"Isn't there somewhere they could go?" the older blue-haired ladies ask in their stage whispers while we pass by.

"Somewhere?" Elle looks at us, alarmed. "What does that even mean?"

"Like a convent," I say.

Autumn grunts. "Or an institution."

But for once, the locals aren't worried about us. They've got their sights set on the cicadas. There are gallons of bug spray and dozens of torches, ready to smoke out those creatures any way they can.

"They just don't get it," I say. "You can't fight nature."

But that's precisely what they try to do. All day and all night, they go after the bugs, burning down the trees where they sleep, slashing down the grass and gardens and wildflowers at every turn. Of course, it doesn't help. The moment the locals' backs are turned, the cicadas emerge from the ash. They fly up pantlegs and down blouses. They turn this town's flesh into their latest hiding spot.

You can't outrun them. They're everywhere at once, descending from the sky.

"It's nice to have friends in town," Elle murmurs. We lie together in the overgrown backyard, as the cicadas cover us like a warm blanket, their tiny legs prickling against our flesh.

"It tickles," Autumn says, and we all laugh together, because the cicadas don't burrow beneath our skin like they did to the others. They just keep enveloping us, twining through our hair, forming rings around waists, until we can sense the buzz of them deep in our bones.

"You belong here," I whisper, and I mean every word.

Cicadas in the sugar bowl and on your wedding gown
Cicadas dipped in flour, fried 'til they're golden brown
Cicadas in the boiling pot, cicadas in the stew
They're rising like the dead, just hoping to meet you

The summer's almost over now, and the cicadas should be ready to say goodbye, their bodies withering, their eyes closing forever. But this time around is different. This year, they're going to stay with us a little longer.

The streets outside are quiet. There's no more graffiti or broken windows or sneers from sour faces. That's because there are no locals left, not really. At least not anyone who doesn't have gashes on their skin, their eyes gone red as hellfire.

On Sunday morning, the three of us walk to the grocery store. Their heads down, mothers and fathers push their carts through the aisles, and little kids watch us with fiery stares, yet nobody ever utters a word.

"We didn't mean to do this," Autumn says, but the three of

us look at each other, silently wondering if that's really true. In a way, this is exactly what we meant to do for years.

As we pay for our groceries, the others gaze back at us, and when we start toward the automatic doors, they open their mouths, but all that comes out is a high-pitched buzz. It's a beautiful sound, the best sound, the only time we've ever liked what the people in this town were saying.

Back out on the street, our blood hums with the melody. It lives in us like a childhood lullaby. Elle begins singing the song we made up as children, all the verses about the cicadas, and Autumn and I can't help but join in, empty husks crunching beneath our feet, wings fluttering all around us.

And for the first time in seventeen years, it feels like we're flying.

🐞 🐞 🐞

Gwendolyn Kiste is the three-time Bram Stoker Award-winning author of *The Rust Maidens, Reluctant Immortals, And Her Smile Will Untether the Universe, Pretty Marys All in a Row, The Invention of Ghosts*, and *Boneset & Feathers*. Her short fiction and nonfiction have appeared in outlets including Lit Hub, Nightmare, Tor Nightfire, Titan Books, Vastarien, Best American Science Fiction and Fantasy, and The Dark among others. She's a Lambda Literary Award winner, and her fiction has also received the This Is Horror award for Novel of the Year as well as nominations for the Premios Kelvin and Ignotus awards.

Originally from Ohio, she now resides on an abandoned horse farm outside of Pittsburgh with her husband, their calico cat, and not nearly enough ghosts. You can also find her online at Facebook and Instagram.

Mightier Than Bullets

Laurel Hightower

"MS. BALLARD?"

Michelle's fingers traced the crumpled edges of the crayon drawing taped to the wall behind her desk. She tried to smooth them out, make the page lie neat and flat as it had at the beginning of the school year. She always started with such good intentions. Fresh supplies purchased with her own funds, new posters tacked on with clean putty. A months-of-the-year mobile constructed from odds and ends she collected over the summer, made with her sister's help while they drank wine and watched travel shows. On the first day her classroom shone with the same energy as the bright faces before her: slates as clean as the blackboard, shy smiles and quiet chatter.

"Ms. Ballard?"

Despite her best efforts, it always got away from her. The room, the lesson plans, her good intentions. The kids themselves. By this time of the year, with winter's slush still melting off and warm weather another month away, all of them, herself included, were as bedraggled as this wilted drawing. It hadn't faded, though. The waxy explosions of red and black were as vibrant as the day they'd been drawn. Her fingers drifted over the figures depicted there, feeling none of the horror the other teachers expressed when they'd seen the art she chose to display.

"Ms. Ballard, what should we do?"

Michelle turned to face her class, their eyes bright with tears, huddled together behind her desk. The lights were off, the heavy door closed and locked, construction paper covering the rectangular glass window inset in the top. It could have been nap time, but it wasn't.

"I'm scared."

The voice was small and high, and her gaze fell on Oliver. Small for his age, with big brown eyes and a head of curly, dark hair. He sat cross-legged on the solar system rug, smack in the middle of Saturn, his skinny arms wrapped around himself. She slid from her chair to settle on the floor with the students. She opened her arms and several of them climbed into her lap, including Oliver.

"I know, Olly. That's a valid feeling right now."

Shouting voices echoed down the hall, followed by scattered gunshots and screams. Michelle took a breath and held the children tighter. They were getting closer.

"Are you scared?" This from Madison, her red pigtails bedraggled around her freckled face.

Michelle smiled and nodded. "Yes. It's a scary situation, isn't it? But we've trained for this."

The children nodded solemnly. They'd hated the active shooter drills at first, frightened of the reality of them, of the realization that they had to huddle beneath their desks because other people had lost their lives. Kids, just like them, as young or younger. Coming face to face with mortality at the age of five wasn't something they should have had to do, but Michelle reflected that kids never had any choice in the matter of their surroundings. Almost worse was when they grew bored of the risks. The threat of death got old, became rote. Another shooting? Yawn. Happened every day, and it was hard not to settle into the idea that it was only a matter of time.

What made the drills easier were Michelle's own additions at the end. The Ballard Battalion they called themselves, the extra steps she taught them giving them courage and confidence some of their peers lacked. It wasn't enough to tell children not to worry when the truth of the world was broadcast on every platform. They needed ways to fight back, to feel prepared, and that was what she taught them. Which was why it had come down to this, she supposed. They were the only ones who could take their own power back. Something about this age was special.

"Now. Who should it be?" Her gaze traveled the haphazard circle of eighteen students, locking eyes with each of them before moving on. It was best if she could get a volunteer—making the choice themselves was part of getting their power back, and they'd be less frightened that way. But they were only kindergartners, so it didn't surprise her when no hands went in the air.

"Can't you do it, Ms. Ballard?" asked Oliver from her lap, his curly head pressed into her shoulder. "It's too big for us."

Several heads nodded, and Michelle's heart ached. She wished more than anything that it could be her, that she could take the place of whichever student was selected to save the rest of them. But it didn't work that way. She shook her head gently.

"I wish I could, kiddos. But the truth is, I'm too big for the job. It's got to be one of you. And I promise—I'll be with you every step." She wanted to go farther than that, to promise she would keep them safe. She hoped she'd be able to, that her own body as a shield would be enough, but there was no way to know for sure, and she wouldn't lie to them.

She gave it another minute—aside from helping the confidence of the kids, the process would be more effective if they chose it themselves. Just as she was about to give up and call on someone, a hand went up from the back of the class, by the papered over windows.

"I'll do it."

Michelle squinted in the dimness. "May? Is that you? What are you doing by the window, honey, come back over here, please. Someone could see you."

May shrugged but came to the rug. "No one ever sees kids, unless we're being bad."

Michelle pried a hand away from Oliver's death grip and reached for the little girl. "Hey, now. What do we always say in the Ballard Battalion?"

"No such thing as a bad kid," intoned eighteen voices as one.

"That's right. But you have a point, May. Grown-ups tend to overlook the smallest members of our society. That's a failing on *their* part." She raised an eyebrow. "But if we can use it to our advantage, let's do it."

May gave a single, solemn nod.

"Are you ready?"

May nodded again, the beads at the ends of her braids clicking together.

"You know how you'll do it?" the young teacher asked.

May smiled. "I had some really bad dreams last week."

Michelle liked that smile. There was an unholy glee to it. "Choose your weapons," she told the girl.

May didn't hesitate. She pushed off the rug and went to the supply cabinet behind the teacher's desk. Michelle always left it unlocked—she couldn't count on being able to get to it in time, in case something happened to her first. It was a harsh reality, but making kids dependent on the adults in their lives could sign their death warrants.

More gunshots sounded from the hallway outside, this time coming from the other direction. Michelle bit her tongue against the sour taste of fear. Either they'd gotten lucky and been passed by, or there was more than one shooter. She wanted to rush the girl, hurry her along in her choice, but eight years of dealing with kindergartners had taught her there was no point in trying, so she bit her lip and kept her shoulders loose, knowing the other kids were watching her for cues.

Finally, May reached into the back corner of the cupboard and retrieved her choice. Several of the kids gave a collective "oooo"—the paints were a bold choice, but May was a bold girl. She could do this, as long as Michelle bought her enough time.

May went to her desk first, but her teacher shook her head and called her over to the floor. "We need you out of sight. Find a spot with enough light for you to see what you're doing."

The other kids made space, each of them focused on the little girl's deliberate movements. Of all her students, May shone the brightest when it came to taking down an enemy. Her imagination was limitless, open and curious. Her creativity hadn't yet been stifled by years of formal education, and Michelle hoped things would stay that way. Her gaze traveled back to the pictures behind her desk. The ones May's parents had expressed concern about, called a parent teacher conference to determine how disturbed their child was. Clawed, hulking, hideous beasts peering from closet doors and under beds. Wounds open and dripping, blood pooled on the floor beside them. Figures splayed with x's for eyes and red tongues stuck out so there was no question of their status.

"What the hell's going through her head?" her mother had asked, fingers curled around a pendant at her neck.

"Why would she draw things like that if she wasn't...disturbed?"

Michelle could have told her it wasn't May who was disturbed. The girl simply found ways to cope in a hostile world that used her for political currency when it was convenient, and ignored her the rest of the time. The images that popped into the girl's head weren't a product of a disturbed mind, but a strong one, and Michelle had capitalized on it.

The argument had gone back and forth between the parents and the principal, each accusing the other of exposing the children to inappropriate media, but Michelle tuned them out. Her own brain was too busy turning the drawings around in her head, putting the pieces together. She'd hoped she'd never have to use the plan she'd developed, but here they were.

"Ms. Ballard? I need to see."

Michelle focused on the girl again, saw the page was already half-covered with something dark, scaly, and filled with teeth. The smell hit her seconds later—something like a zoo cage, an earthy, animal stink with a crust of rancid blood at the edges. The shadows by the window had grown deeper, shifting uneasily when she looked too close.

"I'll go," she told May, and eased the children from her lap. Several of them whimpered, clung to her legs and begged her not to. She removed their hands gently and shooed them to the rug. "You're all being very brave, and now it's my turn. I'll be fine."

She was far from sure of that, but it didn't matter. There had never been any question in her mind of how this would go down. She knew she would step into the line of fire for her kids, would open her arms wide for the bullets meant for them if it would get them away safely, give them a chance to choose their own paths. It didn't mean she wasn't afraid. Her heart beat fast, her palms sweating, and she tried to control her erratic breathing. She crept along the wall, pressed close, disturbing a layer of chalk dust as she went. The classroom had always seemed so small, far too tiny for the many bodies packed into it, but now it seemed to stretch on forever.

She reached the classroom door, still pressed out of sight, and held still at the sound of squeaking shoes pelting down the hallway. She peeled back the construction paper covering the window, scanning the empty hall, looking for a child on their own, but it wasn't a kid running down the hall. It was the shooter, and he saw her.

She wanted to scream, to back as far away as possible and huddle with the children, hoping the door and desk would provide enough protection. The bulletproof windows wouldn't open, and they were too strong to smash. Security protocol that only sealed in the vulnerable classes, trapping them with whoever managed to make their way inside the elementary school with no metal detector at the front door.

"Why would we need a metal detector?" the principal had asked. "These are kids, they're not going to bring weapons to school."

She hadn't been able to make him understand, to break through his willful blindness. And now they were here, in a hell she'd felt breathing down her neck for her entire career.

The shooter's gaze locked with hers, and he stood still, his rifle hanging at his side.

"Ms. Ballard? Please."

Michelle drew a shaky breath. "He's skinny. Kind of tall—taller than me, shorter than Mr. Porter. He has blond hair, shaggy on the top."

The rooms weren't soundproof—he heard every word she said, and had the snarl to prove it. He lifted his weapon and pumped it, baring his teeth. He opened fire at the door and Michelle cried out, barely dropping in time. The cartridge exploded through the door's glass, sending splintered wood and shrapnel flying across the room. The children screamed and scattered, pushing themselves to the far windows. All except for May, who sat with her paints, feverishly adding to her picture.

"A little more," she called, her small voice shaking.

Michelle closed her eyes and tried to picture the young man who'd just taken a shot at her, to see anything in her mind's eye beyond the impossibly dark barrel of the gun. "Uh, he has a mustache, but a really thin one. His face is broken out...spotty, red."

She threw a glance at the girl and saw her bent close to the page, her tongue sticking out as she painted.

The door frame shook, the handle turned one way, then the next, then another blast of gunfire came and metal flew. Something grazed Michelle's head and a searing heat rose from her hairline, a warm swell of blood rising in its wake. She started army crawling back to the kids.

"Tell me about the gun," called May, bent nearly double over her work.

"Pump action shotgun," answered Michelle, her words breathy and short. She couldn't get enough air in her lungs, and blood was dripping from her hair into her eyes. Had she been hit, or was it just panic? "Black, double barrel."

There was no need for more descriptors, not with these kids. They memorized firearm characteristics like other kids hoarded song lyrics or action figures.

A massive *boom* sounded and the door exploded inward, bashing hard against the wall behind. The nightmare sound of children screaming almost froze Michelle in place. She couldn't do this, couldn't bear witness, and for a long, shameful second, she hoped she'd die first.

"Thought you'd be the ones to get away, huh, bitch?" snarled a voice from the door. "Thought you'd be the hero and save all these little bastards?"

Michelle looked again at May. She was still working, her attention only on the reality she created on the page. Michelle took a breath and tried to catch that odor from before, the animal stench, but it was overwhelmed with the copper stink of her own blood. She rolled to her side, blinking up at the man who stood over her. Without the gun in his hand, without the hatred on his face, she'd have called him a boy.

It didn't matter. His age, his reasons, who he was. None of it mattered as soon as he picked up that gun, and she knew better than to try to reason with him. She just needed to buy them some time.

"These kids are more heroes than you'll ever be," she spat. "Take that gun and shove it where the sun don't shine, *bitch.*"

His eyes widened when she threw his own epithet back at him. "You fucking *slut.*" He pumped the gun again and stood over her, straddling her prone body.

She rolled on her back to meet his eye, to keep his attention on her. "The fuck would you know about it? You haven't seen a pussy since your mom's." She had a fleeting thought of the parent calls she'd get if any of the kids repeated her words, and had to stifle a giggle in spite of her terror.

"Cunt!" he screamed, and brought the stock down hard, but he telegraphed the move a mile in advance and Michelle rolled out of the way easily. She grabbed for his ankle, tried to bring him down, but it backfired when he fell heavily on her, his knee driving into her belly. It knocked the breath out of her and she curled on her side, gasping for air.

He got to his knees and reached for his gun.

"Yeah, you...better...get that gun. Closest thing...you've got...to a dick," she wheezed.

"Whore!" he shrieked, pushing the hot muzzle against her chin. "I'll paint these kids with your brains before I kill 'em, one by one."

"Wait," said a soft voice from far too close.

Michelle tilted her head back, blinking blood from her vision. "May, honey, get back, okay? Go where it's safe."

The girl didn't look at her, instead focused on the man with the gun, her painting in one hand, a brush in the other. "What's your name?"

The gunman sneered. "Fuck off, you little shit. Cunt in training, just like your teacher."

Fury rose in Michelle's chest but the little girl held her ground. "Please. I want to know—I made something for you."

The man panted, his snarl frozen in place but a look of puzzlement in his eyes. "Kyle," he said finally.

"Kyle." May nodded and dropped to the floor again, kneeling over the picture and applying the brush once more. "Kyle," she repeated slowly, forming each letter with painstaking care.

Michelle looked at the gunner, surprised to find him engrossed in the child's movements. In spite of himself, he was bending close, trying to see what was on the page.

May stood and smiled. "Kyle," she said once more, but made no move to hand the painting over.

The man sucked in a breath and raised his gun once more. "That's right. Remember that shit so when you're in hell, you can tell 'em who—"

His face froze, his words cut off, the last bit of breath escaping from between them with a small, undignified *poo* noise. Michelle tried to place the sound she heard next, a wet sort of pushing was the only way she could think to describe it. Kyle's eyes grew wider, his mouth moving soundlessly, his collared shirt pooching outward. Rending sounds followed and long, black claws ripped through the shirt from the chest beneath.

Michelle pushed away across the tiled floor, scrambling until she reached May and gathering the girl in her arms.

268

The creature in the shadows wasn't fully visible, but the stench was overwhelming now. A stink of shit and meat and blood and fear, all caked into dark, rough hair turning to scales at the thing's joints. It was tall, this creation of May's, towering over the man-kebab it had made.

"Kyle," it repeated once in a dark and grinding voice. The man screamed, until the creature popped his head into a toothy mouth and bit down hard. "Kyle," it said again, chewing the man's skull.

Michelle didn't bother trying to hide the sight from the children's eyes when they gathered close to watch. They'd seen worse. They'd made worse, and they likely would again. She'd shown them that nightmares could be weapons, that their imaginations could be turned against those who would harm them.

It didn't take long for the creature to eat its fill. There was plenty left for proof, when the time came, if not identification. "Kyle," belched the creature once more before climbing into the cupboard and closing the door behind it. It was the last time the man's name would be spoken. May went to her desk and bent over it, methodically painting over the name she'd drawn so carefully. There was no more Kyle. He wouldn't be politely cuffed and fed and spoken to with respect. He wouldn't have a chance to make an insanity plea or talk about his rough childhood. He might as well have never been, except for the bits of viscera and gristle left glistening on the classroom floor.

Michelle pushed painfully to her feet and limped to May, standing over her shoulder. "Beautiful job," she said, and held her hand out. The girl gave her the drawing, and Michelle went to the wall behind her desk, pulling off two pieces of tape from the dispenser. She gave the painting pride of place, and had May sign it in the corner. For it was the girl's name that would be spoken and remembered in the years to come.

As it should be.

❧ ❧ ❧

Laurel Hightower grew up in Kentucky, attending college in California and Tennessee before returning home to horse country, where she lives with her husband, son and two rescue animals, Yattering the cat (named for the Clive Barker short story) and Ladybug the adorable mutt. She definitely wants to see a picture of your dog, and often bonds with complete strangers over animal stories. A lifetime reader, she would raid her parents' bookshelves from an early age, resulting in a number of awkward conversations about things like, "what does getting laid mean?" She loves discovering new favorite authors, and supporting the writing and reading community.

Laurel works as a paralegal in a mid-size firm, wrangling litigators by day and writing at night. A bourbon and beer girl, she's a fan of horror movies and true life ghost stories. *Whispers in the Dark* is her first novel, though there are always more in the pipeline, and she loves researching anything horror related.

You can find her at https://laurelhightower.com/.

Loud And Clear

Max Booth III

LYNNE SHOULD'VE NEVER GOTTEN out the damn walkie talkie. Some things, they were buried away in boxes for a reason. Sometimes the past was meant to stay the past.

She wouldn't have even gone out to the old storage cabin if she hadn't been drunk, and she wouldn't have been drunk if she hadn't gotten into a fight with her sister. So maybe this was all her sister's fault, when you got right down to it. Except, the more Lynne concentrated, she couldn't remember who'd actually started the fight. Which one of them had initiated the yelling? Lynne was more of a yeller than Mindy, yes, but Mindy was a bona fide professional when it came to passive-aggressive comments.

When Lynne thought about it now, all she could remember about the encounter was how smug Mindy had been acting about her new granddaughter, about her whole perfect family, just rubbing it in Lynne's face like she was expecting her to be jealous or something. Then Lynne got a hold of Mindy's good wine, and things spiraled out of control from there, and instead of trying to sleep off the bad vibes she'd driven the three miles to her house and decided to explore the old cabin they'd designated for storage. See what kinda dirt she could uncover about her dear perfect sister, maybe. Who knew, right? The night was young, and all that bullshit.

Nobody lived on these campgrounds except for Lynne now. Mindy was close, their parents even closer, living in a small building just outside the camp's front gates. But, considering the size of these campgrounds, she might as well had been alone out here. At least that's how she often felt. For the most part, she was okay with it. Living alone was what she preferred. Maybe sometimes she got lonely, but so what? Who decided lonely was such a bad thing, anyway? It wasn't healthy, being surrounded by other humans twenty-four-seven. A person needed to be alone. They needed space to breathe, to think, to figure things out.

So what was she *figuring out* in the storage cabin next to her house? Lynne wasn't quite sure. She wasn't searching for anything in particular, really. She was drunk, but not drunk enough to pass out. The sorta drunk that unearths childhood grudges, that tricks your brain into fixating on the tiniest of unimportant details. But what, exactly, had led her *here*, to this storage cabin, of all places? Something Mindy had said earlier this evening, when they were in the midst of the argument that Lynne may or may not have started.

Admit it, Mindy had said, slurring her words, *you've always been jealous of me. Even when we were kids. First it was that Barbie head Grandma got me, and—*

—Like I could give a shit about some fuckin' Barbie head, Lynne had cut in.

Oh, please. Don't pretend like you didn't throw the biggest fit. Grandma got me that Barbie head and she got you that little stupid troll and you were so angry and cried so hard and Dad had to send you to your room until you could control yourself. You were jealous and you've always been jealous of everything that happens to me, including my family. Including my granddaughter.

And that was when Lynne said the words that had gotten her thrown out of her sister's house: *Why on earth would I be jealous over such an ugly little baby?*

Did she regret saying what she'd said? Only a little bit, but she was still drunk. Come the morning, she might be feeling different. It would take one hell of an apology to make amends with Mindy again, but Lynne knew she'd eventually win her over. They were twins, after all. One couldn't survive without the other, right? Isn't that what everybody always said, especially when Lynne and Mindy were young and swore they hated each other's guts? That was their mom's favorite way of making them patch things up. *Twins are one perfect being. Without both pieces in place, they'd just crumble.*

So, again, what did any of this have to do with why Lynne had decided to investigate the storage cabin at one in the morning? The fucking Barbie head, of course. She was confident it was somewhere in one of these boxes, and she was going to find it, then she was going to drive back down to Mindy's and shove it in her face.

Here, she'd tell her, *you forgot something.*

The plan, as far as her drunken mind could speculate, was flawless.

Now all she had to do was find the damn thing.

Instead she found something else. Something she hadn't thought about for years. Except, no, that was a lie. She'd been thinking about it every day for the last half century of her life.

There, wrapped in old newspaper at the bottom of one of the boxes her father had stored in this building ages ago—the walkie talkie.

The one she'd supposedly "lost" back when she was thirteen.

She'd known what it was even before unwrapping the faded newspaper. Subconsciously, perhaps she'd even known she would find it before stumbling in here tonight. Was it possible she'd used the argument with her twin sister as an excuse to come hunting for this walkie talkie? Lynne failed to think of any logical reason *why* the walkie talkie would've even been on her mind, except for the obvious reason, the reason that only seemed to emerge from hiding whenever her defenses were particularly loosened by alcohol.

In any case, she had found it. The walkie talkie. Who'd stuck it in this box, anyway? Not Lynne. She would've never thought to *wrap* it. Not at thirteen. Her father, then. And where on earth had *he* found the walkie talkie? She was sure she'd destroyed it, or thrown it away, something, *anything* to make sure nobody ever used it again. But what, exactly, *had* she done with it, all those years ago, she couldn't quite say—except for *something.* She'd done *something.*

And now here it was again. Nearly half a century later.

Jesus, she thought, letting its weight make itself at home in her palm, *how the time flies.*

She stood, intending on calling it quits. If her sister's dumb childhood toy was in one of these boxes, she would've come across it by now. Mindy herself had probably trashed it shortly after receiving the gift from their grandmother. This whole search had been nothing but a waste of time. All she'd actually succeeded in accomplishing was creating a total mess in the family's storage cabin. A good majority of the boxes had gotten completely torn open, which Lynne planned on blaming on the booze but in reality she'd just felt the need to *destroy* something, anything, it didn't matter what. The good thing about ripping cardboard was nobody could hear it scream.

Lynne turned off the cabin lights and headed across the gravel walkway to the house she'd claimed after her parents permanently shut down the campgrounds. Sometimes they asked her if she ever considered reopening the place and running it herself, and sure, sometimes she entertained the idea, mostly for her parents' sake. They'd spent so many years trying their best to keep it operational, and she knew they hated to see it so dormant in these later years of their lives. But the truth was, Lynne had no intention whatsoever of reopening the camp. She'd already worked enough in her life. Now it was time to enjoy retirement. Twenty-six years she'd spent in School Food Service, supervising a large urban central kitchen facility which prepared satellite breakfast/lunches for thirty-four elementary schools throughout Northern Indiana. No way in hell was she gonna start running a camp after all that. Some people were fed a lie early in life that told them they were meant to work a nine-to-five forty hours a week from the moment they were legally allowed to work until the moment they died. Some people, they went their entire lives busting their backs just because it was *expected* of them. They ignored any thought of retirement and continued until they dropped dead on the floor of their work station. And for what? The satisfaction of being a hard worker? Whatever that was supposed to mean. As far as Lynne was concerned, she'd served her time. Now she was out. She had a nice place to live. She had solitude. She had nature. And, if she ever felt too lonely, most of her family lived only a couple miles away. What more could a gal ask for in life?

She didn't realize she'd taken the walkie talkie with her until after locking the front door. She could have sworn she'd left it back in the storage cabin with the rest of the other crap. Yet there it was, still in her hand, like it was meant to be here. Like it'd been specifically designed for her palm. Like it had always been in her grasp, from the beginning of time until the very end. Like it hadn't just spent the last forty-five or so years at the bottom of an old, mildewy box crudely labelled "JUNK #7".

So what if she'd brought it into the house? It didn't mean anything other than she was drunk and not paying much attention to her actions. As if to demonstrate she truly wasn't bothered by this discovery, she shrugged and tossed the old walkie talkie on her couch and went off toward the kitchen in search for an abundant amount of H2O and perhaps some sort of sugary treat. She'd foolishly neglected to eat much during dinner tonight, choosing instead to consume as much wine as possible on an empty stomach. The consequences were beginning to announce themselves and she didn't want to be around when they finally arrived.

Despite practically turning the kitchen upside down, Lynne failed to recover any sort of dessert. No pie, no cake, no anything. Which was maybe for the best. Foods packed with that much sugar would not exactly do her any favors in the long run. Instead she pulled down an expired pack of saltines and munched on their stale saltiness. Although she was still plenty drunk, Lynne was responsible enough to predict she'd be grateful tomorrow that she had thought to pad her stomach lining with half a dozen crackers—and water. Yes. Lots of water. Guzzling it down like it was going extinct. She'd already peed three times since returning from the storage cabin, and she imagined many more trips to the bathroom would be in her near future before the night finally gave up the ghost.

Lynne collapsed into a kitchen chair at the oak table that'd been here since as long as she could remember. Her twelve-year-old yellow Labrador, Shylo, nuzzled his head against her shin and begged to be loved. So she sat there, petting her dog, chugging water, cramming saltines down her throat. Thinking ugly thoughts about her sister. Wondering if Mindy was still awake, too, also plagued by irrational rage. Maybe Mindy had every right to be upset with Lynne, in retrospect. She had, after all, called her new granddaughter "stupid". In Lynne's experience, you couldn't really go around insulting infants without pissing off at least a couple people. Had she actually meant what she'd said? No. Of course not. Had she meant to say something that would, without failure, make Mindy completely lose her shit? Well, yeah. Duh. And it'd worked, just as Lynne had known it would work.

Obviously she would've never said something so hurtful in front of the baby's mother—Mindy's daughter, Lisa. Lynne's whispered insult had been strictly meant for one set of ears. Only, the more Lynne replayed the evening in her head here in the kitchen back at her own home, the more she found herself doubting her grotesquely offensive declaration had come off as low as a whisper, after all. There had to be a reason why her throat was so raw, right? As much as she wanted to believe it, there had been no whispering at tonight's little family shindig. And Lynne could tell herself all she wanted that Lisa hadn't been in the same room as them during the incident, but she knew the truth. The real truth. Not the fabricated truth that copious servings of alcohol made easy to believe. Lynne hadn't just said what she'd said to Mindy. She'd said it to Lisa. She'd said it to Mindy's husband. She'd said it to Mindy's other children. She'd said it to hers and Mindy's parents. She'd even said it to the stupid goddamn baby.

The way they'd all looked at her afterward...

Jesus. Nobody had ever looked at her that way before. Not ever.

Well, okay, now that was another lie, wasn't it?

Jeremy had given her almost an identical look.

Before everything happened.

As it was happening.

It was sort of funny, sort of pathetic, pretending like she hadn't gone out to the storage cabin explicitly to find the walkie talkie.

Maybe she should've just headed back to Mindy's and apologized to everybody. It seemed possible that they could all still be there, attempting to recover from Lynne's inappropriate behavior. She could just imagine the kind of shit they might've been saying about her. How they couldn't understand why she never settled down and had a family of her own. How it wasn't healthy, spending so much time alone like she did. That kind of solitude was liable to make someone cuckoo for Cocoa Puffs. The same kind of bullcrap she was sure they always brought up when she wasn't around. Only now, thanks to Lynne's big dumb mouth, they had themselves plenty of justifications for their unwelcomed judgments.

Whatever.

This was all ridiculous, anyway. People Lynne and Mindy's age weren't supposed to get caught up in this sort of petty drama. So many of their arguments could be swept into a trash bin labelled "STUPID HIGH SCHOOL SHIT". Truthfully, there was nothing preventing her from calling up Mindy and apologizing except for her own idiotic stubbornness. All she had to do was pick up the phone and dial. Or, if for some reason making a phone call right then was too physically exhausting, then even a lousy text message would have at least done *something*. Any action—no matter how small—to show Mindy that she already regretted the direction tonight unfolded. The smallest of technological gestures to express even a *hint* of an apology. And yet…she couldn't do it. Her miserable goddamn pride, for whatever it was worth, wouldn't allow it. Refused to even seriously consider it. So instead of apologizing like any responsible adult would've done, what did Lynne do? She threw a couple more saltines in her mouth, peed one last time, then went off to bed. Maybe in the morning she would've managed to stomach the idea of lowering herself at her sister's feet and begging forgiveness, but not tonight. No way. She would have rather marched out into the forest behind her house and drowned herself in the river.

❦ ❦ ❦

The next morning she had completely forgotten about the walkie talkie, but—as it turned out—the walkie talkie had not forgotten about Lynne.

She was in the kitchen again, this time brewing a pot of coffee instead of popping open another bottle of wine. The way her head was feeling, she never wanted another drop of alcohol in her house again, much less in her stomach. She knew she should've eaten something of real substance this morning, but the only food that sounded even a tiny bit tolerable was another stack of saltines, except Drunk Lynne hadn't bothered leaving any extra for Sober Lynne. The bitch.

Okay, fine. A piece of toast then. After all, bread was bread—right?

It might've been strange to admit, but Lynne enjoyed the process of operating a toaster. Unlike most other devices in her kitchen, the toaster really made her *work* for her food. It wasn't as condescending as a microwave. With one of those all you had to do was press a button. Most kitchen appliances treated their users like they were toddlers—old enough to understand they would die without consuming food on a daily basis, but far too stupid to figure out the cosmic complexities involved in properly preparing a meal. There was a reason why toaster companies had to keep warning their customers not to poke silverware into the heater slots of their merchandise. The vast majority of human beings alive today were incredibly dumb. Not as dumb as those who had already died from toaster electrocution, but still pretty damn dumb. And besides, just because a certain person had not yet perished from a kitchen appliance-related death, it didn't mean they never would. In her years on this planet, Lynne had encountered her fair share of people—usually in line at the supermarket—who she suspected would eventually be eliminated by any number of inanimate objects specifically designed to provide ultimate consumer convenience. So yeah. She *enjoyed* using toasters. Specifically, the one she owned. It wasn't a fancy toaster, or anything like that. Nothing you'd see prominently advertised on an endcap at Bed Bath & Beyond. It was as simple as these machines could get. No extra doohickeys or anything like that. Completely bare bones. Unlike the other junk in her kitchen, handling it actually required a brief bout of physical strength. Any idiot baby could press a button on a microwave. But with a toaster, you had to press the levers down. And with Lynne's toaster, specifically, you had to hover over it the entire time and mentally time when your bread was thoroughly toasted, otherwise it'd just keep heating and heating until the bread turned to black ash and the machine itself melted into a hot, sticky goo.

Which was why Lynne didn't hear the walkie talkie at first. She was too preoccupied with ascertaining her childhood (and, now, *adulthood*) home didn't burn down on her watch, that all other background noise became a muffled drone, like it existed in a separate universe from her own, in a land above some distant, unknowable water.

But, eventually, even someone as determined as Lynne could not ignore the noise coming from out of the living room.

It sounded like only static at first, and she wondered if

she'd left the TV on some channel her property couldn't get due to the seemingly endless layers of trees surrounding every direction. Not that she tended to watch much television. Lynne preferred a nice thick paperback over the idiot box any day of the week. But sometimes, sure, she was too tired to concentrate on prose, and some mindless show on Netflix turned out to be exactly what the doctor ordered. But still. She didn't *think* she'd watched any TV last night. *Had* she? Admittedly, the whole night seemed a little fuzzy now, on the morning after, but it wasn't like she had gotten blackout drunk or anything. She would have remembered if she had watched something. So what the hell was that noise then? Last night she'd stumbled in from the storage cabin and marched straight into the kitchen with the sole intention of sucking on as many saltines as humanly possible. Then, at a certain point, she finally made it into her bedroom and passed out. The only time she spent in the living room after returning from Mindy's was when she had drunkenly tossed the forgotten walkie talkie on the couch.

"Oh," Lynne whispered, then flinched at the sound of her own voice bouncing off the walls of her empty kitchen. Even her dog jumped.

All consideration for the bread slowly heating in her toaster seemed to vanish at once. She spun away from the appliance and tiptoed toward the living room, straining her ears, half afraid that any sudden movements on her end would spook away whatever was at the source of the peculiar static noise, and half afraid her added presence would only make it more excited. Whatever *it* was…

Oh, don't be daft. You know damn well what it is.

Only one thing that she knew of could make that noise. That *specific* noise. A noise she hadn't heard in about forty-five years. A walkie talkie, yes, but not just *any* walkie talkie. A *Winslow* walkie talkie. The same brand she'd owned as a kid. The brand that surely no longer existed in the modern world. The brand of walkie talkie that she'd carelessly discarded on her couch last night before falling asleep.

And there it still was, waiting for her.

Emitting static because it was turned on, but Lynne couldn't for the life of her recall twisting the little POWER knob at the top of the device—and even if she *had*, there's no way in hell the batteries inside that thing wouldn't have rotted away by now. Not many things could survive half a century. Most *people* didn't make it that long.

Like Jeremy.

Yes. Jeremy.

Another prime example of something that should have rotted away by now.

And, yet, if that was true, then whose voice did she hear that morning, subtly rising from the distorted static of her old Winslow walkie talkie?

It wasn't a stranger, that was for sure. She couldn't simply dismiss the voice as some trucker passing through town, frequencies overlapping with each other. The voice on the walkie talkie, it was undeniably a man's voice. A man, whispering one word over and over, letting each syllable stretch out like it was his own form of screwed-up torture.

Her name.

The man was whispering her name.

And not just *Lynne*, either. No, he was whispering something she hadn't heard in years. Not since she was a child. The name her twin sister had come up with one day, almost out of the blue, and it'd landed so well all the other kids at camp started calling her it, too—until, eventually, like most childhood nicknames, it kind of just faded away forever.

Forever, or…until…

Until now.

When a man—no, a *boy*—who had been dead for forty-five years decided to start whispering it through a walkie talkie.

"*Lynnnaaarrrd...Lynnnaaarrrd...*"

Lynnard.

She stood over the couch, staring at the walkie talkie, listening to the dead boy's voice choke out of the tiny speaker, and wondered if she was still drunk from the night before. It seemed possible. She'd had a *lot* to drink. Certainly enough to cause a person to hallucinate spooky ghost voices. But she wasn't fooling anyone, including herself. Lynne wasn't drunk. Hungover, yes, without a doubt—but drunk? No. What she was hearing was real. Real, or...or what? Was she losing her mind? Insanity sounded a whole lot more plausible than whatever the alternative might have been. But how the hell would *she* know if she was going crazy? Wasn't that the whole thing about *Catch-22*? If you knew you were crazy, then you weren't actually crazy. Only those truly unaware of their brain's corruption could legitimately claim insanity—except they couldn't, not really, because if they *claimed* anything, then that would imply some sense of awareness, which would only cancel everything out. But that was just a book, right?

Yeah, just like the walkie talkie in front of her was *just* a walkie talkie.

Fuck this.

Lynne picked up the device and pressed the mic button. Waited a moment, trying to calm her heartbeat, then said, "Who is this?"

On the other end of the walkie talkie, the person started laughing.

"Who *is* this, goddammit?" Lynne said again. "This isn't *funny.*"

"Lyyynnnaaaaarrrd," the voice said, "your toast is burning."

She almost said *what are you talking about?* but then hesitated, focused on her house, finally accepting the scent that had managed to infiltrate her senses without triggering any internal alarms. The voice on the walkie talkie was correct. Her toast *was* burning. She raced into the kitchen and found a cloud of smoke drifting out of the toaster's heater slots. Jesus, how long had she even been away? Twenty seconds? No way. Must've been at least five minutes. Where the hell had the time gone? She pried up the toaster slots and two blackened oblong-shaped slices of bread reluctantly regurgitated from its fiery grin. The miniscule appetite she'd forced herself to work up this morning abruptly disappeared. She held the toaster above the trash can and turned it upside down, letting the two destroyed pieces of bread rain ashes into the nearly full bag. God, how could she be so *careless*? If the man on the walkie talkie hadn't warned her, who knew what could have—

But wait.

How the hell *did* he know her toast had been burning, anyway?

Unless he was in the house, too.

Watching her.

Smelling her.

Instincts guided Lynne across the kitchen, back pressed against sink, eyes on both entrances. If someone tried sneaking in here, they wouldn't go unnoticed. But so what if she noticed him? It wasn't like he would say, "Whoops, busted!" and turn back around. If someone had broken into her house, they meant to cause her harm. She needed to be ready. Ready for *what*? She wasn't sure. Ready for *anything*, she supposed. Which was why she slid open the drawer to the left of the sink and snuck out the largest butcher's knife within reach. She'd never stabbed another human being before, and didn't exactly feel any *desire* to do so in her lifetime—but there was something reassuring with her grip wrapped around the handle. Something that added a sense of confidence that hadn't existed until now.

"Who's there?" she shouted to the empty kitchen, and cursed under her breath. That's exactly what every woman in a horror story asked seconds before getting the opportunity to see the inside of her own guts.

From the living room, more laughter over static.

Lynne inched her away out of the kitchen, keeping her back pressed against various counters and cabinets. No way in hell was she going to let someone sneak up behind her. That's what *always* happened in the books she read. The characters get too careless. They think nothing bad can ever happen to them—until it does. Not Lynne. She was smarter than that. If someone wanted to try something with her, she wasn't planning on going down without one hell of a fight.

In the living room, she could make out what the voice was actually saying.

"You're not going to find me until I'm ready for you to find me," he said. "You're not going to find me until I tell you where I am. You got that, *Lyynnnaaaarrrd?*"

She picked up the walkie talkie and spoke into the mic. "Whatever you say, *Jeremy.*"

A long silence followed, and Lynne grinned. Clearly he hadn't been expecting that.

Egged on by the sudden adrenaline, Lynne continued talking, the whole time studying her own reflection in the blade of her butcher's knife. "Correct me if I'm wrong, *Jeremy*, but didn't I already kill you once?"

Another long silence.

Then the static returned, and he said, "You have no idea what I am now. You have no idea what I've become."

"You know where I live," she said into the mic, then twisted the POWER knob off and threw the walkie talkie as hard as she could against the wall and it exploded into a dozen fragments of jagged plastic.

❦ ❦ ❦

The last time Lynne saw Jeremy, they were both thirteen years old. The last time she saw him was also the last time *anybody* saw him. But nobody else knew that but her. She'd never spoken a word about what happened that night to another soul, which made it hard to believe someone might've been messing with her now. Only two people knew the truth about that night on the canoe, and as far as Lynne was aware, only one of them was still alive.

She locked every door in the house and returned to the kitchen, then pulled the table across the floor so she could sit at it without being vulnerable to someone attacking her from behind. Locking the doors wouldn't be very effective if the intruder was already in the house, but what else was she supposed to do? She wasn't going to call the police. What would she say? *Ah yes, I think the boy I murdered when I was a teenager has come back from the grave seeking revenge?* At least she'd finally have confirmation on whether or not she was mentally insane.

Well, okay, maybe *murdered* was a strong word, but what had happened on the canoe…it didn't exactly make her look like Little Miss America. Sometimes she was able to convince herself the whole thing had been one unlucky accident, but not for very long, because if it'd only been an accident, then how come she'd never told anybody about it? Why did she *hide* it? Because, despite what she liked to tell herself, Jeremy hadn't just *slipped*, had he?

She'd pushed him.

And when he tried climbing back into the canoe, had she reached out a hand to help him up?

No. Of course not. If she helped him, then she wouldn't be hearing fucking *voices* on a walkie talkie forty-five years later.

It only took one whack with the canoe paddle to keep him down. Then his head disappeared in the water, and the water turned a dismal red, and she never saw him again.

Nobody did.

She got a glass of ice water and sat at the kitchen table and waited for something to happen. After an hour, nothing did, and she had to pee again, so she decided to hell with it and went off to the bathroom. She brought the butcher's knife with her, in case the intruder was hiding behind her shower curtain. He wasn't. Another hour passed and she concluded that, besides herself and Shylo, the house was empty.

And besides, considering how calm Shylo had been behaving all morning, how likely was it really that someone had broken in? The first sign of an unsourced noise or weird smell and he would've started barking until his voice went hoarse. Which meant there was no way the voice could have known her toast was burning, right? Which meant...what, exactly? That she'd hallucinated the whole episode?

Out in the living room, the walkie talkie was still smashed to pieces. For a brief moment she feared it'd still be on the couch, perfectly intact. But no. At least she hadn't imagined *that*. And everything else? Had that also been real, or...?

She returned to the kitchen and called Mindy. It rang four times before she answered.

"Wow, you usually don't apologize for being an asshole until after at least twenty-four hours have passed," she said. "I'm impressed."

Lynne bit her lip. With everything else going on, she'd blissfully forgotten about last night's incident. "Have you noticed anything weird today?"

Mindy hesitated, then said, "Uh, weird like how?"

"I don't know. Just weird."

"Are you still drunk?"

"I don't know."

"Don't you have anything to say for yourself?"

Lynne knew the smart thing to do would have been to apologize, but she just couldn't. Not with the way Mindy was speaking to her. The smug tone she used while asking that last question. *Don't you have anything to say for yourself?* Lynne could just about vomit, and not only because she was still nursing the hangover from hell.

"No," Lynne finally said, "I sure don't," then ended the phone call. Next she called her parents, but all they did was give her a lecture about last night's behavior, so she found a quick escape route from the conversation. Whatever was happening, it was targeting Lynne and Lynne alone.

It?

No, *he.*

Jeremy.

Her mind kept trying to branch out into other theories, but her gut knew the truth. Despite how illogical it sounded, there was only one person who could've been on the other end of the walkie talkie this morning, and that was the person who'd drowned with the companion walkie talkie still clasped around his belt loop. She could sit around the kitchen all day trying to figure out how something like that could've been possible, and she'd always land on the same answer: *who fuckin' knows?*

One thing she *did* know, however, was this: if Jeremy wasn't in the house, then he was somewhere outside. Somewhere close. Watching. Waiting. What he certainly wouldn't expect was for her to come out and try to find him. Only a crazy person would do that.

"C'mon, Shylo," she said, tightening her grip around the butcher's knife. "Let's go for a walk."

* * *

It was a nice day out, which was a shame. Lynne was a nature girl, through and through, and she would have loved to enjoy such perfect weather without a nasty hangover gurgling around in her stomach. Plus the whole walkie talkie stalker situation going on. It was difficult to really let loose and participate in the joys of nature when your entire body and mentality were consumed by fear.

Shylo sprinted ahead, sniffing out the trail, and only then did it occur to Lynne that whatever out here trying to taunt her might also serve as a threat against her Labrador. But she couldn't just leave him inside by himself. It was better being out here in the open. If the shit suddenly hit the fan, there were plenty escape routes. He could pick any direction and take off without looking back. Unlike the house, where they were restricted by walls and doors.

Still, though. She made sure to keep calling his name, reminding him to keep within sight. The last thing she wanted was for him to disappear and then have to spend the rest of the day looking for him. She loved that dog more than anything else on this planet. And, she liked to think, he loved Lynne just as much, if not more. They'd lived together for almost twelve years now. That was a long time to be with someone, especially a dog. The bond between a human and dog was impossible to force. It came naturally, if it ever came at all, but when it did—oh, boy, there was nothing else like it in the world.

Lynne didn't have a plan, really. Her thought process hadn't extended past going outside and possibly coming upon her stalker by surprise. Plus, scary situation or not,

Shylo was still a dog, and as much as Lynne would have liked it, dogs could not exactly operate a toilet. He'd have to do his business sooner or later.

If something *did* happen, at least she still had the butcher's knife. Could she actually *stab* someone, though? If you'd asked her yesterday, she would have said *no way*. But now? Now she didn't *what* she could or couldn't do. Maybe nobody did—not until the opportunity presented itself, and you either did what it took to survive, or you didn't.

Lynne wondered if the man was watching her now. Hidden somewhere in the trees, studying her every movement. Was he confused that she hadn't called the cops? Had he expected her to stay hidden inside all day, like a scared little woman? Fat fuckin' chance. Let him try something. Just let him try.

He wasn't going to sneak up on her. Not with Shylo nearby. Nothing went past her dog. She just hoped this guy didn't have a gun. Then she wasn't sure what she'd do.

This guy.

Thinking like it's some stranger again.

Like it wasn't someone she'd already killed once.

Which meant…what? That he was a *ghost*? Ghost didn't need guns. Could dogs sniff out spirits? Chills went down her spine, realizing she had no goddamn idea exactly what they were dealing with here. She was hit with an irrational urge to scream Jeremy's name. To taunt him into showing himself. But if he was something beyond human—which, the more she thought about it, was the only logical explanation, as illogical as that sounded—then maybe she wasn't ready to confront him just yet. Maybe she needed a little bit more time to prepare herself.

Before going back inside, she collected the SD card from a nearby trail cam that she'd hooked up to a tree a few feet away from her preferred hiking path. She doubted she'd caught anything incriminating, but hell, who knew? Today had been full of surprises so far, so why would they suddenly stop?

❧ ❧ ❧

Once, a few years back, she'd caught a cougar on one of the trail cams. Since then, every time she plugged an SD card into her computer, she experienced a confusing mix of both hope and fear that she'd see one again. Hope because it'd been the most exciting discovery of her life. A real-life-honest-to-god *cougar!* Her nephews and nieces had begged her to let them see the photos any time they came over. Not just any person caught a *cougar* on their trail cams. But Lynne had, and yeah, she was *proud* of what was—realistically—pure luck. But at the same time, she was also terrified of finding another one, because that would mean it wasn't just some... fluke, that cougars actually lived on her land. The same land she frequently hiked through with Shylo. It would make her entire property completely unsafe. What would she even *do* with a back yard full of cougars? Call animal control? They'd probably tell her to piss off. No way they got paid enough to handle freakin' *cougars.*

Until today, she couldn't imagine finding anything scarier on her trail cam than another cougar.

Now she could think of something a lot worse.

Now she was praying for something as pedestrian as a lousy old cougar.

Within the last twenty-four hours, her trail cam had snapped nearly a thousand pictures, which was not unusual. It was motion-sensored and programmed on rapid trigger, so if *anything* moved in front of that screen, the device would go off like a machine gun.

The first couple pages of pictures contained nothing

more than random wildlife. Predictable animals like birds and squirrels. The occasional fox. Some turkeys.

But the last hundred or so pictures?

Something different.

Something bigger than the average animal.

Standing straight on two legs.

Staring directly at the trail cam.

Something that wasn't an animal at all, but a man.

Long, thick strands of hair hung from his face, down his head, over his body. The word *caveman* shot to the front of her mind, but she couldn't process what it meant. Not yet.

In every photo, the man's right arm was raised. Palm pointing toward the trail cam. And each photo, the hand was in a slightly different spot.

Waving.

He was waving at Lynne.

And, as the photos neared the end, behind that bush of facial hair, the faint shape of a smile started to emerge.

The man was grinning.

Seeing what he looked like, she had no idea if he was Jeremy or not. Before uploading the SD card, she'd possessed the utmost confidence in her theory. But this man…he looked like nobody she'd ever seen before. Of course, the last time she'd laid eyes on Jeremy had been forty-five years ago. They were both thirteen. She didn't exactly look like how she looked back then, either. But she also hadn't *died* like Jeremy had.

Unless…

Unless he never died.

On the last photo that he appeared in, the timestamp said **1157**. Which was less than fifteen minutes ago. After collecting the SD card, Lynne had gone straight to her computer and inserted it into the drive.

Meaning what?

That the man had been standing in the same spot Lynne stood in, only minutes apart from each other? *Seconds*?

How had she missed him?

And, more importantly, how had *Shylo* missed him?

❦ ❦ ❦

There was a hunting store a few miles down the road. Lynne never paid it much attention until the day she decided to catch the man in the woods. The man who'd been watching her, every day, waiting for...what, exactly? Lynne didn't intend on letting him show her. Not the way he wanted to, anyway. When you were a woman who lived alone, in the middle of nowhere, you couldn't afford to take those kinds of risks.

So she went to the hunting store.

She didn't know what she wanted to buy. Sorta figured she'd know it when she saw it. Roaming down the aisles, she giggled to herself, imagining how the clerk might've reacted if she asked him about the best tools available to catch another human being. Would he have assumed she was joking, or would he have fled to the back room and called the police?

If she'd explained the situation to someone else, that might've been their first question, too: Why *not* call the police? Why deal with this yourself?

And her response probably wouldn't have made much sense to most people—that she preferred to handle things by herself, that she chose to live out here in the woods for a reason. That it wasn't the cops' business what happened out here. All she needed was some state trooper snooping his nose around these parts, unearthing secrets meant to stay buried. Like hell. So what if there was a man in the woods? If Lynn couldn't handle something like this, then what was she even doing living out here on her dad's old camp-grounds?

And besides, if the man really was the person she suspected, then it would do her no favors to round up the law. Otherwise she might end up being the one leaving the campgrounds in the back of a squad car.

She could have spent all day at the hunting store, trying to make up her mind, but in the end she decided to keep things simple and purchased the following items: one bear trap, one canister of pepper spray, one machete, one pair of handcuffs, and several lengths of rope.

The cashier gave her a weird look while ringing up her order, so she added a pack of bubblegum to throw him off her scent.

"You planning on hunting someone?" the clerk asked her, and she almost had a heart attack.

"What?"

"You know," he said, then scanned the store real quick to make sure someone wasn't eavesdropping, then leaned in and whispered, "they say man's the most dangerous animal to kill."

"Oh yeah?" Lynne said, not sure why she was entertaining someone who was clearly a psycho, except for maybe the fact that it was like talking to her own reflection.

The clerk nodded. "They say, when you kill a man you can see his soul drift out of his body. Usually through the mouth, if it's open."

"Who says that?" she asked.

And he smiled. "*They.*"

"Oh." She waited for further explanation, and when he didn't give one she decided it was best to get the hell out of this place, so she swiped her debit card and booked it through the exit without bothering to wait for the receipt.

❦ ❦ ❦

Instead of driving home right away, she pulled into a fast-food drive-thru. Her stomach still felt like shit from the night before but she also hadn't eaten anything since waking up. With everything going on, she'd forgotten about one of the most basic necessities of survival: food. She would have preferred going inside a coffee shop or something, but didn't feel comfortable leaving Shylo in the car that long. It was bad enough he'd stayed outside while she shopped in the hunting store.

So she got something in the drive-thru and then found a nice isolated spot in the back of the parking lot. She put her car in PARK and turned up the radio, listening to one of the classic rock stations that played the same seven songs on a loop. Most of these songs she could remember coming out when she was in her twenties or thirties. How were those considered *classics*?

The world moved on, with or without you.

The songs you grew up listening to became classics and then, before you knew it, those songs were replaced by other songs that didn't come out until after you graduated college. Eventually those would be replaced, too. Everything was replaced. She ate her fast food and pondered the reality of an uncaring universe. She loved nature, but also knew if she ever died in the woods behind her house, nature would not hesitate to feed off her decomposition. That was the way the world worked. In the end everything was compost.

She didn't realize she was crying until the tears were rolling down her face. All she could think about was the boy she'd left to die forty-five years ago. How quickly the rest of the camp had moved on without him. How, over the years, everybody forgot about him except for his family, and she was sure even *they* had eventually moved on. You had to, after so long. Nobody knew the truth. How could they? How could anyone? She'd never uttered a single word. All these years, and she'd kept it a secret. She'd swallowed the truth and the truth had been rotting away inside her stomach ever since, poisoning anything it came in contact with.

And what *was* the truth, anyway? That Mindy was correct? That Lynne *was* jealous of her? That she'd always been jealous? First the stupid goddamn Barbie head, sure, but had it stopped there? Of course not. The jealousy only got worse as they got older. When she found out Mindy and Jeremy were dating, Lynne would've turned green if she wasn't already so red with rage. Mindy had *known* Lynne had a crush on him, but did she care? Ha! When had Mindy *ever* taken Lynne's feelings into consideration? When had she ever truly given a shit about anyone besides herself?

So yeah. Fuck it. Lynne took Jeremy out on the lake. She told him to hold on to the companion walkie talkie, told him she'd radio when everybody else was asleep and it'd be safe to sneak out. She pretended to be Mindy. They pushed the canoe down the large concrete ramp in the middle of the night and drifted out into the water. Barely made it five minutes before he caught on, realized who she really was. He freaked out. Started calling her a psycho.

What does it matter? she asked him. *Don't we look alike? Isn't that enough?*

And what had that little ghoul done?

He'd laughed.

Laughed right in her face.

Said she was nothing like her sister.

Said she never would be.

Nobody ever saw him again, except for Lynne, who encountered him in her dreams every night after the incident.

Replaying the moment over and over.

Every time, smacking him in the face with the canoe paddle.

Watching the blood turn the lake red.

Then paddling back to camp, sneaking into bed and pretending like nothing happened.

She'd even helped post the MISSING PERSON posters around town.

Nobody'd ever accused her of anything.

Nobody so much as *suspected*.

Not even Mindy.

And now the little shit was back. She didn't know how, but he was back. In a way, she'd always known he would return. Something like what she did, you couldn't just not face consequences.

The past always caught up with you, didn't it?

And now here it was, finally ready to punish her.

Ready to make her suffer.

What the hell was she supposed to do? Kill him all over again? And then what? Spend the rest of her life continuing to feel guilty?

No.

She couldn't do that.

She *couldn't*.

She didn't *want* to kill anybody. She never did. What had happened…it wasn't her fault. It was an accident.

Except, no, it *was* her fault.

She'd spent the last half a century pretending like she wasn't truly responsible, and look at how that had turned out for her.

Running away from her actions.

Acting like it'd been out of her control.

No. Fuck that.

Lynne was tired of running away.

Lynne was so goddamn tired.

She put her car in DRIVE and pulled out of the parking lot. She was going to put an end to this once and for all. She was going to do what she should have done in the first place. She was going to *fix things*, as much as she could fix them.

She drove right past her own driveway. If Jeremy was waiting for her, he could keep on waiting. There was something far more important to take care of first.

Down the street, she pulled up in front of Mindy's house and sat there behind the wheel, trying not to cry, but it was useless. She was a mess of tears and snot and they weren't going away any time soon. She wiped her face with a napkin from the fast food bag and got out of the car. Shylo plopped out with her and followed her up the porch. She was going to be able to do this alone. Not without her dog. Not without her good boy.

Lynne knocked on the door and together they waited.

It was time to make amends.

❦ ❦ ❦

Max Booth III is a writer, publisher, editor, podcaster, and indie bookstore owner. They are the co-founder of Ghoulish Books, a publisher/bookstore hybrid specializing in horror.

Born and raised in Northwest Indiana, they now live in San Antonio, TX.

Find their work at www.TalesFromTheBooth.com.

You can also visit them at their bookstore: Ghoulish Books, 9330 Corporate Drive, Suite 702, Selma, TX 78154.

Better by You, Better than Me
Rebecca Rowland

THEY DIDN'T DISCOVER the body until the middle of the morning. 9:25, to be exact. In Todd's estimation, that would have been the beginning of second period, his Contemporary American History course. It was a class populated mostly with apathetic seniors who hadn't been quick enough on the draw to make it into Jessica's Psychology course or the other, more interesting electives, like The Law and You, The Economy and You, or even the nebulously narcissistic class titled simply, America and You.

The police would be interviewing him, he was certain. That's what they did when a person was found dead: they questioned the last individual who'd seen the victim. *Victim.* Was that the appropriate term in a suicide? Todd didn't think so. In any case, he'd be questioned, and Todd wasn't sure he had the energy to conjure up a sufficiently believable countenance of concern. He hadn't shed a tear when Jessica sat across from him at the restaurant table the evening before, sobbing quietly into her dinner napkin. He hadn't even blinked. By the ripe old age of 46, Todd had taken his capacity for empathy, given it a good shag against the wall, then put it in a cab to go home, never to be seen again. He was fresh out of fucks, as the saying went.

Just moments earlier, Todd had poked at the soggy manicotti plate with his spoon, his eyes unable to flit away from the water stain on the utensil's stem. Jessica was talking to him, chattering on about some godforsaken nonsense like she always did.

"I caught that old movie *Tarantula* on tv last night," she said, twirling her fork so that it spun a rapidly growing football of linguini on her fork. "That scene where the big spider is in the fish tank of the lab? Scared the bejesus out of me." She shoved the pasta into her mouth, a dribble of olive oil leaking onto her lower lip.

Todd watched her masticate her food, the globule of grease inching toward her chin until she flicked her tongue out to catch it. Before she could swallow, he placed the spoon carefully on the edge of his plate and told her: simply but firmly, so that there was no mistaking his declaration. Jessica's mouth paused in mid-chew. A millisecond later, it distorted into a quiet wail.

"Is everything all right?" The waiter appeared out of nowhere, his eyes focusing simultaneously on Jessica and on the growing number of nearby patrons staring at their table with concern. "Perhaps Madam would like…" He gestured toward the back corner of the restaurant, the dark hallway leading to the bathrooms.

Todd reached over and placed a cold hand on Jessica's forearm in an awkward tableau of mock concern. "Madam is fine, thank you," he said. "I'll take the check when you're able."

When the server disappeared, Todd moved his arm and edged his chair closer to Jessica's. Her face was buried in the shroud of polyester table linen she clutched tightly in both hands. Todd leaned his head so that he could whisper in her ear. She wore a perfume he'd never smelled on any other woman, a mixture of crushed funeral flowers and leather. She smelled like a new car: a dead hooker in a new car.

"You want to know why? Shit like *this* is why," he hissed. "Pull yourself together. We're leaving."

And that was that. Jessica said nothing on the ride home, just stared blankly out of the passenger window, her swollen red nose glaring back at her from the side mirror. When Todd reached her house, she opened the door, walked purposefully across her front lawn, and disappeared into the darkness of the enclosed porch without a word. Todd did not wait to see her inside.

"Jackson says it was hanging." Terri, the French teacher whose last name always escaped Todd, lit a cigarette and leaned backwards into the corner of the well-worn couch. She stared at Todd for confirmation. It was lunch period, Todd's preparation block, and he eyed the microwave on the counter nearby, waiting for his leftover manicotti to reheat. The space-aged oven had been a recent acquisition for the teachers' lounge. Todd managed to survive most of the 80s without one at home and still relied on tin foil and a wall oven to warm up food, but truth be told, he usually just ate it cold from the refrigerator.

"I heard," he replied. The microwave emitted a long beep and Todd opened its door to retrieve his dish. He didn't want to talk about it, but the news was inescapable. He and Jessica had been openly dating for months; of course the schaden-freude junkies would be coming out of the woodwork to poke their forks in him.

Terri blew a billow of smoke in his direction. "So?" she prompted. "What gives?"

"You're such a goddamn vampire." The union steward with the ponytail sat down next to Terri, a pile of disheveled mimeographs on his lap. "Leave the man alone. This is a sad day."

Terri pulled a long drag. "Check her album collection. I'm guessing she was a Judas Priest fan?" She tapped her ash into a ceramic tray on the rickety coffee table. The cigarette was extra-long and skinny: one of those Virginia Slims, Todd thought. He concentrated on cutting up his pasta with the edge of a plastic spoon and did not look up, even as the tobacco cloud mingled with the steam drifting from his lunch.

Ponytail clucked his tongue. "Too soon," he chastised.

Terri stretched her arms wide. "That song they're being sued over?" she continued. "I've listened to it. I'll admit: it's catchy." She was still holding the cigarette, its smoldering tip hovering dangerously close to the couch covered in Midcentury Modern upholstery. Todd wondered if the fabric was flame-retardant. He doubted it. "Not sure it causes people to off themselves, but who the hell knows what subconscious commands they slipped into the music?"

Ponytail cleared his throat. "*You're* still here, aren't you?" he said, the impatience heavy in his voice. "Besides, the case was dismissed. It was on the news last night."

Terri rolled her eyes and took another drag. "Doesn't mean they're not guilty. Or won't be punished." Todd could feel her staring at him. He continued to focus blankly on his plate, refusing to give her the satisfaction of his annoyance.

It wasn't until he'd eaten the last mouthful of his meal that he realized the room had gone quiet, the only sound the incessant hum of the nearby refrigerator. Todd looked up, and his eyes drifted immediately to Terri.

Only, she wasn't Terri; at least, not the Terri he'd seen five minutes earlier. This Terri looked an awful lot like Jessica, and she stared at him, unblinking, from the far corner of the couch. Her face was bloated and had flushed an unnerving purplish-blue, a hue of insidious rot. The lids of her large brown eyes were pulled back in a menacing yet surprised expression, her garishly lipsticked mouth gaped slightly open, and her tongue, an alarming shade of bright red, peeked out from between her teeth, grazing her lower lip.

On reflex, Todd turned away and shut his eyes. A second later, the vapid banter of his colleagues resumed around him, and when he opened his eyes again, Terri—old Terri—was leaning forward to stamp out her butt in the ashtray. Ponytail had disappeared. Todd's takeout container lay slightly askew in his lap, leaking a small bit of leftover white ricotta onto his khakis. Had he fallen asleep?

He collected his belongings and dumped his trash, not bothering to say goodbye to Terri who had already moved on to gossiping with a math teacher. The hallway was surprisingly empty, a ghost town of flickering fluorescent bulbs and scuffed beige tile. He reached his classroom and peered through the chicken-wired window. It was empty save for four individuals, three huddled closely together by the windows and the last sitting perfectly still in the row closest to him.

Todd opened the door slowly and slipped inside. As he did, all four women turned to face him in unison. Only then did he recognize their faces. "Mom?" Todd croaked hesitantly. His mother died when he was in junior high, a single car crash on her way home from work after a shortcut through the local pub. By the time the firetrucks arrived with the jaws of life, her pale blue Volkswagen Beetle had fervently fucked a large oak tree, the orgasm of twisted metal, blood, and Mom parts shot in a load along the edge of the road and into the brush.

And yet, there she was, still wearing the polyester pant suit she'd sported in the giant portrait displayed next to her closed coffin at the wake.

Stranger still were her two companions. He hadn't seen them, hadn't heard head nor tails of them in, what—ten years now?

"How—" Todd rubbed his eyes, then leaned forward and rested his palms on his thighs. He looked back at the visitors. The three women at the windows were smiling, his own private episode of *This is Your Life:* his ex-wife, dead mother, and estranged daughter all lurking in this makeshift green room, waiting for the chance to pop out and surprise him to the cheers of tinny applause.

Closer to him sat Jessica, her face purple and bloated, slumped in the audience's front row, slapping her two hands together in mock appreciation. The frayed ends of the rope around her neck bobbed in time to her clapping. He was close enough to see that the whites of Jessica's eyes had been swallowed by broken capillaries, her brown irises now rimmed in thick halos of pink and red. As she continued to stare at him, her mouth remained agape, a bright red tongue lolling lazily atop her bottom lip.

Todd shut his eyes again. "This isn't happening," he said out loud. His voice echoed slightly. "This is stress. A stress response, some sort of panic attack." He'd never had a problem with anxiety before—nothing formally diagnosed, but hell, he was rounding the corner toward fifty. He could feel his body dismantling bit by bit. Surely his mind could be affected as well.

When he opened his eyes again, Jessica had moved. She was no longer lackadaisically lounging in a student desk; she was standing directly in front of him, the tip of her nose only inches from his chin. He could smell her perfume again. Dead hooker, new car.

Dead girlfriend, *new car*, he thought, and chuckled slightly at this.

"Dead *ex*-girlfriend, you mean," Jessica corrected. Her

mouth formed the words, but the voice that resonated sounded wet and gravelly as if swimming through chunks of spoiled milk.

Todd steeled himself. "I don't know what's going on here," he said, the nonchalance in his tone taking even him by surprise, "but you aren't welcome here." Jessica did not move. He swallowed hard. "You need to leave."

The three women stood silent on the other side of the classroom, watching him intently. Jessica seemed to consider his command, but after a long moment, her expression changed. Her mouth opened wider, revealing more of her tongue, and for a moment, Todd thought she might be preparing to cry. Instead, she laughed. Not a guttural chuckle or a half-hearted snicker but a full-on, hearty cackle, her body convulsing with the sheer intensity of it.

Todd turned to leave, but he was yoked back. Jessica had lassoed the end of her rope around his neck and was quickly securing it into a slipknot. As Todd leaned away from her, the rope tightened, the scratch of the sisal pricking and burning his skin. He instinctively clawed at his throat to loosen the noose just as Jessica kicked him, hard, in the back of his knee, sending his body crashing to the linoleum floor in an awkward heap.

❦ ❦ ❦

Todd awoke on a cot in the nurse's office, his head fuzzy and thick as a square of shag carpet. A student, her face flushed with fever and her mouth crusted with dried vomit, peeked from behind the curtain between them, then darted out of sight. He ran his hands over his face. Above him, an exposed pipe ran along the drop ceiling tiles. Speckled memories of what transpired swam up to the surface, gasping for air, and he touched his neck, unnerved to find that the area was indeed sore.

The face of Miriam, one of the guidance counselors, appeared in the space where the student's had been. "How are you doing, Todd?" she cooed, less like a concerned colleague and more like a dog catcher luring a rabid hound from its hiding place.

Todd sat up and swung his legs onto the side of the bed. In response, the room tilted on its axis and a searing pain shot through his skull. "Fine, fine," he said, trying his best to sound professional, business-like. Nothing like passing out in your classroom in the middle of the day to instill confidence in one's abilities as an educator, he thought. Had one of the administrators found him on the ground? Worse yet, had the students? "I have to get back to class."

Miriam slid the curtain sideways a foot. The child who'd spied him earlier was nowhere in sight. "Jackson has people covering your classes for the rest of the afternoon. Nothing to worry about." She sat daintily on the edge of the mattress, maintaining a clear physical distance from him. "You've experienced a major trauma, Todd. Your physical response is certainly normal." She picked at imaginary pilling along the bed sheet. "The police arrived a half hour ago. They've been speaking to the admins and want to talk to you, but if you aren't feeling well—"

Todd pressed his feet into the floor and slowly rose to standing. "I'm fine." Around him, the crispness of his surroundings softened slightly as if someone had lowered the lighting to a more romantic wattage. He blinked rapidly, trying to clear his vision, then sat back down, willing the room to right itself again.

"Mr. Osbourne," the police officer materialized without warning at the edge of the opening in the curtain. "I understand you had a bit of a fall earlier today."

Earlier today? Todd thought. *How much time had passed since he was in his classroom?* He frantically scanned the space behind the policeman but did not see a window. To be fair, the officer was as wide as a Mack truck and it was difficult to see anything but a wall of dark blue uniform sandwiched between the two edges of yellowed cotton drape.

"I was hoping I could ask you a few questions about your friend…your colleague: the teacher who was found dead this morning in an apparent suicide." The officer clutched a small notepad with his left hand; in his right, he held a small pen. As he readied the writing instrument to write down Todd's responses, a third hand reached from around the curtain and pulled.

Beside the cop stood Jessica, the same Jessica Todd had seen in the teachers' lounge and his classroom: purple and swollen, mouth agape, tongue wagging. "Correct him, Todd," she gargled. "I'm not your friend, Todd. Am I?" She bent down to whisper in his ear, her musky perfume filling his nostrils. *"Not anymore."*

Beside him, Miriam busied herself with a study of the bed linens again.

In front of him, the police officer rhythmically clicked his pen.

Tick-tick-tick.

Jessica reached out, encircling his neck with her cold hands. Todd pulled away and ducked his head, causing the pain in his temples to throb and the horizon of his brain to tip drunkenly sideways. Todd slid downward and pressed his cheek against the cold floor. "Go away!" he cried. "It's over! We're done! Just go the fuck away!"

He felt the meaty, firm hands of the police officer on his shoulders, trying to lift him back onto the cot. "Hold on, Mr. Osbourne. Just hold on."

Jessica crouched next to him, rubbing the dead flesh of

her face against his. "Let go," she hissed and began to laugh. "Just let go." She laughed and laughed, and Todd pressed his face harder into the floor.

And in that moment, Todd finally understood.

❧ ❧ ❧

For one quick moment, he was weightless.

Todd stepped from the edge of his teacher's desk, an electrical cord knotted around his neck and secured to the long metal pipe running the length of his classroom's ceiling. His arms flailed wildly, his body rebelling against the decision to strangle himself. This would show her, though. She would remember how she hurt him. She would be sorry.

On the far wall, a large analog clock read 9:25, its thin red hand sweeping the last seconds as they leaked from Todd's body. *Tick-tick-tick.*

Around him, the teenagers gasped in horror. Some stood from their seats, staring helplessly at him; others hid their heads in their hands. A boy in a Pink Floyd t-shirt turned gray and vomited onto his desk, a splatter of regurgitated cereal and milk that dripped onto his jeans below. One girl began to scream.

Jessica appeared at the door; her fair, immaculate complexion blushing with alarm. "No, no no!" she cried, pushing a student out of the way and running toward the front of the classroom. "Oh, Jesus! Jesus, Todd, what have you done?!" She turned back to the hallway door and called for help. Then, she was somewhere below him. He felt her warm hands on his leg. "Oh, God—Todd, I didn't mean it. Please…please stay with me. Please—"

The union steward with the ponytail rushed past her, grabbed hold of Todd's waist, and hoisted him upward, trying desperately to fight gravity as it insisted on tightening the noose. "Hold on, Mr. Osbourne. Just hold on," he called. "Jessica, get security! Call an ambulance! Call…"

His voice drifted softly away, the fade out of a record track disappearing into grooves in the vinyl.

The sun streaming through Todd's classroom windows grew hazy as a thick, dense cloud blanketed the sky. Todd felt his eyes roll upwards as his body melted downwards and dripped onto the cold tile below. From the shadows crept a shadow in the shape of a giant spider. It climbed onto Todd and smothered his face in its soft belly, a swaddle of innumerable legs wrapping themselves around his torso, finally cocooning him to sleep.

❧ ❧ ❧

Rebecca Rowland is a Bram Stoker Award-nominated editor (*American Cannibal*) of seven anthologies and a horror cocktail book and a Shirley Jackson Award-nominated author (*White Trash & Recycled Nightmares*) of three short fiction collections, one novel, and too many novellas and short stories, one of which, *Optic Nerve*, snagged a Readers' Choice 666 Award from Godless Horror.

Despite her love of the ocean and distaste for cold weather, Rebecca makes her home in a landlocked and often icy corner of New England (USA).

To indulge in her tomfoolery, follow her on Instagram or visit RowlandBooks.com.

A Nightmare on Elm Lane
Richard Chizmar

My FATHER and I started digging the day after school ended.

I had just finished the seventh grade at Edgewood Middle School and was looking forward to a summer of fishing, bike riding, and playing Magic the Gathering with my friends. If I was lucky I might even run into Katy McCammon at the creek or the swimming pool and finally summon the courage to ask her out to the movies and to get ice cream. Charlie Mitchell had bet me twenty bucks on the last day of school that it wouldn't happen. I was determined to prove his fat ass wrong, even if it meant crashing and burning with Katy. After all, I would have the entire summer to get over it.

My father had just finished his millionth year of teaching upper-level science at the high school and evidently had other plans for the first week of my summer vacation.

"I'm homeee," I announced and flung my baseball hat on the foyer table.

"Don't let the door—"

The screen door slammed shut behind me.

"—*slam!*" my dad finished from the next room.

I walked into the family room, flashed a sheepish grin at my mother, who was reading a magazine on the sofa, and shrugged at my father, who was kicked back in his recliner watching the Orioles on television. "Sorry...I forgot."

"You forget one more time, you're gonna be sorry," he said, a hint of a smile betraying the tough-man attitude. My dad was a lot of things—a terrible singer in the shower, a horrible driver, often embarrassing in public, an ace Scrabble player—but tough wasn't one of them. My mom always called him a Disney Dad.

I plopped down on the sofa and started taking off my shoes. "Who's winning?"

"Don't ask," my dad grumbled

I laughed and made a face at my mom. She rolled her eyes. My dad was also a lifelong Orioles fan with, how shall I say this, unusual views regarding baseball managerial strategy. He believed in three-run home runs, double steals, and two out bunts. Sometimes all in the same inning.

"My God, what'd you boys do tonight," my mom asked, wrinkling her nose. "You stink."

"Played whiffle ball at Jimmy's," I shrugged. "Then went down to the park."

"You boys catch any fireflies?"

"Yeah, Mom. We all ran around and chased fireflies and stuffed them in an empty jar. Then we played hide-and-go-seek and tag and did a sing-along. What are we, five years old?"

She swatted me on the shoulder. "Don't be a smart aleck."

I grabbed my arm and pretended to swoon.

She laughed. "Go put your shoes on the back porch and take a shower. You're making my eyes water."

I jumped to my feet and gave her a salute—"Yes, ma'am, Janet, ma'am."—and headed for the kitchen and back door.

My father's voice behind me: "Don't call your mother by her first name."

I opened the back door. "Sorry, Henry, won't happen again."

I heard the squawk of the recliner as my father released the leg rest and got to his feet in the next room. I hurriedly tossed my shoes on the porch, slammed the door, and took off for the back stairs…

…just as my father, all five foot eight and hundred-fifty pounds of him, scrambled into the kitchen, nearly slipping in his socks on the linoleum floor and landing on his ass. "I'll teach you not to backtalk your parents!"

I bounded up the stairs, giggling, and locked myself in the bathroom.

"You're lucky today's the last day of school, you little communist!" my father bellowed from downstairs.

🍂 🍂 🍂

I tossed the wet towel on the floor next to my dirty clothes and climbed into bed. The sheets felt cool on my bare legs. I used the remote to click on the ten-inch television on my dresser and found the Orioles game. They were losing 8-3 in the bottom of the seventh. It was going to be another long season.

My dad stepped into the doorway. "Hey, I know tomorrow's your first full day of summer vacation, but I need your help for a few hours."

"Help with what?" I asked, dreading the answer.

"I have a little project for us. Won't take long."

"Oh, boy," I said, remembering the last little project. My dad had come home one afternoon with blueprints for a fancy tree house. We'd spent almost two weeks sawing boards and nailing them into place in the old weeping willow tree in the back yard. When we were finally finished, it looked more like a rickety tree-stand for hunting deer than it did any kind of a tree house, and it had cost my dad over three hundred and fifty bucks in materials.

My father laughed. "Now you sound just like your mother. Get some sleep, Kev. I'll see you in the morning."

🍂 🍂 🍂

I rubbed sleep from my eyes and walked across the patio to the picnic table tucked in the far corner. There were two shovels and a pick-ax leaning against the table, and a couple pairs of work gloves and a sheet of what looked like complicated directions sitting atop the table.

"Not more blueprints," I grumbled.

"They're instructions, smartie pants," my father said from behind me. "How do you expect to do a job correctly if you don't have instructions to follow?"

I resisted the urge to look over at the weeping willow tree.

"You get enough to eat?"

"Yeah," I grumbled.

He picked up the instructions and work gloves. "Grab those tools and follow me."

I cradled the shovels and pick-ax in my arms and followed him into the back yard. He walked past the backstop I used for pitching practice, past the two-tier bird bath my mom loved so much, underneath the drooping branches of the weeping willow tree, and stopped just short of the vegetable garden that lined our back fence.

"You can put them down here."

I dropped the tools onto the grass. "Okay, now can you tell me? What's the big surprise?"

My father smiled, spread his arms wide, and turned in a slow circle. "This is where our brand new goldfish pond is going."

"Goldfish pond?" I wasn't sure I had heard him correctly.

"That's right," he said, pointing. "Twelve by six foot pond there, complete with miniature waterfall. Rock garden there. Couple of nice benches there and there. It'll be a thing of beauty when we're done."

This sounded like a lot of work. "Mom know about this?"

"'Course, she does. Whose idea do you think it was?"

I knew better, but wasn't about to say so. "How long is this gonna take?"

He tossed me a pair of work gloves, started pulling his on. "Don't worry, Kev. I only need your help with digging the hole and laying down the liner. I can handle the rest."

I breathed a sigh of relief. Not to be a jerk about it, but I *was* thirteen years old and it *was* summer vacation. I had a lot of important stuff to do.

"We've got two days to get that done. After that, the pump and circulation kit will be here, couple days after that, the live plants and fish." My dad was grinning like a kid in a candy shop. He got a little nutty about things like this, but I sure loved him.

I slipped on the work gloves and picked up a shovel. "Well, what're we waiting for? Let's get digging."

He slapped me on the back. "That's the spirit."

🍂 🍂 🍂

A couple hours later, Mom brought out glasses of lemonade, and my father and I sat in the shade of the weeping willow and took a much-needed break. We were dripping with

315

sweat, and despite the gloves, we both had blisters on our hands.

"Not bad," my father said, taking a long drink and eyeing our progress.

The kidney-shaped outline of the pond was complete. Chunks of sod and dirt were piled off to the side on sheets of clear plastic. Later, when we were finished digging for the day, we would take turns filling up the wheelbarrow and humping loads to the driveway where we would shovel the dirt into the back of my father's pick-up. I wasn't looking forward to that part of the job.

"How deep do we have to go?" I asked.

"Thirty-six inches from end to end."

I looked at the hole. It was maybe six inches deep in most places.

"Take a few more minutes," my father said, putting on his gloves. "Finish your lemonade."

I watched him pick up a shovel and start digging. I sat there in the shade and drank my lemonade and thought about Charlie and Jimmy and the rest of my friends. They were probably down at Hanson Creek right now fishing. Or playing ball at the park. Or betting quarters on the shooting games at the arcade. Or...

My father slung another shovelful of dirt over his shoulder, grunting with the effort. I finished my lemonade and hurried to his side. I figured I had plenty of time for fun and games later on.

❦ ❦ ❦

"You poor boys," my mother said, watching us struggle to grip our forks at dinner.

She had made my father's favorite, beef stroganoff, and

even though we'd worked up quite an appetite, the blisters on our hands made eating a slow process.

"I told you we're fine, honey," my father said. "Few blisters never hurt anyone."

I stuffed another bite into my mouth and nodded agreement. I felt strangely happy and proud of myself. I felt content.

"Well, maybe you should take a break tomorrow and—"

"No way," I said, my mouth still full. "We need to finish digging, so we're ready for the pump on Thursday."

My father beamed. "That's right."

We finished our stroganoff and wolfed down two slices of chocolate cake each for dessert, then we all moved to the den to watch the start of the Orioles game. I was in bed and snoring by nine-thirty. It was my last peaceful night's sleep.

🕮 🕮 🕮

We were up and digging by eight the next morning, energized by a big breakfast and a good night's rest. Dad brought out a radio, and we listened to callers complaining about the Orioles' lack of pitching, hitting, and coaching for the better part of an hour before switching over to an oldies rock station. We were making decent progress on the hole. I figured we'd be moving dirt right up until dark tonight, but we would definitely finish. We were determined.

By late-morning, my father was working his way in from one side of the hole while I attacked the other side. The plan was to meet in the middle, and then use the tape measure to see how much deeper we needed to go. The work was methodical and mindless, but oddly satisfying.

A Led Zeppelin song was playing on the radio when my shovel hit something solid. I wasn't surprised. So far, we had unearthed about a million rocks of various shapes and sizes, an old toy truck, a rusted-out lid from a Speed Racer lunch box, and a few tangles of copper wire that my father said was probably left over from when the house was first built. I had even found a keychain in the shape of a miniature horseshoe with an old key still attached to it. I'd stashed that in my pocket to show my friends later. Maybe it opened a treasure chest somewhere.

I looked down and saw something small and pale in the dirt. Then, I saw another one. Maybe three inches long.

I lifted my shovel for a closer look — and my breath caught in my throat. I'd never seen one before in real life, but I had seen plenty enough on television to know what I was looking at.

They were bones.

"Umm, hey, dad."

The volume on the radio was loud, so I called again, "Dad, I think you should take a look at this."

This time he heard me and came right over. "What's up, Kev?"

I raised the shovel to give him a better look. He squinted in the morning sun, then reached down and picked up one of the bones. "Huh. Probably the previous owner's dog or cat."

He dropped the bone back onto the shovel and hopped down into the hole next to me. "Where'd you find it?"

I pointed out the spot with the tip of my shoe.

He carefully dug a wide circle around it. "I saw this on a National Geographic special about dinosaurs." He dropped to a knee and started sifting through the dirt with his hands.

"Jurassic Park on Golden Elm Lane," I laughed.

"Bingo," my father said, holding up another bone for me to see.

"Kinda gross, don't you think?"

"Just part of nature, son. You're the horror movie freak,

how can you think..." He didn't finish his thought. He knelt there, perfectly still, his shoulders suddenly rigid.

"What's wrong?"

He leaned closer to the dirt.

I tried to see around him. "What'd you find?"

My father stood and turned to me, a strange expression on his face. "Let's take a break and go inside and cool off."

I moved to the left to try to see around him. He moved and blocked me. "Kevin—"

"What is it, Dad?"

He let out a long sigh. "Put your shovel down. Carefully. I'll tell you in the house."

"Tell me now," I begged, laying down the shovel on the grass and peeking behind my father into the hole.

Several slender, pale bones lay atop the pile of dirt.

June sunlight glinted off something shiny encircling one of the bones.

It was a dirty gold ring.

❦ ❦ ❦

By dinnertime, there were three police cruisers parked in front of the house and a police van parked across the street. The back yard was swarming with officers and detectives. Some of them investigating the hole and bagging evidence, others just standing around, talking.

I sat on the patio and watched everything. All of my friends had stopped by at one point or another, but my mother had shooed them away with the promise that I would call them later that night. Most of them spent the evening texting me and watching from across the street, their bikes parked on the sidewalk.

A police detective had interviewed my father and me, first in the living room, and then again as we showed him what we'd found in the back yard. He'd asked us a lot of the same questions two or three times, almost like he didn't believe us. When the other cops showed up, he quickly finished with us and got to work with the others.

Both my mom and dad must've asked me at least a dozen times throughout the day if I was all right. Each time I reassured them I was fine. The truth was I was more than just fine. I was excited and anxious to find out even more about what was going on.

I eavesdropped on every conversation I could. I offered policemen drinks and made other excuses to talk to them. I even used the zoom on my phone camera to try to get a glimpse of what was going on over by the hole.

Finally, around the time it started getting dark and two policemen started setting up portable lights, I climbed the weeping willow and perched myself inside my tree house. I couldn't see much from up there, there were too many branches in the way, but I was comfortable enough and could hear a lot better.

Around nine o'clock, I heard a cell phone ring somewhere below me.

"Sharretts," a voice answered, and then there was a long pause. "Make sure you check with Henderson first. He left here fifteen minutes ago."

I recognized the voice now. It was the detective who had interviewed my father and me earlier in the day. He obviously didn't realize I was in the tree above him, listening. I knew this because of what he said next.

"That all depends on what Cap says. I think they're gonna GPR the whole damn back yard in the morning."

Another pause.

"Three skeletal right hands so far."

I realized I was holding my breath.

"That's right. No other remains. Just the hands."

I could hear his footsteps moving away from the tree.

"Someone's checking on that right now. Okay, talk soon," and then there was just the muffled chatter of the policemen below and the soft whisper of a breeze in the weeping willow.

A short time later, I crept down from the tree and went inside. I hurried to the bathroom to pee — I'd been holding it for what felt like forever — and realized that I still had the horseshoe keychain in my pants pocket. I knew I should probably go back outside and give it to the police. It could be important evidence.

Instead, I went to the kitchen and ate a snack and used my phone to look up what GPR stood for: *Ground Penetrating Radar.*

They were going to x-ray the back yard tomorrow. They were looking for bodies.

❦ ❦ ❦

I was too tired to call my friends back that night, so I called first thing the next morning. I started with Jimmy.

"My mom says you can maybe come over tonight, but just you, not the rest of the guys."

"Awesome. My mom said she saw the story on the news last night. They had pictures of your house and everything. Golden Elm Lane is famous!"

I'd watched the same news story this morning during breakfast. It felt weird seeing my house like that. Not a good weird either. It was almost like they were trespassing or something.

"What are they doing now?" Jimmy asked. "They find any more skeletons?"

I walked over to the window and looked outside. "A couple vans showed up a little while ago…"

I told Jimmy what I'd overheard the night before about GPR and how there was a guy in regular street clothes pushing something that looked like one of those portable golf caddies with three wheels back and forth across my yard. A cop in uniform walked alongside him, carrying a clipboard and a fistful of little red flags attached to wire stakes. Every once in a while, they would stop and the cop would take a knee and plant one of the little red flags in the grass, and then they would move on again.

Jimmy was fascinated — "it's just like a freaking movie, man!" — and made me promise to text him a photo from my phone. I told him I would. I didn't say a word about the other thing I'd overheard while sitting in the tree house: about the police finding three right hands. Just like with the keychain, I hadn't even shared that information with my parents yet. I didn't know why, but I'd kept that to myself.

❧ ❧ ❧

First thing in the morning, the police had asked my parents to make sure everyone stayed clear of the back yard, so I was forced to watch from my bedroom window. I pulled my desk chair close and cracked the window a few inches, but I still couldn't hear much. To make matters worse, the weeping willow blocked a good portion of my view. I was flying blind today.

I sent Jimmy a blurry picture of the cops operating the GPR machine and did my best to keep up with my other friends' text messages. I ate a ham and cheese sandwich and Doritos for lunch and skimmed a couple articles in the new issue of *Gamer's Monthly*. I almost fell asleep twice after lunch and took the fastest bathroom break known to man for fear of missing something important. I counted four red flags sticking out of the ground. No telling how many more there were behind the tree and around the hole we'd dug.

The hours dragged on. I started thinking about sneaking outside for a closer look. I even considered sneaking up into the tree house again. What were they going to do, arrest me?

I had just about convinced myself to go for it, when there was a knock on the door behind me. I turned and both my mom and dad were standing there.

"Hey, Kev," my dad said. "Got a minute?"

They walked into the room and sat on my bed.

"Did they find something else? Did they—"

My dad put his hands out. "Whoa, slow down." He glanced at my mom and continued, "We just finished speaking with one of the detectives, and we thought we'd share with you what he said."

"If anything we say upsets you," my mom said, "just say so and we'll stop."

I looked from my dad to my mom and back to my dad again. "Just tell me!"

"This stays inside the house, Kevin. It's family talk, not for your friends. Got it?"

"Got it," I said, nodding and sitting on the edge of my seat.

"According to the detective, they've found skeletal remains from at least three different people in the back yard."

No duh, I wanted to say.

"They've also marked some additional areas they plan to search later this afternoon. The detective told us the lab ran some tests on the bones we found and they came back as more than twenty years old, so fortunately they know we had nothing to do with this."

I hadn't even thought of that. "Wow, we could have been suspects!" I blurted, putting an immediate frown on my mom's face. Wait until Jimmy heard about that.

"They also pulled property records and discovered that

the sole owner before us of 149 Golden Elm Lane was a man by the name of Walter Jenkins. By all accounts, he was a friendly, well-liked man with no complaints against him and no arrest record. He was retired from the Navy and worked at the hardware store in Dayton. He was widowed when he was in his sixties and moved to a nursing home about ten years later. That's when we bought the house and moved in."

"Is he still alive?" I asked, my mind working.

My dad shook his head. "Died six years ago. Didn't have any children and no living relatives nearby."

"So, if he didn't do it...who did?"

"That's what the detectives are trying to figure out, Kev. Detective Sharretts said they might have a few more questions for us in the days to come, but mostly they'll be looking around for folks who knew Mr. Jenkins back when he lived here."

"You know some of the world's most famous serial killers were normal and friendly on the outside, right?" I asked, remembering some of the books I'd read. "They weren't all weirdos like Dahmer and Gacy and—"

"You hush now," my mom interrupted, getting up from the bed. "No more talk about serial killers. Get yourself washed up and help us prepare dinner."

"But, Mom..." I whined, looking at my dad for help.

He stood up from the bed. "You heard your mother, Kev. Let's go."

So much for help. I groaned and followed them downstairs.

❧ ❧ ❧

That night, I dreamed Walter Jenkins was chasing me.

The house was dark, and Jenkins was old and wrinkled, but incredibly fast and strong. No matter where I ran or hid, he kept finding me. He had a hideous grin and an evil laugh and a long, wicked-looking knife. He wanted my right hand.

Terrified and cornered, I crept into the basement.

"Come out, come out, wherever you are," he called in a gravely, sing-song voice.

I sat perfectly still in the space between the washer and dryer, afraid to breathe. I had piled several dirty towels on top of me. I couldn't see a thing.

"I know you're down here," he said, and I could hear the shuffle of footsteps getting closer.

"C'mon now, Kev, I'm not going to hurt you."

The footsteps stopped right in front of me. I felt a whisper of cool air as one of the towels was removed from on top of me.

"I promise I won't hurt you."

Another towel gone.

"I'm just gonna kill you!"

The last towel was snatched away, and I saw that evil grin and long, shiny blade slashing—

—and that's when I woke up in my dark bedroom, sweaty sheets clenched in one hand, my other hand the only thing stopping the scream from escaping my mouth.

❦ ❦ ❦

"Dude, you're like a celebrity," Doug said. "Everyone's talking about you."

Charlie rolled his eyes. "I wouldn't go that far."

"Don't be a douchebag," Jimmy said and punched Charlie in the shoulder. "You're just jealous."

"The day I'm jealous of gay boy Kevin here is the day you get to bang my sister."

"Already banged her," Jimmy said, pushing off on his bike. "And your mom, too."

Charlie's chubby face went red. He jumped on his bike and started chasing Jimmy down the trail. "Take it back! Take it back!"

Jimmy just laughed and kept on peddling.

It felt good to be with my friends again, instead of locked up inside the house. The police had left a couple days ago, and even the news crews had stopped coming around.

"So they have no idea how they got there?" Doug asked for at least the fifth time that morning.

I shook my head. "It's a big mystery."

"You mean a nightmare," he said, and then his eyes flashed wide. "A nightmare on Elm Lane!" He hooked his hands into claws and started slashing at me. "Maybe Freddy Krueger did it!"

I laughed and pushed him away.

"My dad says they should check out the folks who own the house in back of you," Doug said, still giggling.

"Police already did that. The current owners and the previous two owners."

"And?"

"And nothing, I guess."

Doug grunted and looked around for Jimmy and Charlie. "It's hot as piss. Wanna go get a Slurpee?"

"Sure."

Doug put his fingers to his mouth and whistled. Thirty seconds later, we heard a returning whistle from deep in the woods. A few minutes after that, Jimmy and Charlie came racing down the trail, both of them red-faced and sweating. We all set out for 7-Eleven.

🍂 🍂 🍂

The four of us sat on the curb outside the store and drank our Slurpees and opened our packs of baseball cards. Charlie and Doug got into an argument about who was a better third baseman, Manny Machado or Kris Bryant, and that turned into a pebble fight until Charlie plunked Doug in the eye. Jimmy and I were content to sit back and watch the spectacle and drink our Slurpees in silence.

A car pulled into a parking spot nearby, but none of us paid it any attention.

"Hey there, boys," a voice called. "Hot enough for you?"

We all looked up. Mr. Barnett from down the street was leaning out his car window, the stub of a cigar poking from his mouth. It smelled like cat shit.

"Sure is," Jimmy answered.

Mr. Barnett looked at me. "Kevin, you're quite the celebrity these days, aren't you?"

Doug gave Charlie a smug look: *I told you so.*

"I dunno about that, Mr. Barnett."

"I saw you and your dad on the news a couple times, walking around in the background. Pretty exciting stuff, huh?"

I nodded, but didn't say anything. Mr. Barnett was the first grown-up to use the word exciting to describe everything that had happened. Of course, all us kids thought it was exciting and cool, but the only words I'd heard other grown-ups use were horrible and terrifying and dreadful. But Mr. Barnett was like that. He wasn't like the other adults I knew. He always drank too much at the neighborhood block parties and shot off too many fireworks on the Fourth of July and my mom was always complaining that he was breaking the speed limit on our street.

"Sooo...the police find anything else that hasn't made the news or the papers?"

"My parents aren't really telling me much," I said. "They're afraid I'll have nightmares."

Mr. Barnett's face tightened, and I could tell he didn't

believe me. "So they found the remains of three hands, and that's it?"

I nodded again, worried my voice would betray me.

"You know I asked my father about the guy who used to live in your house," he continued, "and my father knew him."

Now he had my attention. "He did?"

"Said he was a nice enough fella but kept to himself. Said he even had a photograph of him somewhere, from an old Veteran's Day parade."

I thought about telling Mr. Barnett that he should have his father call the detectives, but I didn't. I had finished my Slurpee and just wanted to get out of there.

"Well, boys, I better run. Kevin, Jimmy, tell your folks I said hello. Looking forward to the cookout on the Fourth."

"Yes, sir," Jimmy said.

I waved as he pulled away.

We all got up, tossed our trash into the can, and mounted our bikes.

"That was weird," Doug said.

Jimmy shook his head. *"He's* weird."

"No, that's not what I meant. He pulled up and talked to us and left without even going into the store."

Jimmy thought about it for a moment and shrugged. I thought about it the whole way home.

❧ ❧ ❧

That night, I heard something in the back yard.

A thunderstorm had rolled in after dinner, dumping nearly an inch of rain and dropping the temperature by twenty degrees. My mom had opened all the upstairs windows, and I had fallen asleep earlier to a chorus of crickets and bullfrogs.

But something else woke me up.

I wasn't sure if I had dreamt or imagined it, but I got out of bed and went to the window.

The back yard was cloaked in darkness, the weeping willow a towering shadow against an even darker backdrop. A lonely bullfrog croaked somewhere in the weeds and I could hear the muffled barking of a dog from the next block over.

I was just about to return to bed when I saw it: a shadow breaking away and moving independent of the other shadows around it. The shadow was in the shape of a person.

And then I heard it, the same sound that had woken me earlier: a *thump* followed by another *thump*, and then the sound of two feet landing on soggy grass.

Someone had just climbed over the fence in the back yard and jumped to the other side.

❧ ❧ ❧

I sat on the front porch and watched the sanitation guys emptying our trash cans into the back of their truck. I wondered if they ever found anything valuable in the garbage. It seemed like such a cool job.

I hadn't told anyone about what I'd seen and heard the night before. First of all, I wasn't one hundred percent sure I hadn't dreamt the whole damn thing. My head was still fuzzy. Second of all, I didn't want to worry my parents. They were tense enough with everything that was going on. I'd even heard my mom after dinner last night blame my dad for picking that spot for the goldfish pond.

The street was quiet today. No police had come by the house for almost a week, and the news people hadn't been by in even longer. It had been an exciting adventure while it lasted, but I was glad life was getting back to normal.

"Caught you daydreaming, didn't I?"

I looked up and saw our mailman, Mr. DeMarco's, smiling face.

I laughed. "Guilty as charged."

He stepped past me onto the porch, stuffed some mail into the box, and plopped down next to me on the stoop.

"I'm getting too old for this job." He took a handkerchief out of his pocket and wiped the sweat from his face. As usual, I caught a faint whiff of his cologne. It was the same stuff my father used to wear. Blue Velvet or something like that. He looked over at me. "You doing okay, partner?"

Mr. DeMarco had been asking me that ever since it all happened. He said finding dead folks in your back yard was no joking matter, and I shouldn't hide my feelings if I was struggling. Mr. DeMarco was cool like that. All us kids loved him. He was old, had to be at least sixty, but he would still toss his mailbag under a tree some days and play whiffle ball or kick ball with us. Other times, he'd treat us all to fudgesicles if the ice cream man was making his rounds.

"I'm doing good," I said.

"Any plans for today?" He glanced up at blue sky. "Looks like it's gonna be a good one."

"We're going fishing down at the creek. Just waiting on Jimmy to finish mowing his lawn."

He got to his feet with a groan. "Now that's a great way to spend a day like today. Even if they ain't biting."

"Oh, they'll be biting all right," I said, grinning. "We've got our secret bait."

He squinted at me. "Lemme guess…cheese balls?"

"How'd the heck you know?!"

Mr. DeMarco tilted his head back and laughed. It was a good, happy sound.

"I know because that's exactly what my friends and me used for bait in that exact same creek fifty years ago! Those fatty carp love cheese balls!"

I laughed.

"As a matter of fact," he said, face turning serious. "I told that police detective pretty much the same thing when he asked. Me and my friends used to run this neighborhood just like you and yours. Fishing, kick the can, racing our go-karts down Golden Elm."

I imagined Mr. DeMarco cruising down the road in a go-kart. Then, I thought of something I'd never thought of before.

"Did you and your friends know Walter Jenkins?"

Mr. DeMarco nodded. "Sure did. Even raked his leaves and cleaned his gutters once or twice. Me and Kenny Crawford, God rest his soul. Told the detective that, too."

"What was he like?" I asked.

"He was a good man, Kevin. Don't you listen to any of the rumors going 'round." He paused, thinking for a moment. "Mr. Jenkins reminded me a lot of my own father. That's how highly I thought of him."

I nodded and was about to respond — when a loud whistle sounded from somewhere down the street.

I whistled back and jumped to my feet. "Gotta go, Mr. DeMarco."

"Summer awaits, Kev. Those carp won't wait forever!"

Later that night, I sat by my bedroom window and watched over the back yard. After nearly two hours of seeing and hearing nothing out of the ordinary, I returned to my bed and was asleep within minutes. I didn't have any bad dreams that night.

Two amazing things occurred later in the week.

The first happened on Thursday morning while I was eating breakfast on the back patio with my mom. My phone buzzed in my pocket. I went to take it out and my mom said, "Uh uh, no phones at the table, remember?"

I put my hands out proclaiming my innocence. "I was just gonna turn off the ringer. Geez."

"Don't you geez me, mister."

I smiled and switched off the ringer on my phone — and saw the text.

I thought I was going to faint right on top of my plate of French toast.

The text wasn't from Jimmy or Charlie, as I had expected.

The text was from Katy McCammon.

Kevin, I'm having a pool party this Sunday at 2. You should come. Lemme know. Katy

I placed my phone beside my plate and read the text a second and third time from the corner of my eye. Then, I broke the world speed record for eating French toast and dumped my dishes in the kitchen sink. I yelled goodbye to my mom and ran down Golden Elm Lane as fast as I could to show Jimmy.

The second amazing occurrence happened on Friday evening, just before dinner. My dad and I were watching a *Seinfeld* re-run when the phone rang. My mother picked up in the other room. A moment later, she came in with the cordless phone pressed against her chest.

"It's Detective Sharretts," she said in a low voice, handing the phone to my father.

"Hello?" My father mostly listened, every once in awhile punctuating the conversation with an "uh huh" or a "no kidding" or an "okay."

After several minutes of this, he finally hung up. "Well, that was interesting."

Stone faced, he walked back to his reading chair and sat down. Turned up the volume on the television. Stared silently at the screen.

My mother (*"Honeyyy!"*) and I (*"Dadddd!"*) erupted at the same time.

He cracked up laughing.

"Tell us what he said!" I begged.

It took another thirty seconds for my father's giggling to wind down, then he filled us in. "Detective Martin said they have a person of interest in custody."

My mother clasped her hands together. "Thank God."

"A former resident of Dayton who moved away a long time ago," my father continued. "Evidently he admitted to everything. The detectives are going over his story to make sure it all adds up, but Detective Sharretts thinks it will. In the meantime, they at least have him on a weapons charge, so he's not going anywhere…"

🍂 🍂 🍂

I had a hard time falling asleep on Saturday night — I kept telling myself: *In fifteen hours, you'll be looking at Katy McCammon in a bikini; in fourteen hours, you'll be sitting in Katy's back yard with all the cool kids; in thirteen hours…* — so I found an old movie to watch on television. When the credits rolled at one a.m., my eyes were finally getting drowsy.

That's when I heard the footsteps. Not outside in the yard, but inside the house this time.

I held my breath — and heard it again.

A creak on the stairs. Getting closer.

My entire body broke out in cold sweat.

It's just Mom coming back from getting a drink of water, I thought. *She has trouble sleeping.* But I knew better. My mom hadn't woken in the middle of the night in forever, not since she'd started taking sleeping pills. And forget about my father, he slept like a bear in hibernation.

Another creak and the whisper of a footstep on hard-wood floor. Someone moving slow and stealthily. Someone creeping.

The house was silent for the next minute or two, and I was just beginning to believe I'd imagined the whole thing, when I heard a quiet *thump* from down the hallway, from the direction of my parents' room. And then I heard a second *thump*. Like something heavy hitting the floor.

I snatched my cellphone from the end table next to my bed and pulled the covers up over my head like I used to do when I was a little kid and afraid of the monster that lived inside my closet. I punched in the security code and keyed in 911, but I didn't press SEND.

My bedroom door creaked open.

Even underneath the blanket, I could hear someone in the room breathing.

Something unnamable — no, it had a name; it was *terror* — stopped me from pushing SEND, stopped me from leaping to my feet and trying to flee.

It's Walter Jenkins and he has a knife.

My heart was beating so hard that I couldn't hear the footsteps shuffling closer. I couldn't hear the breathing growing more labored.

But nothing was wrong with my nose — and that's when I smelled it.

The faint scent of cologne. Blue Velvet or Blue Ice or whatever the hell it was called.

Now I knew who'd buried the hands in my back yard all those years ago.

Now I knew whom the keychain belonged to.

He wanted it back.

🌂 🌂 🌂

RICHARD CHIZMAR is the *New York Times* bestselling author of the *Gwendy Trilogy* (with Stephen King), as well as *Becoming the Boogeyman, Chasing the Boogeyman, Widow's Point*, and many other books. His next novel, *Memorials*, will be published by Simon & Schuster/Gallery Books in October.

He is the founder/publisher of *Cemetery Dance* magazine and the Cemetery Dance Publications book imprint. He has edited more than 35 anthologies and his short fiction has appeared in dozens of publications, including multiple editions of *Ellery Queen's Mystery Magazine* and *The Year's 25 Finest Crime and Mystery Stories*. He has won two World Fantasy awards, four International Horror Guild awards, and the HWA's Board of Trustee's award.

Chizmar (in collaboration with Johnathon Schaech) has also written screenplays and teleplays for United Artists, Sony Screen Gems, Lions Gate, Showtime, NBC, and many other companies. He has adapted the works of many bestselling authors including Stephen King, Peter Straub, and Bentley Little.

Chizmar's work has been translated into more than fifteen languages throughout the world, and he has appeared at numerous conferences as a writing instructor, guest speaker, panelist, and guest of honor.

The Visitor

Philip Fracassi

THE PRIEST, squinting at the starfield of snow blowing at his headlights, twists the knob that speeds up the wipers, rubbing away the melted ice sticking to the windshield. On the seat beside him is a black leather Bible. The only one he's ever owned, given to him by his mother nearly thirty years ago on Christmas day.

Jonathan, may this Holy Book bless you and keep you, she'd written inside, her handwriting elegant and tidy, her message a constant source of comfort each time he opened the front cover.

He says a silent prayer for her soul, then follows it with another for his own safety on these hazardous roads. The house has to be close now, but it's dark, the weather has turned for the worse, and beyond the reach of the white headlight beams there's nothing to indicate where he is, nothing but the never-ending ribbon of pavement rolling beneath him, the constant stream of snowflakes attacking the car and distorting what little vision he had to begin with.

It had been his choice to do this, so he had no right to

complain. The call from Bishop Freeman had been brief, and skeptical.

A parishioner had called the church multiple times over the last week—a mister Richard Quinn, who lived in the country just outside of town with his family; a wife and two small children. He'd begged anyone he could get on the phone for help, claiming a demon was nested in his house, plaguing the family, terrifying his children, keeping him and his wife up at all hours.

"He wants someone from the church to go out there and pray with them, bless the house. Drive the devil away, I suppose," the older priest had said. "Of course, I thought of you."

Since he was a child, Jonathan had felt a certain sixth sense for things. Finding lost keys, waiting by the front door minutes before his mother arrived home. As a priest, he'd participated in exorcisms, seen and heard things deemed impossible by the secular world. Now, when something... irregular came up, he was usually the one called upon.

"So, you'll go out there," the bishop continued. "Sprinkle some holy water. Speak some Latin, perhaps?"

Jonathan could hear the tinkle of ice cubes on crystal from Bishop Freeman's favorite vice: a nightly glass (or three) of single malt scotch.

"You seem unconvinced."

"It doesn't matter what I think," the bishop said tiredly. "We are instruments of the Lord, and we do what is right, without judgment, without rancor."

Bishop Freeman had suggested he call the family later in the week, but Jonathan hated the idea of waiting. Hated the idea of young children being tormented—be it by demons or something else. Something more human.

That morning he tried to call Richard Quinn and introduce himself, but received only a busy signal in reply. He wasn't overly concerned, not at first. But after a few more attempts throughout the morning—still getting that same *beep beep beep* each time he tried the house—he grew worried.

Cursing under his breath, Jonathan checked the address the bishop had given and estimated the drive would take no more than an hour (even in bad weather). Then he donned a tab-collar cleric shirt and collar, black slacks, and a fleece-lined overcoat. He glanced out the window at the darkening sky, the already fluttering snow, and figured no one would mind if he wore his rugged, waterproof work boots. It wasn't as if he were going to church, after all.

And now, out in the middle of nowhere, surrounded by darkness and blinding snow, he feared he was lost; that he'd missed the driveway's entrance jutting off the lightless road. He checks his gas gauge, no problems there—and decides to give it ten more minutes before turning around...

There!

He stomps the brake pedal—too hard—and feels his stomach rise into his throat as the tires slide instead of stop, if only for a moment. When the treads finally catch pavement beneath the thin sheen of invisible ice, he lets out a relieved breath. To his left is a narrow gravel driveway. A dented, gray mailbox lingers on a post, rocking in the wind, the address he searched for stenciled on its side in weary black ink.

He'd found them.

☙ ☙ ☙

The house was large in the Victorian style, and old. The windows facing the front drive were dull, mustard-colored eyes browed by snowfall. There was no porchlight, nothing indicating that the people inside were expecting company.

Jonathan sits in the car a moment, letting the heat run

over his boots and exposed fingers as he grips the wheel and stares at the house, waiting for the front door to open, for some sign of welcome. After a minute, he shakes his head, grabs his Bible, and shuts off the car. A few moments later he's climbing the steps, eyeing the windows for signs of movement, signs of life. He knocks on the door and waits.

"Come in!" a man's voice yells from inside, a voice Jonathan assumes to be the homeowner, Richard Quinn.

Jonathan takes a last look back toward his car, lets out a bemused chuckle, stomps the snow off his boots, and pushes open the door. "Hello? It's Father Hall."

He takes half a step into the house, hesitant to close the door behind him, as if sealing himself inside would be a permanent decision, unrepairable. There's a slam from his left and he turns his head to see an empty, dimly lit kitchen. A piano plays a fragmented melody from his right; less a song and more a cacophony of disjointed notes, as if a cat had run across the keys. Jonathan begins to sweat beneath his heavy coat. His fingers grip his Bible tightly.

"Mr. Quinn?" he calls out, hating the weakness in his voice, the unease in his heart.

Straight ahead is a staircase leading to a darkened second floor. Next to the staircase—running deeper into the house— is a narrow hallway with crimson wallpaper, a dark wood floor, and a milky white ceiling. Jonathan can't help thinking of it as a throat, growing darker the further it recedes from the foyer, ending in dense shadow.

Something stirs, then slowly emerges from the black gullet of the corridor. Footsteps against the hardwood. Jonathan takes half a step back. A cold wind blasts through the door, chilling his exposed neck. He opens his mouth to call out a greeting but the words catch, a dominating inner voice interrupting before he can speak.

Run! Leave this place.

The piano plays again, louder this time. Another *slam* from the kitchen, as if someone is opening and closing cupboard doors in anger, or searching...

"I..." he stammers, and is about to turn away when the shadowy hallway flickers with light, a fixture on the ceiling blinking with worry, or possibly aggression. A second later, a man emerges from the dark, wringing his hands on a dirty towel, his face pale and strained with a mixture of embarrassment, fear, and apology.

"Father Hall?"

Jonathan exhales a held breath, wipes sweat from his brow with the back of a hand and nods, doing his best to work his mouth into a smile. "That's right."

The man extends a hand, looks down at it, then pulls it back. "My hands are filthy. We've..." he stops, wincing at the sound of the piano. "Jenny, can you give it a rest, please!" The piano goes quiet, and the man offers a watery smile. But his eyes, Jonathan notices, are dark and grave with exhaustion. "We have a visitor."

Jonathan glances to the right as a young girl—perhaps ten years old—steps into view. She wears blue jeans and a stained white T-shirt.

"Hello," Jonathan says to the girl, who does not respond.

Richard Quinn grins, as if putting on a happy mask in the presence of his daughter. "You'll have to forgive us," he says, spreading his arms to emphasize his pit-stained, half-buttoned shirt, dirty trousers, disheveled hair. "Been hell around here these last couple days."

Jonathan turns and shuts the door. The whistling of winter is cleaved away, and the boards beneath his boots creak in welcome. "It's quite alright, Mr. Quinn," he says. "I'm here to help."

❦ ❦ ❦

The kitchen is messy, but not disastrously so. There are dishes lumpy with half-eaten meals on the dining table, and more in the sink waiting to be scrubbed, dried, and put away. Beth Quinn leans against a counter holding an unlit cigarette, blonde hair pulled back in a frayed knot, her face without makeup. She wears tights and a hooded sweatshirt. Her feet are bare, and Jonathan wonders how she stands it.

The house is freezing.

A boy, perhaps a year or two older than his sister, stares at the priest with hard hazel eyes. Like the others, he looks tired. He's holds open a cabinet door, gripping it tightly by the handle. As Jonathan begins to greet his mother, the boy slams the door closed with such force that it causes all three adults to hunch their shoulders in unison. Beth shakes her head, eyes closed tight, but says nothing.

"Mrs. Quinn," Jonathan finally says, moving to shake her hand, but she thrusts the cigarette forward, stalling him.

"Got a light, Father?"

Jonathan looks at her a moment, wondering if she's joking. Then he glances at Richard, who looks downcast, perhaps in embarrassment.

The boy slams the cabinet door again.

Discordant sounds from the piano float in from the other room like dead, wind-blown leaves on a cold autumn day, the chords jagged and tuneless.

Jonathan feels tension crawl up his spine and across his shoulders. He takes a steadying breath and turns his attention to the husband. "Mr. Quinn, why have you called me here? You told Bishop Freeman something about a demon."

Quinn sighs heavily, shakes his head. "Started when we heard noises in the attic. I went up there, thinking we had varmints. Nothing. Then the kids..." he swallows hard, and Jonathan sees tears forming in those burdened eyes. "The kids said they'd wake up in the middle of the night and see someone standing in their room, watching them while they slept. A man made of shadows, they said. Crazy, right?"

"Make him leave," Beth says angrily, then turns her back to the two men.

"Look... Father Hall," Richard says, ignoring his wife. "We need your help, okay? We just need you to bless our house. We're so tired..."

Jonathan nods, horrified at the despair of this family. "Yes, well, I can certainly do that," he says. "Why don't we all go sit in the other room? I'd like to speak to your whole family, find out more..."

SLAM!

"I... young man, would you mind not..."

SLAM!

"You need to bless this house," Richard Quinn repeats. "We need you to do it now. Before it's too late."

"Too late for what?" Jonathan says, sweat running at his temples, his Bible clutched to his chest like a shield. "Please, Mr. Quinn, I need to understand."

Beth turns from the counter, eyes blazing at the priest, lips curled with hate. "Make him leave!" she screams, then storms from the kitchen. Jonathan hears her yelling at the young girl. The piano stops momentarily.

"Bless our house, Father."

"Fine," Jonathan says curtly, then closes his eyes and takes another large breath, tries to calm his frayed nerves. "I'm sorry, I mean... of course. Why don't we all go in the other room and I'll say a prayer for the family."

Jonathan turns and leaves the kitchen. He hates to admit it, but the boy is scaring him a little. The repeated slamming of the door, and the parents doing nothing, saying nothing. As if they didn't hear, or care.

What was happening to this family?

As he steps into the foyer, another eruption of loud noises come from the upper floor. Just near the top of the stairs. Or... the attic?

Jonathan looks up toward the murky darkness, but sees nothing.

"Father, please..." Richard Quinn stands beside him, imploring him to follow into the next room, where the piano has begun playing once more—louder now, as if the little girl is throwing a tantrum.

"Who is upstairs?" Jonathan asks.

"You can't go upstairs," Quinn says, a pained look on his face. "You *must* bless this house. That's why I called, you see? But now days have passed, and nothing's changed. You must..."

Quinn's words are cut off by another series of loud noises from the second floor, followed by another sound...

Footsteps.

"Mr. Quinn, who's up there?"

"Please, Father..."

Jonathan, the tension and bizarre actions of the family having taken a toll on his patience, simply scoffs in irritation and moves toward the stairs.

He climbs the steps slowly, letting his eyes adjust. He waits to hear Quinn yell for him to stop, to come back, but he doesn't. When Jonathan reaches the top of the stairs, he can make out the gloomy outlines of doors along the second-floor hallway. He turns back, wondering if he's been followed, and sees the entire family standing at the bottom of the staircase, watching him. The piano, along with the slamming of the cabinet door, have ceased.

Well, that's something anyway, he thinks, then moves deeper into the house.

The Visitor

He waits to hear the banging sound again—similar to a hammer pounding a nail—but there's only silence. There's a sickly smell in the air, as if a small animal had crawled between the walls and died.

Pushing forward, he walks past two closed rooms until he reaches the last door in the corridor. It stands slightly ajar, and a misty light comes through the opening.

"Hello?" he says, and pushes the door inward.

Beyond is a small bedroom with two single beds, side-by-side.

The children's room.

Moonlight pours in through a window, but it's still quite dark and he can only clearly make out the room's larger objects. Beds, dressers, a cluttered desk. He feels the wall for a switch, finds it, and flicks it on.

The beds are neatly made. One is covered in a green quilt, the other in a duvet designed with a pattern of small cars. The identical wooden headboards are pushed against the far wall so the ends of the beds face the door. Face Jonathan.

Protruding from beneath the ends of each bed—heels resting on the cold hardwood —are a set of small, bare feet, as if the children were sleeping on the floor, rather than the mattress. As if they were playing a game.

Of course, that can't be.

The children are downstairs.

"Hello?" Jonathan says in a hoarse whisper, heart frozen inside his chest, his breathing fast and shallow.

He walks to the first bed—the first set of feet—and bends down. The bare legs do not stir. He sets his Bible on the green quilt and, with a shuddering breath, gently touches two fingers to one of the ankles.

He is not surprised to find the skin cold to the touch, and it's only now, close up, that he notices the bluish hue of the flesh.

Jonathan stands, bends over to grip the ankles, then slowly shuffles backward, sliding the body from beneath the mattress, past the fringe of the draping green duvet.

It's the girl, he thinks, even though all that remains of her head is a dented, deformed mask of a face and a halo of blonde hair, clumpy and dark with dried blood.

He feels eerily calm as he walks to the other bed and repeats the action, this time with the boy. There are no hazel eyes left to glare at him, but he'd swear it's the child from the kitchen, the one fond of slamming cabinet doors.

"Mr. Quinn!" he yells, his eyes not leaving the two parallel bodies. He guesses they've been dead for a day at least. Perhaps longer.

He stumbles out of the room, shuts the door. For a moment, gorge rises in his throat but he forces it down, clutches his Bible tightly, as if it is an anchor in a storm. Stumbling, he moves to the next door in the hall, opens it to find a darkened bathroom. Again, he turns on the light, and part of him—that small, hidden part residing behind consciousness, the part that sends red flags and raises the hair on the back of one's neck—already knows what he'll find.

Beth Quinn is in the bathtub. Her naked body is strewn like a broken doll, her head bent at an impossible angle, the kind that comes from having a badly broken neck. A thin wire is wrapped repeatedly around her throat, her face. A piece of bone juts through an exposed forearm and her eyes are open wide, her face a mask of pure terror.

Jonathan does not go in any further, but instead backs into the hallway.

There's one last door.

In the master bedroom he finds Richard Quinn. His hands and feet are splayed wide, his wrists and ankles tied with wire—identical to that used on his wife—to the bedposts. His neck has been opened from ear to ear, his stomach from chest to groin, his insides...

This time, Jonathan *is* sick. He vomits on the bedroom's hardwood floor and runs from the room, slapping madly at walls to keep himself from falling.

I've got to get help... I've got to... I've got to get OUT.

He lurches toward the top of the stairs and there, waiting for him at the bottom, are the four members of the Quinn family, alive and... whole.

Jonathan halts on the first step, his mind spiraling, afraid to go further, afraid to find out what the people at the bottom of the staircase really are.

If they're really alive... or something else.

"I told you to bless us," Richard Quinn says, his mouth set in a hard grimace. "To bless this house."

"I don't..." Jonathan starts, trying to find words that make sense, that will breach the hurricane of confusion shredding his mind. "I don't understand."

The little boy turns and runs, howling, toward the kitchen. Almost immediately the cabinet door begins to bang again and again and again.

The girl drifts away, back toward her piano, seemingly eager to create the discordant sounds of the tortured keys.

"I told you, but you didn't listen," Richard Quinn says.

It's only then, in that moment, that Jonathan realizes he's not alone at the top of the stairs. Behind him, wooden floorboards creak beneath heavy feet, and someone—someone very close—is breathing heavily.

"I told you," Richard says, as if annoyed. "We have a visitor. And now it's too late. Too late for all of us."

A thin wire, round as a halo, slips over Jonathan's head and snugs tightly to his neck, cutting into his windpipe. As he's pulled backward he drops the Bible, freeing his fingers to claw at the wire digging through flesh, cutting off his air. Killing him.

As his vision blurs and tunnels, he can just make out Richard and Beth staring up at him from the first floor. Beth shakes her head in disgust and stomps angrily toward the kitchen, where she will wait for eternity, holding a cigarette that will never light, listening to her poltergeist children create havoc—a juvenile response to their anger at being taken from this world so soon, so brutally.

Soon, he knows, Jonathan will join them, his soul held captive by a house of horrors that will remain cursed by murder and blood, unblessed, forever damned.

❧ ❧ ❧

Philip Fracassi is the author of the novels Don't Let Them Get You Down, A Child Alone with Strangers, Gothic, and Boys in the Valley.

His other work includes the story collections No One Is Safe!, Beneath a Pale, and Behold the Void.

For more information on Philip and his work, visit his website at www.pfracassi.com

Lips Like A Scythe

Steve Van Samson

SHAKRA DANE TURNED from where she was sitting on the cliff.

She squinted into the growing darkness between the trees, wondering if the sound had been her imagination. As a gust of wind blew up from the vista below, it set a chill upon her bones. With a sudden shiver, she shifted her gaze to the end of a forest path.

It was only a quarter mile hike back to where her boyfriend's pickup was parked. And though she could picture her jacket lying on the backseat, leaving it there had been intentional. At the time, she was hoping that something else might keep her warm.

"Bren?"

The large boy of nearly, but not quite eighteen was crouching beside the fire he was still trying to start. Looking up, he threw on a goofy smile. "Yeah?"

Shakra knew he'd go and grab her jacket if she asked, but that wasn't the only thing on her mind.

"I… uh," She began to bite the left side of her bottom lip in that way she sometimes did. "Did you hear that?"

"Hear what? The chirping?" He smiled. "Aw, that's just frogs."

Shakra looked again to a spot in the woods that now seemed especially ominous. "No... it was something else. Sounded kind of like someone was shaking a milk jug with sand in it."

Brennan turned to look where she was looking. Then he raised an eyebrow, "That's weird. Can you hear it now?"

Seeing his disheveled blonde hair and consternated expression made the girl feel a bit better. She listened for a few more seconds, then ultimately shook her head.

"Well," Brennan Matthews returned his attention to the pile of wood. "Nature sounds pretty weird sometimes." He proceeded to reposition the logs for what was probably the ninth attempt. "This one time, when I was a kid... I heard these crazy noises outside my bedroom window. I swear to God, it sounded like Godzilla was fighting the Prophecy bear out there. You ever see that movie?"

"Godzilla?"

"No, *Prophecy*! It's got this super gross toxic waste bear that goes crazy and starts killing people! *In one scene*, it finds these campers and..." Seeing his girlfriend's nervous expression and remembering what they were both about to do, Brennan's smile drained away. "Anyway," he cleared his throat. "Turns out the racket outside my window was just a couple of racoons going at it."

The girl stared for a few seconds before giggling. Then, shaking her head, she looked to the lopsided tent that was just big enough for two. Again, her heart was picking up speed. She couldn't believe they were really here. Just her and Bren. That they were actually doing this. And the fact that they were breaking a bunch of posted rules—or laws? Were they breaking the *law* by camping overnight at Reaper's Bluff? Aw hell, she didn't care. Illegal camping wasn't exactly the same as going on a murder spree. Of course, seeing as how Shakra had lied to her parents about where she was, they might be inclined to disagree—both on that point, and her choice of company.

Brennan was what most would refer to as *a big boy*. He was tall and fairly massive—built like the linebacker he'd been for the past two years. A stark contrast in all ways to the petite, caramel-skinned, Junior class president before him.

Shakra's eyes moved to the circle of rocks that the boy was kneeling beside. She had never personally started a fire before and based on how long this was taking, neither had he. Donning a hopeful expression, Brennan tossed another match onto the pile. Like the previous three, it smoked for a few seconds and promptly died.

"Maybe the wood is too wet?" She offered.

The boy gave a lazy shrug. "I mean… it *shouldn't* be. I got it from the shed." He sighed, looking thoroughly underwhelmed with himself. "I don't know what I'm doing wrong here, Shak. I swear. I've seen my dad do this a thousand times and it's always zero to hellfire in sixty seconds."

The boy stood, contemplating the thin thread of smoke for another few moments before abruptly standing. He turned then to the girl with a devilish grin, as his eyebrows performed a quick double hop. "Of course, we've still got my secret weapon."

Before the girl could protest, Brennan had already picked up the full-sized gasoline can.

"No!" She exclaimed with the start of another giggle on her lips. "I told you before—you're going to blow us up!" Shakra stood up and walked over to where he was standing. Gently, she lowered his hand with hers until the volatile object was back on the ground. "I don't know why you even brought that thing."

"I dunno…" he suddenly looked like a sad puppy. "It was already in the truck and, well…"

As Brennan looked down, the girl's eyes pulled him in. Stealing the rest of his words as well as the breath from his lungs. In his reckoning, the boy had never seen anything more mind-numbingly beautiful in all his admittedly privileged life.

Back in eighth grade, Shakra Dane had been the new girl in town. A transfer student from all the way from Boston. And while she probably wasn't the only half-Indian girl in the whole state of Oregon, she could definitely vouch for Willamette High.

At first, Brennan Matthews had seemed like just another southern-fried meathead. But as time went by, she came to understand that the boy's bravado was manufactured. A thing that'd been forged in the flames of parental expectations and tested every day of high school. It was a concept that Shakra understood all too well.

SMACK!

"Ugh, these things." Brennan pulled a small flattish insect off the back of his neck. "These stupid *stink bugs* are everywhere up here."

"Well?" Said Shakra with a completely straight face. "Maybe they can get this fire started for us."

"Shit, there's enough of 'em. Think if we ask real nice?" With a warm smile, Brennan put his arm around the girl. Melting into the gesture, Shakra leaned into her big linebacker—pressing her face into his chest until it replaced the world.

This was supposed to be the big night. She'd felt it all week. The two had been dating for the last six months of junior year, and now here they were—defying rules of her parents as well as the United States Forest Service.

And so what if they were?

The fact was, they were seventeen. That magic age where you can still get away with some really dumb shit. Another year and they'd be *who knows where*. Off to college, probably in different states. Possibly about to become completely different people, or worse… *their parents*.

"You know…" Bren's voice reverberated through his chest and the lips of the girl. "There's still time to bail. We could always just pack up and go home. I mean, if you're having second thoughts."

The question made Shakra pull away and gasp for air. In the back of her brain, she could hear her parents cheering for this far more sensible decision. Unfortunately for them, she did not want to go back. What she wanted was this. To spend her first night with Brennan Matthews on the top of a mountain. Alone and together, holding each other's naked bodies until dawn broke the Oregon sky.

Lifting herself up on tiptoes, the two kissed for a long while.

"You know what?" She gently pulled away, only an inch or two. "I think I'm good right here."

"Really? Even if there's no fire and we freeze to death?"

Shakra gave an alluring little shrug. "I mean… who says we need a fire to keep warm?"

Hearing this sent the young man's heart jackhammering inside his barrel chest. As the two kissed again, time slipped over them like a river around a stone. This embrace was more impassioned than the last. Sadly, it was cut short.

"*CH-CHT CH-CHT CH-CHT CH-CHT…*"

The sound was like a bucket of ice water. A humming laser blast that shot through and turned their stomachs to stone. The two stopped what they were doing and turned immediately in the direction of the trees.

"Okay, you heard it that time. Right?" Shakra's heart was pounding for various reasons.

353

But before Brennan could answer, the sound happened again. It was louder this time or maybe only closer. A burst of low rattling like someone was shaking out a sheet of newspaper—only that wasn't quite right. Breaking from the embrace, he turned and stepped forward. Placing himself between Shakra and the sound.

"*CH-CHT CH-CHT CH-CHT CH-CHT…*"

"Is it… a rattle*snake?*" The girl was starting to sound worried. "Are they that loud?"

"Naw. No way." After a few seconds, the boy's expression turned to an angry scowl. "Damn it," he said. "I know what this is."

He turned to see Shakra's big brown eyes. They were wide with something close to fear. A fact which made him all the more pissed off as to what he was suddenly sure was happening.

"Friggin' O'Grady."

"What? You mean Tommy?"

Brennan nodded then looked back towards where the sound had been. "Gotta be. He's the only one I told where we were going tonight. That dumb-shit. I swear to God, I'll—"

The chittering, rattling sound came again and it was in a very different place. Whatever was making the sound was either movie fast, or it wasn't alone.

"*Tommy! Hey, who's out there with you, man?*" Brennan's volume was impressive when he wanted it to be. His bellowing filled the would-be campsite—reaching the trees and plummeting over the drop-off. "Is it Harry? Beaumont? Little Big Mac? Listen, I'm gonna give you assholes exactly one chance to pack it in and get the hell out of here. I hear that rattling shit *one more time*… y'all gonna be hurting worse than that night we got shut out at Beaverton."

Again came the sound and Brennan's head jerked in another direction. His eyes were dinner plates. Not wanting to show how freaked out he really was, the boy tried to find his previous volume.

"Alright, you jerks," His voice was shakier than he intended. "You asked for it."

Brennan plodded forward a step, but quickly discovered something was holding him back. He looked down to see a small hand on his arm. A lovely caramel-colored thing that was pulling in the opposite direction.

"Don't," Was all Shakra could manage at first. Her eyes alternated between the large boy and the still darkening woods. "This doesn't feel right. I changed my mind, Bren. I think we should—"

As the girl's next word froze in her throat, her eyes darted to what had just exploded out of the woods. It was an animal, though its frantic movements made it hard to identify in the low light. Shakra tried to point, even to simply breathe, but there wasn't time. She was propelled violently through the air, soaring past the spot they had chosen to spend the night —hopefully entwined in an act she'd been dreaming about for months. After a jarring landing, the girl rolled to a stop near the cliff and scrambled to her bloodied hands and knees.

Any pain she was feeling was swallowed by a sudden rush of adrenaline. Whatever the animal was, it had hit them like a runaway bus. And it was Brennan who'd taken most of the blow.

"Oh God," She gasped, trying to recapture her breath and see what was happening. "Bren?" Her voice was so thin. She strained to see—blinking, trying to rub away the phantom flecks of light which hung there. "Bren, come on! Answer me!"

But the only answer Shakra received was a low rustling rattle. It was softer than before, deeper in pitch, but also close enough to touch. With a shiver that racked her body from chin to heel, the girl began moving around the lopsided tent. With effort, she managed to blink the boy's legs into some semblance of focus, though the rest remained obscured. It was almost as if living shadows were covering his upper half like a blanket… or a shroud.

When the scene finally became clear, Shakra wished desperately that it hadn't. The darkness covering most of her boyfriend wasn't made of living shadows but, it was *most definitely* alive. The creature was black—possessed of an oily iridescent sheen which slid up and down its length. Given the overall posture and shape, *panther* was her first thought, but there was no fur. Also, the legs were wrong—segmented like those of an insect.

Though frozen in horror, Shakra tried to make out the thing's head. But this was obscured by great pointed shoulders and a distinctive dorsal crest. It almost looked like someone had jammed a giant circular saw blade, complete with teeth into the thing's upper back. The crest seemed to be vibrating—emitting a softer, more contented version of that terrible rattling.

"Bren?" The name slipped out. Horrified, Shakra clapped both hands over her mouth but, the damage was already done.

Next came a flash of something long and red. Something which was connected to the front of the thing's skull. Moving on some biological hinge, the scythe-like appendage swung outward. It was the last thing Shakra Dane ever saw.

🍂 🍂 🍂

Patrol Captain Heather Finch had spent twenty-one minutes in a deep, restful sleep, but it had taken her almost three hours to get there.

When the phone rang, the woman's slumbering brain immediately assimilated the sound. One by one, the dream-marigolds she was planting started to sing like little bells. Red and yellow petals were visibly vibrating from the noise, but Finch took this in stride. Lazily, she turned to regard her only companion in the dream-garden—a living, breathing, three-dimensional representation of Botticelli's Venus. She was around nine feet tall, fully nude, and standing upon an enormous Dorito. With a distant expression, the Goddess of love and beauty rolled her eyes. Then she spoke in a familiar, if incongruent, voice.

"*Chief?*" Said the Venus in the voice of Ranger Todd Peveril. "Captain Finch? *I'm sorry to bother you so late but... oh dang, we got a real emergency over here...*"

The woman's eyes shot open. Finch immediately folded herself into a sitting position and looked at the blinking red light on her answering machine.

"*Oh come on, Chief. Please? If you're there, could you just pick up?*"

The woman lunged forward, reaching the bedside phone just in time. "Todd, are you still there?"

The man on the other end made an audible sigh of relief. "Oh dang... it's good to hear your voice, Chief! Listen, I'm sorry to bother you. I... know you've had a hard time sleeping lately and..."

"Forget it," Finch threw her short legs over the mattress edge. Shivering as a cool draft passed over her toes. "Alright, Ranger. What are we looking at?"

"Some kind of animal attack. At least, I hope that's what it is. Hate to imagine the person who could do what I just saw," Peveril said, releasing an audible shudder. "It's uh... bad, Chief. Real bad."

As bitter wakefulness returned, the Patrol Captain's heart balled up like a fist.

"Okay," she said firmly. "I'm listening, Todd. Tell me what you saw."

"Well... there are two victims. They're *kids*, Chief. Just a couple of damn *teenagers* by the look." Suddenly, the Ranger's voice had become a thin, fragile thing. "Listen... I'd rather not say more over the phone because I don't think you're gonna believe me anyhow. Probably best if you see this for yourself."

Finch took her time letting go of the breath she'd been holding on to.

"Goddamn it." Finch dragged the curse out into a three second affair. "Alright. I'm on my way. Just hang tight. And, Todd?"

"Yeah, Chief?"

"Did you alert Fish and Wildlife yet?"

"No... they're my next call."

"Good. Just do me a favor and wait ten minutes, alright? The last thing I need is Jack Hawley mucking things up before I get eyes on the scene."

The pause which followed ended in a reluctant response.

"Alright. Ten minutes. Just get here fast, okay?"

After hearing the telltale click, Finch cradled the handset and hopped off the bed. As she began pulling her unwashed uniform off the floor, she couldn't help but scoff. It was all so clear now. The Icarian levels of hubris she'd entertained to think that a nonstop eighteen-hour shift might be rewarded with a couple hours of sleep.

Looking once more at the phone, she had a fierce urge to flip it off... but no. That would feel too much like she was offering the gesture to the man who'd just been on the line, and that wasn't fair. Todd Peveril was just doing his job—and by the sound of things, the guy was having an even worse night than she was.

It was 11:53 pm when Finch pulled off the main road and into the parking area by Reaper's Bluff.

The place had taken its name from a farmer who had lived in the mid-1800s. According to local legend, Eamos Whitlock had the idea to exploit the lush grasses which grew naturally in the area. After a harvest, he would dry, bale and sell the grass as what he called *mountain hay*. And despite initially being called a loony by locals, Whitlock's gambit actually paid off. His product was said to be of a superior quality and for three years, demand for mountain hay grew. All that ended rather abruptly however, when the remains of the man were discovered one day. Whitlock's body was found frozen and pinned beneath an equally frozen horse. The prevalent theory at the time was that a rattler had bitten the animal, which reared up, fell atop its rider and promptly died. After that, though his special hay was missed, no one ever tried to follow in Eamos' footsteps.

The name Reaper's Bluff came into use sometime in the early 1910s, due to the fact that the man had used a long farming scythe to reap the grass. Kids today, however, typically forget all that boring history stuff. Instead, they tend to equate the name with a more famous scythe carrying reaper. The ebony-robed personification of death itself. It was for this reason that the bulk of the duties carried out by Rangers like Todd Peveril, tended to involve the removal of various spray-painted skeletons.

Finch shifted her truck into park and released the safety belt. With a sigh, she glared over at the glove compartment, knowing that it still contained three home-baked Snickerdoodles in a small plastic bag. For seven whole seconds, she considered reaching out for some buttery-cinnamon courage. But after patting herself on the stomach, she swiped her flashlight off the seat and left the cookies where they were.

Outside, the night was cold. After once more checking the Glock on her hip, she zipped up her jacket the rest of the way. With a shudder, she thumbed the flashlight on and pointed it towards the toll booth. The small structure was where Todd would have called from, and she expected him to be there still.

"Ranger?" She called out only a dozen steps away. "Ranger Peveril? Are you in there?"

There was a soft glow coming from inside the booth, though no answer came.

"Todd?" She said, as her anxiety began to simmer.

When she reached the door, Finch discovered it was ajar. Suddenly, her nerves went straight into a boil.

The booth's interior looked to have been ransacked by a bull that'd mistaken it for a China shop. The desk lamp was turned on but tipped over onto a mess of strewn paperwork and manilla folders. More startling than this, was the far wall. It'd been a while since she'd seen it, but Finch was fairly certain the gaping hole was new.

"Oh crud," said Finch.

Frantically, she looked around the tight space—eventually stepping on a smashed bit of plastic. Stepping aside, she frowned at what remained of the toll booth's telephone.

"Double crud."

Without another word, the woman backed slowly out of the booth. The shock of mountain air made her spin—first clockwise, then counter—pointing her government issued firearm at every sound in the order they reached her ears. Suddenly, she wished she hadn't passed on the Snicker-doodles.

"Get a hold of yourself, Chief." Heather Finch said this

aloud through clenched teeth. "You're spiraling. Just get a grip and breathe."

It was good advice. And breathe she did. In through her nose and out through her mouth, just like they'd taught in gym class.

"11:59," she squinted down at her watch. "Reaper's Bluff toll booth has apparently been vandalized. No sign of Ranger Peveril. I am proceeding to investigate further."

Narrating her own findings and actions was a trick Finch employed often. Initially, she reasoned that doing so made details easier to recall later, when it came time to type up the actual report. In certain rare instances however, she found that the narration also provided a calming effect.

Glock in hand she stalked around the toll booth. On the other side, there was plenty of debris, but no sign of the missing Ranger. The view from this side confirmed that the hole in the wall was definitely an exit. And as the flashlight's beams fell upon the freshly disturbed ground, more became clear. The tracks were grouped in a pattern similar to a mountain lion's... but whatever had made them didn't have paws. The footprints were strangely V-shaped—like nothing she'd ever seen. And worse, whatever had left them, was apparently dragging something. Something roughly the size and weight of a man.

Heather Finch swallowed hard. Then she aimed the beam of light along the tracks, which led to and promptly disappeared at the beginning of a paved parking area.

The woman swallowed hard. Then she forced herself on. Moving slowly onto the asphalt and past rows of white lines on either side. Out here, surrounded by so much open space, Finch was the textbook definition of exposed, yet somehow, this felt safer. There was no cover in the parking lot for her, but neither for whatever had just Tasmanian-Devilled the toll booth. If a bear appeared out of the tree line, even going full speed, she'd have plenty of time to react. And though she loathed to shoot anything, especially an animal... the job had to come first. If there was a killer bear or cougar loose on Reaper's Bluff, it needed to be dealt with. Hell, that was the job.

Acknowledging this caused a shock of clarity to strike the nerves of the Patrol Captain. Suddenly, her senses felt hyper aware of everything. The non-directional insect song, the chirping tree frogs, the crunch of pavement underfoot, every lick of wind—these resounded in her hearing like the various sections of an orchestra. Out here, the flashlight was doing far less work than the moon, so she clicked it off. Allowed herself to become one with the mountain. This was, after all, her domain. And she, its great protector.

SNAP!

With a sharp inhalation, she swung the Glock in the direction of the sound. Finch's breathing spoke of a recently finished marathon. She clicked back on her flashlight, but there was nothing there. At least, nothing she could see.

"Just breathe, girl." She reminded herself, "It'll all be fine if you just keep breathing."

Ahead, two vehicles sat nestled into the far end of the lot. These she approached with heightened caution but, also the hope that at least one would contain her missing Ranger. The first was a state issued Crown Victoria with Forest Service printed on the side. Next to that was a lime green pickup. Seeing the vibrant color of the thing made her heart sink. There was just one person she could think of with a truck like that. Not wanting to, her eyes shifted to the 'Matthews Hardware' sticker on the tailgate.

"Shit," she said, frankly—sadly.

Shining the light around the truck's interior, she spotted a jacket on the backseat. The garment would have been a smart thing to remember on such a chilly night, but it was far too small for the Matthews boy.

"So that was the plan," Finch shook her head. "You took a date up here, didn't you kid?"

Deeply saddened by the implication, Heather moved her hand down to her pocket. Out of this she extracted a small rectangular object and held it to her chest. After a few seconds, she opened her hand to look at the thing. A final memento of the habit she'd fought so hard to kick, and yet missed just about every second of every day. The Zippo lighter featured an image of a gorgeous brunette with ice blue eyes. The incomparable Bettie Page was clad in lacy red negligee that matched her lipstick. Finch hadn't bought a pack of cigarettes in almost eighteen months, but parting with her old flame proved a more difficult affair.

"What do ya say, lady? One for good luck?" After planting a quick kiss on Bettie's cheek, Finch dropped the lighter back in her pocket.

"12:14 a.m." The narration resumed. "Ranger Peveril's vehicle has been located beside one lime green Chevrolet C-10, which I have reason to believe belongs to the son of 'The Lug Nut King' Vernon Matthews. Both vehicles are empty and there are no signs of foul play."

She walked faster now. Headed up the quarter mile of dirt path to the initial overlook.

"It has been approximately sixty minutes since Ranger Peveril's phone call. Given the state of the front booth, locating him is my prime concern. I'm continuing up the mountain now with weapon in hand."

As she moved along, she gripped both Glock and flashlight as if they'd been fused into one. And though the safety was on, that gun-light was pointed at every snap, crackle and pop that came from the surrounding woods. Holding the two things together like that was something she'd seen in a couple of cop movies. Back when it'd been just her and Bettie and the full flavor of a Consulate Menthol held alluringly between two fingers.

Shit, maybe it's the damn cigarettes? Yeah—maybe, despite what all the experts were saying, smoking wasn't bad for you at all because when you gave them up, you started baking way too many batches of cookies and got a son of a bitching case of insomnia for the bargain?

SMACK!

She slapped one side of her neck, pulling away one of those flat stink bugs that seemed to be everywhere these days. After flicking it away, she brought her fingers to her nose and inhaled. As always, the scent reminded her of summers at her grandfather's farm and of staining the front porch. Though the memory was a good one, she shook it away. Willing her feet to keep moving. Pushing onward into the dark unknown.

🍂 🍂 🍂

The next fifteen minutes passed without incident, though this did little to stop Finch from narrating.

"12:35 a.m." Visible breath puffed from her mouth and nose. "I've just reached the boundary of site one. Am proceeding to investigate."

As she stepped, the dirt under her boots seemed to crunch with the volume of small hydrogen bombs. Suddenly, the woman was very aware of how exposed she was, and unlike in the parking area, this notion was far from a comfort. Except for the drop-off, trees were on all sides. And in the superb dark of just past midnight, trees could hide a lot.

"Approaching what looks to be an intended campsite now. There's a tent, a fire pit and…" Her foot connected with an overturned object. It was rectangular and red, with a spout sticking out of one side. "What the Christ were they trying to do? Burn the whole mountain down?" Finch started mumbling under her breath "Damn teenagers. At this age they think the rules apply to everyone but them. No matter how many signs you post or how official you make 'em look. None of it matters because…"

She stopped grumbling as soon as she saw the dark splatters that could only be blood. Suddenly, her mind raced back to the phone call that had ripped her from her hard-won slumber. Ranger Peveril hadn't gone into detail… he'd just said it was bad. Real bad.

"Damn it, Todd… where are you?"

In answer, the night offered a new sound. A chilling, unnerving, rattling kind of sound which cut through the omnipresent insect song to pierce the woman's heart.

"CH-CHT CH-CHT CH-CHT CH-CHT…"

Her first thought was that someone was shaking dice around in a bedpan—only that wasn't quite right. She whipped around—simultaneously aiming both Glock and flashlight in the direction of the sound. She'd never heard anything like it before, and with nearly two decades of service in the United States Department of Agriculture, that was saying something.

She stood there for almost a full minute—practically reaching out with both ears for something to focus on. Then something asserted itself. From a spot she wasn't watching came a dark kinetic blur. This registered vaguely in the woman's periphery, but not enough to count.

Finch was knocked off her feet and sent tumbling over the cold ground, in the direction of the overlook. Frantic hands flew out, desperately trying to grip something—anything that might stop her momentum before it was too late.

She gasped with the realization that she was no longer moving. When both eyes shot open again, they were met by flashing lights. It took a few seconds to understand that the sudden disco show was being caused by her own flashlight. It had been dropped and was currently rolling around in circles somewhere close by.

And, because of course it was, the Glock was gone too.

As the light spun slower and slower, Finch could see something walking toward her. Something with the silhouette of a pitch-black cougar. Bizarrely, the animal approached in a drunken, zig-zagging gait—almost as if it was still trying to decide if she was a threat.

"*CH-CHT CH-CHT CH-CHT CH-CHT…*"

That horrible dried out rattle was louder and closer than ever. It stabbed at her brain like an icepick. Still on her hands and knees, Heather Finch began backing up but quickly realized just how close she was to the edge of the cliff. As real panic set in, she searched for a rock or stick—anything she could use for a weapon.

"*CH-CHT CH-CHT CH-CHT CH-CHT…*"

Looking up, she was met by a pair of eyes. Not cougar eyes, but inky orbs that bulged out the side of the ugliest face she had ever seen. While the overall shape and stalking locomotion *was* cat-like, this was some kind of gigantic insect. Other than the eyes, its smooth, oblong head seemed featureless. And on its back was a tall crest, set between the shoulder blades. This looked paper thin from directly head on, but as the animal turned, she could see more. The crest was actually disc-like—rimmed with little nodes, like the teeth of a circular saw, but twice as large as the biggest Zildjian cymbal she'd ever seen…

"*CH-CHT CH-CHT CH-CHT CH-CHT…*"

The animal was less than twenty feet away now, still approaching in that unnatural way. Heather swallowed, tried not to blink. The only thing she'd found was a rock about the size of a baseball. As a final weapon, this felt woefully inadequate, but she didn't care. She reeled back and hurled the rock with every bit of strength she had.

The animal stopped, poised itself into a crouch. Then there was a flash of red. Something from underneath the thing's neck had swung out and swatted at the speeding projectile—turning it into a foul ball. Finch didn't understand what she was seeing. It was like the animal had a huge crab-leg attached to where its chin should be. One that was still on full display.

The thing turned back to face the woman as that long red appendage swung slowly outward on an unseen hinge. In her gut, Heather Finch knew it was reaching for her. Just as she understood that the animal's current posture meant that it was about to pounce.

BAOWW!

There was a bright flash in the darkened path. Someone was firing a rifle.

BAOWW! BAOWW! BAOWW!

The animal unleashed a hog-like squeal as one of the bullets hit home. Folding the red scythe back under its throat, it scrambled away. Disappearing into the nearby woods.

"Todd?" Finch barely managed the name before keeling over.

The shooter was running. Shouting her name. But Finch was having trouble staying conscious. Fortunately, when she passed out, Heather Finch fell into a pair of arms instead of the scenic overlook behind her.

🍂 🍂 🍂

367

It was raining in the dream garden. Not water, but large drops of vanilla extract. And not that fake stuff they sell at the grocery store either. Real Mexican vanilla like that bottle she brought home from Playa del Carmen back in '71.

When she opened her eyes, the face of Botticelli's Venus was less than six inches from her own. The Goddess looked very concerned.

"*Cap?*" Said the Venus in a low Texas drawl. "I said, are you okay?"

When Finch failed to respond, the living Renaissance figure reached back, snapped a snack-sized piece off her giant Dorito and took a bite. "*Captain Finch,*" The Goddess crunched as she spoke, "*I need you to answer me, okay? Are you hurt?*"

❧ ❧ ❧

With a splash of cold air, Heather Finch awoke in a sitting position—cradled by someone she had yet to identify. After many purposeful blinks, she looked up at the blurry shapes that were trying to become a face.

"Todd?" She said hoarsely.

"Who's *Todd?*" The man repeated the name in the same low drawl of Botticelli's Venus. "I think you're delirious. It's me Jack. Officer Hawley."

"Oh," The woman sounded disappointed. Grateful but disappointed. "Hey, Jack."

"Hey?" The Fish and Game officer's long ago broken nose was now fully in focus. "Is that all you have to say? Christ, you almost just... I mean—*what the hell was that thing?!*"

"I..." Finch remembered the horrible animal, those bulging black eyes and the flash of red. As the appendage struck out in her mind, she couldn't help but flinch away.

"Whoa, it's okay," said Hawley. "It's gone. It ran off."

"Yeah but for how long?" Finch sighed and promptly held out a hand as if she expected something to happen. "Do you mind?"

Obliging as fast as he could, the Officer helped Finch to her feet. The man was a transplant. About as big and loud as they made 'em back in Texas.

"Here," Hawley handed over a flashlight. "You dropped this."

"Thanks," Finch accepted the object and switched it back on. Then she released a long breath. "Really... if you hadn't showed up when you did."

Hawley waved away the gratitude. "It's alright. You'd have done the same for me."

Finch just smiled at this and forced a nod.

"I got a call from one of your Rangers..." Officer Hawley stopped to produce the name but was having trouble.

"Peveril," Finch asserted. *"Todd* Peveril."

Hawley snapped his fingers. "Right. Ranger Peveril. He indicated that there'd been an animal attack, but Christ... I've never seen anything like that thing! Have you?"

"No. No way. When it stepped out into the moonlight, it was almost like..." Finch began shaking her head, but this turned into a full-body shudder. "Do they have wheel bugs in Texas?"

"Wheel bugs?" Hawley sounded a little confused. "You mean those ugly gray little bastards that got stingers on the wrong end?"

Finch nodded. "That's what it looked like. Some kind of jumbo 1950s B-movie version of one of those, but black. It even had the stinger-mouth! I can see it now in my head. That blood red thing, how it folded out from under the throat—long and curved like the blade of the Grim Reaper himself. Only it wasn't a blade. I think that was the thing's proboscis."

Jack scratched under his hat. "Say again?"

"*Proboscis*. It's what certain insects have instead of lips. Think of it like a cross between a straw and a hypodermic needle." She shrugged. "Butterflies have 'em too."

"*CH-CHT CH-CHT CH-CHT CH-CHT…*"

The sound was far away, but not far enough. Both officers swung their lights to the same point, but could see only trees and the voids of deep space between them.

Jack Hawley shook his head. "I don't think that's a Goddamned butterfly."

"You know, Officer… I'm inclined to agree." Heather's light swung again—this time to the ill-fated campsite. She'd dropped her gun when the thing had tackled her, but knew it couldn't be far.

"Well," said the man, sounding strangely guilty. "Since we're on the subject of impossible B-movie stuff… there's *probably* something I should mention. Now, I know how this is gonna sound but, hear me out, alright?" Hawley sighed and took his time doing it. "About a week ago, there was this guy who came into the station, right? He was weird. Tall, skittery —with a foreign accent. Name of Johanne Bauer. He came in real quiet and polite… then all at once he started hollering about how a bunch of people were gonna die. We all thought he was a nut—all that stuff he was spouting. Mad doctor this and mutated science experiment that. Something about those flat stink bugs you got around here. You know, the ones that smell like Minwax when you squash 'em?"

Though Finch hadn't stopped looking for her Glock, Hawley had her full attention. She gave a wary nod.

"Right, well he said those things aren't supposed to be here. In America, I mean. That they probably hitched a ride in a shipping container or some such. Bauer said the guy he'd been working for was some genius-level science wiz who was trying to solve the problem once and for all."

"Genius science wiz?" Finch raised an eyebrow. "Around *here*?"

"I know how it sounds, but yeah. A man by the name of Deemer... or Gleamer, maybe. Bauer said the guy had been trying to make something that would be able to wipe every one of them little stinkers out. Some kind of super predator they'd grown in a test tube. He called it... the *rattleback*."

"*CH-CHT CH-CHT CH-CHT CH-CHT...*"

The sound appeared as if on cue. It was still some distance away, though the animal was definitely moving—circling them. Finch remembered the crest on the animal's back. Pictured it vibrating like a buzzsaw.

"Well..." Hawley proceeded. "According to Mr. Johanne Bauer, this... *rattle-thing* got out. Escaped into the wild green yonder. But... not before it killed the head-scientist-boss-guy." Hawley's eyes turned up in thought. "Beemer? Femur? Lemur? Man, it's on the tip of my tongue."

"Are you sure it wasn't *Frankenstein?*"

"Yeah, I'd remember that for sure." Said Hawley, apparently missing the dig.

"Perfect." Finch was no longer able or willing to hide her frustration. "So, tell me Jack, what did you and your fellow officers do after hearing this incredible story—because I know you didn't alert my office! Let me guess... you all laughed in the guy's face before sending him on his merry way? Am I getting warm?"

"Well... I mean, we did do the first part." Hawley looked a little wounded. "After that though, we had him sit in a room for a couple hours while we tried to authenticate his story. Turns out, the head scientist guy was real. Professor *what's-his-name* owned a cabin in the woods outside Cottage Grove."

"Jesus, that's only twenty miles from here."

"Don't I know it," Jack nodded enthusiastically. "Thing is… when we went to the address, there was nobody home."

"And?" Heather demanded. "Did you even look around? Go back for a search warrant or whatever you guys do?"

"Hey, ease up, alright? We did what we could. Remember that we're *Fish and Wildlife*. Shit, just by being there, we were probably stretching the limits of our purview by a measure of fifty-five. Look… I passed the whole story onto the local police myself. Course… I'm pretty sure they thought it was a prank." He looked deflated. "I definitely would have."

Finch stopped searching for the Glock. Eventually, she sighed. "I guess I would have too. So what happened to Mr. *Johanne?*"

"Had to let him go. We told him not to leave town, but he just laughed. He knew damn well we couldn't do anything to stop him. For all I know, he left the station and hopped on the next plane to Denver… or Switzerland."

For a short while, neither party said another word.

"Well, that is a hell of a story, Jack."

Hawley chuckled. "Worst part is, we ain't gotten to the end yet. Hey, lookie here," The beam of his own light was hovering on Finch's missing Glock.

"Oh, thank God," Finch began to walk, automatically swinging her light to the same point. But there was something that caught her eye. Raising her arm an inch higher caused the circle to illuminate what was standing in the shadows beyond her dropped weapon.

The bulging hammerhead eyes stole her breath but seeing that flash of red again nearly stopped her heart from beating. Like a deer in headlights, all Heather Finch could do was freeze as the sound she'd come to dread, rattled once more in her ears.

❦ ❦ ❦

Jack Hawley was already firing his rifle, but the horrible thing was too fast. The so-called rattleback darted in its unpredictable zig-zagging way, causing every blast to hit dirt.

Before Finch could form a cohesive thought, the thing tackled the big man from Texas. For a second, she thought he was going to absorb the blow, but the impact was too great. With an animal the size of a mountain lion attacking his upper torso, Jack Hawley teetered, stumbled. Then he disappeared, monster and all, right over the cliff.

For many seconds, nothing felt real.

Finch stared at the place where Hawley had been, but no matter how many times she blinked, the man did not magically reappear. Shock fell upon her then, dulling all sound and thought. Through this, she could just make out a kind of skittering sound. A frantic scritch-scratching coming from just past the overlook. It was as if something was clawing its way back to the top. Something that she was pretty sure didn't wear an Oregon Fish and Wildlife badge.

The woman's breathing was so intense, the cold air felt like it was sawing at her throat. Turning, she darted to where she had spotted her state-issued firearm. Running turned to stumbling, but at the last second, muscle memory she hadn't needed since little league kicked in. With a dramatic slide, she snatched up the Glock and pointed both it and her light at the space above the cliff.

Finch's hands quaked with emotion, but she fought to stay strong. She knew her next shot had to count because a miss would mean the big game over. At the first sign of the thing, she had to blast its ugly face off and that's all there was to it. Unfortunately, as she came to realize, the scrambling skittering sounds had stopped.

Afraid to take her next breath, Heather Finch licked her lips. The taste spoke of salt and fear, and this made her angry.

She didn't want to see Jack Hawley in his current state. In fact, right then, she wished very much that she was still at home in bed. Perhaps tending her dream garden while Botticelli's Venus lazily munched her unrealistically large Dorito. Only this was no dream. No—from the moment Todd Peveril's frantic call had ripped her from a sound twenty minute slumber, this night had been nothing but *a bad monster movie.* Some would-be-Frankenstein's nightmare brought to life. It was all insane... impossible. But it was also happening on *her* watch.

So she kept her feet moving. Bringing her closer and closer to the edge of the scenic overlook with each step. Because Heather Danielle Finch was the head LEO for all six districts of the Willamette National Forest. Already no less than four people had been hurt or killed by this thing but, by God, the list of victims was going to stop there.

She pointed the weapon over the cliff. With it and the flashlight pointed down, Finch's wide eyes drank in the mountainside. Unfortunately, the only thing out of place was the body of a man she knew. A man who, up until two minutes earlier, she'd held no particular affinity for.

"Jack?" She whisper-shouted the name, receiving no response.

Officer Hawley was down there, but he wasn't moving. At least not at first.

"Hey, ease up," He lifted an arm. "Would you mind getting that light out of my face?"

"Jack!" Finch practically squealed, which was something that she absolutely never did. "Holy crud, are you okay?"

"Well," said Hawley. "I'm *alive.* But... that thing... I saw it climbing. *Oh God, Heather, I think it's back up there with you right now!*"

With wide eyes, Finch spun around.

Despite the lack of rattling fanfare, there it was—practically on top of her.

She could see the red bit unfolding but before she could line up the Glock's barrel for a shot, that scythe-like proboscis shot out and stabbed downward—sliding neatly between a radius and its matching ulna. Feeling the pain, watching the organic blade pop out the underside of her right arm, redder than when it went in... the Patrol Captain's only recourse was to scream.

❧ ❧ ❧

Heather Finch was being dragged over hard rock-laden earth. And then, quite abruptly, she wasn't.

When the long blade-mouth was unsheathed from her arm, the woman's agony was renewed. Through tears, she saw that it had pulled her away from the cliff. Close to where its earlier victims had been trying to start a fire. It was easy to forget them—the teenagers. They who had set this whole night into motion. Had the rattleback dragged them away too? And Todd?

Finch cradled her arm and forced her vision into focus. Past a gasoline can and some toppled firewood, was the beast. The rattleback was pacing like a tiger in a cage, but with a noticeable limp.

"Didn't like that fall much, did ya?" Finch sucked air in through clenched teeth. "*Good.*"

Without a second's hesitation, she pointed her Glock at the thing and fired. Squeezing the trigger again and again until the action produced only clicks.

The echoes of her reports rolled away—leaving behind an omnipresent tone in her ears. With no small effort, she managed to get to her knees where she stopped for a breath. Once back on her feet, she felt like a decrepit ninety-two-year-old. With every joint screaming and her adrenaline spent, the empty Glock felt impossibly heavy. And so, she allowed it to drop.

When the gun hit the ground, the animal flinched. As the woman approached, all it could do was watch. Still alive, but twitching—its scythe-like mouth part flapping ineffectively against the ground. When the woman was reflected in those bulging lidless eyes, the shattered crest on the thing's back began to vibrate.

CH-CH-CH... KK... CH-KK... CH-CH...

The sound was different than before. Weaker. Like the engine of an old Dodge trying to spin back to life.

"So..." Finch wiped some blood off her lip. "Seems the rattleback has a death rattle."

THWK! The red proboscis stabbed the ground near Finch's boot.

"Jesus!" Shooting back a step, her heel connected with one of the firepit rocks and caused Finch to lose her balance. As her ass returned to ground level for what felt like the umpteenth time, every inch of Finch exploded in fresh pain. When she looked, the rattleback was pulling itself straight for her. That was when instinct took over. From Finch's gullet came a primal yell as one foot shot out in a tremendous kick. The boot hit home, sinking deep into one of the animal's softball-sized eyes.

Her hard rubber heel came back wet as hog-like squeals rang in her ears. Finally, that blood red proboscis failed and came down one last time—piercing the forgotten gas can as if it were made of butter. The rattleback made a curious little squeal. Then, discovering a reservoir of sweet liquid inside, the damn thing began to drink.

Finch winced at what she was seeing, but knew exactly what needed to be done. Despite her own pain, she reached for her pocket—confirming the small rectangular object was still within before pulling it out. By the light of the moon, the woman in red negligee looked more beautiful than ever.

After flipping the top, Finch thumbed at the flint wheel. On the third try, a flame appeared. Then her eyes turned to the rattleback. Though broken and bleeding, the impossible thing refused to die. The eyeball that had met her boot looked like a crushed grape and was leaking colorless fluid. For the briefest of moments, Heather Finch considered feeling sympathy for the lab created monstrosity. Then she remembered Todd and Jack and those stupid kids.

"What do ya say, darlin'?" She winked at the bisected image of Bettie Page. "One more for the road?"

The resulting explosion wasn't exactly the Charger in Bullitt... but right then, Heather Finch felt a little like Steve McQueen. Watching the cougar-sized monstrosity burn, she had a fierce urge to flip it off... but no. Whatever it had done, the rattleback wasn't a monster—not really. Created in some mad-science lab or not, it was an animal. Utterly unnatural and yet driven by needs that were anything but.

Besides, McQueen didn't flip off the Blob. That would have just been crass.

❧ ❧ ❧

For a time, the night was quiet. As for Finch, her body felt like it had been freshly trampled by wild elephants. But that was fine. Reaper's Bluff was safe, and that was what really mattered. Hell, that was the job.

"Uh... *hello*?" The voice of Jack Hawley sounded like it was a million miles away. "What the hell was that?"

After hobbling to the overlook, Finch took a draft of mountain air. Letting out a cloud of visible breath felt pretty good, though it made her yearn for the full flavor of a Consulate Menthol.

"That..." She shouted over the edge. "Was our science experiment. I may have caused it to explode."

"Well shit," Jack said a few seconds later. "How'd you manage that?"

"Tell you later. Listen, I've got to call this in and get us some help, alright? But I'm coming right back with some first aid. Just gotta grab the kit from my truck."

"Uhhh... okay." Hawley sounded unsure. "I'll just... stay here then."

"You do that." She smiled.

"Hey, uh, Heather?"

"Yeah?"

"I'm glad you're okay."

The woman's smile grew. "Back at ya. Hey... you like Snickerdoodles?"

There was a long pause, but eventually Hawley simply managed a confused, "I guess?"

"Alright!" Finch clapped her hands. "Because *boy howdy*, have we earned them buddies! Just hold tight, Jack—I'll be back in a flash!"

The Patrol Captain wasted no time. Her wounds hurt more and more with every step but she tried not to think about it. She had to get to her truck and drive to the nearest phone. The State Police would be her first call but there were a few others. She'd leave out the science fiction stuff for now —concentrate on the victims. The officers who were down, or in the case of Ranger Peveril... still missing.

As she hobbled down the path through the woods toward the parking area, she tried to concentrate on the positives. Specifically on the two-day old cookies in her glove compartment. In fact, it was the Snickerdoodles she'd been picturing when the impact came from above.

The woman's head had banged off the ground, causing comprehension to go south. Her vision blurred and swam while her hearing was more deadened than ever. What she knew for sure was that something had been dropped upon her as she'd been passing by. Something that was now laying on top of her. Only it wasn't just some-*thing*... it was her missing Ranger.

Frantically, Finch tried to free herself, but Todd Peveril had never been one to skimp on the baked goods. As things stood, there may as well have been an Angus bull on top of her for all the progress she was making. Unable to do much else, Finch cried out—bellowing her well-earned outrage into the cold Oregon sky. Her mind raced over the incredible series of horrific labors the night had forced her to perform already. It was more than most Patrol Captains did in an entire career and by God, nothing could take that away from her.

It was about then that she heard it. That rattling rustle she had come to know and dread so well. Blinking up into the branches, Finch's vision focused just enough to make out a shape. There was an animal up there—something about the size of a cougar.

"*CH-CHT CH-CHT CH-CHT CH-CHT...*"

The woman renewed her struggle, finally unpinning her one good arm. And as things came into focus, she could see more of what was in the branches above. There were people up there. All neatly arranged and laid out with their faces pointed down. They were staring at her almost expectantly— asking for help with their dead eyes. Finch's eyes darted between them. Shifting from face to face... to face. There were seven at least.

"*CH-CHT CH-CHT CH-CHT CH-CHT...*"

With another of its warnings, the second rattleback climbed farther out on its branch. This one was larger and paler than the one she had killed. Grey, maybe, though it was hard to tell in the diffused moonlight. Based on its posture, the animal was about to pounce, and she could already see the red piece unfolding from beneath the throat.

Recognizing this and what it meant, Patrol Captain Heather Finch averted her eyes. But as she turned her head to the side, her unique angle afforded a perfect view of something else she hadn't noticed before. There, spray painted upon the trunk of an old tree was a robed skeleton holding a long, crooked scythe. Death was looking her right in the face —glaring through hastily rendered eye sockets. Seeing this final infraction, the corners of the woman's mouth turned down in a deep, defiant scowl. When she looked up, it was just in time to see the thing above her leap from its branch. But before it hit, Finch's one good arm shot out, and she extended a firm middle finger.

🍃 🍃 🍃

A fierce proponent of character diversity & of avoiding cliché like the plague, **Steve Van Samson** is the author of the novels "Mark of the Witchwyrm", "The Bone Eater King" and "Marrow Dust", the collections "Black Honey and Other Unsavory Things" and "Year of the Rattlesnake" and a comic book or two. Aside from writing, Steve co-hosts the long running nostalgia podcast Retro Ridoctopus and watches way too many black and white movies.

White Pages

Clay McLeod Chapman

Is your refrigerator running? Total amateur hour. You're just begging for them to hang up before the fun's even begun. You got to trick them into sticking around. Stay on the line. The longer you keep your target talking and keep yourself from cracking up, the bigger the bragging rights. Glory is yours!

Confusion is the key, so I always start with—*Who's this?*

Turn the tables. Totally throws them. They're the ones answering the phone, right? Aren't they supposed to be asking *you* who *you* are? Aren't you the one who called them?

Who's this?

You could be anybody. Any *body*. Just a voice. Nothing but a breath of air expelled from the lungs, all that air pressure building up below the larynx, until it blows the vocal folds apart, reined in by your tongue and teeth. Becoming words. Becoming someone.

I've been a bible salesman, I've been a newspaper reporter, I've even been FBI… I've been just about anything I can think of on the fly, but for that first inhale, that very first breath of silence before the air leaves my body and becomes the voice of whoever I'm pretending to be, asking—*Who's this?*—I'm anybody, nobody, everybody, all at once.

So… who am I tonight?

"Showtime," Connor coos just next to me. He wriggles his tongue between the orthodontic bands in his braces. He's slipped them back on after dinner, just like his mother always instructs him to do, in hopes of correcting his over-bite. So far, no dice.

"Let's do it."

I pull out the White Pages, that massive tome of phone numbers, plopping it down between us on the kitchen counter. It lets out a hefty *thwack* the second it strikes the Formica. I run my thumb up the book edges, that thin skim of its pages fanning across my skin, like I'm shuffling a deck of the flimsiest cards, letting out the faintest fanning sound.

fffffwwwwwip

We're cranking at my house tonight. Mom and Dad are in the basement, watching Cosby. He'll keep them busy long enough for the two of us to get some solid calls in.

Who's this?

Who am I?

Anyone.

No one.

You'd never guess I'm twelve. That I'm in the seventh grade. That me and Connor crunched through a whole DiGiorno pie tonight, the rubbery cheese still coating my tongue.

None of that matters when I pick up the phone. Cracking that book open, shuffling the deck, I close my eyes, flip to a random page and run my finger down the listings until…

Bingo. William Pendleton. Shoreham Drive.

You're mine tonight, Billy-boy.

It doesn't matter who this guy is. Where he lives. He's in

my sights. First target for the evening. The White Pages is our guide to finding our quarry. Fate picks our prey for us. We leave it up to destiny to decide who to call. You don't know them; they don't know you.

It's the anonymity that gets me.

Imagine: A space that erases your identity. Completely wipes your face, your whole body, your entire being. You're nothing, nothing at all. You can be whoever you want to be.

Where else could you do something like that but over the phone?

Just as long as it's local. You don't want to go long distance. That's when Ma Bell charges you. Suddenly you're leaving a paper trail. Those numbers end up on your parents' phone bill, racking up the long-distance rates, calling out of state, and suddenly your mother is wondering who-in-the-heck is calling up folks in Fresno. Winnipeg. Albuquerque.

The White Pages serves up targets within a three-county radius. Those numbers don't cost a dime. And believe me, there's plenty of fish in this sea. You just have to reach out and touch someone.

Let's see what Mr. Pendleton's up to on this fine Thursday evening...

"Ready?" I ask Connor, my squire. He nods, giggling already. He's not as good at cranking as I am. One day, maybe, the White Pages will be his. I'm teaching him every-thing I know. The tricks. The tactics. The ways to keep your mark on the line, luring them in.

"Listen and learn," I say.

I dial up the number, flossing my finger through the rotary phone, one digit at a time, watching the plastic shield whirl before settling back down and dialing the next digit. That vortex of numbers keeps whirring, creating a portal to exhale into. Let my voice dive in and transform into something different. Someone new. I'm divested of my flesh. I'm reborn.

It's ringing. One chime. Then another. Then—

"Hello?" It's a man's voice on the other end. Probably Mr. Pendleton. Probably watching Cosby right now, too, just like everybody else out there. He's distracted. Mind elsewhere. On the Huxtables. Eyes on the television. One ear on the laugh-track, the other pressing against the telephone, that colander in the receiver opening up. All those holes.

"Who's this?" I deepen my own voice, dropping it down an octave, just so I don't deep six my chances straight out of the gates. You got to keep them on for as long as possible. Keep them on talking. See how long you can keep it up without busting a gut.

My record? Two minutes. Kid you not. I'm going for three minutes tonight. I'll be in the Guinness Book of World Records for longest crank call before we're done.

"Pardon?"

"Who is this?" I ask again, doing my damnedest to keep from cracking up. Connor's leaning in so he can listen to the conversation. I push him away. His pepperoni breath's throwing my mojo. I need to focus. He keeps dry heaving these silent laughs, sounding like a donkey with colic, his whole chest rocking up and down in this silent conniption fit. I can't look. Seeing him guffaw is going to make me laugh and then we're done for. *Game over.*

"I think you have the wrong number," the man on the other end says.

"William? Is this William Pendleton? It is, isn't it?"

"Well… yes? How did you—"

"Your name was selected to be a part of a very exclusive telephone survey. We are asking some of our most loyal customers if they may be interested in—"

"Hold up. Customers? What customers?"

"Our records show that recently you purchased a lifetime supply of—"

"*Lifetime?*"

Connor can't keep it together anymore. He snorts right at my shoulder. A big ol' trumpet blast from his nasal cavity. *Shit, shit, shit.* He brings his hand up to his mouth, cupping his palm over his lips, eyes going wide with panic, staring back at me.

Too late. Pendleton's onto us. "What's going on here? Who is this?"

"Sorry about that, sir. Must be a bad connection." It's so hard to hold onto the ruse. "I was wondering if I might interest you in..." That snickering is infectious. "Interest you and your family in a... a..." Once you start cracking up, brittle giggles, there's no controlling it.

"Don't call back here again."

Click. The line goes dead. Nothing but dial-tone, humming back.

Now we're both busting a gut. Tears in our eyes. Connor's lips split, revealing the gleam of his teeth, all metal, the braces laced to his incisors pushing his smile up and out. I spot a creamy wad of chewed pizza dough still clumped up between the brackets, a lump of leftover DiGiorno stuck in his mouth.

"My turn! My turn!" Connor reaches for the phone.

"Hold up." My elbow goes up high, blocking him like we're on the basketball court. I've still got the receiver in my hand. The phone is bolted to the kitchen wall, just underneath the cabinet where all the snacks are. There's a yellow notepad mounted next to the phone. A Bic rests on the lip of the pad, for whenever people need to take a message.

"Give it to me!" Connor cries, a little too loud. We got to keep our voices down.

"That was just a warm up..." My arm goes out at my

shoulder, holding the phone away from Connor. There's about a mile's worth of coiled cord connecting the receiver to the base, a pig's tail going on for an eternity. An infinity piggie. The more Connor grabs for the receiver, waving his arms in the air, the more the two of us tangle into its tail.

"That's no fair!"

"Quit it!"

"Dick."

Cheers is up next. I hear the rumble from the basement. All that canned laughter. There's a studio audience downstairs. Mom and Dad won't wander into the kitchen until there's a commercial break, which gives us just enough time for one or two more calls.

Back to the sacred White Pages. That mystical tome. An ancient registry of names. Talk about a real cinderblock of a book. It's got enough heft to make Tolkein blush. Every name, every phone number, address, is here at our fingertips, listed in alphabetical order. If that's not a work of magic, a spell book that summons up the suburbs, I don't know what is.

Poring over its pages, I can't help but feel the necromancy resonating out from it.

It is a holy relic. An ancient opus.

A grimoire.

The Yellow Pages are less magical to me. They're strictly for businesses listings, not as much fun to crank. But the White—the blinding white—Pages, with all of its mystical listings, this telephone book is where it's at. I hold its power. I possess its majesty.

Only I can summon the names.

The book is flimsy. Its pages barely hold themselves up, limply curling under their own weight. We're talking hundreds—*thousands*—of names and numbers, right here.

Home phone numbers. Portals to travel through. To enter

the homes of others. To slip into their lives, their very existence, invisible to them, nothing more than a voice.

Every year, they update this book. A new edition finds its way to our doorstep. It's a living, breathing book. People die. People move. People change their phone numbers.

The White Pages changes with them. Erases their names.

This grimoire lives.

My fam's in the book, to boot. I've looked. Gone down the row of M's before landing on our listing. I'm not name-checked, but it's our family right there. Dad's there. Mom, too. I'm there merely in implication, in between the lines. Nobody would ever be able to find me.

At least, I don't think so. Not yet, at least.

One day, I'll be somebody.

I'm thinking about all the people in this book. Every last one of them has a life. A home. There's that bit in that movie —*The Jerk*—where Steve Martin starts jumping up and down, so ecstatic over the fact that his name is finally, *finally*, listed in the phone book.

He's somebody now. He *exists*. He's got a name, a number —a testament to being real, bound by flesh and blood and his very own telephone number. I remember laughing my ass off at that when I first saw the movie with Mom and Dad, but there's some truth to it. It's not just a joke. From the moment you end up in the White Pages, you belong to this world. You're not untethered, unmoored. You are here... and anyone can call. Seek you out.

So let's let our fingers do the walking.

I lean over the White Pages. I feel its power rising up from the paper, the ink itself radiating in some strange dark energy. It's majesty, blindingly white. I have to close my eyes. Shield myself. Flip through until I settle on a page. Run my finger down the length of names, any name, the tip of my index finger slowly sliding down the column, feeling the faint rub of newsprint paper, the pages so thin, rough against my skin, before finally stopping at—

"Grayson. Harold. Montague Street."

This White Pages have offered him up as our next target. His name materializes beneath my finger, as if it were written in blood, rising up from the masses.

"Hello, Harold… Here we go."

I dial, watching the rotary whirl, nearly getting hypnotized by its revolutions.

The vortex opens.

I exhale, my breath stepping through the portal, vaulted through that winding coil of cord, spiraling for miles and miles as destiny connects me to my mark. My next target.

It rings.

Once.

You found me. The voice on the other end is calm, smooth.

I don't know how to answer that. My brain short circuits. I can't come up with something to say. How am I supposed to respond to that? *You found me?* Who says that?

I was wondering when you'd call.

That voice. It belongs to a man. That much I can tell. He's not old. Not dotty. There's a softness to it, a gentle tide of kindness, that slithers through the receiver at my ear.

I don't like it. I don't like it at all.

I've been waiting…

Connor's looking confused. He can't hear the voice on the other end. He's got no clue what's going on here. I'm not saying anything, simply listening to this man. This voice.

Can I come over now?

The receiver gets heavier in my hand. The phone feels stuck to my skin. I don't know why, I don't know what to do, I don't know what I'm supposed to say.

So I hang up.

"What the heck happened?" Connor asks, confused. "What did he say?"

"Nothing."

❦ ❦ ❦

Our phone rings around ten. I'm already in bed, but I can hear the peal reach out from the kitchen and crawl down the hall, the chime clamoring all the way to my room.

I don't think much of it. It's kinda weird to get a call at this hour, but it happens. Sometimes one of Mom's sisters wants to chat about their siblings, get their gossip on.

"Sean?" Mom shouts. "It's for you…"

…Me?

By the time I make it to the kitchen, in my PJs, Mom's holding the phone out for me. I give her this guilty look. Like I'm in trouble. Her eyebrows lift, impatient with me. She's miffed she had to climb out of bed to answer the phone. She stretches her arm out further, as if she were saving up this extra inch just for this moment. *Just take it,* that gesture says.

When I don't, still won't, she says, "It's Connor. He's asking about homework."

Homework? What homework?

I take the phone and bring the receiver to my ear.

"Hey," I say, defenses down. "What assignment are you talking about?"

Why'd you hang up? The voice could belong to anybody. I don't know who this person is. A voice. It's just a voice. But the softness belongs to the same man as before.

It's him again. He called back.

Can I come over now?

I hang up. My body's just been jolted, my arm bolting out at my shoulder and slamming the receiver down on the phone's cradle, practically cracking the plastic. So hard, the

389

bell within the phone rattles upon impact, a dwindling echo of its chime clattering out for lingering moment.

"Don't break it," Mom warns. "That's not one of your toys that you can just destroy..."

I don't know how long I stared at the receiver, breath held in my chest, unable to exhale until I knew for certain they weren't going to call back.

"Want to tell me what that was that all about?" Mom asks.

"Nothing," I manage.

"Did Connor get what he needed?"

"Yeah."

"Tell him next time not to call so late. Whatever it is, it can wait until the morning..."

❧ ❧ ❧

The phone's ringing the second I get back from school, plowing through the front door and plopping my backpack down. I head to the kitchen to get some chips. Mom's out at the grocery store—or so says the note she left just next to the phone. Dad doesn't come home from work until six thirty, so I have the run of the house to myself for at least an hour.

The phone keeps ringing. It was ringing when I walked up the front porch. I could hear it resonating through the windows as I unlocked the front door, nearly felt the chiming reverberating through the key itself, the metal vibrating between my pinched fingers like a tuning fork. I didn't think much about it (*that's a lie*) as I stepped in. Walked down the hall.

How long has it been ringing?

Most days, I don't answer. Not like it's for me. Who's gonna call for me?

Who am I?

No one. I'm not in the phone book. Not yet. I'm just a

nobody. Just a kid. I'm not even listed in the White Pages. Nobody knows who I am. *Nobody.* No one's going to call for me.

But the phone keeps ringing.

This month's issue of Ranger Rick came in the mail today. I try to occupy myself by flipping through, crunching down on a Tostito.

The phone won't stop ringing.

Instead of giving in and hanging up, whoever it is, they're just going to let it keep on ringing and ringing and ringing. They're not gonna stop until someone answers.

Until I answer.

So I lift the phone off its cradle. I get my grip around the plastic, fingers tightening, like I need to hold onto something to keep myself from falling. A handle to stay upright.

I take a breath before bringing the receiver to my ear.

I don't say anything. I just listen.

Breathing. Someone's breathing on the other end. They're not saying anything, either. Not at first. Who's going to break the silence? Who's going to fill the silence?

There you are.

What am I supposed to say? I'm afraid to hang up. He's going to keep calling, isn't he? Now that he has my number, now that he knows who I am, he's not going to stop.

You have no idea how lonely it's been.

I just let him talk. I barely say a word. I don't need to. Once this guy gets started, whoever he is, he just talks and talks and talks. Really chews my ear off.

What was the name again? What listing did I pick from the White Pages?

Grayson, that's it. Harold Grayson.

"Are you Harold Grayson?"

The voice on the other end doesn't say anything at first. I hear his breath. It picks up.

Laughing. He's laughing.

The people who lived here... they seemed like a nice family. At first. They had a little girl. Younger than you, I imagine. She wasn't allowed to answer the phone. Talk to strangers.

I've left them in their bedroom. Together. Tucked them all in.

They didn't want me to be a part of their family.

I thought I could make their house my home, but... it doesn't feel right. Now I've just been waiting for a new home. It's so hard to be outside, don't you think? In your body. In your skin. I don't like my skin. I've never liked my skin. I wish... I wish I was nothing but air.

I've lost count of how many houses I've been in now... None of them are home.

I don't want a house. I want a home.

I keep looking for a home. I wander through house after house after house but none of them are home and then I wait and wait until someone reaches out and invites me in.

The phone finally rang... and there you were. There you were.

You found me.

My arm's all tangled in the phone's coiled cord, wrapping around my wrist, a serpent slithering up my forearm. There's just enough length to make it to the center of the kitchen before the cord went taut. I want to run, but for some reason I can't let go of the phone, caught in this snake's grip, the cord tightening like a noose around my throat, choking me.

Have you put any thought into the possibilities, how fate brought us together? Of all the combinations of numbers, of all the people you could have dialed... you found me.

Doesn't that feel like destiny? What else could it be?

I know the answer. It was the White Pages. The telephone book brought us together.

*There's a new feature here on phones... Last call return. Have you heard of it? Press *69 and the operator automatically dials the number of the last person who called... You.*

White Pages

Can I come to your house now?

❧ ❧ ❧

I don't want to be anybody.

I don't want to be anybody.

I don't.

The most recent edition of the White Pages just arrived. It landed on our front doorstop with a hefty *thwump*, pounding the porch. Mom asked me to grab it, bring it in.

I didn't want to touch it. I kicked it into the house, letting it skid down the hall, punting it all the way into the kitchen.

Then I ripped it in half.

I grabbed a handful of its pages in each hand and tried ripping it down the middle, but it was too thick. So I grabbed several sheets and wadded them into a ball. Peeling the White Pages away, layer by layer. Gutting it from the inside out. I kept going back for more and more, tearing pages out by the handful, balling them up and throwing them across the kitchen. All those names. Those numbers. I didn't want them reaching out. Reaching me.

The phone's stopped ringing. We don't get that many calls anymore. Just the normal amount of salesmen, telemarketers, always asking if we'd like to subscribe to this. Offering us that.

He hasn't called back. It's almost been a week now.

Yesterday, while we were all eating breakfast, just before I was about to head to the bus, I noticed the headline in the newspaper: *Family Found Slain in their Own Bed.*

Dad's barricaded himself behind the paper, walling himself in with the business section, so I can read the article without him noticing.

It mentions a girl. She's missing her eyes. Someone plucked them out, then tucked her in between her parents

393

in their bed. The tongues of her mother and father were gone.

Can I come over now?

I'm not afraid of the phone ringing anymore. Now I'm more worried about the doorbell.

❧ ❧ ❧

Clay McLeod Chapman writes books, comic books, children's books, as well as for film and television. His most recent novels include What Kind of Mother and Ghost Eaters. You can find him at <u>www.claymcleodchapman.com</u>.

Afterword
Tom Deady

I hope you've enjoyed your visit to THE RACK. This book is special to me for so many reasons. Most of all, it is my tribute to the fond memories I have of running to Woolworth at the Wellington Circle Plaza in Medford, MA to spin THE RACK. That's where I fell in love with horror.

It was late, a weeknight, and I wanted a book to read. I walked (or maybe rode my bike) to Woolworth with enough money to buy a paperback. Yes, I spun THE RACK, spun it until something caught my eye. An all-black cover with a face embossed on it and just a single red drop of blood. It was, of course, Stephen King's *'Salem's Lot*. I devoured that book and was forever a horror fan.

That was the first book I remember buying from THE RACK, but it was far from the last. So many hours of enjoyment were found reading those magnificent, crazy books and visiting all the possible worlds they availed to me. It was a great time to grow up.

Things are very different for today's readers. Bookstores are fading away and finding paperbacks in drug stores or supermarkets is mostly part of history. The limited horror sections in the surviving bookstores and internet searches fall short of the wonder of spinning THE RACK. This book is my chance to give a piece of my childhood back to those who might share some of those memories, or maybe those who never experienced the fabled RACK.

My role in this was easy. All I had to do was ask these many talented authors to write great stories in the vein of those wonderful mass market horror novels. And man, did they come through! I owe any success this book has to them; it is their worlds you are visiting.

Special thanks to Richard Chizmar for connecting me with the people necessary to get permission to include a Stephen King story. The thirteen-year-old who first picked up 'Salem's Lot is forever grateful.

I also need to mention Christa Carmen and Larry Hinkle. They were my secret collaborators and advisors for the long duration of the project and their input and encouragement made this anthology better than I ever could have alone.

Will Errickson deserves much praise. He is a true historian of the genre and his foreword added exactly the insight I was hoping for.

Speaking of capturing the vibe of the anthology, how about that cover? Lynne Hansen must have gone to the crossroads and made a deal with the devil to come up with that. It looks like it was pulled off THE RACK fifty years ago. I am forever in her debt.

Last but not least, my lovely and talented wife, Sheila Deady, did all the interior design and formatting, as well as supporting, and putting up with me throughout this labor of love.

I won't say putting together an anthology was easy, but working with all these wonderful artists was a dream come true. This book is everything I envisioned it could be, and I

Afterword

truly hope you enjoyed it. Perhaps we'll meet again for another spin of THE RACK.

Tom Deady
Tucson, AZ
August 2024

Tom Deady (Editor)

Tom Deady is a Bram Stoker Award winner (2016) for Superior Achievement in a First Novel, and has since published several novels and novellas inspired by his love of horror.

Tom was born and raised in Massachusetts, not far from the historic town of Salem.

He resides in Arizona, where he's working on his next novel.

Shop for signed copies and more at
https://www.tomdeady.com/
Subscribe to my newsletter to get exclusive updates!

facebook.com/tomdeady

instagram.com/tom_deady

tiktok.com/@tomdeadyofficial

bookbub.com/profile/tom-deady

Also by Tom Deady

Shop for signed copies and more at

https://www.tomdeady.com/

Subscribe to my newsletter to get exclusive updates!

Novels

Haven

Eternal Darkness

The Clearing

Those Left Behind

Novellas

Weekend Getaway

Of Men and Monsters

Collections

Tales from Circadia

The Edgewater Chronicles

Printed in the USA
CPSIA information can be obtained
at www.ICGtesting.com
LVHW091336051024
792969LV00001B/54